ANNE WHEELER

VORTEX

THE BRIGHTEST VOID

I looked on the earth, and lo, it was waste and
void;
and to the heavens, and they had no light.

Jeremiah 4:23

CHAPTER ONE_
NIMBUS STATION, ETRIK

CORALIE WOKE TO THE BENIGN AMBER ILLUMINATION that was her constant companion. It was becoming easier to sleep in the small capsule that had been her home for as long as she could remember, and that recent effortlessness was disheartening. Truthfully, it was surprising her body had lasted this long, trapped and used and bled like a piece of meat. Of course, they weren't bleeding her dry, but having half one's blood sucked out at a time, stripped of its criexain, then replaced, did a number on one's body. Even an augmented one.

So, too, did the isolation. The maintenance on the medical equipment was done from outside the capsule; the sealed door ensured no one could speak to her, and that all but her loudest cries went unheard by the staff and her fellow captives.

And cry she did, or, at least, had at first. The entire situation was unreal. Leaving Mars behind, first as a volunteer, then as a . . . what was she supposed to call herself now? A prisoner? That implied she'd done something wrong. A subject? That implied they were testing something on her, which they weren't. They knew exactly what they were doing. A blood donation center? Perhaps, if she wasn't strapped down in this silken cocoon, only able to move her head a few centimeters to each side.

But she *was* trapped here, and scrutinizing her physical status upon waking each time had only grown more difficult. She went through the procedure anyway, from her toes on up. There was nothing else to focus on, no other way to keep her cognitive abilities intact.

Her toes didn't move much anymore. The medics had wrapped them in some kind of corrosive bandage when she'd first come here, and she was halfway grateful for that—her nails hadn't grown long enough to curl into her skin, even if she could feel her skin eroding along with them.

Her legs were weak. Atrophied, most likely, because she'd been unable to shift them for as long as she could remember. No point in focusing on them for long.

Her lower back was cramped. It had been cramped for several sleep cycles now. On Mars, she'd be looking for a massage, or perhaps a zero-g yoga studio. Here, she could only cry in frustration.

Her bladder didn't burn today—tonight?—which meant the antibiotics they'd started last week had done their job. The catheter was still in place. Whatever they were doing with her urine, she didn't want to know.

Her vision was useless. The inoffensive cream plastic ceiling was only ten centimeters above her nose, and her ability to focus at a distance had deteriorated to the point she couldn't see over her chest, except as a beige blur. Even the ocular implant she possessed had difficulty focusing so close. She'd snapped a few pictures of the plastic early on, then deleted them when they'd revealed nothing thought-provoking.

Her cinnamon hair had grown long, a sign of how much time had passed, but she could still blow it out of her face. That had become a game, a way to keep her lungs strong. Coughing also helped, but coughing gave her fits, made her chest muscles ache.

Cautiously, Coralie shifted her head to the side to stare at the IV line that ran through the wall into her left arm. The muscle in her neck that was always knotted upon waking eased as she rolled her head back to center. No blood rushed up the tube coming from her left thigh, which meant this was her week off. At least, it was what she'd taken to calling a week, since there were no such time periods on Etrik. It wasn't Earth, after all. Not even Mars.

Truthfully, there wasn't even such a thing as time inside her capsule prison. She slept, she dreamed —though they were regular dreams, not the intense and hyper-realistic ones she'd had inside the wormholes between here and Earth. Then she woke and cried some more. Sometimes she listened to the man next to her—or above, he could have been above—scream.

Even eating was taken care of through a large-bore IV in her right arm, and forgiving them for taking that away from her seemed impossible. Being able to eat meant she was human, that she could mark time, that she still had some semblance of self-determination. Maybe that's why the bastards wouldn't let her do it.

Her own colleagues.

While she'd dreamed her way through the last two wormholes, before she'd noticed the silver eyes that were a hallmark of their condition, they'd *changed*. She wouldn't use the word vampire, because that was ridiculous, but they'd become immortal—or at least, that was how Thomas Kinnard, Nimbus Station's new director, had explained it before bringing her to the surface from *Triumph*'s orbit and shutting her in this capsule. Kinnard, the scientists, and everyone else here needed the criexain in her blood to stay alive, but other than that, they'd found themselves near-immortal.

She herself was mortal, augmented with illegal body modifications or not. How much longer did she have? A hundred years? Only fifty? A hundred and fifty was supposed to be the usual life span for augments on Earth, which was partly why bodily modifications like hers had been banned a century ago. But the doctors had never considered that her blood would be removed and scrubbed, or that she wouldn't be able to move, or that she'd be prevented from eating and drinking.

Perhaps her extended life wasn't a threat to anyone anymore.

A cry sounded from somewhere around her, jerking Coralie from her thoughts. One of the others was awake, and he was terrified. Maybe angry, but the quality of this sob sounded frightened. Did she sound like this when she cried? Did they listen to her, wonder if she was hurting or lonely or had finally lost her mind?

She closed her eyes and listened. The sound was closer now, and growing louder.

What—

A wisp of hair blew in her face, and she tried to blow it back. It landed in her mouth, and she coughed, then inhaled. The air smelled different now: crisp, with a hint of antiseptic.

Her brows drew together.

The door.

They'd unsealed the door.

Her heart skipped a beat, and the monitor above her head reacted. Calm, she had to be calm. There were all kinds of ports entering her skin, and if she panicked, if they thought she was a threat, she would be unconscious in seconds.

Breathe.

Just breathe.

She closed her eyes. Imagined the beach, the rolling waves, the call of gulls. The monitor ceased its beeping, then a hand fell to her forehead.

"Good," said the voice. "Very good. I didn't want to have to sedate you right away."

Kinnard.

She couldn't see him, but his voice made something in her chest flutter in fear. He'd said goodbye when he shut her in here so long ago. Implied she would die in this capsule, perhaps of old age, perhaps when her heart gave out.

So why was the door open?

Was this it? Was she finally useless to them?

The cocoon that had been her home slid out of the capsule effortlessly, and she blinked in the bright light. Kinnard's blurry shadow flittered about her, surrounded by a few others—likely medics, the ones responsible for this torture. She hated them all. Before all this, she could have killed them all without breaking a sweat. Now she could only lie still and blink up at them.

"Is she conscious?" Kinnard's voice was louder than anything she'd heard in months. "What's wrong with her?"

"Stunned a bit. Sensory overload after her time in the capsule." The medic's voice dripped condescension as he draped a thin piece of fabric over her. "Plus, she can't see very well. But that means it's as good a time as any to move her."

"Moooo—" Her lips moved, but the sound that came out wasn't her voice.

The medic laughed and moved toward her feet. His hands, gloved and warm, felt around her leg, and a sharp pain traveled upwards, toward her heart.

She cried out loud, out of pain, shock, and fear. If they were removing the tubes, that meant they had no further need of her. It didn't take a genius to figure out they were going to kill her.

The same warm hands stuck a pressure bandage on her wound, and the tears stopped, though a few leftovers tracked down the corner of her eye, itching as they settled behind her ear. Maybe she was wrong. Hope was futile, but it was human, and she . . . she was still human. If they didn't intend to let her bleed to death, maybe things weren't bad as they appeared.

The medic moved to her other side and repeated the procedure as Kinnard hovered. It hurt more the second time, probably because she was expecting it. Coralie wanted to fling her legs upward, catch both of them under the chin, but there seemed to be a disconnect between her brain and muscles. Atrophy, yes, now she remembered. But she could overcome that. She *would* overcome it, and then she could get out of here.

Kinnard reached for her cheek, and the medic brushed his hand away.

"I'll insert a port when I'm through," he said. "She'll just clot right up again from those coagulant capsules in her bloodstream otherwise. Besides, it's best not to get carried away before she's fully recovered. She's weak enough as it is."

Something croaked in her throat.

"If you insist." Kinnard looked down at her, his unnatural silver eyes at odds with the distinguished wrinkles forming at their corners, though they matched his graying hair. Coralie had once thought him handsome despite his age, with his patrician nose and high cheekbones, but none of that mattered anymore. "I suppose I should be the one to tell you . . . I finally decided that I wasn't adequately using all the benefits they promised me when we left Mars. Can you guess which one I'm missing out on the most?"

Her throat closed up again as she stared at his blurred form. He couldn't be serious. This was some sick joke. A hallucination. Any moment now she'd wake up back in the capsule, and wouldn't that be better than this nightmare?

"No? It's my personal criexain source, naturally." He laughed, and with a sharp look at the medic, otherwise occupied with patching up some IV site or another, scratched at the delicate skin on the back of her arm. "And I've chosen you."

* * *

She couldn't walk to his quarters, of course. Some part of her mind doubted she'd ever walk again. Kinnard walked beside her floating gurney, carving long scratches in the skin her thin hospital gown didn't cover—it seemed the medic's warning had been in vain. He'd inserted a port above her right breast, but Kinnard couldn't drain anything from it while they moved, so he scratched and licked the blood off his nails. He stared at the port while he did so, and Coralie decided that would be her first training goal: to move her hand enough to cover it. Just to aggravate him. But since she couldn't do that yet, she didn't worry about his stare. She watched the dark ceiling instead, and the lighter walls—though that motion hurt her fresh wounds—but she couldn't see much of anything at all besides the change in illumination.

What she *could* make out through the blur that had become her life was what she'd expected. Materials from each ship that had arrived here from Mars and Earth formed a modular base that seemed to go on for kilometers. It was then she realized her chest was moving up and down. She was breathing real oxygen, outside of her capsule, and that didn't make any sense. The atmosphere on Etrik was low, much too low for her to survive for long. The v-words didn't need as much oxygen as she—Kinnard had mentioned that when he'd shut the door—but she was breathing now, so they must have pressurized the station.

For her?

She blinked in the diffuse light, trying to focus on the present. Maybe none of it mattered. She'd trained for this. Well . . . not *this* exactly, but at least a vague impression of this nightmare. Maybe that was how she'd get through this. Her body might be broken and her mind might be in shambles, but she could retrain everything. Could strengthen both.

A door opened behind her—they were pushing her head-first—and she tried to twist to see what new module they'd entered. Kinnard urged her head straight with a gentleness that surprised her at first. But it made sense. Naturally, he didn't want his source of criexain damaged. The gurney came to a sudden stop, and she shivered.

"Keep her warm." The medic pulled another blanket over her, and she gave him a grateful look before his silver eyes came into sudden focus. "I'll be back tomorrow with an anti-clotting injection, but call if you have any issues before that. I don't expect her to be fully mobile for another few cycles, but now that she's off the life support, she needs to work on getting up and around. Don't want to risk blood clots."

"I'll keep that in mind." Kinnard's gaze didn't leave her upper chest.

"Very good."

The door at her feet hissed shut, and she squeezed her eyes closed again.

Kinnard chuckled as he pulled her gown to the side. "I'm not going to hurt you. What would be the point? But I need a drink. Just a tiny bit. Now that you won't be getting it back, you won't lose as much at one time. That should calm you."

Glass clinked somewhere to her side, and she turned her head. Kinnard, to his credit, had put on gloves before attaching the sterile tube to her port, but he'd rested the other end in a crystal glass now sitting on her chest, and she couldn't stop a shudder.

"You—" Coralie forced her lips around the word.

"I what?" He clamped the tube, then removed it and tossed it into a hole in the bulkhead, along with his gloves. "No, tell me . . . I'm really very curious."

It was all the energy she could muster, even as her heart raced out of control. Kinnard shrugged, then leaned back, glass in hand, on what looked like a leather settee. The glass was dark red on the bottom—that much she could see when she squinted—and her stomach rolled. He was a set of contradictions. Though he wore a plain gray jumpsuit that engulfed his willowy frame, she could just as easily imagine him sitting in a dark library, clad in a velvet jacket, with a glass of scotch beside him and a cigar in hand.

"I suppose you'll need rest. And you'll get it. You're no good to me dead or even sick. How's your vision?

"Bad." It came out slurred, like she was drunk. Like the sound of a sheep bleating, though she hadn't seen one in years.

"It'll improve in time." He took a sip, then bared bloodstained teeth as he spoke. "I know you can't see it now, but this really is a good ending for you, Coralie."

"Ending," she repeated. Her tongue moved this time, and that was an improvement. But why wouldn't her throat work?

"Well, technically it's not an end—it's not as though you're going to die anytime soon. But it's an end to who you were on Earth, isn't it?" He took another sip, and she looked away. "That's not supposed to frighten you. You're valuable to me. More valuable than you can possibly understand."

"I—I do understand," she croaked. And she did. Pure blood was likely healthier than the refined pills the rest of the station took. Why wouldn't Kinnard want it? She just wished he'd chosen someone else.

Or did she?

"Oh?" Kinnard poured a bit of water into the crystal and swished it around before polishing off the diluted blood. "Then we won't have any trouble, will we?"

Coralie shook her head.

"Good." He reached for a clean glass and poured something in it. "Here. Just a little. Don't want you to overdo it."

Those silver eyes were too close when he stood, and more of the liquid splashed on her lips and face than into her mouth, but what little she tasted felt like heaven. She hadn't realized how good water could taste, especially the filtered stuff the station provided.

"More?" Her voice was a little stronger now.

Kinnard shook his head and pulled the glass away. "It'll make you sick. You can have more tomorrow." He watched her for a moment, then headed to a small alcove halfway into the room from the door. A bed sat inside; a narrow table about the width of her hand ran along its length against the wall. "Yours," he said, pointing. "There's a curtain for a privacy, and a force field to . . . well, to keep you in until you regain your strength. I doubt you could keep yourself from falling if you managed to roll over."

"And af—after?"

He chuckled but didn't answer, just lifted her from the gurney as effortlessly as though they were in zero gravity and deposited her on her unported side. Coralie wanted to scream at him for touching her, but he'd laid her head on a pillow, and oh, it felt so good to be off her back that silent tears formed. She closed her eyes so he couldn't see her gratitude.

"That's right. Rest. Tomorrow you start what the medic said, work on gaining your strength back. And your eyesight. I won't have time to shepherd you around everywhere."

His tone had changed from hungry to matter-of-fact, so she pried one eye open. The lust in his eyes was gone, but instead of being reassuring, the change made her heart beat faster. The creep really did just want her blood.

"I—" The last of the moisture on her tongue evaporated. "Could. Kill myself. Like the. Others."

"You won't." Kinnard stopped, his hand on the curtain, all too composed. "You would be back in that capsule before you did it. And you wouldn't ever be coming out. No second chances. Think about that. Think about staring up at that ceiling and never again being able to move your legs. For the next hundred years."

He pulled the curtain across the bed, leaving her in the dark with images of that horrifying future.

CHAPTER TWO_

USOGC BAYONET, SECTOR
BONNEVILLE ORBITAL DOCKS, MARS

Far below Josiah's boots, the red dust and white icecaps of Mars filled the window of *Bayonet*'s aft observation deck, sending a familiar wave of disorientation through him. It was always the same way when he looked down upon a planet, so he shifted his gaze to the right, toward another United States Orbital Guard cutter slipping through the orbital docks as silent and graceful as a shark through the open sea—and as deadly, if anyone's calculations were off.

Just like the planet down below, the other ship was so close he couldn't see the entirety of her. But no loud crunch reverberated throughout the hull as he held his breath. No klaxons rang in his head like they had aboard *Vigilant*. Yes, for the moment at least, *Bayonet* and the thin metal that separated him from the void were intact.

"Captain?" Over the intercom, the voice of the officer of the deck startled him as the other cutter drifted into open space, clearing the dockyard. "Lieutenant Commander Ahn is aboard, and we've been cleared to undock."

Josiah couldn't prevent his shoulders from sinking in relief as he reached above his head for the intercom button to reply to the OOD. He knew his new executive officer, unlike most of the rest of *Bayonet*'s crew. He'd known Patrick Ahn forever, in fact, even if they'd never actually stepped aboard the same cutter at the same time. But their years had overlapped at the Academy; they'd fished all over Long Island Sound together, had known each other for years before the—*before*. Ahn was more of a friend than most anyone else in the system these days and would keep him sane, just like he always had. Yes, it was odd to see him aboard *Bayonet*, but he wouldn't question his good fortune now.

"Very well," he replied, all too conscious that he was about to give his first order as *Bayonet*'s commanding officer. "Commence pre-release procedure. I'll be there momentarily."

"Aye aye, Captain."

Voices in the passageway behind him interrupted his thoughts, and he turned to see Ahn wave off his escort and rap his knuckles on the edge of the door, his stiff posture suggesting he was committed to ceremony, even in private.

You're enjoying this entirely too much, aren't you, Patrick?

"Come on in. But you really don't—" Josiah cut himself off and sighed, then jerked his chin, motioning Ahn inside. There was no point in arguing with a man who equally relished military discipline and winding up his friends. "Get it over with."

Ahn took three steps inside, dropped his bag, and came to attention. "Sir, Lieutenant Commander Ahn reports as ordered."

"We didn't run fast enough to avoid the Martian riffraff, I see." Josiah extended a hand. "Welcome aboard, but never do that again."

"No promises." Ahn's bearing dissolved into laughter as he gripped Josiah's hand in a firm hold. "As for the running, I had to see what was so important that I could scarcely step foot aboard before the clamps released. Sprinting to catch a ship is different from waiting around just to wait around some more."

"Sorry about that." Josiah turned toward space and waved at the planet below, in the direction of the people who made such decisions. "I'm surprised they didn't give you more notice."

That was mostly a lie. He'd only had a few weeks himself, but he couldn't fault anyone for this hastily planned mission. The Orbital Guard didn't have anyone past the second wormhole, much less the fifth, and they needed those ships and personnel where they were. More and more traffic was transiting these days, and Mars Area Command was . . . concerned, to say the least.

"They practically hauled me out of bed this morning." Ahn ran a hand through his dark hair. He'd somehow managed to avoid any gray, and Josiah couldn't help a familiar pang of resentment that had only strengthened as he approached forty with more silver than he approved of. "Showed up in person and banged on the door. Cassandra wasn't thrilled. The girls have a dance recital in a week—they've been looking forward to me being there for months."

Sounds about right.

"I only read our orders a few hours ago, so I'm as much in the dark as you. The National Space Research Council transport ship *Triumph* has gone missing in the Etrik Zone with four hundred seventeen aboard." It was hard to suppress a frown at that. "We're to locate it, rescue the crew, and return them to Mars. Or Etrik, if circumstances and desires permit."

"Etrik?" A raised brow.

"Etrik. Six wormhole jumps, the last two a first for us. Or anyone besides NSRC, to be completely accurate."

"Fun." Ahn's brown eyes glittered. "And we get to burn like hell in between, aboard a ship that smells like fresh paint and sweet, sweet ozone. This was worth getting out of bed for."

"Too true. For some of us, at least." He exhaled, delaying the worst news. Well, the most personal news. "Patrick . . . Hope's on board."

"Hope?" Ahn let out a low whistle. "That's fortuitous."

"*Lousy* is the word you're looking for, I think." Josiah gave a strangled laugh. Seeing his ex-wife on the manifest had ruined the rest of his day.

Maybe even his year. "Or rotten. Unsatisfactory. Even desperate. I could think of a dozen words."

"Not that I want to make a habit of disagreeing with you, especially five minutes in, but I'll have to take exception to *desperate*. You have to admit, if you need a skilled navigator for wormhole travel —" Ahn raised his hands defensively. "It doesn't get much better than her. Besides, if it bothers you that much, you know you'll barely see her most of the time, much less have to interact with her."

They still could have found someone else, was on the tip of his tongue, but he forced his jaw shut. He'd lost that fight with Ahn after the divorce, and rehashing it again was pointless. Especially knowing where his loyalties lay—with Hope. Always with Hope. Josiah supposed there was a reason for that, but what did it matter?

"I suppose you're right." He ran his hands over his face—the beard he'd grown during rehab was gone, and it only emphasized his return to his old life. Temporarily freed from the memories of Vigilant by the sheer formidableness of the current mission, his heartbeat returned to normal again. "It'll work out, I'm sure."

"Seen her yet?" Ahn asked.

He shook his head. "She's been in the navigation hole for hours, working calculations. Wormhole travel is apparently different from slinging around Saturn and back. I don't want to interrupt."

Besides, I'm fairly certain she's avoiding me.

"Ah." Ahn cleared his throat. "Well, you've always been professional, and so has she. You'll work it out."

"Problem is, she's not even the strangest part." Josiah leaned against the window and folded his arms, more to prove to himself the fused glass would hold. "I don't suppose I'm the only one wondering how all three of us ended up on the same patrol?"

Ahn laughed out loud. "And get an answer from the clowns in Assignments? You know what they say—a monkey banging on a keyboard for an infinite period will eventually produce the works of William Shakespeare. It was bound to happen eventually."

"Fair enough." He knew his face was dark. "But I don't like coincidences."

"Not every cruise ends in disaster. In fact, the great majority don't. *Vigilant* was an anomaly, you know. If she'd been built ten years later, her hull would have held."

Ahn had always been the optimistic one. But he hadn't been aboard that elderly cutter when she'd been torn to pieces in port by a civilian skiff that had slipped through the security perimeter, loaded with explosives. He hadn't spent almost six months in a hospital and another four months learning to walk again.

Josiah sighed. Maybe that was why he was so uncomfortable right now—he'd fallen asleep on a dinosaur and woken up in the future, aboard one of the Orbital Guard's newest cutters. Unlike *Vigilant* and her constant gremlins, all of *Bayonet*'s systems were fully functional, and stale fuel, oil, and sweat hadn't yet attached themselves to the sleek white bulkheads, inset with panels of centuries-old Coast Guard red. Like aesthetics and history mattered on a law enforcement ship.

Or maybe they did, in a way he hadn't grasped yet. The hospital on Mars had been gray. The walls, the ceiling, the shades that prevented him from seeing anything outside of his box. Maybe they hadn't wanted their patients to recover? Maybe they'd wanted them to forget the vast expanse of the solar system, the oaths they'd taken?

Compliant patients were easy patients, weren't they?

And compliant cutter captains are easy cutter captains?

Paranoid. He was becoming paranoid, and Ahn knew it.

"Yeah," he replied. "Maybe you're right. Maybe *Triumph* had communications problems, and with any luck, this will be the epitome of a tedious and mind-numbingly dull SAR mission with four hundred confused souls on the other end." Hell, they'd already gotten farther than *Vigilant*'s last patrol. "And none of us will even get to include it in our next promotion packages for fear of putting the board to sleep."

"Sounds like a deal, and I'll hold you to it." Ahn hauled his bag to his shoulder, then wagged a finger at him. "I believe they're waiting for you on the bridge."

With that, he disappeared down the passageway to the XO's quarters, leaving Josiah to make his way to the bridge alone.

CHAPTER THREE_

USOGC BAYONET, LEAVING MARS
ORBIT

JOSIAH LAY ON HIS BUNK FOR OVER AN HOUR BEFORE the door chimed, clutching a rosary over his closed eyes. The familiar words hadn't come, just like they hadn't for months, as if a barrier between his soul and mind had sprung up while he'd been on the surface. Whether it was the responsibility of commanding *Bayonet* herself, or the vastness of space that threatened to swallow them all whole if he made a mistake, or something even more distant and unthinkable, he could only repeat the same phrase over and over:

Please don't let me screw up that badly again.

The unwelcome chime that usually meant bureaucratic nonsense of some sort was followed by a pounding that thwarted further introspection, and that kind of insubordinate disruption could only mean one person. Well, maybe two, but Ahn had enough post-departure paperwork to keep him occupied for at least another hour. Which meant this had to be—

With a groan, he shoved the rosary into his pocket. This was best dealt with sooner rather than later.

"Enter," he called toward the intruder.

The door opened as he pushed himself to his feet. Hope stood in the passageway just like he'd predicted, that same strand of caramel hair he knew so well escaping from the knot at the back of her neck. He wanted to tuck it back in, cut it off, do *something* to keep himself from touching it. Instead, he clenched his hands at his sides, wishing he hadn't answered the door in the first place. Jonathan's hair had been that color, and he didn't need or want the reminder of his marriage or his son.

"Good evening, Captain." Her expression was blank, but she'd always been good at hiding her emotions. "Do you have a moment?"

His stomach flipped.

Hell.

How long had it been since he'd heard her voice? Six months? Her easygoing Pass Christian drawl, untarnished by four years in New London and a new life on Mars, still did things to him—and it wasn't just because she was one of the few aboard born on Earth.

"Commander . . . O'Donnell." He narrowed his eyes at his name on her chest, then forced his gaze to settle on her green eyes and nothing else, a feat that was startlingly difficult even after a year. "Is something wrong?"

"On second thought, let's cut the crap for five minutes, Josiah." She pushed her way inside without waiting for him to invite her and collapsed in his desk chair before replacing the loose piece of hair in its prison, an action that quashed the rest of his desire. "You knew I'd show up."

"Not quite so soon, to be fair." He closed the door and sank onto his bunk again, wrinkling his nose at the curious smell of coffee that followed her. She rarely drank the stuff. "Truthfully, I was afraid we'd spend the next few weeks skulking around and avoiding each other in the wardroom, so hashing this out now is probably best for everyone on board."

"Yes. It probably is." The answer was short.

"But the flight plan?" Anyone else would have seen it as a non sequitur, but after all these years, he could still read her mind, and she wasn't going to discuss *them* without discussing *Bayonet* first.

"You gave me quite a bit of extra work to do once the new orders hit, but it wasn't that complex in the end." She tried for a smile that didn't quite materialize, and he knew it was his fault. "Even if Etrik isn't exactly Saturn."

And Hope could find Saturn with her eyes closed and none of *Bayonet*'s systems operational, which was probably why she'd been assigned in the first place. He hadn't told Ahn, but he'd fought that when he'd first seen her name on the crew manifest; first vaguely, then, when that hadn't gotten him what he'd wanted, with as many specifics as he could muster. Having one's ex-wife aboard led to . . . problems. Everyone knew that. But Captain Anderson had shaken her head and said, *Lieutenant Commander O'Donnell is going with you. Figure it out and make it work.* As if one could simply forget the best eighteen years of their life, especially when they'd been followed by one of the worst.

"And I'm certain you've already got it figured out, no matter how much work it was."

"With the help of the NSRC data and the beacons they've been dropping on the far side of each wormhole." Hope hesitated, obviously wondering if she could dumb it down enough for him. Apparently deciding that wasn't possible, she hurried on, and he couldn't find it in himself to be offended. She wasn't wrong about his lack of navigation skills. "It was no problem, just a bit tedious to program at first. The real fun will come once we approach the first wormhole."

"Then that's good enough for me. I trust you."

And it was, and he did. Having her focus on the *real fun* of navigating meant he could concentrate on the mission. Not his previous failures, not *Vigilant*, not the mistake the Orbital Guard had made in giving him *Bayonet*—not to mention a promotion to commander—and definitely not the way her shapeless midnight blue uniform stood no chance of hiding the curve of her hips.

"So?" she asked.

"So what?" He arched a brow. "You're wondering what you're doing here, too? Believe me, I argued against it."

He'd meant it in the most *I'm-as-confused-as you-are* way possible, but a flash of pain shot across her face, then vanished.

"No. I don't care about that. I just go where they tell me to go and do what they tell me to do, and if that means . . . well, anyway, I don't question it." She swallowed. "I mean, so what's the real story? The last I heard, *Bayonet* wasn't set to be underway for another month, and she didn't have a captain."

Josiah blew out a breath.

"You know exactly as much as I do. Fifteen days ago, Mars Area Command received word from the NSRC research station on Etrik that one of their transport ships—*Triumph*—is overdue. Very much overdue, actually, because Nimbus Station waited months to send a probe with the news, then said probe took another seven weeks to reach Mars because of vortex instability. Finding her is our priority, but I'll be honest with you, the lack of comms from *Triumph* herself after she transited the first wormhole bothers me. And no distress signal, not even the vac alarm?" All ships had them encoded to send an auto-distress signal when exposed to vacuum. All legal ships, that was, and *Triumph* wasn't some system-skimming hulk crewed by bandits.

"We would be chasing debris strewn across a thousand square miles," he went on, "or something even worse. The Navy has secured the entrance to Wormhole Bravo, but what if something happened on the other side?"

"If that communication probe had trouble getting through the wormholes, a distress signal would have had no chance." Hope scratched at her forearm through the fabric of her sleeve. Her skin had always been dry in space, and he hated himself for remembering.

"Perhaps." She wasn't exactly wrong, but his gut said otherwise.

"You don't believe it's just a SAR mission then. Why not?"

"Hell if I know. I'm sure it is. It has to be." He shrugged off the claim. Search and rescue, though one of the Orbital Guard's primary responsibilities, turned into otherwise all the time. The last one had. Had almost killed him, too. Hope knew that. "I'm just chasing ghosts same as always, right? I'm sure there's an explanation for everything."

"I'm sure there is. And you?" Her expression grew soft. "How are you? Really?"

His gut tightened. For a fraction of a second, she'd looked at him like she used to, and she just couldn't—

"You know I'm fine." The doctors and psychologists had made sure of that. He was sick of them all. "I wouldn't be here if I wasn't."

"And you wouldn't be hiding in your quarters if you were." Her palm settled on the worn copy of *Great Expectations* lying on his desk, dog-eared to the same page it had been for years. He'd never read it, but it came along, every time.

"Where else would I be?"

"I don't know." She hesitated. "The bridge. The wardroom. Strolling around your new command. You must be proud of it. I'm proud for you, and she's not even mine."

Terrified, more like.

"They don't need or want me on the bridge right now," he replied. "There's nothing I can do there that I can't do here, anyway. And the wardroom is the size of this bed." He knew her well enough to know she wouldn't argue, especially since it was mostly the truth. "Look, it was a long trip from the surface, and I haven't even settled in yet. I'm tired, and I'll have plenty of time to explore once I catch some sleep." If he could convince her, he could convince herself. "Honestly, I'm fine."

"Are you? I know that look. You're not fine, so don't lie to me, Josiah O'Donnell."

Why had he bothered to lie to her? Wasn't that one purpose of marriage, to know someone as well as—or better—than they knew themselves? And she did. Knew his weaknesses, his strengths, every little thing that made him tick and lose sleep at night.

Everything, that was, except why he'd really left her. He could scarcely remember himself, some days.

"Well, then, I confess. It's an adjustment." He waved at the bulkhead, hoping she'd take the hint, then at the silver oak leaves on the collar of his blue blouse, folded on the table beside the bed. It was a half size smaller than the one he'd worn aboard *Vigilant*—maybe he'd overdone things in his recovery, especially the running. He'd have to work on that. "All of it's an adjustment. Walking, being back on active duty, a promotion, having command of a cutter . . ."

"You deserve it." She sighed and leaned forward in the desk chair, elbows on her knees. "You need to believe that. Unless you can, things will never get better for you."

Or us, he almost heard her say, but that was a fantasy.

"Hope—" His voice broke. She would never understand why he'd left, that his decision didn't even have anything to do with him, really. It had all been for her, and since he couldn't even tell her that much without inviting questions he refused to answer . . . he just needed to shut up before he said too much.

Another knock. He opened his mouth to protest, but Hope shook her head and sprang to her feet, making the identity of his newest guest obvious. Ahn also swept inside without waiting to be invited, then, after flopping onto Josiah's bunk beside him, propped his boots on the desk chair.

"What did I miss?" he asked. "Clothes are still on, mostly"—this with a brief glance at Josiah's plain undershirt—"so looks like I've interrupted shop talk. What a shame."

"You'd think two years at headquarters would have taught you a little something about discretion." Hope tossed a stylus at his head, but Ahn caught it with one hand before it hit the floor. "Don't crush my delusions like that."

"And almost twenty years says we're way past discretion where some things are concerned." He sobered. "We all thought if anyone would make it, it would be you two," he added quietly. "Though I'm glad to see you haven't killed each other yet."

"Ancient history," Josiah broke in. If he said it often enough, it would become the truth. He could pretend. "And get those filthy utilities off my bed."

Ahn sprang up with a mock salute. "Aye aye, Captain. I suppose we all know who you'd prefer in your bed." Another stylus hit his head, Josiah's own, and he chuckled. "So? What's the rest of the story?"

"There's no rest of the story until there is, apparently." Hope reclaimed the desk chair. "Glad I'm not in charge."

Ahn's expression turned gleeful. Being pulled from surface duty, Josiah was beginning to understand, wasn't the drudgery he'd first claimed. Some people were like that—craved excitement, no matter what. And Ahn had always been that way.

"Restricted comms?" he asked.

Josiah nodded. "Beginning of the next watch. Don't let any rumors get started, but let everyone know to get their messages out soon." If nothing else, the order would allow Ahn's wife to receive her last message for a long while. He had no one to say goodbye to himself, but his crew deserved more. "Hopefully that's an overreaction and we can rescind the blackout as soon as we find *Triumph*, but I don't want word of four hundred dead to hit the media without some damage control."

"Comm blackout until further notice, aye."

"And Patrick?" Josiah rolled his shoulders back and forth, trying to defuse the tension there. The response, more detached and professional than he'd thought Ahn capable of, unnerved him. "I want all security wearing a sidearm once we're through that last wormhole. Let them know." It was an unconventional order, even on a ship tasked with law enforcement throughout the solar system, but Ahn didn't blink.

"Aye aye, Captain." His lip curved upward. "You know, taking orders instead of giving them is a pleasant change. Practically a vacation."

"You wouldn't know a vacation if it bit you in the face," Josiah replied. "When's the last time you took Cassandra to Earth?"

"Six years ago." Ahn frowned at the floor. "Kids are expensive. Deimos Station is as far away as we'll get unless those orders for New London come through."

Dammit.

His gut tightened. He'd languished long enough in a rehabilitation center on Earth to care much about going back anytime soon, but Ahn just had to bring up kids.

The cabin seemed to chill twenty degrees, and Ahn cleared his throat. "Well. I'm going to catch some shut-eye while I can. Be good, okay?"

Josiah laughed out loud, and Ahn shot him a grin and disappeared. Hope didn't make a move to leave.

"It's been a while since Ceres." Hope glanced toward the door. "I've missed him."

His breath caught. "Just him?"

"I . . ." She waved her hands about anxiously before clutching the bottom of her shirt. "Ancient history, remember? You said so yourself."

He'd lied. She must know he'd lied, and yet . . . and yet what was the point? There was no going backward, especially not while he had command of *Bayonet.*

But afterward . . .

He shook off the dream.

"I did," he replied. "And it's true."

"Good. Then there won't be any issues working together, right?"

Josiah shook his head, acutely aware of how he was no longer controlling the conversation. No, she had steered it directly away from their marriage, from emotion, from *them*. And that, to be sure, answered everything.

"There never have been before."

"No," she mumbled, seemingly torn for once. "I suppose there haven't. But we haven't worked closely before, either. Which is why I think it's best if we make every attempt to avoid each other from here on out. As much as possible, at least." Then, a bit more brightly, she added, "I'm going to get some sleep. I'll see you around, sir."

I'll see you around, sir?

He could only nod at her betrayal. With a single word, she'd spun the relationship they'd once had into something formal and aloof, and he had to admire the effortlessness of it. She hadn't given him any opportunity to respond, either—and something had changed in her expression, like she'd decided a long time ago how this would go, no matter how much he tried to change her mind.

There was nothing else to say. The door closed as she stepped into the passageway, and he closed his eyes once more, visions of wormholes taking her place.

CHAPTER FOUR_
NIMBUS STATION, ETRIK

THE HARNESS WAS AN ANNOYANCE. CORALIE KNEW this, and yet at this point it was the only thing keeping her upright on the treadmill. Hundreds of years of space exploration had eliminated the need to strap oneself in while exercising during zero-gravity operations, but the advantage of that kind of system couldn't be denied right now. She lifted her feet and let herself hang until her breathing returned to normal. The Earth-like atmosphere in Kinnard's cabin helped with that.

It had taken weeks to get to this point. At first, she'd lain in her bunk and cried when the only thing she could move was her big toe. Leg lifts came eventually, and when she could finally place her feet on the floor on her own and walk with Kinnard's help, it didn't matter that he was touching her. Walking was a gift, one she'd never take for granted again.

Besides her initial rehabilitation and his weekly feedings, he had paid little attention to her, and that was the way she liked it. He left each morning for whatever duties he had aboard the station, returned late at night, and didn't care what she did in the meantime. That was usually calisthenics, as much as she could handle until she collapsed. It was the only thing that took her mind off the nightmares and his next feeding.

Those were painless, at least, and she could tell the time was coming by the way he'd begin to look at her—like a piece of meat. That rare, juicy, perfectly cooked steak she still hadn't eaten. He'd begun apologizing for those looks, and she hoped that sympathy meant he would free her, but the next day he'd always sit her down in the chair that had become hers and begin his process.

Coralie had taken to trembling the entire time.

Kinnard didn't seem to mind her reaction, though. He'd drain her—just a little, for it seemed whole blood was more powerful than the scrubbed kind they'd taken from her before—then lean back with his glass, like he'd done that first night. While he drank, he talked to her like he never did otherwise

—about Earth, about her family, about the things her former crew was doing at Nimbus Station. She only half-listened, unable to move her eyes from her blood in his glass.

The treadmill completed its pre-programmed routine as Coralie hung above it, and she lowered the harness, testing her weight. When she'd first started this routine, she'd had to crawl back to her bunk on her hands and knees, and that was a humiliation she'd never subject herself to again. But today her muscles cooperated, even letting her stumble to the bathroom for a shower.

They'd been competent enough in constructing Nimbus Station, for the recycled water was hot, and it soothed the soreness that came with re-learning how to be physically fit. Yesterday she'd tried pull-ups on a bar Kinnard had installed when she'd asked, but the motion had pulled on the port in her chest. Coralie leaned her forehead against the metal shower surround and brushed her hand over the bump under her skin, wanting nothing more than to rip it out.

She wouldn't, *couldn't*, die like this.

It wasn't the first time the thought had popped into her head, but this time she felt it somewhere deep in her soul. There was hope, yes, but underneath that was more fear, more resignation. For resignation was why she was still here, wasn't it? For her, Earth might as well not exist anymore. There were six wormholes that separated the two planets, and more light-years than she could re-member. She supposed she had known at one time, but lying in the capsule for long had shrunk her world even further.

In any case, Etrik wasn't somewhere she could live if she managed to escape. While the gravity was almost the same as Earth, the atmosphere wasn't nearly as conducive to human life. Or most other kinds of life, really, though she wasn't sure exactly why bacteria and tiny insects flourished and larger animals could not. On Mars, that kind of thing made sense. Here, it was just one more question.

Coralie slammed off the shower and pulled a non-regulation tank over her head before slipping into the same jumpsuit almost everyone else on Nimbus Station wore. It'd taken her a while to figure out a way to cling to any semblance of modesty when Kinnard pulled her jumpsuit down to draw her blood, but she'd asked, he'd dug through a few of the cargo containers for some clothes. He'd only found a few tanks with low enough necklines, so she only wore them when she expected him to feed, and judging by the way he'd looked at her yesterday, he was very close.

Trying to ignore her immediate future, she combed through her damp hair and hoped for the best. It was becoming thick and long—a product of better food—and soon it would need to be cut. She would have to beg for a pair of scissors for that, because Kinnard thought letting her have anything sharp was dangerous. She didn't want to admit he was probably right.

Presentable again, she glanced around his quarters. Her chest ached around the port, so more pushups were out of the question. There was a selection of books stored in the public computer, but they only reminded her of Earth—and though she hated to admit it, her eyesight wasn't quite back to normal.

Flopping onto one of the leather chairs, she sighed. Kinnard hadn't actually said she couldn't leave the room, though she'd never given leaving any serious consideration. Was there even enough atmosphere out there? That didn't matter to some extent, since she could breathe in Etrik's atmosphere for a short while, so maybe it was cowardice on her part. Those were her former colleagues out there, and seeing them—having them see her like this—well, which was worse?

She found herself in the corridor anyway, eyes wide and chest heavy with anxiety. It was empty, which made sense since it was the middle of a shift. The door slid shut behind her, and she sucked in a few lungfuls of air as she turned, committing the number on the door to memory.

23-9-16: section 23, deck 9, room 16. Finding her way back wouldn't be difficult. It would be even easier to find her way back if she was limited to pressurized parts of the habitat. Kinnard couldn't possibly intend to let her go far.

"Coralie?"

Coralie jumped at her name. The blonde who'd turned the corner behind her smiled, then narrowed her silver eyes.

"Helena?" It felt strange to call one of *them* by their name, even the woman who'd once been a colleague. A friend.

Helena brushed the untamed curls Coralie had always been jealous of from her face. "Kinnard let you out."

"He never said I had to stay inside. I figured if I could breathe when I opened a door, then I was welcome." A shiver ran down her spine. For the first time, she wondered how safe outside was.

Was Helena hungry? "But you know, I'm pretty tired. I think I'll go lie down."

"No, you're not. You're pretty scared of me." Helena cocked her head to the side. "I'm safe. I've had my daily dose, and I'm not interested in taking what's Kinnard's, anyway."

"I'm not his." The dizziness intensified, but she was certain it was from Helena's comment and not a lack of oxygen.

"No, but your blood is, so no one's going to drink from you behind his back. Come on, since you've decided to brave the outside." She gestured down the corridor. "I'll show you around."

"I don't think so." Coralie put her hand on the door. "I really am tired."

"You can't stay in there forever. Let me show you the workout facilities. And the greenhouse. Kinnard had them pressurized for you, so you won't have to wear a suit." Helena's silver eyes became plaintive. "Please?"

"Why?" Suspicion was going to be the one thing that kept her alive.

"Because we were friends once." Helena shrugged. "And maybe I'd like to explain."

* * *

They visited the greenhouse first. Outside, terraforming was well underway, and scientists had predicted a full Earth environment in another two hundred years. Faster than Mars, even if travel here hadn't been possible until the wormholes were discovered. A few v-words were visible through the large glass windows, but that was only possible for changed humans. Her own body wouldn't last long.

But here, in a single module built just for fresh vegetables and even fresher air, Coralie felt like she might live. Humans had been coming to Etrik for five years now, and that had allowed for the growth of quite a few large trees—cheap, live-fast-and-die ashes, to be sure, but they were *living*. Seventeen of them poked up through the gantry from the first floor, and she reached out to touch a silvery jade leaf. Only Helena's sharp glance stopped her from plucking one, so she sat on one of the benches and considered her feet.

"Looks good, doesn't it?" Helena asked, sinking down next to her.

"It does." Coralie's gaze shifted to the large pot of cherry tomatoes next to her. Their scent was recognizable even this far from Earth, homey and comforting. She chanced Helena's wrath and picked one, and the risk was worth it. "These taste good, too."

"They're some exotic heirloom variety. Seeds are cheap."

"Yeah. And they travel well."

Their eyes met, and Coralie blinked to keep from looking away. She knew seeds were cheap. Helena knew they traveled well. But small talk was all that was left.

Helena broke the stare first. "I'm sorry, you know."

"You knew." Rage like she hadn't felt except toward Kinnard built. "You never bothered to warn me, just let me wander in this nightmare, and now you want to sit here and talk like we used to." She brushed away a tear as the feel of the capsule's silken cocoon against her skin flickered through her memories. "I don't know how you can live with yourself. Do you know what they did to me?"

"It was necessary." Helena raised her chin, though her voice had weakened.

"Necessary," Coralie repeated. "Let's review what you say is necessary, shall we? Lying to me about what I would be doing here. Telling me there was something wrong with *me* once we'd transited that wormhole, and that's why I needed to be restrained and stashed away in a makeshift sick bay by myself. Locking me away in a capsule for eight months, intending on doing it for another hundred years. Do you know my eyesight still isn't perfect, even with my implants? Or that I had to crawl on the floor for almost a month before I was strong enough to walk again? Or that I stutter sometimes after going months without talking?"

She pulled her jumpsuit aside and pointed at the port.

"Is this necessary, too? What the medic did to me, what Kinnard does to me every few days? He drinks my blood, Helena. He sits there with a glass and drinks it in front of me like we're having a pleasant cocktail together, and there's nothing I can do about it. I can't even move. My entire body freezes, and all I can do is sit there and stare at him. And it's going to happen until I die!"

"You don't understand."

"No, *you* don't understand."

Helena stared off into the distance, out through the glass toward the red rocks outside. Etrik looked like Mars in the photos, Coralie had always thought, but being here . . .

It's not Mars at all.

"It was a mistake, everything that happened at first." Helena sighed. "As the first group to colonize was going through the second to last wormhole on the Etrik route, they realized almost immediately that something was wrong. The eyes, the physical deterioration. They knew they were dying—slowly. All but one, a botanist from Mars. The entire way to Etrik, he remained healthy until succumbing to an aneurysm a few weeks after arrival. The autopsy showed a congenital defect that was missed in the medical screening. Nothing sinister, but it ruptured when he did his first walk outside in a vacuum suit. Bad luck for him, I suppose. But the doctor who performed the postmortem hadn't used gloves out of some misguided sense of pessimism and impending death, and when a bit of the botanist's blood got into a scrape on his hand, he began to heal."

Coralie's stomach dropped. It wasn't hard to figure out what Helena wasn't saying.

"So they all drank a dead man's blood." Her stomach lurched. "And then conveniently forgot to tell anyone what had happened. Including me."

"Would you have done differently?" Helena asked. "Everyone wants to live, and death was certain for everyone who'd passed through that wormhole, whether from the lack of criexain or what anyone on Earth would do when they found out. You know the NSRC would send the military to exterminate us if they knew. So, after a bit more research, they figured out there was a gene that had prevented him from changing when the rest of them had—and then they set about finding more of those people whose blood could be used. Things were getting dire, and there was really nothing else they could have done. Problem is, that gene is rare. Incredibly so."

Helena wasn't wrong. Would Coralie have done things differently had she been in their situation? Not likely. No one wanted to die if there was a way to save themselves.

"Fine," she replied. "They did it to save their lives. Even if I couldn't fault them for that, and I'm not saying I don't, what about the rest of them? It's been five years! Five years that more people have been coming here, allowing themselves to change like this, lying to the NSRC, lying to the government, doing horrible things. Beyond horrible, Helena. You know what they did to me, and you did nothing to stop it!"

"They're scientists, mostly." Helena lifted a shoulder. "What kind of scientist wouldn't want the chance to live forever, especially on a new planet? All that research, all these new innovations to discover . . . and here we are, all the way out here with no one to bother us. Etrik's at the end of a wormhole sequence. There's no strategic value. The military doesn't want it, so it's the perfect place."

The logic was irrefutable. And intolerable.

"But you're not a scientist, Helena. Neither are half the people here."

Helena tucked her hair behind her ear. "The year before *Triumph* left Mars, my mother died. Pancreatic cancer. It was worse than I ever imagined. Kinnard knew—lots of people did—and he asked if I wanted to be part of something that would prevent that from happening to me. I jumped on it."

"Without asking questions?"

"They wouldn't let me." Her expression became distant. "It was 'sign up, no questions asked', for a chance to avoid my mother's fate. I assumed it was for some sort of medical research. By the time I knew differently, it was too late."

"You could have told someone."

"And risk them withholding the criexain from me? Besides, you know communications with Earth are limited. Until they can install a stable communications line through the wormholes, we've got limited comms—just expensive probes, and believe me, no one here wants to use one unless absolutely necessary."

"They need me, though." Coralie's heart skipped a beat. "I could try contacting NSRC on Mars. I could warn them."

Helena's hand closed over her wrist. Coralie tried to pull away, but the hold was steel. It felt like Helena could break bones just by pressing, and maybe she could.

"Don't make me tell Kinnard you're plotting something." She twisted a bit, and Coralie bit the inside of her cheek to stifle a yelp. "He may need you, but he can still make the rest of your life miserable."

CHAPTER FIVE_
NIMBUS STATION, ETRIK

KINNARD WAS SITTING ON HIS USUAL SETTEE WITH A glass of vodka in his hand, tracing the scrolling numbers on the tablet beside him, when Coralie entered. The lust in his eyes made it clear he'd have preferred something other than alcohol, and she made slow work of closing and locking the door. If she could just delay turning around . . . maybe she'd turn around into a new world. Earth, maybe. Home. A time and a place where people with modifications like hers didn't exist, and *Triumph* had never gone through the wormhole, and there wasn't a man sitting there on the couch, salivating for her blood.

But when he cleared his throat, and she turned toward him, she realized how foolish that had been.

"You went exploring." Kinnard licked his lips; his gaze dropped from her face to her port. Better than her breasts, if she was being honest with herself, but she might have preferred that. Human men stared at breasts. Monsters stared at the hole in her skin from which they drank blood.

"I was out wandering around with Helena Roscrow. I know her from Mars. We were just in the greenhouse, really. She wanted to show me some more of the station." The audacity with which he was staring emboldened her. "You never said I couldn't leave your quarters. In fact, Helena said you had certain parts of the station pressurized just for me."

Kinnard watched her for a long time, like he couldn't believe she'd pried that bit of information out of Helena.

"Indeed," he finally replied. "The pressurization annunciators are functioning as you'd expect— you can go anywhere you can still breathe. And if you can't, you might reconsider the validity of your reasons for being in a certain location."

"Can you give me a hint of where the off-limits sections are?" She suspected she already knew, but she wanted to hear him *say* it. Maybe he would narrow down the important compartments in the station—besides the capsule room, there must be several, and if she wasn't allowed there, she'd need to find a way.

"I think you know." He shrugged, then tossed back the vodka and set the glass down. "Sit. I'm hungry, and I'm sure you'd rather just get this over with."

Time to give in . . .

For now, at least. She would think of a way out later. Still, her legs shook as she walked to her chair and unzipped her jumpsuit. She placed her palms on her knees to stop the trembling. It never hurt, but there was another kind of pain than physical, she'd learned—one that was harder to recover from.

"Do you know why you were safe wandering around the station?" Kinnard asked, attaching a sterile length of tubing to her.

Coralie shook her head. Pretended she was anywhere else.

"I threatened to withhold the criexain if anyone touched you."

Blood flowed from her body, and she closed her eyes. Sometimes she made herself watch to remind herself just what a bastard he was, but tonight she couldn't even do that.

Wouldn't do that.

Her palms began to sweat, but she couldn't move enough to wipe them on her pants. Of all the things. Any sane person would have expected her to be claustrophobic after being in that capsule, but so much time in space had dulled her to small spaces. But the tubing Kinnard held against the edge of the crystal reminded her too much of the tubing that had gone into her leg, and those memories were enough to make her sick.

"It's happened, you know," he went on.

"What?" Despite her vow, her eyes flew open. "No one's touched me. Believe me, I would never let—"

"Oh, of course they haven't, not that you'd have a say in stopping it if it had. But one of the astrophysicists—Mario Alvaro—threatened it. Talked a good game in front of the wrong people. He's in the lockup now, just begging for one more dose."

"Why don't you give it to him?" The question was shaky.

Kinnard removed the needle from her port and rinsed the residual blood into his vodka glass as he sat. "Call it our new form of execution," he replied, taking a sip.

"You're horrible," she breathed. She shouldn't care about the fate of someone who'd wanted to attack her for her blood, but Kinnard was . . . he was a monster.

"Not horrible." He finished her blood in one swallow. "Judicious. We must maintain order here. We exist on the edge of the knife, and no one and nothing can be allowed to threaten our stability."

He moved toward her again, and Coralie jerked her jumpsuit back up. "You're sick. Executing people for mere words, freeing me while the others suffer—"

"Pull the jumpsuit back down."

Her palm settled protectively on the zipper. "You already had your drink."

"I need to flush your port," he said patiently, pulling on another pair of gloves.

"No." Coralie stood, ready to bolt. "A medic can do it tomorrow. I can't stand the sight of you."

Kinnard reached for her anyway, and she grabbed him by the wrist before she realized what'd she done.

Amusement flared in his expression as he stared at her grip. "You think you're stronger than me, hmm? Let's make a deal, then. I know you've been working out. I know how strong you are. You take me down, and you can wait until tomorrow. I take you down, and I flush it right now—after one more sip."

"Fine."

Coralie yanked her hand away and wiped her palms on her pants. If he wanted to believe she was still afraid, well . . . he didn't know her very well, then.

Augmented, she was augmented. She could take him.

Kinnard's amusement turned to an all-out grin. He darted at her, and she stumbled backward before catching herself, blocking his punch with her forearm. It hurt, but his grin faded, and she knew she'd hurt him just as badly. That was something, at least.

"Very nice." He put his weight on his rear foot and gestured to her with his hands. "You try now."

Something was wrong. He was inviting an augment to come at him? Well, she wouldn't think twice about that. She would hurt him, make him pay for everything. She'd regret it later, but it would feel so, so good tonight.

With a scream, she lunged at him, but he grabbed her outstretched hand like a frog snatching a fly from the air.

Her mouth fell open. His grip should have been impossible. She'd never practiced close combat with a v-word, but humans were humans, weren't they? Tales of inhuman strength outside the augmentations she had were just that. Myths. Lies. Scary bedtime stories parents told their children. They weren't true. And . . . a wormhole had done this? It shouldn't be possible. Physics didn't allow for this sort of thing, biology didn't allow for this sort of thing. The very nature of the universe—it had betrayed her and everyone else who'd thought they'd had a handle on things.

Kinnard spun her around as she debated and pulled her against him, her arms pinned behind her. "That was fun," he whispered in her ear. "Maybe we can do it again sometime. Now let's get one thing straight. I'm in charge here. I make decisions about my personnel, and I make decisions about your medical care. Now sit. I've changed my mind, and I think I've worked up a bit more of an appetite."

He hadn't hurt her. The modifications done to her body back on Earth had ensured his strikes hadn't even bruised her. But as he drained another tablespoon of her blood and prepped the flush she'd declined earlier, she didn't care. She hated him more than she could hate anyone, and there were only three other people aboard Nimbus Station —*humans*—who could help her take him down.

The other three in the capsules.

CHAPTER SIX_

THE WORMHOLE HUNG THERE IN SPACE, TWO hundred nautical miles in front of them, invisible to the naked eye in its current unstable state. Only the display in front of Josiah's chair, projected above the helmsman's station as well, showed the anomaly, a shimmering sphere emitting wispy tendrils of emerald and indigo. They curled more the farther they drifted from the center, like smoke out of a chimney on a cold Illinois morning. He watched them coil and twist, his sense of marvel building. How had he ended up here from the cornfields of a Midwest farm?

"Nice." Beside him, Ahn brought his coffee to his lips and drained half the mug in one long gulp. "Just like the pictures."

Josiah choked down a laugh. "If I didn't know better, I'd say you were underwhelmed."

"Nothing to be overwhelmed by. We're not the first to go through," Ahn reminded him. "Not by far."

He was right—*Bayonet* wasn't. There were thousands who'd made their first jumps by now. Some had remained on the far side for good—the NSRC scientists on Etrik, for example—and even more had jumped and returned to Earth to talk about it. Hell, Canada ran Bondar Station just on the other side, and both the US Navy and Chinese PLAN had permanent fleets stationed past Wormhole Alpha, a kind of combined customs base and last-chance protective buffer for whatever might come through the other way.

Probes hadn't seen anything, of course. Heaps of nebulae. A few deserted planets. Some dead-end wormholes—the Etrik System was at the termination of one of those. With zero strategic value, the Joint Wormhole Organization had designated it as "scientific interest only" and promptly handed it over to the NSRC. No one had minded. Giving civilians their own planet kept them out of everyone else's hair.

"Well, overwhelmed is probably the wrong word, too. Impressed, maybe." Josiah peered over his mug at the back of Hope's head. She was muttering bearings and headings to herself so quietly no one could hear; that much he knew. The coffee beside her, though—that was strange. She'd never been much of a coffee drinker, but perhaps preparing for the first transit had kept her up late the night before. Or perhaps, though he hated to admit it, he didn't actually know who she was anymore. Had he ever?

"I'll buy that, I suppose," Ahn replied. "It's astonishing that's it been right here all this time, and we never knew."

"Humans are limited." Josiah tapped on the station in front of him. Forty-five seconds until the next vortex stabilization, an opening that would last for almost an hour—plenty of time for *Bayonet*'s transit. "Which is probably for the best, given the trouble we cause."

"There's that cynicism I've missed so much. I was starting to think you'd become an optimist." Ahn chuckled as he grabbed his cup and disappeared down the passageway, waving his watch at the sensor that logged his departure from the bridge.

"Someone needs to be cynical for both of us," Josiah replied under his breath. He motioned with his chin toward the forward windows, toward the nothingness of the wormhole. "Okay," he added a little louder, leaning forward in his chair. "Let's do this."

"Aye aye, Captain." The OOD—Ensign Ethan or Evan Valdéz, Josiah suddenly found himself unable to remember his name—sucked in a breath and glanced to his side, at the coordinates and thrust information Hope was feeding him through the navigation system. "Helm, come right five degrees, ahead slow."

"Right five degrees, ahead slow, aye." Boatswain's Mate Second Class Hales didn't sound nearly as nervous as Valdéz.

Attitude thrusters hissed, followed by the rumble of the main engine firing somewhere far behind him. *Bayonet* tilted in response, but her integral stability system meant Josiah didn't so much as shift in his chair, though he grabbed his coffee out of sheer habit—*Vigilant* hadn't had such innovative technology. The sphere in front of them grew larger until Hales flicked the adjustment switch, shrinking the display and allowing a miniature of *Bayonet* herself to appear. The wormhole dwarfed her, and Josiah looked away.

"Ten seconds to stabilization," Valdéz added. "Nine, eight, seven . . ."

His voice drifted into the background. The wormhole out the window didn't change—the void couldn't—but on the display, the tendrils became rigid, taut. They stretched forward, reaching out as if to grab *Bayonet* and her hapless crew, a kraken waiting to pull its prey underwater forever.

"Mark," Valdéz finished.

The tendrils disappeared into the sphere as he spoke, swept backward by an invisible force Josiah supposed he had learned about in physics and promptly forgotten. Light curved around the sphere, creeping around the circumference until ring upon golden ring floated through it. In the center, the shadows of deep space smoldered, untouched by the luminosity of the Sun.

"Sir?" Valdéz asked.

Josiah glanced at the scanner beside him for any visual targets. There were none coming from the opposite direction, of course. Bondar Station controlled traffic through Wormhole Alpha, and *Bayonet* was transiting under the highest priority, traffic already cleared for her high-velocity burn to Wormhole Bravo.

"Take us in," he replied, wetting his mouth with coffee that had suddenly turned stale.

"Aye aye, Captain." Valdéz's left hand worked his control pad, typing in his instructions for the log. "Helm, continue on course, ahead half."

"On course, ahead half, aye."

The engine vibration strengthened as the wormhole loomed large in the display once more. *Bayonet* was only thirty nautical miles away now, and the sphere expanded, the number and size of the curved light rings ever-increasing. Josiah glanced out the side window, toward Saturn's rings and the Sun, cold and distant, then back to the darkness ahead.

Before he could tell himself to blink, *Bayonet* was inside. Rings of light spiraled about them as the black sphere opposite them became visible to his naked human eyes at last. Speed? What did speed matter now? He couldn't decide if they were drifting, or being propelled by the plasma engines that normally powered *Bayonet*, or falling into an infinite void beyond anything he'd ever imagined. Before he could panic at the idea of the first instance of an Orbital Guard ship colliding with itself, *Bayonet* penetrated the second sphere.

Stars materialized, alien constellations he'd never seen except on the charts in front of him. Josiah pivoted backward for an instant to catch the retreating wormhole, forgetting there was no aft window on the bridge. Ahn was getting a hell of a show from the aft observation deck right now, though. His hand touched his coffee mug. Still warm, even after jumping fifty-plus light-years from his home system.

So unnatural.

And yet . . . and yet, it felt *right*.

"Helm, all stop." Valdéz's voice shook, just enough to be noticeable. *Bayonet*'s engines cut, and silence filled the bridge. "Captain, we're receiving a comm."

Josiah could have sworn he heard his heart beating. "Very well. Put it on speaker."

"*Bayonet*, this is Bondar Station, how do you read?"

He picked up the microphone and took a breath. *Easy.* The first jump had been easy, and all this worrying had been for nothing.

"Bondar Station, *Bayonet* here," he replied. "Loud and clear."

"*Bayonet*, radar contact seventy kilometers from VAGES. Confirm if able."

Josiah squinted at his screen, half expecting to have to estimate their distance to the nearest waypoint, but Hope had already sent the location confirmation to his station, along with the metric conversion. He stifled a laugh at that.

"Reading the same, Bondar, bearing 325 and seventy kilometers."

"Good deal, *Bayonet*." The initial crackle of an unsecured pulsed laser transmission stabilized as the modulation keyed into *Bayonet*'s encryption system at last. "Proceed on course for Wormhole Bravo—and welcome to the New World."

CHAPTER SEVEN_
NIMBUS STATION, ETRIK

Coralie slept in the next morning, long after the morning alarm had sounded in the hallways outside, notifying the station of the beginning of the second watch. Kinnard thought she was hurting, had apologized when he'd left, which just proved he had no idea what she was capable of. Every injury from last night—the ones he'd inflicted on her and the ones she'd caused herself—had healed: from the multiple needle sticks in her port, to the bruise on her forearm, to where he'd scratched her on the shoulder with his thumbnail while grabbing her. The scratch was an accident, of course, now that he could drink and not just lick.

She shuddered at the thought as she pulled her hair into a low ponytail. For the first time in days, working out wasn't the first thing on her mind. Becoming stronger hadn't stopped Kinnard, and after tossing and turning all night, abusing her body further wasn't appealing. She deserved a break, and she needed to explore all she could if she was to free herself and the others.

Visiting the security center on deck seven was out of the question unless she wanted to find herself back in that capsule—if she could even breathe there—so she strolled to the facilities department instead, stashed in the corner of a module two levels below Kinnard's quarters. It took longer than she'd expected, since she had to stop at each door and check for atmosphere, but in the end, she'd made it. Had Kinnard expected her to?

Perhaps he had, though he likely had an idea that it was a close second choice to security for her, if in fact it was second best at all. On the far wall from the entrance was a map of Nimbus Station, lit with colored bulbs—power distribution, life support stations, fire detection and suppression locations, comm sites. Coralie stared at it for a moment, memorizing what parts of the labyrinth she could and taking photos of what she couldn't with the ocular camera in her left eye. The v-words would kick her right out and snitch to Kinnard if they thought about it long enough, but she'd been marked as one of the associate engineers in this very department. Her appearance wouldn't be that suspicious to them.

Shouldn't.

"Excuse me," she called out. "Can someone help me?"

Four sets of silver eyes swiveled toward her.

"Coralie." Henk Scheper, the man who'd have been her supervisor had things gone according to plan, blinked at her, as though he'd forgotten she'd ever existed. "What are you doing here?"

"I'm bored," she replied flatly. Henk's betrayal stung. On Mars, they'd been friendly enough to have the occasional drink together after work.

"You already have a job." He twisted back toward his station and tapped at a list of water purification statuses. "Go do it."

"Only once every few weeks." She managed to contain her gag. "I'm bored in between."

"Well, there's nothing for you to do here." He focused on his screen. "Go bother someone else."

"Henk, hold on." Riley Shaw sounded irritated as she stood, but then, she always had when Coralie was in the same room. Going through the wormhole might have changed Riley's eyes from dark brown to silver, and the lack of sunlight on Nimbus Station might have turned her warm sepia skin ashen, but her lip still curled in Coralie's presence in much the same fashion as it had on Mars. "There's always the fire detector inspection. It's due in two days. Kinnard wouldn't mind if she did it, and we do need the help."

Coralie's heart skipped a beat.

Yes.

"Won't mind?" Henk brushed his shoulder-length blond hair behind his shoulders. He'd always curled it on Mars, but here on Etrik, he seemed to have little concern for its appearance. "He'll be pissed."

"So what?" Riley's tone suggested exactly what she thought of Kinnard and his approval of her activities. "He'll never find out as long as she's back to her quarters before he wants her."

Henk turned, looked Coralie up and down, and sighed. "I suppose it doesn't make that much difference. Fine. Procedure is to start on deck one and work upward. You know the drill. Make a mistake, and you'll be restricted to your quarters so fast your head will spin. No being nosy, either. Follow the map. You're banned from section two on deck two and section seventeen on deck four, you understand?"

Coralie grabbed the tablet he held out and nodded. Henk might as well have told her where she really needed to snoop around. "You'll notify the departments I'm coming?" The last thing she needed was to surprise a group of v-words by appearing in their doorway again. Her own department was one thing. Strangers were another altogether. "And pressurize the compartments?"

"I suppose I'll have to."

With that, Henk's silver eyes flickered back to his screen, like she was offending him by asking such a legitimate question, and Coralie padded out into the steel hallway, tablet under her arm. No one stopped or even gave her a second look as she wandered down the corridor, counting the sections down to one, and she couldn't believe her good fortune as each door revealed a glorious new world full of oxygen and possibilities.

Free.

She was free. Free from the capsule where they'd tortured her for over a year, free from Kinnard's quarters, free from . . . well, fear and anger and homesickness, for now.

Even with the snapshots she'd taken, it took almost ten minutes to find the elevator that led down to deck one. The orbital station on which she'd trained above Mars was a similar tangle of hallways, and she'd always suspected it was some kind of subtle evaluation—get lost, and you were out of the Nimbus program. But she'd always had an eerily accurate sense of direction, and it was only the disorientation she'd struggled with since Kinnard had freed her that made her lag along more slowly than she would have otherwise.

So did the cold. This part of Etrik was about the same as winter in the Ontario forests where she'd done part of her survival training. Outside of Kinnard's obviously heated quarters, the thin jumpsuit she wore wasn't nearly warm enough to compensate for the chilly corridors, and though she'd survive, it wasn't pleasant. Maybe the v-words didn't get cold like they had before they'd changed.

Coralie shivered and pulled her hands inside her sleeves as the elevator headed downward. When the doors opened, she was underground—or at least felt like she was. The lights were brighter down here, and she stood on the institutional flooring, gazing down the t-corridor. Left seemed to lead to a mechanical room, and she made a note of that. Useful now? No. Later? Quite possibly. Right was unlabeled, and at first she was suspicious of the lack of information, but that was probably the norm for a base that had only been built a few years earlier.

She mentally scanned through the snapshots of the map and came up empty once more, which meant this was an older section of the station, one not monitored regularly enough to be shown on the primary map. That meant straight, for now— straight was a good foot wider, and she slunk down that corridor, still unsure of what to do when a v-word found her down here.

Hi, I'm just checking the smoke detectors didn't seem like it would go over so well, even if it was the truth. But each bulkhead down this way was neatly labeled with the deck and section number, and as she counted down from thirty, her apprehension eased. No v-words in sight helped with that, and doing what she'd expected to be doing aboard Nimbus Station was comforting, even if things had gone so very badly in the end. No one confronted her as she walked, and when she arrived at Deck 1, Section 1, Room 1, she was almost disappointed.

It was just a storeroom, cool and almost empty. A few rows of inoperative computing equipment were stacked in the corner, two office chairs in front of them. She considered digging through the stacks for some sort of weapon, but that would be shortsighted. There would be more fertile hunting grounds for that, and she needed to earn Henk and Kinnard's trust before she ran off and did something rash.

With a sigh, she dragged a chair under the first smoke detector and pulled the scanner from her pocket.

* * *

The good thing about the chill was that she hadn't broken a sweat checking the first thirty-two sensors. No one had bothered her as she proceeded down the first set of doors, all empty offices and storage rooms. She had rummaged through a few of the containers, finding nothing but wiring and printer paper. She'd laughed at that. What did they plan on doing with something as obsolete as printer paper? The answer was obvious, of course —some checklist or another said to bring printer paper to the edge of the universe, and so they had.

Coralie leaned against the wall as she waited for the elevator to take her to deck two. Henk had told her to stay away from some section or another upstairs, but she didn't remember. Memory issues, naturally, weren't something she or any of the augmented ones normally dealt with, but Kinnard—curse him, his torture had been ruinous enough to affect her mind. Would it return? She didn't even want to contemplate the alternative.

Still, as the elevator zipped upward, she ran through Henk's words and warnings one more time, then, finding nothing, she shrugged it all off. They'd remind her if she wandered into the wrong area, and if they didn't? And if that happened, she would plead ignorance. What else could Kinnard do?

A few v-words passed her as she turned right out of the elevator and proceeded to section one. Her amplified hearing picked up quiet whispers.

She's Kinnard's, you know. Still human. Well, mostly still human, I suppose.

Do you think she's angry about what happened?

I don't see why she would be. She's free now, isn't she?

I suppose it doesn't matter if she is. She's not a threat. She's weak, comparatively.

Coralie's stomach churned at the casual manner with which they discussed her predicament. Even Helena had been . . . well, not apologetic, no, she hadn't been that at all. But she hadn't been *nonchalant* like this.

Shaking her head at how she was the weak one once more, amplified hearing or not, she turned the next corner in the dense labyrinth.

And froze.

Two v-words stood in front of a steel door. They weren't dressed in the usual gray jumpsuits of the scientists and support staff, but black utilities with a gold shield on the left chest—Nimbus Station Security. Both stiffened when she appeared, and a quick glance at the blank location plate told her exactly why.

Deck two, section two.

Where they keep the others.

Her mouth went dry, but she forced her heart rate back to normal. It thudded once as the pacemaker complained of the rapid deceleration, then obliged. She'd never gotten used to that part of her augmentation. It was physically uncomfortable, a constant reminder that she was no longer fully human.

Well, more human than everyone else on Etrik now.

"Ms. Frazer," the one on the left began, "you're not allowed to be in this section."

"The fact I'm able to breathe suggests otherwise." Coralie held up the clipboard. "I'm conducting fire alarm testing. The inspection is in two days, and we're in a rush."

His brows drew together over silver irises that matched the gray streak in his dark hair. "Nonetheless . . ."

She swallowed. Did she dare mention Henk's name? It might get her in, but if security contacted him, she'd end up locked back up in Kinnard's quarters once more.

"Hold on, Sanchez." The other man—except it was so hard to think of him as a man—shifted his ample weight to his opposite foot. "It's not even about the inspection. Think about it. What if there's something wrong with the alarms in there?"

Sanchez's gaze snapped to her.

That's right. It'll kill them, and then you'll die.

In an odd way, it was comforting to know the others were protected. Physically, at least.

"I can't allow it," Sanchez finally replied, after looking her up and down with the same *nice steak* expression Kinnard sometimes wore. "Kinnard left orders, and she's not to be allowed anywhere near this section. She's too close as it is."

Coralie took a step backward and gave him an innocent smile.

So close . . .

"But what if we escorted her?" His colleague turned a bit more frantic. "She can't overpower us. And she certainly can't get them out of here on her own. Where would she take them, anyway?"

Sanchez bit his lip.

"No," he finally drawled. "She doesn't come in. Facilities can send someone else. And if you come back here again, Ms. Frazer, I'll tell Kinnard. If that happens, you won't have to worry about batting your eyelashes for access since you'll be right back behind this door in a capsule." He stepped toward her and put a hand on her forearm. "Now get out of here. And don't come back."

CHAPTER EIGHT_
NIMBUS STATION, ETRIK

Henk stared at her for a long time, and it took a great deal of effort for Coralie to not avert her gaze from his silver eyes. One slight change in her DNA, a fluke of her birth, and that could have been her. Well, maybe not, because she would have had to decide to go along with it, just like the rest of the scientists had. Would she have made the same decision? Or changed her mind upon reaching Etrik?

And if she'd done that, would they have killed her for not going along with their plan? Why was she even asking herself such inane questions? She had the faulty gene, she couldn't be changed by whatever sorcery the wormhole held, and she'd come through with her humanity intact. Second-guessing the future was pointless.

"Don't think for a second that security has forgotten you showing up at that compartment a few days ago. Kinnard will kill me if I allow you back there." Henk tapped a pen on his console. "And you know what he'll do to you."

"He can't kill you." She swallowed. *Not directly, at least*. "I thought that was kind of the point. And as for me, I'm willing to take the chance he's enjoyed having me so much that he won't want to go back to pills of refined criexain."

Well, technically Kinnard could threaten all he wanted, but he wouldn't resort to *that* unless absolutely necessary. And pulling another human from the capsules? He was already running low.

"He can withhold criexain from me." Henk narrowed his eyes. "And I personally don't care to die that way. Why are you so excited to get in that compartment, anyway?"

"I'm not." She dropped a bit of her enthusiasm, and it wasn't difficult. The nightmares were frequent. "It's the last place I want to be. Or so I thought. Turns out it's only second to last if you count Kinnard's quarters."

"Cabin fever, huh?"

Coralie nodded. "Of the worst kind."

Come on . . .

"I suppose we've all got it, especially here." Henk clicked his pen a few times and narrowed his eyes at her. "I can't blame you for wanting to get out."

"I also have a vested interest in making sure the station's not going to burn down," she added. "A large one."

That wasn't a lie. She'd glimpsed the other v-words working outside in the limited oxygen atmosphere that would be the eventual death of her and the others. Like the north of Greenland where she'd done some of her hazardous environment training, fire was deadly on Etrik.

"I suppose that's true, too." He clicked the pen a few more times, then sighed. "Take Riley with you."

"Henk!" A pen clattered to the desk as Riley's black braids appeared from the other side of the console. "I'm not a babysitter."

"Just do it. It won't take long, and then you can come back here and get back to making our lives miserable."

Coralie suppressed a grin. Henk had never been known in NSRC for his diplomacy and had the written reprimands to prove it. Agreeing with him made his candor even more amusing.

"Fine." Riley sighed with the heaviness of someone who'd just been ordered to float her way back to Earth in nothing but a spacesuit. "You're going to call those goons Kinnard has stationed out front and let them know we're coming? I don't feel like an argument this early in the morning."

"Yeah." Henk raised his hands. "Sure. If it'll make you happy."

Thank you, Coralie mouthed at him before darting into the corridor. She was already behind Riley's pace, apparently chosen to minimize the time spent with a *human*. It wasn't as though she and Riley had been the best of friends on Mars, but this was positively miserable.

But unlike when she'd run across Helena and talked with her in the greenhouse, she had no desire to kindle a friendship now. Even making small talk was unappealing today, especially with Riley, whose sole personal discussions prior to Etrik had revolved around Coralie's implants and how they lowered her value among men. Coralie was certain most men didn't care, but in any case, it wasn't a discussion she wanted to have. Not with Riley, at least.

They marched in silence to deck two, ignored by Nimbus Station personnel who otherwise looked on in curiosity. The silence, desired though it was, gave Coralie too much time to think of what she was about to see, and her heart—the real one, no pacemaker required today—was thumping away by the time they reached the compartment that still gave her nightmares. Sanchez stood at the door like before, and he loosed a pained sigh when she and Riley rounded the corner.

"Look," he began, "I really don't know how many more times I have to say this—"

"Fire alarm inspection," Riley interrupted in a bored tone. "Scheper approved it. You can call him if you want."

"And you had to bring her?" This with a nod at Coralie.

"It's her job. She's one of the few who knows how to do it. I'm just the babysitter."

"How hard can it be?" Sanchez narrowed his eyes. "Don't you just push a few buttons?"

"No." Coralie met his gaze. "You don't."

He steadied his stance, then nodded. "Fine. But you're responsible for her."

"Yeah, you be sure to tell Kinnard that." Riley rolled her eyes. "Open the door."

Sanchez mumbled something unflattering about Kinnard under his breath, then turned and keyed in a code, following it up with a fingerprint scan. His broad shoulders and ample weight prevented Coralie from seeing the code, and she wouldn't be able to duplicate the prints. Not easily, at least. Cutting off his hand would work if it came to it.

"There you go." Theatrically, he swept a hand toward the open door. "Enjoy."

Right.

Enjoy.

Coralie crept into the darkness beyond Riley, her implants adjusting as she blinked. She knew from experience that the capsules were soundproof, but the steel floor somehow softened her footsteps, taking away any chance for hearing, every possibility the others might be reminded of anything but their own misery. What was the point of that kind of torturous isolation, anyway? It was bad enough to be locked away like a piece of meat.

The yellow glow from occupied pods caught her attention, but she kept her mind focused on the fire detectors, keeping her gaze away from the sides. She didn't need to look to know that rows of capsules marched down the edges of the room, some with humans inside, some waiting for more victims, Kinnard had said. But who? One volunteer a voyage wasn't enough to sustain the Etrik colony for long.

"There," she whispered to Riley, too anxious to speak louder. "First one is above that access panel there."

Riley made a noise of agreement and stood back to let Coralie climb the wall ladder. The panel slid to the side almost silently, and she hopped up, settling her weight on the beam that ran down the center of the compartment. Above the capsules was open space, with a bulkhead at one end. It was even darker up here, but with a quick blink Coralie's implants caught up. So did her mind—from up here, she could explore the compartment without Riley breathing over her shoulder.

"Riley," she hissed down the hole, "I screwed up. Wrong access panel. The first detector is another five meters aft. I'm just going to crawl down there and check it."

Riley didn't answer, so Coralie balanced on the beam and tiptoed aft, casting quick glances at the machinery that rose through the ceiling. Tubes and cables intertwined in a perverse dance she didn't have a chance of understanding, especially since her body had suddenly become both heavy and insignificant.

Coralie sank to her knees and took a breath. The tube in front of her—filled with an easily identifiable dark liquid—mocked her, and when she went to stand, she found herself almost incapacitated with fear.

Just like in the capsule.

She glanced down, under the beam.

It was dark.

Steel.

Not the cream plastic.

It was enough that she could force her muscles into action. She found the detector where it was supposed to be and knelt beside it to run its self-test process. Riley would be able to see the flashes and hear the beeps through the ceiling, allaying any potential suspicion. That completed, she crept back to the hole with her eyes closed to avoid seeing the tubes again, then slid down.

"Two more," she told Riley, who was leaning against a half bulkhead checking her nails. Riley simply waved her away, so Coralie proceeded, her eyes on the floor. Maybe by the time they left she'd be brave enough to glance to the side, at the others who hadn't been as fortunate as she.

No.

She had to look, no matter how much she didn't want to.

The second detector checks went faster than the first, and her heart, which had finally settled down, pounded again as she descended for the last time. She took a breath, intentionally slowing it, but her training didn't work as well as usual. One quick look to her right revealed an empty, dark capsule, so she focused on her feet again.

Next row. There has to be someone in the next row.

Coralie took five more brief steps, then stopped. Yellow light flooded her left eye. Riley was leaning against the open door at the end of the compartment, seemingly so far away, so she swiveled to her left and braced herself.

A clear plastic door greeted her, locked with a keypad that looked like the one Sanchez had let her and Riley in with. A row of lights flashed above, yellow and green, and a medical screen of some sort hung to the right. Heart rate, brain activity, and other scans she couldn't identify flashed at her, but it was the man lying in the cocoon inside who drew her attention and held it.

He was naked, like she had been, and his azure eyes stared up at the ceiling just centimeters from his nose, aimless and lost. His hair was longer than hers had been when Kinnard had released her, but that didn't necessarily mean anything. No ship had arrived on Etrik since *Triumph*. It was tangled, and though he wasn't her type, she wanted to run her hands through it, make him presentable, force him to remember his humanity with her touch.

His mouth opened in a silent scream as she stared, followed by sobs that shook his entire body. Coralie took a step forward, wondering if he was the same one she'd heard crying another lifetime ago. She felt no judgment, no mental accusations of weakness of even the slightest sort, for hadn't she done the same? Didn't she still, if only in her dreams?

Words punctuated his cries, but she couldn't hear or interpret them as she approached his capsule. Before she could think of what Riley might do, she placed her palm against the plastic door. There was no way he could see her standing behind him, but as she tried to project her presence, she was certain he felt it. He must, for as he closed his eyes, his sobs faded away and his heart rate returned to normal.

"I'm Coralie," she whispered, even though the door blocked all sound. "And I'm going to help you."

"Coralie!" Riley's screech made her jump. "You can't be near him!"

"I didn't do anything." With one last sigh, Coralie turned toward her. "It's not like I touched him."

"You shouldn't even be that close to the capsules." Riley dragged her toward the door. "If Kinnard were to find out—" She stopped in her tracks, then shoved Coralie behind her. "Kinnard. What—"

Coralie peeked out from behind her. Kinnard stood in the doorway, his arms folded over his gray jumpsuit and his smooth face drawn into a frown. Her heart skipped a beat, and she coughed as the pacemaker responded. Didn't it realize humans could skip a heartbeat and still live?

"Sanchez called me." His tone was cool. "What's she doing in here?"

"Fire detector inspection," Riley replied, less bored than when Sanchez had asked her the same. "Had to be done."

"Then Henk should have found someone else to do it." His gaze swept toward Coralie. "You knew what would happen if you crossed me."

"I didn't cross you." Coralie crept out from behind Riley. Hiding implied guilt, and she could imagine how Kinnard would deal with guilt. "I'm doing my job."

"Last I checked, there weren't any fire detectors in that capsule you were staring into." Kinnard jerked his head at Sanchez and the other guard, and iron hands grabbed her by the arms. "But no matter. You'll change your mind about snooping soon."

CHAPTER NINE_

THE BRAVO, CHARLIE, AND DELTA TRANSITIONS HAD gone much like Alpha, though Josiah had witnessed the last two from the rear observation deck, leaving the bridge in the capable if anxious hands of Ensign Valdéz. The young officer had paled when he'd realized he would be in charge of taking *Bayonet* through the next wormhole himself, but there had been no time like the present and no wormhole like Charlie. Josiah supposed some charitable senior officer had done the same to him on *Munro*—thrown him in the deep end and let him swim or drown—but his memory had grown foggy in recent days.

Most of his memory, at least. Because in the silence of his stateroom, he couldn't help but think of the way Hope had looked at him yesterday when he'd wandered into the wardroom at the same moment she'd been sitting down with a muffin. Like he was a stranger. Only that wasn't right, because she'd have been more welcoming to a stranger. Instead, she'd stood, greeted him properly—he couldn't fault her etiquette—and then disappeared, leaving her meal untouched on the table.

With a yawn, he tried to focus on Ahn's words once more. Last night's sleep had been fitful, and he didn't hold out much hope that tonight's would be any different, though for once he actually intended to sleep as they transited Wormhole Echo. There was exhaustion, and then there was the exhaustion of captaining a starship. He was learning the difference.

"Sorry," he said as Ahn cleared his throat again. "I'm focusing. Really, I am."

Ahn raised a brow. "Looks like you're yawning to me."

"Just—" Oh, hell. What was the point in lying, especially to Ahn? "I'm just a bit worn out. Thinking about things. Sorry about that."

"What things?"

"Ah . . . Hope?"

"Is that a question?" Ahn asked. "From what I hear, you and Hope have been doing a wonderful job of avoiding each other, which makes my life a hell of a lot easier, so thank you for that. I've had nightmares of having to pry you two from each other's throats in the wardroom every morning. Try again."

The unmistakable sensation of thrusters firing as *Bayonet* fine-tuned her course to enter Wormhole Echo drew Josiah's attention to the starboard bulkhead. He leaned back in his bunk and tried to ignore the sound, his hands behind his head. It was an intentionally casual move, one that would never fool Ahn, but he had to try.

"I've just been thinking about what we'll find there, I suppose," he replied.

"Look, no one wants to see this turn into a re-covery operation. But even if *Triumph* had a catastrophic structural failure in deep space, you've seen worse."

"Yeah." He sat up. "I have."

But how was he supposed to explain to Ahn that it wasn't *Triumph*'s fate that had him so worried? Yes, he'd seen worse. Space was unforgiving, and everyone aboard *Bayonet* with the barest amount of SAR experience had seen things they'd rather not. Nightmares? Sure, he had a few of those every once in a while, but they didn't bother him. He woke up, prayed, showered, and moved on to the things he could still do something about.

No, there was something else stuck in the back of his mind, something he couldn't quite identify.

Ahn took a gulp of his own coffee. As long as Josiah had known him, he hadn't minded it cold. Or burned. Or bitter. Or sweet. Coffee was coffee, and Ahn never turned it down.

"Remember," Ahn said, gesturing with his cup, "when I spent those nine months aboard *Hamilton* turning circles in the out-system? Some Neptunian port made a report of an overdue merchant vessel out of Oberon, so we burn out there, hailing her the entire time. Had to divert half the power to the engines, because, you know, *Hamilton*. No hot water, no hot food, the entire time we ran like that. I am telling you right now, it was worse than a six-month cruise." He paused, considering. "Well, damn near might as well have been six months before we got back. I swear to you, if I never see Neptune in person again, it'll be too soon."

"No hot food for weeks on end." Josiah chuckled. "However did you survive without coffee?"

"I made a few thermoses before they diverted power. *Semper paratus.*" Ahn gave him a look. He'd always been sensitive about his habit. "Anyway, we show up, and the thing's docked right there, plain as Saturn's rings. Couldn't believe it. But she didn't respond to any of our local hails, and the dockmaster gave us a story that didn't add up, so we sent a team over. And her skipper, get this, he actually meets us at the hatch and admits he tried to slip in without telling anyone because he was trying to evade a rather large customs duty he owed when he'd left Pallas over a year and a half before. He never expected us to actually come after him."

"And what happened?"

"He bitched about the fines for a long time—light ones, I might add—then gave up when we threatened him with criminal charges, including every single one we wrote up for not carrying enough vacuum suits and having out-of-date star charts. Point is, things happen. People are forgetful, messages get passed incorrectly."

"Patrick." Josiah ground the heel of his palm against his eyes in a vain attempt to stave off the developing headache. "While I'm thrilled to listen to you grumble about how victimized you were on that patrol, that entire story is literally the opposite of people being forgetful and passing messages incorrectly."

"Eh, you know." With a remorseless laugh, Ahn chugged the rest of his coffee. "Close enough."

"Yeah. You're right." He'd chased down enough of the same in his time. Just not through a bunch of wormholes. "I'm sure it's all some sort of misunderstanding."

"Likely." It was Ahn's turn to yawn. "We've got another two items on the agenda, but I think we best table those until tomorrow's meeting. You're fading, and it won't look good if you fall asleep tomorrow on the bridge."

"Nice to have someone else taking care of my schedule for once." Josiah glanced at his empty cup, then nodded. "All right. Tomorrow, then. Same time, same place."

"Wouldn't miss it." Ahn stood. "See you tomorrow."

Josiah tapped on the desk as the door closed behind him. Ahn was an optimist, and he'd never won an argument against that sentiment. But then, Ahn lived a charmed life, had a charmed career. A loyal wife, two lovely children, an actual home on Mars, and command prospects within the next two years. Maybe sooner, if *Bayonet* fulfilled this mission. Could it get much better? Likely not, and that's why Ahn would never understand his cynicism. Or cynicism at all.

No. That wasn't fair, Josiah realized, as he stripped off his uniform and fell into bed in nothing but his underwear. He'd had a loyal wife, still had a promising career, and weren't homes overrated, anyway? His small flat was good enough for one person. Ahn had nothing he didn't. Children, maybe, but even after nine years, they hadn't been blessed with more than one, and that was that. No, Ahn was just *confident*.

He closed his eyes and considered Hope's earlier words.

Where else would I be? he'd asked.

I don't know, she'd replied. *The bridge. The wardroom. Strolling around your new command. You must be proud of it. I'm proud for you, and she's not even mine.*

For one brief moment, he considered getting up, getting dressed, and taking that stroll she had suggested—forty-eight people were probably wondering why they'd seen only the most ephemeral sightings of their captain since departing Mars. But *Bayonet*'s thrusters fired, and she rolled once more as he lay there, lulling him to sleep like he imagined the ships of old did to their captains upon endless, undulating ocean waves.

The dreams came almost immediately.

* * *

He stared at his bunk, steel and cold and hard, then tossed his brand-new sea bag to the floor next to it. The stiff white canvas looked ridiculous next to the chipped gray locker, so he sank to his knees and began to unpack. The specter of his mistake hung over him, a gray cloud of uncertainty and doubt. He didn't belong here. The other midshipmen were cool and confident, and he was still trying to adjust to his first sight of the ocean in his long eighteen years. Except for space, his ultimate destination, New London was about as far from a farm in Illinois as one could get, and in the five hours he'd been here, he felt the scarlet letter of his past on his chest.

Farm boy.

Hick.

He'll never make it.

Things would have to change. He'd show them he could learn, that just because his only exposure to the wider galaxy was the stars over the cornfields didn't mean he couldn't succeed in space. But he'd worry about getting unpacked before he worried about any of that.

"Hello."

He jumped to his feet at the voice—the past hours of being hollered at had already beat that into him. But to his relief, it was another mid who stood in the corridor outside, her uniform unrumpled and a piece of hair escaping from her bun. His eyes must have lingered on it longer than appropriate, because she reached up, cheeks red, and tucked it back in.

"Hi." He brushed floor dust from his palms and stuck out his hand. "Josiah."

She smiled, and he wanted to turn away so she couldn't see the fool look in his eyes, but he already knew he never wanted to look at anything else.

"Hope."

* * *

Water lapped against his feet.

A breeze tussled his hair.

Above him, some sort of seagull screeched. His limited travels before now hadn't prepared him for the beauty of it, even if he'd pouted about this particular school being on Earth. Sure, they'd had a few four-day deployments to orbit—and he'd spent most of that time sick—but most of the past six months had been spent right here. In the classroom. On the ground.

"You awake over there?" Hope waved her hand in front of his face.

"Yeah." He couldn't believe he'd forgotten she'd come to visit. "Just thinking."

"About?"

He chuckled. "How I didn't want to come here, even for training. How they could train us in space right away, but they don't."

"Bold words for someone who's spent most of his time up there throwing up." Her words were gentle through the teasing.

"True." He glanced sideways at her, then at the large boulders strewn across the beach. Soon it would be too cold to come here. Soon they'd both be gone, scattered throughout the system. "But I'm glad it happened."

"Really? You could have fooled me."

"I mean, I want away from Earth. Everyone here does, don't they?" His heart pounded, but he had to tell her sooner or later how he felt. "But I wouldn't have met you if things had gone differently. And that means something."

Her eyes widened, and for the longest moment ever, he thought his heart was going to crack.

Then she smiled.

* * *

Munro was a large cutter; his first real experience in space had made him sick. Green in more ways than one, he'd reported to her XO, then spent his first watch throwing up in a garbage can on the bridge. He'd done two short orbital cruises during his time at the academy and a few more during various schools, but there was something about knowing he wouldn't be standing on solid ground for the next six months that screwed with his mind in ways he could have never imagined.

Wiping his mouth for the dozenth time that day, he reached for a clean blouse, then set it aside and picked up his tablet. No messages from Hope today, but that wasn't a surprise. She was underway, out past Mars, and messages were only sent in bulk a few times a week. He re-read her last one again and again, wishing his own ship had the capacity to allow for video calls. Not that he'd forgotten her voice or the way she said his name or the way her eyes lit up whenever she saw him, which was less and less often these days.

How long had it been? Only six weeks since they'd said goodbye? It felt like six years, and even though his shipmates laughed and told him he was too young to be focused on one woman, he knew better.

He brought up her photo on one half of his tablet and closed his eyes. Writing messages was getting harder and harder. The idea of being hundreds of millions of nautical miles apart for the next however many years was sickening, and worse, he knew she felt the same. She said as much in her letters, even though, as she pointed out, they were both stuck where they were.

But that would have to change.

And he was going to have to be the one to set them in motion.

* * *

Mars wasn't where he'd ever planned on doing this.

Where exactly he *had* planned on doing it, he wasn't sure. Somewhere with oxygen to breathe outside, probably. But that meant Earth, and neither of them had been near the planet in over a year, so Mars it was.

It could have been worse, he told himself repeatedly, trying in vain to settle his nerves. There was an impersonation of a small pine forest—under a dome, of course—and there was a small store outside the station that sold more jewelry than he thought made sense out here, and most importantly, they were finally on the same space station.

It was time.

His palms sweated as he touched the ring in his pocket. He wiped them on the inside, terrified she'd see. Only because it would give his surprise away, of course. He wasn't afraid of her. Wasn't afraid of her reaction.

Hope squeezed his hand. "I can't believe we're finally together."

It was the same thing they'd both been saying since she'd arrived earlier that afternoon. He'd been there to greet her ship, but so had several dozen others, and he hadn't been able to concentrate on anything but this evening since.

"I know." He sat on a fallen log, an aesthetically odd choice under a dome where everything was controlled, and she sank to his side, her head on his shoulder. Her touch, her presence, how could he ever want anything else? He took a deep breath. "What if we were together, um, more?"

She scoffed. "Good luck with that. Assignments hasn't been happy with my requests lately. We're on different career paths."

His heart sank. She wasn't understanding, and he was going to have to spell it out for her. "Right. I guess I didn't mean in the same location. I mean . . . what if we could be together differently, I guess is what I meant."

She pulled her head off his shoulder. "Josiah, what exactly are you saying?"

He pulled the ring from his pocket and twirled it around his thumb, staring at it. "It's been such a long time. And I love you. I love you so much it hurts. And I would never ask you to give up your career, and I know things would be difficult if you say yes, but I don't want to be with anyone else. Ever. Even if we have to go months without seeing each other. I don't know if you feel the same way, but we keep dancing around this relationship, and . . . and I need you to know how I feel."

Her mouth opened and closed a few times, so he rushed onward.

"I'm fouling this all up. I think I'm supposed to be down on one knee while I do this, but that seems like a strange, old-fashioned custom when we're here in these fake woods on another planet, and I suppose . . . I suppose I should actually ask you a question, if I'm going to do this right."

"Yes. You should."

She blinked at him, then glanced upward, at the glass dome and red atmosphere above it, and he wished he knew what that uncertainty meant.

"I'm afraid of the answer."

"You shouldn't be."

He took a deep breath, then forced himself off the log. There was mud underneath his leg when he knelt, strange on a planet that was mostly dust, and he had to force himself to focus.

You're almost there.

"Hope, I can't imagine going forward in this life without you by my side, no matter how far apart we are. You are the other half of my soul, the one who makes me a better man than I am on my own, the one I want to wake up next to whenever I can. Marry me. Please."

"Yes." She kissed him once, and then again, and before he could get a word in edgewise, yet again. "Yes, of course I'll marry you."

* * *

Josiah's eyes snapped open.

With the reluctance of a man who knew he'd fallen asleep only six seconds before, he felt around the panel above his head for the direct comm to the bridge. The dreams had been so real, he had been convinced he'd been reliving the past, Hope's touch and all, but here he was, lying on a thin mattress in his quarters, light-years from Mars and even further from Earth.

"Bridge." Valdéz sounded like he'd found a bit of confidence hiding somewhere in the last wormhole.

"Status?"

"We cleared the exit sphere three minutes ago, sir." A pause. "And, uh, seventeen seconds."

Not even three and a half minutes? *Bayonet* had been making maneuvers to line up with the entrance when he'd fallen asleep, hadn't she? He couldn't remember, but it had to have been longer. Damn, he was truly exhausted to be this disoriented.

"Very well." He clenched his jaw lest Valdéz hear his apprehension. "Next high-velocity burn to commence in?"

"Ninety-seven seconds, sir. Spooling up for it now."

As if on cue, a resonance vibrated deep into his bones, painful yet soothing. He could laugh at Ahn about his love for speed all he wanted, but *this* was what had made him fall in love with space. For the next ten hours, *Bayonet* would run as fast as the plasma engines would let them, nothing in their way but hard vacuum. It had always done it for him, or at least it had before *Vigilant* had made him nervous around other spacecraft.

"Very well. Notify me once we reach . . ." He searched the screen above him, placed specifically so he could see all of *Bayonet*'s systems without getting out of bed. *A good waypoint, a good waypoint . . .* "Once we reach ELKON."

"Aye aye, sir."

The click of the mic signaled the end of the conversation, and he squinted at the screens over his bunk. He'd slept long enough, should get up and —and, well, do something. He rolled to his side and reached for his shirt, and his gaze landed on his watch.

How had he dreamed almost half his life in less than four minutes?

CHAPTER TEN_
NIMBUS STATION, ETRIK

They pulled her through a door into a dim room, and for a moment, Coralie couldn't see a thing, so confused by the alternating light and dark of the compartment with the capsules, the corridors, and now wherever they'd brought her. The environmental system was reduced or not working well here, for it was mold, not the sterile clean of scrubbed air, that filled her nose.

She blinked twice, and the implants sprang to life. Rows of—well, she couldn't call them anything other than cages—lined each side of a wide aisle. Chain-link fences, like the NSRC security people used to keep their dogs in on Mars, except these enclosures ran all the way from the ceiling to the floor, where large bolts appeared to prevent any sabotage. Since the v-words were stronger than any dog that had ever existed on Earth, they had to be strengthened, though she couldn't tell how. Unlikely even she could just bend the metal and walk out, but once the security guards left, she would investigate. Every system had a weakness, even this one.

"Like it?" Sanchez pushed her toward the third cage from the door, then shoved her inside and secured the door with a flashing lock.

There.

That lock, which relied on technology rather than brute strength, would be her way out of here, but not until she convinced them she wasn't a problem any longer. With a long look at the door, she crept back to the steel wall and settled down on the floor.

"Guess so," he replied before she could answer. He snapped at the others, an almost disappointed look on his face. "Enjoy your new quarters. I'll be back for you when Kinnard needs his next drink."

The door slammed, and Coralie closed her eyes, all thoughts of escape taking a backseat to a new emotion—rage. Screw Kinnard. What would he do if she drained herself first? What could he do if she made sure he couldn't use her? The others who'd killed themselves had died while under more restrictions than she was dealing with right now. Surely she could come up with something.

Unless he simply took another victim from their capsule . . .

Slowly, she scooted toward the fence on her left. The untreated edges of chain-link fence were sharp. It would take a while to bleed out with the coagulation capsules that floated in her bloodstream, the same ones the medic had been so worried about when Kinnard had shown her mercy, but did it really matter in the end? She wanted to live, yes, but she wanted to take the bastards out even more. Anyway, living on Etrik as Kinnard's prisoner for the rest of her life wasn't all that appealing, and he had just committed a grave error in judgment by leaving her unsupervised.

There.

Against the rear wall, she found the end of a wire, sharp and rough. She gripped it, trying to bend it at the right angle to scrape her wrist. It resisted even her augmented strength, and she swore to herself, then froze as a rasping sound on her other side echoed throughout Kinnard's makeshift brig.

She wasn't alone.

With more reluctance than she could afford, she turned, still crouched on her knees. There was a hulking figure in the enclosure next to her, so shrouded in the shadows that even her implants hadn't given her warning. It dragged itself toward her, stopped only by the metal that five seconds before had seemed impenetrable.

"This—" The voice was raspy, and she still couldn't make out his features. "This is his idea of a joke. Isn't it?" A pause. "Or just more torture?"

She swallowed. "Who are you?"

"Mario Alvaro. Astrophysics."

Mario Alvaro. The man Kinnard had mentioned.

Coralie backed toward the opposite side of her cage. The scientist, a man she'd only seen once from a distance, had nothing to lose. He was weak, yes, but just her being here was dangling a steak in front of a starving man. Her heart thudded, and she was certain it was the real one, not the pacemaker.

"You're the one who wanted to kill me," she replied, steadying her tone. "I would think this is torture for me to be trapped in here with you, not you with me."

"Who said I wanted to kill you?" Alvaro coughed. "I only wanted a drink. One I never took."

"Because you didn't have the chance." Arguing with him was probably a bad idea, but what else was she supposed to say? That she was grateful to Kinnard for protecting her to a point? "I know Kinnard's got security following me around when I'm outside his quarters."

That was an odd thing. On Mars, she'd have been flattered by the protection. Here, it was just one more reminder that he wanted her for one reason only.

"It was just talk," Alvaro gasped as he pushed himself up against the wall. "Locker room talk, if you want to view it that way."

"Oh, sure." She couldn't help the frantic laugh. "Just talk."

He crept closer on his hands and knees, and she slammed her mouth shut when his features became clear in the single bulb that hung by the entrance. Sallow skin drooped from a face that might as well have been etched in chalk by an artist who'd never wielded a chisel. His eyes were a deep yellow spotted with black instead of silver, a combination she'd never seen before, except maybe in sunflowers. Lack of criexain must damage the liver. Well, it made sense. Without it, the immune system turned against the v-words; she'd known that much. Perhaps it had some sort of affinity for that part of the body.

"Do you think," he said, choking on what sounded like mucus, "that I'd want to die like this, even for a taste of your pure blood? How reckless do you think I am?"

An uncomfortable emotion she hadn't felt in a long time wound through her mind, freezing her.

Pity?

It couldn't be. She didn't feel compassion for any of them, even Helena, not even after her story about her mother's death. She certainly didn't feel it for this *thing* that had treated her like she was something for him to use, even if he hadn't actually done it.

"How much would it take?" she asked.

Alvaro blinked. "How much?"

"How much of my blood would it take to cure you? I know it's not too late, as long as you're alive."

A cough. "You can't—"

"I can." Coralie yanked at the chain-link fence. It gave, just enough. "Kinnard never said I couldn't let anyone else drink my blood."

Alvaro narrowed those unnaturally yellow eyes. "I suspect that was understood. Besides, a drink from you here would only prolong the inevitable."

She let out a deep breath. He was right. There was the slim possibility she'd be able to sneak in and continue to feed him for a few days, but to what end? Kinnard would find out eventually, and when he did, he'd separate them, and Alvaro would die regardless. Besides, he was her enemy. Why should she want to help him?

"It would make you feel better, wouldn't it?" she asked before she realized what she was saying. "Wouldn't it help the pain?"

"I can't ask you to do that." His shoulders sank. "Not after what we did to you. Not after what we did to the others."

"You didn't ask me." She yanked at the metal again, then clenched her teeth and drew the sharp edge against her forearm. Of all the ways to die, liver failure must hurt. It was definitely more painful than the scrape—the scrape that would heal in the next five minutes if he didn't take advantage of her mercy right away. "I offered."

Alvaro sucked in a breath and focused on the cut, his eyes gleaming with the same hunger that was usually in Kinnard's.

"This is a trap." He licked his lips. "And you know there are cameras in here."

Of course there are.

"It's not a trap." Coralie held out her hand, cringing inside. "But if you're worried someone will notice, I'd lick it off before they can stop you."

His tongue scraped across her skin, then he closed his eyes and took another ragged breath. "Hospice care on Etrik. Who'd have ever thought that would become a thing?"

"How fast do you think it'll work?"

"Five seconds, apparently." He swallowed a few times. "Some of the pain has faded, at least. Took the edge off."

"Good." He still didn't look like he was capable of much physical strength, so she leaned against the wall and yawned. "I'm glad. Once this cut heals, if they don't bust in here to stop me, I'll give you another sip. And I'm sorry. For whatever that's worth."

"It's worth a lot."

She wasn't sure how to respond to that. And when his breathing became regular, and soft snores sounded throughout the makeshift prison, she was grateful she didn't need to.

* * *

The lights flicked on.

Coralie squinted at Kinnard's figure in the doorway, then next to her. Alvaro was lying on his side, pale. She reached through the fence, but there was no pulse on his neck.

"Couldn't make it through the wire, could he?" Kinnard sounded too nonchalant over the death of one of his own men. "Good for you, I suppose."

He didn't unlock her cage like she'd expected, but sidestepped her completely and unlocked Alvaro's, then pushed his limp body with a boot. Alvaro didn't move, and she rested her head against the wall. Tears? That wetness tracking down her cheeks couldn't be tears. Why would she cry for someone like him?

"Well?" Kinnard's voice broke into her grief. "Are you just going to sit there?"

She hadn't even realized her door was open. Shaking her head, she stumbled to her feet and followed him out. Kinnard didn't speak as they walked through the maze of tunnels. He didn't lead her back to his quarters, either, and though part of her felt she needed to run, what would be the point? He'd already punished her for her imagined crime, so this was something different. When he stopped in front of a door on deck four, she frowned up at him.

"I don't want you in my quarters anymore," he said, as though that explained everything. "You're a distraction I don't need."

He pushed the entry switch, and Coralie peered around him into the narrow cabin. It was scarcely big enough to accommodate her height, but the single bed to her right and wet bathroom at the rear spoke volumes. There was no window, but the viewing screen opposite the bunk cast a promising, indistinct glow across the deck. She'd be able to program it to show almost anything—space, Mars, the Everglades. After the capsule, it might as well have been the entire universe.

"Mine?" she asked.

"For now."

Her brows drew together as she slid by him and inside. "Even after—"

"Perhaps I've gone about things the wrong way." Kinnard leaned against the doorframe and pushed his sleeves up. "I assumed negative reinforcement would be best to start your new life here, and maybe that was unfair to you. Until yesterday, you were compliant enough. Consider this a favor, one which I hope will earn me a little more cooperation in return. Do you like it?"

Coralie nodded, too afraid to speak. It would betray her emotions, and more than that, her plans.

"Good." He stepped inside and closed the door. "Because I need a drink."

There wasn't the usual pre-feeding hunger in his eyes as he spoke, but if it was cooperation he wanted, she would give it to him for now. She was too tired to fight, too wordless to argue, and though she would have never admitted it to him, this gift meant something. It had given her a bit of her humanity back, and she had to struggle to not feel grateful to him for it. She lay back on her new bed and closed her eyes as he drained half a glass of blood from her port. She'd expected him to leave afterward, but he settled into the desk chair on the opposite wall and stared at her.

"Where are you from?" he asked.

Blast it.

Coralie yanked her jumpsuit back up over her shoulder and sighed. Not one of these conversations again. That first sip had turned him into a normal person, and while Kinnard the thirsty almost-vampire was bad enough, there was something just as bad about Kinnard the satiated almost-human.

"The Mariner Valley," she replied wearily. "I went to university there."

His brows rose. "Not Earth?"

She shook her head.

"But your personnel file—"

Her stomach clenched. Everyone who noticed the discrepancy became curious.

"I was born in Florida and was raised by my maternal grandparents in a small town in northern Mexico," she admitted. "But they resented everything about me. The money, the time, the fact that my parents had the audacity to die in a decompression accident somewhere high above Earth and ruin their peaceful retirement."

"Ah." Kinnard swirled the glass of blood as she headed to the washroom to splash cold water on her face. "I thought I detected a hint of an accent."

The water did little for her flush of humiliation. Thinking of those years always did it.

"Most think it's the Mariner Valley, but it's Mexico." She patted her skin dry and stared at herself in the mirror. She'd lost too much weight, had become much too pale. But that was everyone's fate on Etrik, wasn't it? The lucky ones who'd survived the trip here, at least. "I don't like talking about it, so now I just say Martian. Pretty much everyone believes it. Sometimes even I do."

"I'm surprised you can tell what part of you is you anymore."

Coralie's eyes narrowed as she sank back down onto the hard bed and tossed the thin gray blanket to the side. She didn't need him to clarify his comment to know he was referring to the augmentations in her body. It was an NSRC program, emergency research to determine if humans with modifications would survive long-distance space travel better than normal ones.

And yet, it was also technology that wasn't accepted among normal people, probably never would be. Most countries had gone through a period of . . . well, regression wasn't exactly the right word. Technology still flourished; the research station on Etrik was proof of that. But a century and a half ago, a series of events had made them realize the sprint toward transhumanism was detrimental to humanity in the end. Even the military didn't have modifications like she did, except perhaps a few purchased and installed on the black market. Perhaps some elite special forces teams as well. But not *normal* people.

"I'm still human," she replied. It was true, even if she questioned the claim. But really, who cared about a pacemaker and a few ocular implants? Those had been in use on Earth for over four hundred years. Hardly controversial. Some of the others . . . well. "More human than you."

"You're missing out." Kinnard gave her a slow grin. "Do you know what it's like to live without worrying about death?"

"But you do worry about it. It's hovering right over you, all the time, as much as you like to claim otherwise. Why else would you threaten your people with it? Use the criexain to kill them? I'll take sudden death from a virus or stroke over worry about what you can hold over your people . . . almost eternally. Mario Alvaro died a horrific, painful death, and I somehow doubt he'll be the last." She blinked against the memory of his sallow skin, but it didn't disappear. Real memories couldn't be deleted like the photos in her data chip.

"I think that might be the most words you've ever said to me." In the mirror, he leaned back in her chair and bared bloodstained teeth. "Even on Mars."

"I was afraid of you on Mars." She folded her arms protectively across her chest. If he wasn't going to argue about what he'd done to that man, she wouldn't keep prodding him. Maybe later. "Most everyone was intimidated, at the very least. You had so much power, so much control over assignments and what research was prioritized, and they knew they needed to keep you on their side."

"And now?"

Coralie pulled at a hangnail on her left thumb.

"Now," she replied, "I just hate you."

CHAPTER ELEVEN_

USOGC BAYONET, PAST WORMHOLE
ECHO

Josiah's stomach growled as he keyed in the code to his quarters a full two hours after his shift ended. But the paper envelope and sealed package on his desk called his name, so instead of changing into a clean shirt for dinner, he sat in front of them and slid a nail through the envelope's seal. A wisp of dark powder flew out, caught in *Bayonet*'s overzealous air currents, and he stared, unnerved, at the remaining ashes inside. The day had always sobered him before *Vigilant,* but if there was anyone not in need of a reminder of their own mortality this year, it was him.

Remember that you are dust . . .

"Merciful Father, forgive my failure that cost seventeen their lives," he whispered.

Hope would have raised a brow had she heard the plea, but no matter what, he asked forgiveness for what had happened to *Vigilant* during each confession, every prayer, each haunting silent moment when the memories became too much. Begging was the least he could do—but there was never an answer, nothing beyond the frivolous promises of absolution he was supposed to believe and would never admit he couldn't anymore.

He took a breath and forced her disapproval to the back of his mind. She'd declined his invitation to join him, after all. Not that he blamed her.

"Have mercy on me, O God, according to your steadfast love; according to your abundant mercy blot out my transgressions. Wash me thoroughly from my iniquity, and cleanse me from my sin. For I know my transgressions, and my sin is always before me . . ."

The rest of the psalm came in a halting whisper, though he could have never explained why the same words he'd recited with such sureness for years seemed to be hiding somewhere deep in his soul now. He suspected it was the unease of doing this alone, but perhaps it was only the chimes in the passageway, meaningless to him at the moment, yet an insistent disturbance. Maybe it was that he was sitting here without Hope beside him, a husband pretending he no longer had a wife.

No matter his initial thrill over the high-v burns, his growing unease with the entire situation wouldn't settle, and he knew exactly why: he wasn't supposed to be here. Not only that, but *Bayonet* wasn't supposed to be here. None of them were. Not out in deep space, an expanse of nothingness surrounding them, a blackness where only a few hundred people had dared to tread.

He sprinkled the ashes over his head, then stared at the vacuum-packed wafer and juice beside the empty envelope. Just like himself, wasn't supposed to be here, either. Even the Orbital Guard chaplain on Mars who'd heard his confession and then handed him the package—a hundred years after the Sixth Vatican Council had made such formerly unorthodox things permissible—had given him a wry look.

You're going deeper into space than most can imagine, much less have traveled before, and this is what you ask for? he'd asked. *You'll be seeing God Himself out there.*

God or hell?

He hadn't seen either, to be fair. Not yet, at least. Nightmares of his failure aboard *Vigilant*, the constant reminders of his failed personal life, and the never-ending sameness of a cutter on patrol—yes, he'd seen those, even when no one else aboard seemed to struggle with the same. Not that they'd tell him if they did.

But what was so wrong with him? Was he supposed to feel like Columbus right now, reaching for an unfamiliar planet with unimaginable promise? If he was, he didn't, for just a few decades later, Cortés's men had brought so much death and destruction that entire civilizations were on the verge of ruin. Was that what he'd done to this untouched part of the galaxy?

You aren't Cortés. A bunch of scientists and technicians beat you through the wormholes.

His heart settled a bit.

An untold number of humans had already spread throughout the farthest reaches of the universe, and so far, there was no war, no genocide, no strife. Well, perhaps there had been strife of the diplomatic sort: a few skirmishes between the Navy and the PLAN, and even more groundwork to prepare for worse, but no. He was nothing like

Cortés. He was out here in this vast, dark void to *save* people, not destroy alien cultures—if they even existed at all.

"But Bondar Station did welcome me to the New World."

Feeling ill once more, he tugged the rosary from his pocket and closed his eyes. He finished the prayer hastily, too aware in his gut that *something* was going on outside, then unwrapped the top wafer and peeled the lid off the small cup. Two knocks sounded at the door in Ahn's usual pattern, but he ignored him and pressed on. The wine was bitter, like it always was in space, something he'd never understood. The knock echoed again, but he ignored it once more as he swallowed the wafer.

"Almighty God, the one Light in the darkness, grant me Your presence and keep me in Your sacred mercy on this day and all others to come. Amen." He swirled a bit of water in the cup and drank it, then hit the unlock button from his desk and pushed himself to his feet. Somehow, he knew there would be no time for further reflection today. "Come on in."

Ahn slipped inside and closed the door behind him, giving Josiah a grin that morphed into an expression of contriteness when he saw the packaging on his desk.

"Sorry," he said. "Didn't realize you were busy, but this can't wait."

"Wasn't." Josiah swiped the remains of the observance to the side. "Don't you ever sleep? What's up?"

"I just swung by the bridge. We may have a problem."

A laugh broke through. "Just one?"

"Well, we'll ignore the rest of them for now." Ahn pointed at the screen, humorless for once. "Bring up the local area."

Josiah waved at the screen. Unfamiliar stars appeared on the bulkhead above his desk, and he searched through his memory for the charts he'd studied before leaving Mars. Celestial navigation had never been his strongest ability, so he searched for the nearest waypoint—there. That oriented him, at least. *Bayonet* was still over twenty-four million nautical miles from the next and final wormhole in the sequence, and not closing fast enough for him. Every hour they spent dithering around and not racing toward it was time that could be fatal to *Triumph*.

"Okay." Ahn hovered over his shoulder and read the coordinates off his comm. "Fifteen minutes ago, we picked up a beacon. Ship's called *Kamorta*, Indian-flagged, out of Ganymede."

Lightweight Merchant Vessel *Kamorta*'s profile appeared at the sound of her name. Not something Josiah would have expected to see much past Jupiter, let alone in deep space and through a bunch of wormholes. She was, allegedly, capable of carrying fifteen passengers and crew.

"Any response to hails?" He scrutinized the ship's schematic. For all the Indian Empire hadn't wanted their private citizens this far into space, they'd recently decided to require vessels transiting past the first wormhole to provide additional capability and passenger data to military agencies. It was something, at least.

"None."

"No vac alarm either, I take it." He blew out a deep breath. It didn't necessarily mean anything, especially if someone aboard had seen fit to manually trigger the emergency beacon. "How long to intercept?"

"Three hours, forty-five minutes at our present velocity."

Josiah clenched his jaw as he ran the numbers in his head. The recklessness of bringing a merchant ship through this many wormholes with no escort —preferably someone who'd been here before, which meant NSRC and NSRC only—grated on him. Didn't they know how risky it was? Or were they up to something so nefarious that they didn't care? After all, it had been pirates, not virtuous explorers, who had been the first to visit the outer stretches of the solar system.

Still, whoever was aboard and whatever they were searching for didn't matter in the end. *Triumph* was the mission, and she was waiting, but there was no part of him that could leave *Kamorta* stranded here in what may as well be another universe, waiting for help that would never come. No matter how reckless her crew was or what they might be up to out here.

That mercy I asked for? They could probably use some right now.

"All right," he told Ahn. "Slow us down. We'll take a look and hopefully be on course again in less than six hours." He stretched, but it didn't do much for the creeping fatigue that had taken over. "I'll be in the back."

* * *

As Josiah marched to Rescue Bay A two and a half hours later, *Bayonet* made her final deceleration, so violently he had to grab for a handhold in more than one spot. A glitch in the stability system—it happened. Still, they were in deep space, and being a relatively short distance away from their target didn't give them much time to stop. Thrusters helped with that, and their hiss echoed throughout the passageway as he tried to keep his balance.

He stumbled into the hangar bay, the sudden victim of yet another of *Bayonet*'s less graceful lurches, and Master Chief Jakob Blayne, Raider 1 team lead, squashed a smile as he entered. He could. His boots were magnetized to the deck here, in preparation for boarding a ship where gravity might not be so existent.

"Got an extra pair here if you decide you value your dignity, sir," Blayne said.

"If only they worked outside the bridge." Josiah steadied himself as the cutter tilted again. "Thrusters keep kicking off, and I almost split my head open as soon as I stepped outside."

"No blood, so it couldn't have been too bad a spill." Blayne laughed out loud. "Happens to us all."

There it was again—that overbearing concern for his well-being that radiated from everyone who knew about *Vigilant*. Josiah shook off the reassurance. It was accurate enough, especially for the boarding teams. While the rest of the ship had been strapped in for deceleration, they'd been in Bay A preparing for the past two hours. It was the rare crewmember who didn't have at least one scar from being flung around the rescue bays.

"Too true," he replied. "How's it looking over there? Engines making any power?"

He already knew the answer, or at least thought he did. *Kamorta* wasn't moving, he'd been able to tell that much from the window; her thrusters were cold and silent. His heart went cold, too. How long had she been out here like this?

"Minimal power from the reactor, enough for life support if they're lucky. Still no response to our calls, but there's a single heat signature moving around." Blayne lifted a shoulder. "Could be a single crewmember who brought her all the way out here alone, but we'll go in assuming the worst."

Josiah didn't bother to ask what *the worst* was. The definition depended on the person, and though he hadn't known Blayne long, he could already tell the man would rather face armed brigands than a privately owned starship full of bodies. Not for the first time, he was relieved his place was on *Bayonet*. Watching disaster from afar was bad enough.

"Two airlocks," added Lieutenant Roselyn Graham, the officer in charge of both Raider 1 and 2. She flicked her fingers in the air, projecting a picture of *Kamorta*'s hull onto the screen next to *Bayonet*'s own airlock. Her dark hair was already tucked into her helmet, its visor raised. "One on the side of an aft cargo bay and one directly into the flight deck. We'll enter through that aft bay, give ourselves space to handle a potentially hostile welcome."

"Fair enough." Josiah hit the comm button next to the airlock. "Bring us alongside."

Bayonet shifted downward and forward just fifteen seconds after his order was acknowledged, and he grabbed the handhold beside him once more. *Kamorta* became large in the window, and he wiped a bead of sweat from the back of his neck.

She's not even under power. She's not going to run into you. If anything, you'll run into her.

"Fifteen seconds," Blayne called out.

The reminder of who was actually in control here helped a bit, as did Blayne's curious stare. Yes, by this point there was no question he knew about *Vigilant,* and there was also no doubt he was questioning his captain now.

Graham lowered her visor and ushered the rest of the team toward the sleek red and white Mark-XVII OPS boat in the corner of the bay—the team who'd done this a hundred times before, though perhaps not light-years from Earth or Mars or wherever else they'd all considered far-flung until now. But it was that distance that allowed *Bayonet* to board *Kamorta* in the first place. Had they been in orbit around Saturn and registered the same distress beacon, they'd have heard from the Indian Empire about harassing their starships, no matter how dire the situation might have been.

What was the old saying? That no good deed went unpunished? That was doubly the case when it came to stepping on political toes in space, but what had people expected when nations had made it into space separately over the course of a hundred years, colonizing their own regions of Mars and then Saturn's moons? He cared about politics, yes, like anyone else who'd lived through the rise and fall of empires, but cooperation was necessary for effective SAR.

He trudged into the passageway outside and watched Rescue Bay A depressurize and the boat make her approach toward *Kamorta*. He'd been aboard a few of these undertakings, sometimes missed the exhilaration. But it felt different now, after Jonathan's death, and he was relieved to be remaining aboard *Bayonet*.

"And there's hard dock." Graham's voice crackled out of the speaker above his head. "Captain?"

Josiah squared his stance. "Give them one last chance before you blow the hatch."

"Aye aye, sir," Blayne replied. "*Kamorta*, this is the US Orbital Guard cutter *Bayonet*. We received your distress signal and have a boat docked at your aft airlock. Acknowledge and release your locks if able."

There was no response over the course of the next minute—not that Josiah had expected one. *Bayonet* had been trying to raise the ship for three hours now, and even if they were dealing with something as trivial as a communications failure, they weren't going to get an answer. His gut, though, said it was something else altogether.

"All right," he said when the crackle of static became too unnerving. "Do it."

He couldn't see most of *Kamorta*'s hull from this angle, but he could hear the crew banging on her hull—a sound that would wake the dead. There was still no reply, so they proceeded to blow the airlock off its hinges with a small charge. The crew might object to having to make repairs, but at this point, he'd stopped caring.

He turned to the boarding control technician beside him. Security Specialist First Class Brigette McArthur hadn't said much of anything as the rest of her team had prepped, and now she was just as quiet as her eyes flickered between the visor readouts from the six inside the boat.

"Atmosphere's intact, sir." She let out a breath. "No microbes detected so far."

"Copy that."

Blayne and his team slipped through *Kamorta*'s passageways almost silently, flashing yellow emergency lights illuminating their faces. McArthur switched between the cameras on their suits, giving Josiah a constantly changing view and allowing him his own analysis of the situation. He wanted to chew on his nails. He'd watched boardings before, dozens of them, but always within spitting distance of Earth—or at least what passed for spitting distance now.

"Blayne," McArthur called into her comm, "you've got a shadow fifteen paces ahead and to your right, approaching the flight deck."

He didn't know how she'd seen it since the flashing emergency lights hid all shadows from him, but Blayne froze. Pointed left, toward the third in line. He—or she, Josiah couldn't read the name on the back of the helmet in the dim passageway and didn't want to look away to check the beacon—dropped to the back, ready to lay in covering fire.

"Come on out," he hollered, taking a step forward. *"Baahar nikalo!"*

"He speaks Hindi?" Josiah asked under his breath.

"Enough." McArthur didn't look away from the screens as she muted her microphone. "Something about a few years on Titan. He doesn't like to talk about it. Blayne, that shadow has stopped, now at your three o'clock." Her gaze flickered toward Josiah for the first time. "It appears to be . . . short."

Graham, halfway through the line, looked up at that, as if she could reprimand McArthur for the vagueness through two hulls and a gap of vacuum. "Short?"

"Uh, yeah, ma'am." McArthur gestured in the air, switching through cameras. "I think it might be a kid."

Blayne swore under his breath, then lowered his rifle and took a step forward, his free hand in the air. He called out a few more words Josiah couldn't understand, and the shadow grew larger on the bulkhead in front of him as the figure shifted.

Have mercy.

It was a small girl with tearstained cheeks who stepped forward into the flashing lights. Her long hair was knotted, and the cream jumpsuit she wore—an impractical color aboard a starship at the best of times—was streaked with grease and what looked to Josiah to be food stains. She glanced at the figures and took a step back, her eyes wide.

Blayne said something else Josiah didn't understand, then knelt in front of her, his hands outstretched. He spoke; she nodded, but his communicator scarcely picked up the whispered conversation. Didn't matter. It was recorded and could be translated later.

"All right, here's the deal." Blayne stood, guiding the girl back toward the airlock. "She says there's six others on board, but there's something wrong with them. Doesn't know what." His tone indicated that even if the girl didn't know what was wrong, he knew exactly what it was.

One heat signature.

McArthur looked toward him, and Josiah sighed. It wasn't the ending any of them had wanted. But one survivor was better than none, wasn't it? Especially when no one else was out this far to begin with—diverting from their pursuit of *Triumph* had saved a life. But dropping the girl off at the nearest Indian spaceport wasn't an option now, so it was back to the search for *Triumph*. They would make up the time somehow, even if he had to run *Bayonet*'s engines harder than planned.

"Scan her and send her over," he said, turning around and heading for the bridge.

* * *

The lights in the sick bay were dim when Josiah stepped inside an hour later, having made certain the engines were up for another high-speed run. The engineers weren't happy, and neither was he, truth be told, but he trusted them to keep *Bayonet* moving and her reactors from imploding. It had to be done.

"How's she doing?" he asked Laurel Somerset. He'd served with the corpsman during his second tour on *Munro*, just prior to his ill-fated *Vigilant* assignment, though he didn't know her well. He had, unfortunately, only met her while suffering from a stomach bug that had swept through the entire ship.

"Sleeping, sir." Somerset turned from her desk and waved at the bed in the corner. A small lump was hidden under the gray blanket, rising and falling with what he assumed were the girl's breaths. "She's fine. Scans were clear, she has no complaints. Absolutely normal, despite having to eat freeze-dried rations for the past four days, she says."

"Four days." Josiah scratched his chin. "And the others? How long has it been since—"

She gave him a *quiet, sir* look and motioned him into the passageway. "We'll know more once they bring them over and check *Kamorta*'s logs, but it's going to be difficult to tell anything about the rest of the passengers and crew as long as we have to keep them down in quarantine." *On a cutter in the middle of deep space*, he swore he heard her add mentally. "It might be difficult to learn anything if the Indian Empire wants them back prior to full autopsies."

Which they would, if they found out about this. But communications were limited past the first wormhole, and even the Indians wouldn't blame them for not passing information like this through Bondar Station.

"How much can you find out once they're aboard?" he asked.

Somerset glanced down the corridor. "Once the scans clear them of anything critical, I can see what I can figure out—but it's probably going to be limited until we make it back to Mars. I don't want to risk releasing anything that could spread."

He didn't ask—he already knew she was thinking of the freighter *Simon Marius*, which had suffered an outbreak of smallpox before spreading it to a commercial space station in orbit around Callisto. Twenty-seven fatalities and eighty years later, everyone had become more cautious about pathogens, both ancient and unidentified. Especially in deep space.

"Agreed," he replied. "And then—"

Blayne's footsteps interrupted his next instructions. The chief's normally ruddy complexion was pale, and he hadn't yet discarded the gear he'd worn while they'd boarded and searched *Kamorta*.

Josiah's skin crawled at Somerset's warning, but then he stopped himself. Blayne wouldn't have stepped foot back aboard *Bayonet* if there was a chance he was carrying a microbe.

"Master Chief?" Josiah asked. "Something wrong?"

Dumb question, O'Donnell.

"We got them all aboard and into the quarantine pods down below. No issues there. But sir—" Blayne cleared his throat. "I might not be a doctor, but there's something really weird about all six bodies."

CHAPTER TWELVE_
NIMBUS STATION, ETRIK

ONLY THREE.

Coralie stared at the pressure suits hanging next to the airlock, as if more would materialize out of thin air if she looked long enough. But why would there be more? The v-words didn't need them, since they could somehow extract enough oxygen from almost any environment, and the prisoners certainly didn't need them. Just her. And Kinnard probably thought that having three whole options was the most she could ask in this new life he'd doomed her to.

"You just going to stare, or are you going to put one on?" Riley leaned against the wall, arms folded, but something about her temperament had changed since Kinnard had caught them in the capsule compartment.

"Just trying to remember how." Coralie grabbed the middle suit and gave it a shake. "And honestly, I'm trying to talk myself into going out there."

"You're the one who wanted a tour." Riley yawned.

"Just a change of scenery, really." Coralie ran her palms down the seams, checking for any snags or holes. Her implants would allow her to breathe outside for a while, but not forever, and there was no point in challenging her body for no reason. Not yet, at least. "How far do you think we can get before they come after us? I'd love to see that dry riverbed north of here."

Riley shrugged and buffed her nails on the leg of her jumpsuit.

Coralie sighed as she stepped into the suit and worked it upward. They hadn't become friends yet, no matter how easily Riley had agreed to accompany her. And on a recreational excursion, no less. But babysitter or prison guard, it didn't matter right now—a walk on the actual surface of another world was reason enough to leave the station for her. Examining the station from the outside was just a bonus. Finding an escape route, somewhere to hide . . . that was even better.

"Have you been outside before?" Coralie struggled to pull the metallicized fabric over her knees. Unlike the old pressurized gas suits, the mechanical pressure on her body allowed for unrestricted movement outside. It just was a bit . . . uncomfortable at first. She'd never truly gotten used to it, even on Mars.

"Yes. Of course." Riley narrowed her eyes. "Why are you so talkative?"

Coralie let the suit hang from her waist and shrugged. "Maybe I'm lonely."

Riley's laugh was a harsh bark. "And I'm the best you've got?"

Silence filled the changing room. She didn't have anyone else, did she? Even Helena had avoided her since that day in the greenhouse, and Coralie hadn't bothered to confront her and ask why. The past was the past, and was there even a future for her? Probably not, but there was a present, and since Riley was here . . .

"Okay." Riley pushed herself off the wall and pointed. "Turn around."

"Turn around?" Coralie asked. Turning her back to a v-word had never seemed like the best course of action.

"It's easier with two people, right?" Riley let her lips curl into a smile, an expression Coralie had never seen, not even on Mars.

"I suppose it is." Her reply was slow. Trust was something not easily given.

She faced the wall and counted the rivets in a bulkhead as Riley worked the suit over her shoulders. There was nothing to be concerned about—they had dressed as teams during training on Mars, after all. It was a measure of trust that didn't quite fit as well as the suit, but when Riley gave her a light punch on the back of her shoulder, her heart didn't so much as skip a beat. It felt . . . friendly?

"There," Riley said, in what almost seemed to be an amicable tone. "You don't need the full pre-breathing protocol, right?"

Coralie slid the zipper to her neck and took a diffi-cult breath.

"About half," she replied. The ability to handle rapid decompression and recompression was one reason for her augmentations, after all.

Still, would Riley want to sit in the chamber for a whole forty-five minutes with her? Coralie wouldn't, if she was in her position. Naturally, there was always the chance Kinnard could have ordered it of her, but Coralie suspected even he didn't worry about her trying anything while she was locked inside with nowhere to go. No, this was something else. Something promising. Even . . . hopeful? She wouldn't argue if Riley were to become an ally.

Riley motioned toward the airlock. "Then lead on."

* * *

The outer airlock slid open fifty minutes later, kicking up a small cloud of rust-colored dirt that wouldn't have looked out of place on Mars. In the distance, an ancient mountain rose, larger than it had seemed from one of the few windows in the station. Millenia of erosion and tectonic uplifts had battered its face, leaving layer upon layer of colorful rock exposed, and Coralie had the sudden realization that everyone aboard Nimbus Station might live to see it disappear altogether if they could procure enough humans to provide them with criexain. How could they refuse to see how abnormal this all was? No one was meant to live long enough to see the seas encroach on land where they had once lived, to see mountains reduced to rolling hills.

She took one step forward, blinking away the incredible idea of the Appalachian Mountains on Earth once standing as tall as the Rockies, then paused, her rear magnetic boot still planted on the steel of the chamber's floor.

"What's up?" Riley asked.

Coralie set her jaw. What indeed?

"I'm afraid of floating away, I suppose," she replied.

"You haven't lifted off the floor yet, have you?" Riley grinned. "You know it's the same gravity as Earth. Same as inside the station."

"Yes." Coralie took another step and returned the smile. "But stepping onto another world for the first time gives you all kinds of second thoughts." *Not that second thoughts are something you would ever understand.*

"Just watch your step. Don't want to have to tape up a hole in your suit out here." Riley gestured toward the mountain in the distance. "But you can breathe for a while if that happens."

Red dirt compressed under her boots as she took another few tentative steps. Yes, Riley was right—the helmet she wore was technically unnecessary for ten or fifteen minutes. But she planned on spending over fifteen minutes outside today, and . . . and no matter how friendly Riley had just decided to be, Coralie didn't trust her. Didn't have any desire to inform her of the limits of her augmentations.

"Not very long. Less than five minutes," she lied. "And it'll knock me out for hours afterward, so it's not something I care to attempt unless otherwise necessary."

Also a lie.

"Great for evacuations, though." Riley's boots—not space boots, but regular work boots—didn't compress the dirt nearly as much as Coralie's as she walked.

"That's the idea." Coralie pointed at a glass outbuilding in the distance. "What's that?"

Riley's eyes glinted. "Worm research. Want to see?"

Not really.

"Sure," she lied.

She followed Riley to the unsealed greenhouse, complete with a door that made little sense to her out here in the limited atmosphere. It clattered shut behind her, and only the red dust through the windows kept her from yanking off her helmet like she'd once pulled off her shoes upon entering that cottage far away in northern Mexico. The greenhouse was nothing like that cottage, though. Instead of warm wood, glass ran perhaps twenty meters to her left, covering racks of what she knew wasn't just dirt.

The worm version of Kinnard's capsules.

Her heart skipped a beat as Coralie picked her way down the center aisle, dragging a gloved hand along the racks. At the other side of the greenhouse, set into the dirt, lay a metal hatch.

She prodded it with her boot. "What's this?"

"The actual experiment." Unhindered by any kind of suit, Riley knelt down effortlessly and lifted the hatch. "Sets of worms go into the ground each month, then the scientists can see how well they're adapting to their new environment."

"They aerate the soil." Coralie stared in fascination at the animals wriggling in the cool ground. Such a small animal might one day contribute more to Etrik's colonization than she ever could.

"And break down organic material," Riley added. "The first step in the ability to grow anything outside. The ground needs the nutrients."

"You'd think NSRC could have found a more suitable planet for supporting life."

"Nothing's been found yet." Riley lifted a shoulder. "We took what we could get, what they gave us. And Etrik was it. Anyway, it's really a blessing. We'll learn how to terraform, and who knows what else will come from that knowledge."

A chill stole down Coralie's spine despite the warmth of the suit. "So you can take more planets?"

"So we can learn." Riley dropped the hatch closed, and the worms disappeared. "Aren't you interested in learning just for learning's sake?"

Coralie had to admit she wasn't—and that Riley's speech was sounding all too much like the one Helena had given her in the greenhouse. But like Helena, Riley wasn't a scientist, and Coralie wasn't going to ask why she was here. Why should she care how any of them justified what they'd done to her and the others?

"If it applies to my work," she replied. "Terraforming is something other people do. It's not something I'm particularly interested in, to tell you the truth."

Riley gave her a small, disappointed smile as she stood. "That's shortsighted."

"Not all of us have a thousand years to be far-sighted." Dammit, her cheek was beginning to itch. She reached a hand toward her head, wishing she could touch her skin. That wasted movement complete, she resorted to the stick inside meant for such a thing—a much less graceful way of scratching.

"Then you must understand why we've done what we've done."

"Is this supposed to be some kind of indoctrination? Make me amenable to everything going on here? Now I see why Kinnard was so willing to let me go out here with you." Coralie blew out a sigh and exited the greenhouse, stopping just long enough to let the fog in her helmet clear. "You're not ever going to convince me that the ends justify these means," she called over her shoulder.

"I'm not trying to change your mind, Coralie."

Riley wasn't the least bit short of breath as she caught up, and Coralie doubted she would ever become used to human beings—or what had *been* human beings—walking on the surface of a planet that would kill her if it had half the chance. Her suit was becoming more uncomfortable by the minute, and her breath was growing short, but Riley didn't look as though she'd have noticed she'd stepped outside the station if Coralie hadn't been with her.

"Yeah." Coralie stalked off toward the mountain in the distance, even though it was days away. How far could she get before Riley caught up to her or Kinnard sent security after her? "You're just trying to explain, right?" she asked scornfully.

Riley's palm touched her forearm. Not roughly, for she probably considered even an augment fragile out here on the surface, but enough for Coralie to feel the sensation and stop.

"No." She strolled off toward the mountains, and Coralie followed. "I'm sure Kinnard's tried. Why would I waste my breath?"

Like you actually need to breathe.

"He hasn't, actually." Coralie shrugged the best she could. "I suspect he knows I'm beyond per-suasion."

"He hasn't?"

"No." Coralie gnawed on the inside of her cheek, her chest tight. "Helena Roscrow has, though."

Riley's brows rose. "Really?"

"Yes." Coralie took a breath, more difficult than the previous one. Helena, in the end, had turned out not to be a friend, and that betrayal, though not as bitter as Kinnard's, had been more difficult to swallow. "A while ago. We used to be friends, and I didn't—" A beep sounded in her helmet, and she glanced at the computer on her wrist and swore. "Leak. I thought I was getting short of breath."

"Let me see." Riley grabbed her wrist and gave the computer there only a glance before pushing Coralie around and toward the station.

"You don't have to shove me around. I can make it." *Maybe.* Coralie forced her heart rate lower, forced herself to take one regular breath. This was exactly what her modifications were for, wasn't it? She wouldn't let herself panic, and then everything would be okay. "I just need to keep calm."

"Here." Riley's hand on her back let up. "Where's the leak?"

"How would I know?" Coralie felt down her sides with gloved hands, but there was no gaping hole, no seam which had come totally undone. A small tear, then—had to be.

Had someone sabotaged the suit?

Of course not. Kinnard would have their head if they had.

"Well, it would be nice if this fancy computer could tell you, I suppose." Riley ran her hands down the seams Coralie couldn't reach. "You don't feel anything? Less pressure, air flowing, anything like that?"

Deciding to save her breath and stay silent, Coralie shook her head and took a step toward the habitat in the distance. Yes, she'd lied to Riley—but it was a long walk with less oxygen than she'd ever been subjected to outside of training. The fifteen minutes of useful consciousness she had in Etrik's atmosphere suddenly felt like thirty seconds.

"Here." Riley stopped on a small seam on Coralie's wrist. "There's a slight cut here. Let me fix it and see if that stops the leak."

"Fix it?"

Riley yanked a white roll from her pocket. "Tape."

"Tape?" Coralie's cheeks flushed, and it wasn't from the lack of oxygen. "You were so concerned about how long I had out here," she spat, rage overcoming her need to conserve air. "You did this, didn't you?"

"Of course not."

Riley ripped a piece of tape with her teeth—a motion that made Coralie's jaw clench inside her helmet. It was unnatural to be standing out here next to someone who didn't need to wear a suit, who could probably float through the vacuum of deep space without so much as flinching. Humans weren't meant to be this . . . alive. Or not alive. Whatever.

"Then why did you bring tape? To scare me? Coerce me into cooperating, into not giving Kinnard more trouble? Make me realize how easily I could die out here by *accident*?"

"I'm responsible for you. Of course I was prepared." A flash of hurt crossed Riley's face, then vanished. "If you'd remembered your training, you would have thought to bring it yourself, and I wouldn't have had to worry about it. Be more prepared next time, okay?"

The rage turned to chagrin between two of Coralie's heartbeats—slow, natural ones. Riley was right. She'd been in too much of a hurry to get outside, had forgotten her training, had forgotten how prepared she would need to be when she came up with a plan to get the others out. There wouldn't be time for forgotten tape and leaky suits or any other mistakes.

But then, that was the least of her worries now. Because there were only three space suits and four of them who needed to escape.

Chagrin became a heavy feeling in her chest that Coralie didn't recognize for a long time. Despair? That didn't make any sense. From the time Kinnard had pulled her from the capsule, she hadn't felt *despair*. Frustration, yes—of course there had been lots of that—but she had never felt hopeless. There wasn't time, and she didn't have the resources to allow for wallowing in self-pity, either.

She took a few slow, deep breaths as Riley wound the tape around her wrist, but the weight around her heart didn't dissipate like her shortness of breath. Still, it had to be the lack of oxygen, and that would resolve itself shortly. But what if she didn't feel better once it did?

"Feeling better?" Riley asked, having seemingly read her mind. "Seems to be sealed."

"Yeah." Coralie glanced at the wrist computer, unable to trust her body any longer. "Looks like."

Riley exhaled, odd for a being who could walk on the surface of this wild and airless planet without so much as breaking a sweat. But then again, they both knew what Kinnard could do to her.

"Good," she replied, a little paler than she'd been when she and Coralie had exited the module. "That means Kinnard won't kill me today."

"I suppose he won't." Coralie examined her sleeve. The tear had to have been small for her to not have noticed, and that meant—well, did it mean anything? Likely not. Just that she'd been in such a rush to get outside and explore that she hadn't done a thorough enough inspection of her own gear. "Good for you, I suppose. That was . . . a horrible thing to witness."

"I'm surprised you're not dying to see it happen to me."

"Seeing it happen to Alvaro was bad enough, and —" She wanted to throw her hands into the air, but settled for raising them to her sides. Riley had never been this inconsistent. Had never been kind or friendly or even cordial, for that matter. "Riley, I don't even know why you dislike me so much. I hope it wasn't something I did."

Riley gave her a small smile. "You walked in that first day, and I knew you'd throw off the entire culture of the department."

"Oh, the entire culture, huh?" Coralie's eyes rolled of their own accord. "Because?"

Riley shrugged. "You were too confident."

For a moment Coralie didn't understand, and then she did. Hadn't she felt the same about various people over the years? Hadn't she judged without knowing, hated without comprehension? How could she blame Riley for doing the same?

"Has anyone ever told you that jealousy is much too human an emotion for a creature who drinks blood?" she asked.

"Well—" Dust flew into the air as Riley dug her boot into the ground. "I was human then."

"Yeah." The confession should have filled her with fear, but Coralie's laugh bounced off the inside of her helmet. "Mostly, at least."

Riley pointed back toward the domes. "We ought to get you back inside, just in case that wasn't the only tear. You may have exacerbated it by moving."

"Oh." She was right, as much as Coralie didn't want to admit it—or leave her newfound friend so soon. "You're probably right."

"I'm usually right." Riley kicked up more dust as she kept pace at Coralie's side. "And about Helena? Don't trust her. Not even a little. Believe me, I'm right about her, too."

CHAPTER THIRTEEN_

JOSIAH SHIVERED IN THE COOL OF THE CARGO BAY ON deck 4 despite his mounting unease. The quarantine pods *Bayonet* carried were already half occupied, something he couldn't remember happening on any other patrol. Oh, there had been a few weird bodies they'd carted off spacecraft in the past, ones that had looked suspicious enough to be isolated inside layers of plastic, but in the end, there had always turned out to be a reasonable explanation for the sores, the rotting flesh, the tumors that covered entire bodies.

There was always an explanation.

"Liver failure," Somerset said, replacing the scanner in its holder. "Not that I needed any kind of equipment or blood tests to tell me that."

And there was the explanation.

She pointed at the body in the second to last quarantine pod, and Josiah didn't need to ask. The jaundice was obvious, especially in the bright lights of the cargo bay. Jonathan had suffered the same as an hours-old newborn, and he'd thought watching his son cry under the lights was the worst thing ever. But even Jonathan hadn't looked like *this*, and it certainly hadn't been what had killed him.

"They're all like this?" His jaw grew taut. If *Bayonet*'s sensors had missed something, if they'd brought a deadly microbe aboard . . . "What's with the silver eyes?"

She shrugged. "Heavy metal poisoning, maybe. It's too soon to know whether it's related or if there's a secondary process at work."

"Heavy metal poisoning would cause liver failure too, right?" It was a guess, but it seemed possible enough to him. "Can you tell what caused it? Sensors didn't pick up anything abnormal on *Kamorta*, and the child seems healthy. Wouldn't a ship-wide biological agent have harmed her as well?"

"Likely." Somerset bit her lip. "But I can't say for sure yet. Hyperacute liver failure is rare, and whatever it is, it came on quickly enough to be classified as such. Just a few days after they passed through Echo, sounds like. I've taken samples of all the medication and opened food found aboard. Eshana says she hasn't taken any meds since leaving Earth, so it's possible something was tainted during manufacture or even after."

Horrific as that suggestion was, it was the best-case scenario for *Bayonet*. Sensors missed things all the time, and while leaving Eshana aboard *Kamorta* was unthinkable, he couldn't help but wonder if he'd doomed his own crew by bringing her and the others aboard. Quarantine wasn't a sure thing, and if this was some sort of alien disease . . .

"How's she doing now?" he asked. "Can I talk to her?"

"Sure." Her gaze sharpened as she motioned with her chin out of the door of the cargo bay and led him back to sick bay. "Though I'm not sure how much help she'll be. She didn't seem to want to talk much about it, except to Blayne about how much she wants her parents. And, you know, translations and all."

Somerset was probably right, though the idea that a human with any innocence left would voluntarily talk to Blayne made him chuckle as they entered. Eshana was sitting up, no longer the frightened gray lump under the covers she'd been at first. A box of children's toys was strewn across the bed, but it was the picture book of the solar system that held her attention. She gave the corpsman a brilliant smile, which immediately fell when Josiah slipped through the doorway. Not a surprise. Hope had always laughed at how much he intimidated children.

"Hi." He perched on the end of the bed, as far away from her as he could get. "I'm Josiah."

She looked up at him with the widest eyes he'd ever seen, and panic shot through him. Dammit, maybe Hope was right, and he should have left this to Blayne.

"Laurel said this is your ship." Her English was better than he'd expected.

"She did, did she?" He'd never really thought of *Bayonet* as his yet. Not in any kind of constructive manner, at least. Hadn't Hope criticized that, too? He shook off the memory and focused on the girl in front of him. "I guess she is mine. And you know what, I bet she's older than you, too."

Eshana gave him a look that managed to be accusing and suspicious at once. "How old is it?"

He smothered a grin at the Indian convention of *it* for ships. "Right around two."

She laughed. "I'm six. So I'm older."

"Six!" He let his mouth fall open in feigned shock. "You're practically grown up, then. Were you born on Earth?" *Kamorta* might have been registered on Ganymede, but that didn't necessarily mean anything.

She nodded.

"Me, too. Illinois. What about you?"

She replied with the name of a city he'd never heard of, but a quick glance over his shoulder verified Somerset had written it down. They'd likely be back to Mars before anyone had a chance to contact family there, but it was a start, at least.

"You're a long way from there," he went on, examining a stuffed bear, then handing it to her. "How'd that happen?"

"I don't know." She clutched at the bear, staring at him over the ears. "I don't remember."

"Okay." Josiah smiled at her. "That's okay. Do you remember everyone else getting sick?"

"Not really." Eshana shook her head. "They told me to stay away from them."

He gave Somerset another look. Had *Kamorta*'s crew and passengers believed whatever had affected them was contagious? Or had they been playing it safe, not knowing?

"Okay," he repeated. Hope was right: he was terrible at this. At least Eshana wasn't crying over his awkwardness. "You sure you don't remember getting on the ship and going up into space? That's a pretty big deal, even for me."

Eshana blinked at him. "It was scary at first. I was sick a lot, but it got better fast, by the time we reached Mars, maybe." She gave him the small smile of a child finally warming up to the strangers surrounding her. "Ravi was still sick when we reached the first wormhole."

Josiah tucked the name away for later and leaned in toward her. "You want to hear a secret?"

She nodded.

"I was sick the first four or five times I went into space. Really sick. Took me months to get used to it. I was afraid they'd send me back to Earth forever, but I got over it."

"They really would have sent you back?"

"They really would have." He could laugh at the memory of the garbage can now. "And it's only been how long for you?"

"December 18." Eshana screwed up her face, thinking. "Three days before my birthday."

He gave Somerset another look over Eshana's shoulder. "Birthday in space? Pretty cool."

"Mummy brought turmeric from home special for it." Her grin turned shy as she dragged a thumb across her forehead. "Do you think you can find it?"

"We can try." It was a lie, and he knew it. Nothing else from *Kamorta* was coming aboard *Bayonet*. They'd taken enough of a risk already. "But if we can't, I'm sure there's some in the galley. Maybe we can get someone to make something with it?"

"Bhindi masala?" She raised a brow like a child twice her age who didn't believe anyone aboard *Bayonet* could make something so exotic.

"We can try that, too." Finally, his smile was un-forced. "Who's Ravi?"

"My brother." The answer was flat, and she grabbed the end of the blanket and held it against her chest.

"I'm sorry about him." His own chest began to cave in. "I bet he loved you a lot."

"Sometimes. Sometimes I think he hated me."

"Oh? I doubt he hated you."

"When I came to live with Mummy and Papa, he did. He was used to having them to himself. He didn't like that they wanted to take care of me, too."

She was adopted? Well, it made sense. *Kamorta* wasn't an inexpensive ship, and after the latest Chinese-Indian War, the wealthy had been expected to care for the children left orphaned. And Eshana was certainly well taken care of, from her physical health to the jumpsuit she'd been wearing, far more expensive than anything Josiah would have picked for a wormhole junket.

"Well, brothers can be like that," he said. "Believe me, I know. I have three."

He hadn't seen any of them in years—two had remained on Earth, and one was a physician out of Mars who seemed to spend more time in space than Josiah himself did, but they'd tortured him for years. Good-naturedly, though, like any torment older brothers would dish out. He should probably send a few messages one of these days . . . though Holden in particular had blamed him for the divorce, and Josiah had little desire to keep arguing about it.

"I miss mine. Even though he was mean."

"I get that." Torn between a chuckle and a tear, Josiah nodded. "Hey, did Ravi take any medicine on the way here? Eat something you didn't eat?"

A crease between her eyes appeared, and he regretted asking. No one Eshana's age should have been capable of that too-adult expression.

"I don't think so," she replied.

"Not even for the motion sickness?"

Eshana shook her head. "Papa said it would make him sick longer. He said if you want the sickness to go away, you just have to deal with it."

"Your dad was a smart man. Sometimes it happens that way." That wasn't true, but it wasn't worth arguing with a six-year-old who spoke with the assumed wisdom of someone six times her age. "Tell you what, you get some more rest, and I'll go see about having someone make some bhindi masala, huh? You let Laurel know if you need anything else, all right?"

Eshana nodded enthusiastically, and he motioned Somerset back into the passageway outside.

"She's adopted," she said under her breath as soon as the sick bay door closed.

"Does that matter?"

"Maybe. It's unlikely, but perhaps there's a genetic component to whatever this is. Maybe they can't process a certain medication they brought aboard, or perhaps there was something in a novel food they brought along for long-endurance travel. A condition similar to phenylketonuria, perhaps."

Josiah gave her a blank look.

"It's a genetic defect that prevents the body from breaking down phenylalanine—an amino acid—with some rather horrifying consequences." She gnawed on her cheek as she thought. "Children who are affected but not treated used to develop numerous physical, psychiatric, and intellectual disabilities."

He couldn't even imagine. As short as Jonathan's life had been, he'd been happy and healthy. Maybe his sudden death had been a mercy, though he'd never believed so until now. Was mercy a word that could ever be used if you lost a child?

"Used to?" he asked. "What happens now?"

"These days parents find out early if their child is affected, and it can be treated with a special diet. Most choose genetic testing and gene editing during pregnancy, so it never becomes an issue. If not, they test newborns at birth."

"I see." He and Hope hadn't done either with Jonathan. He supposed he'd been tested for it just after birth, but those first days as a new father had been a blur. Hell, Jonathan's entire life had been a blur, now that he looked back on it. "Any ideas in this specific case?"

"I don't know offhand of any genetic disease that can be triggered by space travel, but I'm not a doctor. I can do some research, though." Somerset shrugged. "I could be completely wrong. It's quite possible this isn't genetic, and the fact she's adopted is irrelevant."

"See what you can find out." Josiah sighed. "Because if this happens again—"

He cut himself off, pretending the reason for his silence was that he didn't want to worry her.

But the truth was, that for no reason in particular, he was terrified himself.

CHAPTER FOURTEEN_

USOGC BAYONET, APPROACHING
WORMHOLE FOXTROT

"Last one," Ahn greeted him as he stepped onto the aft observation deck. "You know, I think I'm actually going to miss doing this. It makes me understand a little of what Armstrong and Aldrin must have felt when the Moon loomed below them in that tiny window."

"You're talking like we won't be going back home through the wormholes." Josiah forced a laugh as his words caught up with him. Maybe some of them wouldn't. This wasn't combat, not even close, but there was always the chance something might go wrong—hadn't *Vigilant* taught him that? Had he just condemned the entire ship with an offhand comment? "Besides, if this works, they'll let us come back out here. Maybe we could station someone on each side of the wormholes like the

Canadians. If traffic picks up like they're predicting, we'll have to."

And then Cassandra would murder you.

"But transiting would be tedious by then." Ahn grinned. "Been there, done that."

"Yeah. I suppose."

Josiah stared out the window into the void as *Bayonet* slowed for her approach. There was no way he could take this as lightly as Ahn. Earth was somewhere back there, even if *back there* had less meaning now than it ever had before. Armstrong and Aldrin hadn't known—might have speculated about it, but hadn't *known*—that space twisted and curled, folding in on itself like crumpled paper. He hadn't really believed it either, even as *Bayonet* had approached Alpha and he'd watched its tendrils reach for them.

"Captain, we're approaching Foxtrot." The voice on the intercom didn't hesitate. Even the crew was getting used to this, and Josiah wasn't sure he approved of the complacency. But that wasn't fair, was it? They weren't complacent, just at ease. "Stabilization forecast in one hour, seven minutes. Once we transit, Nimbus Station will be twenty-nine million, seven hundred and three thousand nautical miles off the bow."

Just over a third of an astronomical unit—but still so far.

"Very well." He gave Ahn a sideways look. "Contacts this side?"

"None, sir. We'll begin the initial sensor scan as soon as the distortion weakens."

Creepy.

Well, what other word was there? Around Mars, everyone's scopes were so cluttered it took a practiced eye to distinguish anything, and now it was nothing less than disconcerting to be out here absolutely alone. Well, not quite alone, because even if the worst had happened to *Triumph*, there were humans at Nimbus Station on Etrik, weren't there? They were closer to civilization than they'd been since passing Bondar Station. The reminder should have settled his nerves, but instead he felt more alone than ever. If the sensor pods on the bottom of *Bayonet*'s hull found nothing . . .

"Let me know as soon as you pick anything up." The panel above his bunk would alert him of a hit during an active search, but he didn't want to take the chance of missing anything.

"Aye aye, Captain."

The intercom went dead, and he sighed. "I'm going to get some sleep," he said to Ahn. "You might want to consider doing the same instead of staring at nothing."

"Won't be nothing for long." Ahn all but pressed his nose against the window. "You're missing out."

Josiah chuckled and waved goodbye without another word.

* * *

". . . four . . . three . . . two . . . one!" he finished, pulling his hands from his eyes. "Ready or not, here I come!"

Jonathan's happy screech echoed from under the bed in his and Hope's bedroom, and he suppressed a laugh as he headed in the opposite direction, calling his name, pretending he had no idea where his quarry was hidden. Hide-and-seek with an almost three-year-old was the easiest search of his life, and definitely the most fun. The giggles continued as he stomped into the kitchen where Hope was slicing tomatoes. He opened a half dozen cabinets as loudly as he could, then banged around a few pots for good measure as she laughed.

"I know you're in here somewhere," he called out, grabbing Hope around the waist and pulling her into his arms. "And you know what it means if I find you."

"You're clearly not looking hard enough," she replied, pressing her lips against his. "Though I have to admit, I won't argue about your being easily sidetracked."

His hands moved lower. "Drop that knife, and I'll show you just how easily sidetracked I can be."

It clattered on the counter, and he kissed her like it had been a year since he'd last seen her instead of just six months. Of course, six months was on the long side for an orbital deployment, especially around Mars, and it seemed to grow longer each time, especially since his return would be shortly followed by her departure. He didn't mind, but she did, and he couldn't help wishing there was another option. Perhaps the day would eventually come when—

A heavy silence fell over him—the giggles from the bedroom had stopped. He pulled away, the taste of her red wine lingering on his lips.

"I suppose he got tired of waiting for you." Hope extricated herself and glanced around the kitchen for a tiny audience, but Jonathan was nowhere to be seen. "I'll go find him. Dinner's almost ready, anyway."

Humming, he grabbed the knife and finished with the tomatoes, though he grimaced at how his weren't nearly as even as the ones she had cut. Still, there was something appealing about domestic life. He shoved the tomatoes to the side and grabbed the open bottle of wine, wondering why he hadn't thought to bring one home from Deimos last time he'd visited. Hope was partial to the silky taste of wine grown in zero-g.

He'd just finishing pouring her another glass when her scream echoed through the flat.

* * *

Hope smiled at him from the screen above the desk in his cabin aboard *Vigilant*, but it didn't meet her eyes, like it hadn't for most of the past year. He reached out like he usually did, and finally her eyes crinkled as he touched the screen. His insistence on pretending they weren't millions of nautical miles apart usually made her laugh, but laughter was rare since Jonathan's death.

"If only." She reached out toward him too, but the gesture was halfhearted and full of self-consciousness. "Just another eighty days."

"It feels like so much longer."

"Yeah." Her grin faded. "Everything seems longer lately."

She wasn't wrong. Days, weeks, months—all had seemed eternal since he'd found her on the floor of their bedroom performing CPR on Jonathan's limp body. *A previously undetected congenital heart condition,* the doctor had said with negligible compassion. Had he been in a hospital when he'd gone into full cardiac arrest, he might have survived, but at home . . . at home there had been no chance.

"And I should have told you before," she went on, "once we pass Saturn, it'll be back to weekly messages again." She made a face. "They say a comm relay at Io is out, and the backup can't handle personal video chats."

He let his head fall to his hands—dramatically, just to convince her to laugh again. It didn't work, and he sighed.

"Well, you win some, you lose some, I suppose," he replied. "It's a poor substitute for seeing you in person, anyway."

"Two weeks of leave on Mars afterward. Hope you can work yours out for the same time." Hope glanced to the side. "Got to go. I've got the watch in ten. Love you."

"Love you, too."

She waved at him, then the screen went dark.

* * *

Vigilant shifted against the mooring clamps once more, seemingly as impatient to disappear into the void as her crew. He glanced out the bridge's large forward window at the red planet below, ready as well. Stepping aboard *Vigilant* almost a year ago, patrolling the Main Belt for pirates and emergency beacons, it had all saved his life after Jonathan's death, given him a purpose again, allowed him to forget. Being back on Mars—well, above it, at least—was still painful, always would be. It was time to leave once more.

"Bridge, port lookout, target bearing 240, low speed."

The call drew his attention away from the Martian dust. The proximity alarm in the bulkhead above his head beeped once as the OOD responded to the lookout, but likely it wasn't anything critical. The Sector Bonneville Orbital Docks were hectic on the best of days, and with the Sector Elysium docks operating at reduced capacity, things would be even worse for the next six months. False alarms were normal, and Control was capable of keeping underway ships from moored ones. Still, a collision could prove deadly, even in port. Had happened just four years ago to two US Navy cruisers high above Earth.

"What's with the alarm?" he asked. It wasn't his problem as *Vigilant*'s XO—he was only on the bridge to supervise the weapons loading—but his pulse had quickened in a way he didn't like.

"Reported target, appears to be no factor, sir." Nervousness laced the OOD's statement despite her claim of *no factor*.

"I see it now." His gaze danced over the navigation projection. A small ship was heading toward them, below and in nothing remotely like a collision course, but close enough that the lookout had seen fit to mention it and *Vigilant* had protested the nearness. "No transponder. Control didn't say anything about it?"

For a moment she didn't answer, and his thudding heart grew more uncomfortable.

"Unauthorized penetration," she finally replied. "Security is pursuing them."

He stepped away from the weapons station and peered out the window beside him. The target, nothing more than a skiff, had disappeared below, and the only thing he could see were two Orbital Guard patrol boats bearing security markings closing in from either side.

"Sure are taking their sweet time, aren't they?" he asked.

"They want to fire, sir. *Chincoteague* is in the way."

For a moment he thought she was treating him like an imbecile, then he realized she was listening in on the comm traffic. He swore out loud, drawing looks, but what did security know that he didn't? If only they'd share that information, give everyone some idea of what was happening out there. *Vigilant* could outmaneuver most ships, could outgun all but the largest Navy ships as well, but being trapped in these clamps left them with few options.

He paced back to the weapons station and let his hand hover over the button that would call Commander Lewdon to the bridge, then hesitated. If he was wrong, he'd be wasting the captain's time and thwarting the OOD's authority for no reason, and if he was right . . . they didn't need to be in the same place on the ship.

Dammit.

But as he watched the skiff on the screen, it crossed underneath *Vigilant,* pursued by the two patrol boats, then headed away from the docks and out toward empty space. His muscles weakened as he collapsed in the chair and resumed his monitoring of the weapons. *More anxiety over absolutely nothing.* If there was any bad luck following him around, it had to have exhausted itself by this point.

The pilot on loan from Sector Bonneville leaned back in his seat and grinned at him as the last of the alarms faded into nothingness. "Everyone needs a little excitement, huh, Commander?"

"Indeed." He cracked his neck a few times and forced his muscles to relax, letting the last of his anxiety fade away as well. No one needed a fright like that, especially in port. "Though I think I'm getting a little old—"

"Bridge, starboard lookout, target bearing 040, closing rapidly!"

The skiff tumbled toward them, out of control, a fiery glow in the darkness, as alarms blared throughout *Vigilant's* bridge. Whether it had been hit by the patrol boats' fire or lost control on its own didn't matter. It was headed for *Vigilant* and there was nowhere to go.

Nowhere except . . .

"Thrusters from standby," he barked at the OOD through gritted teeth. "Blow the charges."

She looked at him like he'd lost his mind, and he couldn't very well tell her he hadn't. To unclamp under low power—there would be injuries.

Still, she nodded. "Blow the charges, aye, sir."

The charges in the docking clamps fired.

Vigilant fell into the darkness, engulfed in flames.

* * *

When he opened his eyes, the view was the same as it had been for days: the gray ceiling of a medical ward and beeping monitors flashing green and red. He didn't want to know what the red was, but he was still breathing, so maybe it was nothing—or maybe his eyes were as bad off as his legs. He listened to the beeps, which grated on his nerves when he spent too much time focusing on them.

"Commander?"

He ignored the nurse in the doorway, just like he always ignored them when they came in. They were all full of an optimism he didn't feel, and their lies had grown old by the end of the first day. Empty platitudes meant nothing when he could only move his feet a few inches, courtesy of the overhead display that had fallen on him as he lay unconscious on *Vigilant*'s bridge. The emergency undocking had prevented the skiff from making a direct hit, but the explosives in its cargo area had detonated when it skipped off *Vigilant*'s hull, tearing the cutter in half and killing seventeen.

Beep.

Beep.

Beep.

"You have a visitor, sir."

He exhaled, not caring how rude it sounded.

"I don't want to see anyone," he replied. Too many had been by already. The accident investigation people. Investigative Service agents. He didn't want to talk to anyone else. Hadn't wanted to talk to *them*. "Tell whoever it is that I'm too tired to answer more questions."

"Tired or not, I think you'll want to see her."

At that, he turned his head. Hope stood in the doorway next to the nurse, pale, with dark circles under her eyes, like she'd been awake the entire time he'd been unconscious. He hadn't told anyone to notify her, which meant someone had taken it upon themselves, and he couldn't allow that. She was still supposed to be on Io, at arm's length, somewhere she could heal and stay away from the rotten luck he brought to everyone around him. Fatigue turned to fury, and the monitors responded. The nurse glanced over, then, apparently deciding it was only his happiness at seeing Hope, nodded and disappeared.

"Who told you?" he demanded.

A frown crossed her face.

"Captain Kestrel. He'd already made arrangements before telling me. Someone had already packed me a bag." She stepped hesitantly toward the bed, like she was afraid of him. "Josiah, did you expect them to *not* tell me? Did you expect to hide this from me? By the time I left, everyone was talking about *Vigilant*."

"I didn't want you to worry." He glanced at the window, but the gray shades were too closed to see much of anything outside. There was only more red dust outside, sure, but it was something. "You didn't need to come all the way here."

Hope's perfectly groomed eyebrows drew together as she sat, but she didn't touch him. Good. Distance would make it easier to do what he had to do.

"I don't understand," she replied. "Why wouldn't I have come?"

Of course she didn't understand. She didn't know how completely he'd failed, both on *Vigilant* and with her. Well, perhaps she *knew*, like everyone had heard of what had happened in orbit above Mars, like everyone close to them knew about Jonathan, but she didn't know how much of his fault it was. She would never understand how thoroughly he'd failed, even if the chaplain who'd been by his side when he'd woken up had tried to convince him otherwise.

Vigilant wasn't your fault. The full investigation won't be complete for a while, naturally, but it seems that unclamping her when you did prevented more deaths. That skiff would have made a direct hit otherwise. You saved lives.

He'd laughed bitterly and sent the man away. It had been a ridiculous claim. Seventeen dead, and he was supposed to celebrate that? He'd failed them, just like he'd failed Jonathan.

"You have work to do," he replied. "You shouldn't be here."

"Yes. We all have work to do." She half snorted. "But I doubt anyone's upset I'm here. They all know your name now."

Great.

"I can't walk," he said. "I'd rather no one know it."

She stiffened. "You will."

"You don't know that."

"The doctor said once the swelling around your spinal cord goes down, you'll make a full recovery. It'll just take some time, but there's a place on Earth—"

"You talked to her?" Rage mounted, though he knew it wasn't directed at her or the doctors. "Without me?"

"Let's just say I didn't look this composed when I arrived." She stroked the back of his hand, and he couldn't bring himself to move it away. "I think she'd have said anything to calm me down."

He considered that for a long time while the machines beeped in the background. It wasn't something he could argue with, but the longer she sat here, the more she touched him and spoke things that made him think and believe . . .

The harder it would be to say what needed to be said.

"You're on leave?" he ventured.

"Not technically. Not yet." She glanced down, self-consciously, then adjusted her ring. "I'm on my way to request it. For as long as you want."

"Don't."

She flinched. "Excuse me?"

"Go back to Io." He took a deep breath, and the red beeping in the corner of his eye quickened. "I don't ever want to see you again."

CHAPTER FIFTEEN_
NIMBUS STATION, ETRIK

KINNARD WAS ANXIOUS THIS EVENING. WHATEVER was on his mind hadn't stopped him from summoning her to his quarters, and it hadn't stopped him from downing a glass of her blood, but the way he tapped on the desk beside his sofa was odd, especially after he'd drank. Usually her blood calmed him, but tonight it seemed to have done little to take the edge off.

Coralie folded her arms across her chest as he rambled on about how much he missed Mars and its red dust. Complaining about the very slight difference from the rocks outside in the Etrik wasteland seemed pointless, and watching him lick a drop of blood from his lips made her feel nauseated, but the last thing she wanted to do was walk out, only to have him call her back for more. It didn't happen frequently, but he did it often enough that it wasn't worth her energy.

"But it's still better than being stuck on that ship," he added, rinsing the glass with a bit of water from a carafe and drinking that down as well. "I thought we'd never make it here."

She blinked away the memories of *Triumph* and the way she'd been a virtual prisoner aboard, without even knowing it. The voyage had been bad enough, yes, with her strapped down and drained of blood just like she'd been in the capsule, but there had been hope waiting for her. Hope that didn't exist now. Not unless she could make concrete plans for escape.

"Where is she?" A shiver ran down her arms. Nimbus Station turned cooler in the evenings, and the v-words didn't much care about warming it. "*Triumph*, I mean. Did you destroy her and the others?"

It only made sense. What use could Kinnard have for a half dozen Martian ships? Unless—the shiver turned violent—he was building his own fleet in orbit around Etrik? Everyone had claimed they had no desire for a hostile takeover of Earth or Mars, but she'd never quite believed them.

"Most were dissembled for scrap." Kinnard set the glass down on a burnished side table, luxury for Nimbus Station, and smiled at her. "You know we don't care about heading back to the Earth."

"Most?"

"Most." He wandered to the bar on the opposite side of the room and filled the glass with gin.

Coralie blew out a breath. Liquor usually meant he was done with her, but there was something about the way he was staring at her now that meant he wasn't willing to let her go just yet.

"Fine." Her jaw tightened. "What do you mean by 'most'?"

Kinnard leaned against the bar and took a sip. "*Triumph* is still in orbit. She hasn't quite outlived her usefulness yet."

Something about what he was saying was still so very wrong, but her heart skipped a beat at his confession. If *Triumph* was up there, still in one piece, she might have found her way back to Mars with the others. Fuel would be an issue, and so would food and water and actually *finding* the wormholes that would take them back to Mars, but there had to be a way . . .

Coralie shook her head. Stealing a starship was step four hundred seventy-eight out of this place, and she was still at step three. Maybe even step one. She didn't even know how to free the others, much less make her way into orbit.

"What else do you need her for?" she asked. "You really are planning an attack on Earth, aren't you?"

"With a transport ship?" Kinnard chuckled. "Hardly. Every navy still in existence would see us coming as soon as we entered the system. I don't feel like testing my ability to survive being shot at in space. The scientists can figure that one out. No, it's something far more mundane." He took another amused sip of gin. "You know we'll run out of blood eventually."

Her brow furrowed. "In a hundred years, perhaps."

"Which is akin to two or three years of your limited life," he replied. "All this is for naught if a hundred years is all we've gained by doing this. Terraforming will take longer, and I won't give up until we can grow food here at the very least."

"You know"—a yawn split her face—"you're obviously trying to taunt me with something, and I'm much too exhausted to listen to it tonight. Either spit it out or let me go back to my quarters and sleep. It's too late for games, and I have work to do tomorrow."

Kinnard's brows rose, then a chuckle echoed throughout his quarters. "You're less frightened of me, finally. I was beginning to think we were going to sit here for the next fifty years with you shaking every time you glanced at me."

Less frightened? It was an interesting observation, and one she couldn't quite agree with, but she nodded. Anything to keep him talking, as tired as she was. Information was more valuable than most anything else here, and he was about to spill some.

"Does my behavior toward you make you feel guilty?"

"Guilty?" He swirled his glass like he didn't know the meaning of the word. "No. Not even uncomfortable. Just . . . confused. Conflicted, perhaps."

Coralie scoffed out loud. "I can't imagine why you would be."

"You do lack imagination. That's why you're in the position you're in." Kinnard grinned and crossed his ankle over his knee. "But about *Triumph*."

She yawned again, this time for real. Maybe he'd taken more blood than usual tonight.

"Act disinterested all you want, but I know you're dying to know. What would you say if I told you I've found a way to get fifty-some new blood sources here at once—voluntarily?"

Her heart skipped a beat, but the abrupt anxiety was ridiculous. Kinnard was just talking nonsense now. There was no way he could get more than one or two humans with the faulty gene to Etrik at a time, and the NSRC must be running out of people with that gene to begin with. Bringing more through the wormholes, especially in larger groups? Well, the people who *didn't* change would notice when everyone else turned into silver-eyed monsters, and they would never continue on voluntarily.

"I'd say you've had too much gin tonight."

"Even so, your blood tasted better." Kinnard ran his tongue over his lips. "Now, are you ready to listen, or do you want to keep arguing?"

Coralie raised her hands in capitulation. Anything to keep him from asking for more.

"We've known since the beginning that finding more blood would be an issue." He leaned back in his chair. "Bringing one or two people over on NSRC ships was a start, and a good stopgap measure, but for this to work, we need more."

The hair on her arms rose. It hadn't occurred to her until now that there was a reason the compartment with the capsules was so large.

"Our contact on Mars dumped a bunch of money on a group of mercenaries, but they decided one wormhole was enough. Turned around after Alpha and went back to Callisto. Made some excuse about the stars looking too different outside of our own system. I suppose the void frightened them. They lacked imagination too." He shook his head in mock disappointment. "You can't trust anyone these days."

"Yeah, you sure can't." Her sarcasm surprised her, but Kinnard hadn't seemed to notice the irony in his comment. "What's your point?"

"My point is, we had to find someone who wouldn't turn and run at the first sight of unfamiliar stars, people who would be motivated to come all the way to Etrik by something other than money, which, if you can believe it, turned out to be not enough. And so we did."

Kinnard stood and refilled his glass. Her mind raced, but the silence became heavy as he downed one shot and then another. A buzzer sounded in the corridor somewhere, signaling the beginning of the third shift, but he didn't so much as flinch at the sound. In another world? It seemed like he might have been.

"And?" Coralie leaned forward, then back again. Appearing anxious was the wrong move. She didn't know why, but somehow, she knew. "Who?"

Kinnard turned back toward her, poured another shot, and smiled. "Go back to your quarters." He jabbed a finger toward the door. "I have work to do."

* * *

She did not go back to her quarters. Instead, she wandered the gray corridors in a daze, wondering if Kinnard would reduce the pressure and physically force her back. But tonight, her chest expanded and contracted with ease, and there was no blurriness in her vision to suggest he had truly meant what he'd ordered—if he really wanted her back in her room, he'd have depressurized the entire route behind her. And so she meandered, from his quarters to the large window at the end of the hallway where the senior Nimbus Station personnel lived. The moon cast an eerie light on the rust dirt outside, and for a moment, she could pretend she was standing on Mars. Boots echoed behind her—night security, no doubt—then faded around a corner without confrontation. They knew who she was, knew what Kinnard had done to her tonight, knew why she was standing here.

Even if she didn't know herself. The dull pangs of homesickness overcame her as a small dust storm glittered in the moonlight, even though Mars had only been her adopted home. Was it only because it was closer to Earth than this distant planet could ever be?

She yawned once more, then turned and padded back toward her new quarters. Kinnard was just drunk and talking. That had to be it. Because the alternative was that he really had found a way to get fifty more people to Nimbus Station, and that—

She collapsed forward, hands on her knees, retching. The nausea had crept up on her, but it couldn't be anything other than stress. How could she rescue fifty more people if she couldn't even rescue the three already trapped in those capsules?

"Coralie?"

Helena.

Coralie swore under her breath, then straightened, trying to ignore the stomach cramps that didn't feel like they were going to go away. Helena's appearance in a corridor she shouldn't be in didn't help things. Had Riley been telling the truth that day outside the station? Should she be suspicious of Helena? Maybe. She'd appeared twice now in the corridor as Coralie had exited Kinnard's cabin —but then, there wasn't any reason she wasn't *allowed* to be here.

"I'm fine." Coralie spat out the lie with the rest of her nausea. Of all the people she didn't want to be sick in front of, Helena was at the top of the list. "It had to be something I ate. I think I'm fine now."

"Well, let's get you back to your quarters."

Helena pointed down the corridor, but before she could say anything else—or worse, grab Coralie's arm—an alarm blared from somewhere in the ceiling, filling her ears with a painful resonance.

Low atmosphere.

Coralie forced her breathing to remain regular. The nausea hadn't been from anxiety after all, but panic would only make things worse. Maybe Kinnard had been serious about ordering her back to that small compartment, and Riley's warning rang in her ears as she scrambled toward the door, too far in the distance. There was plenty of time before she lost consciousness, but if there wasn't any oxygen on the other side . . .

Helena on her heels, Coralie fumbled at the keypad, praying to whatever god that might exist that the next corridor would be filled with air. The leak in her suit had been insidious, the symptoms slow, but this was something completely different. Modifications or not, her chest was tight, and the numbers on the lock blurred.

"Helena—" She pulled blue hands from the keypad. "I don't remember the code. Is there air on the other side?"

Helena shoved her to the side and entered a sequence that Coralie hadn't a chance of remembering. "No. Near-vacuum, like this one."

"Oh." Coralie leaned against the wall and forced her heartbeat to slow. Was there an emergency mask in the next hallway? It hadn't occurred to her to memorize the locations, but if she survived, she would remedy that first thing. "How far to the next door?"

"Ten meters, I think." The door slid to the side, revealing the longest gray corridor Coralie had ever seen. "You've got plenty of time left. I'll follow behind. Now go!"

Somehow, she forced herself upright and placed one foot in front of the other. The corridor darkened as she stepped through the door, but still she plodded on, watching the emergency lights flash as she passed underneath. Did the v-words still find it odd to walk in an environment that would have killed them five years ago? She would never be able to get used to it, ever.

There.

That dark square up ahead. Her mouth full of the metallic taste of cold, Coralie stumbled toward it, gasping for air despite the certain knowledge there was none to be found. A gray figure prowled in the shadows of her vision, speaking words she could scarcely hear and could understand even less. Why wouldn't the figure help her? Open the door that held the mask and emergency oxygen supply? Was she imagining her companion?

Her trembling hand hit the glass, feeling the latch that would save her life. Training, she'd had training in emergency procedures like this. The box was designed for humans in trouble, panicky ones who couldn't even remember their name. And she'd been through worse, had wanted to live more desperately than this. She could figure it out.

The latch slipped from her fingers, and she hissed out a curse through gritted teeth as she reached for it once more. The shadow behind her grew smaller, but there was no time to worry about that. Hypoxia caused hallucinations, and she wasn't special enough to be an exception.

The panic slid away as she fought for a grip on the latch, and she turned around, looking for the source of the sudden giggles. The gray shadow? Was it laughing at her? Or were they her own?

"Shut up." The order was slurred as her grip slid off the metal once more. "Stop laughing." She was rewarded with more giggling.

"What the hell?"

The voice boomed behind her as she clawed at the glass, laughing at her own incompetence.

Kinnard?

Suddenly nothing was funny anymore, least of all her inability to draw a deep breath. Wavering, she turned toward the sound, then crashed against the wall and slid to her knees. Kinnard's figure knelt next to her and swore at someone behind him. Silicone hit her mouth, but when she took a breath, there was only more of the vacuum that had advanced upon Nimbus Station.

Kinnard stood, a hand on her shoulder, then swore again.

"I'll get her to my quarters," he shouted into nothingness. "At least the door there will seal. Have a medic meet us there with oxygen."

Coralie wanted to fight him, but self-preservation won out as he lifted her up and half dragged her down the hallway back toward where she assumed his quarters had disappeared to. It was hard to tell, because everything had gone blurry, hazy, an icy death she hadn't truly understood was so close. Her augmentations had made her brave, the leak in her suit when she'd stepped outside the station with Riley had made her bold, and now she only wanted to take a deep breath that would never come.

The lights in Kinnard's quarters assaulted her eyes as his door opened, and she closed them as he dumped her on the sofa. She'd always suspected he cut the atmosphere after she left, but as his door hissed closed, the unmistakable scent of gin and soap—not vacuum—filled her nose.

"It's not so funny now, is it?"

On her back, she opened her eyes and looked up. Kinnard was watching her with . . . well, not concern. He would have to be human to show an emotion as trite as concern. But there was apprehension in the way his shoulders slumped as he took his usual seat in the chair across from her.

"Don't tell me you've never seen someone euphoric with hypoxia," she mumbled, laying a palm over her head.

"In a corridor that was supposed to be pressurized?" He raised a brow. "No. I'll be quite honest with you, I have never seen that."

Said corridor must have been repressurized after Kinnard had carried her inside, for the medic rang the doorbell, then entered without closing the door. Coralie took two deep breaths from the mask he pressed over her face, then waved him off, grateful he disappeared without further argument.

"I was just looking out the window," she said to Kinnard, trying to ignore the new headache. "And then—"

And then Helena had materialized.

Had Helena been the gray figure in the side of her vision as she'd struggled to unlatch the emergency oxygen cannister in the second hallway? Her mind was too muddled to remember the details; everything after she'd watched the dust devil outside seemed like a ghastly dream.

"I told you to go back to your quarters. Why were you lingering outside mine?"

"Then you knew the corridor would depressurize." The dream became even more dim, stolen away by what might as well have been his confession.

"No." Kinnard frowned, and for a moment, she felt guilty about her accusation. "They know what would happen to them if you were harmed like that."

"Someone was in the corridor with me." Coralie pushed herself to a sitting position and gazed at the photo of Mars that hung above his desk. She wasn't quite willing to accuse Helena yet, but perhaps she could arouse Kinnard's own suspicions. "Maybe someone doesn't care."

He scoffed out loud. "You've forgotten what happened to Alvaro?"

"Hardly." She couldn't help the horror that crossed her face. "But you were threatening me. It's quite possible someone else doesn't know how bad their death might be."

"Hmm." Kinnard scratched his chin with his thumb, then leaned back in his chair. "I suppose you have a point."

"Then you'll check the security tapes? Whatever security the environmental system has? See if someone emptied that oxygen cannister in the hallway?"

Dammit, she would have to check the rest of them. She hadn't realized how much she'd emotionally relied on the cannisters' presence, and now that they'd proven themselves unreliable . . .

"Of course."

He sounded miffed, and somehow, that amused her.

"You looked so worried when you found me by the emergency oxygen," she said, "and you swore when you realized it was empty, like you'd also realized you liked me enough to not let me die."

"Don't be ridiculous. That's the hypoxia speaking." He crossed his arms and settled into his chair once more. "I just like your blood."

CHAPTER SIXTEEN_

USOGC BAYONET, PAST WORMHOLE
FOXTROT

Hope stepped inside Josiah's quarters and fixed him with a skeptical look. Since the last wormhole passage, she'd been standing watch more than usual, and yet in all his wanderings, he hadn't seen her in three days. There was no doubt that was intentional on her part. So much for the pleasant working relationship she'd claimed they were capable of.

But whatever promise she'd made and then broken didn't matter anymore, at least as far as he was concerned. Before they found *Triumph*, before life intervened once more, there were things that needed to be said—and soon, since *Bayonet* was less than a day from her last known location.

Yes, it was time.

"Ahn said you were looking for me," she began, the vacant expression he hated so much sliding into place. "Is something wrong, Captain?"

Well, that formality answered his first question. No loose strand of hair was visible today either, like she'd made certain to dredge up the most professionalism she could before knocking on the door to his quarters. It didn't bode well for her reaction to anything he wanted to say. Then again, she was starting another shift in two hours. Maybe she was just prepared.

Does that mean she thinks this is going to take two hours?

Hope cleared her throat and folded her arms in a decidedly insubordinate manner, and he tucked the panic away where it belonged, caught his thoughts once more before they went racing away to a place they didn't need to go. Anderson had been a fool to allow them on the same planet, much less the same cutter.

"Close the door, please," he told her.

She did so, and he could almost hear her mind spinning.

"I had a dream the other night," he said, pretending nothing about his thoughts were untoward. Normal, he could sound normal. Always had, right? "About you. About us."

Hope sighed and made to turn toward the door once more. "Josiah, this isn't really a good time."

"Not like that." *Not only like that.* "The problem is how real they were. The day we met—do you remember?"

Like she was giving in to a toddler, Hope sank onto the spare chair that Ahn normally occupied and raised a brow.

"Do you?" he asked once more.

"That was literally two decades ago." He didn't say anything, and she waved her hand at the bulkhead. "Okay, fine. No, I don't remember the day we met. I'm sure I was terrified and overwhelmed and trying to figure out exactly what I was doing in Connecticut."

"I remember you being overwhelmed." He gave the bulkhead a smile, too afraid to direct it straight at her. "Well, I didn't until recently, I suppose. But the dreams I've been having lately have been so realistic that I could have sworn you were standing right there in the hallway in front of me. I saw a mole on your wrist and the way your hair wouldn't stay out of your face, even then."

Her forehead creased as she ran a hand across her temple, checking for loose hair. "I had that mole removed two weeks after I got to the Academy. The flight surgeon thought it was suspicious for skin cancer, and before I could say it had been there forever and hadn't killed me yet, he was slicing it off. I think I'd met you all of three times at that point. There's no way you remember that."

"And yet ever since we transited Echo, I dream about that vividly. Usually about you. Once about Jonathan. The last one was about *Vigilant*, and—and what happened after."

"I'm sure you've had lots of nightmares about *Vigilant*, and I'm sorry it's been so difficult on you. I'm sure time will help." Hope swallowed down what he knew was a lie, then brushed her throat with a light touch. "But I don't think we should talk about the rest."

She was wrong. She was so, so wrong. And somehow, he had to convince her of that.

"I'm talking about the dreams." *Right now, at least.* "I need to know if anyone else has been having them."

"Tell me you're not serious." He could have sworn she'd started to roll her eyes but stopped just in time. "Lots of people have weird dreams like that, especially when they're working twelve-hour shifts in artificial gravity. You know that."

"Have you?"

Her eyes flashed a warning. "Maybe."

The reply was just shy of rude, and her defensiveness gave the actual answer away.

"What are yours about?"

"Josiah . . ." Her tone and the way she was saying his name with such exasperation was a warning. He knew that from long ago. "It doesn't matter what they're about. They're just dreams. The content is meaningless. I always dream like that when I'm exhausted, and this has been—let's just say getting through the wormholes has been rough. I didn't want to be the one responsible for collapsing *Bayonet* in on herself . . . I started having nightmares about it as soon as I found out what we'd be doing out here."

It was as close as she'd ever come to complaining, and he didn't know how she did it. He'd have been a nervous wreck in her position. Watching her work from across the bridge had been bad enough—but also intimate, in a strange way. He'd never had such a clear window to her professional life before.

"Can you find out if it's happening to anyone else?" he asked. "I need to know. I can't poke around and ask questions like that, but you could. You were always discreet like that, and people who won't talk to me will talk to you."

Hope tapped her nails on her thigh and gazed at the bulkhead behind him. Zero eye contact. This wasn't good.

"Being your ex-wife is more isolating than you seem to want to believe. People don't speak to me much—I'm pretty sure they're afraid I'll report everything they say back to you." *Little do they know,* he could almost hear her think. "Besides, you should be asking Patrick to do this."

"I'm asking you."

"Asking or ordering?"

"Whatever it takes."

"You're serious about this." Hope let her head fall backward, closed her eyes, and mumbled a few choice words to the overhead under her breath. "Fine. All right. You're assuming a lot, but I'll see what I can find out."

"Thank you." He leaned back, inexplicably re-lieved by her cooperation. She was right—he should have asked Ahn, but this was something he wanted to keep close for now. Besides, if she'd admitted dreaming of him and Jonathan . . . "Speaking of that, how much is being talked about regarding *Kamorta*?"

"If you're asking if rumors about an entire starship's worth of people dead of liver failure are spreading around the ship, then yes, they are." She chewed her lip, then shot his mug a jealous look. "Minus one passenger, of course. I've been trying to ignore it."

"Curious how true rumors can be." *Kamorta* obviously wasn't why he'd ordered the initial communications blackout, but that decision had already worked in their favor. At least he'd done one thing right. "But Somerset couldn't find anything amiss with any of them. Maybe back on Mars, with better equipment . . ."

He tried not to think of Eshana, and he knew Hope was doing the same.

"At which time *Kamorta* won't be our problem any longer," she reminded him. She'd always been too pragmatic. "We did what we could. The Indian Empire will request that the bodies be repatriated, and then they'll come get their ship, too. Eventually."

As well they should, he knew she was thinking. That was Hope—pragmatic and not so curious about the odder things in space, most of the time. He understood, even if he didn't feel the same. To her, everything in space had a reason, something scientifically provable. How else could she rely on the stars to guide her around? He understood that, or at least his brain did. But his gut . . . that was something else entirely. Because Hope hadn't seen the horror on Blayne's face when he'd come off *Kamorta*.

"Maybe you're right." He hated to admit she was. It was true that they'd already done what they could. More than some would have expected of them, even. "Let someone else deal with the fallout."

"Right."

Her reply was even shorter, and he drummed his fingers on the blue fabric of *Great Expectations* in response.

She's going to walk off any second now. Stop her.

"You still haven't read it, have you?" he asked.

Hope heaved a sigh. "I'm not exactly a Dickens enthusiast—and I know you're not, either."

She glanced toward the door, clearly done with the conversation, obviously waiting for permission to escape. It was now or never. Well, not never, but he certainly wasn't getting braver as the days wore on, and once their search for *Triumph* started in earnest, there wouldn't be any free time. Now that they were through the last charted wormhole, *Bayonet* was already blasting away through space with her sensors. Things could become chaotic in the span of just one hour.

"I somehow forgot." Another lie. He folded his hands in his lap. "Hope, there was something else I wanted to talk to you about."

Her jaw clenched. "What now?"

Yes, he was definitely pushing things.

Oh, well.

"There's something I have to tell you. Something important."

Bayonet's thrusters fired as they reached the end of their current search track, and his inner ear chose that very moment to not cooperate with the stabilization system. Or maybe the sudden dizziness and nausea wasn't from the turn after all. Because once he finished the sentence, there was no going back. No more pretending. No more lies. And it was her who held his future in her hands now.

One last chance . . .

Hope raised her brows again.

"I—" He closed his eyes, as though that would make what he was about to say easier, and the words tumbled out as *Bayonet* and his heart leveled out once more. "Hope, I still love you."

CHAPTER SEVENTEEN_
USOGC BAYONET, PAST WORMHOLE
FOXTROT

THE AIR IN HIS CABIN SEEMED TO DISAPPEAR INTO the ether as Hope stared at him, pale and wide-eyed. He'd made a mistake, that much was clear by the way her shoulders sagged as she sat there, like he'd just given her the worst news of her life. Well, no. He'd done that before, in a hospital far away on Mars, and even then, she'd been more stoic than now.

"You what?" It was scarcely a whisper.

"You heard me." He'd say it as many times as she needed him to. "I still love you, I still want you, I still need you, and I'm asking you to give me another chance."

"Josiah." The look of incredulity on her face as she sat frozen on his spare chair sent a spark of agony through his soul. "What you did to me . . . I couldn't eat the entire way to Mars after I got word about *Vigilant*. I was terrified you'd die before I got there—or that they'd lied to me and you already had. But you told me to go back to Io, and then you *filed for divorce* before we'd even docked. Are you honestly going to sit here and act like none of that happened?"

"I know it happened." Even if he hadn't remembered, the dreams would have reminded him. "And I know you have every right to be angry, no matter how much I beg for your forgiveness. But Hope—"

"I have to go." She stood, fairly tripping over the chair as she did. His muscles tensed, ready to spring, but he caught himself just in time. Even if she'd smashed her head on the deck, even if there was blood, helping her now would be . . . idiotic. She would bite his head off before she accepted his help. "I was supposed to relieve Valdéz ten minutes ago."

His brow creased. "You have two hours."

She backed against the door. "I—"

"Just lied to me," he replied as evenly as he could. "Like I can't tell time."

"So what if I did?" Her hand grappled behind her for the lock switch. "I don't see why it's any of your business where I'm supposed to be right now."

For a moment, the entire universe stood still as her façade crumbled in front of him—though she couldn't know yet that it had.

"I don't think you quite understand how this goes." His chest threatened to cave in on itself. "If you're going to act like I'm nothing to you but your commanding officer, then it damn well is my business where you're supposed to be right now!"

Hope opened her mouth, her cheeks as flushed as though he'd slapped her.

"Don't think I haven't noticed your insufferably faultless protocol," he went on before she could speak, "and if that's the game you want to play, I'm more than happy to play along, but I won't allow you to be surprised when I do. You don't get to have this both ways." He took a breath. Maybe he'd gone too far, especially when he'd just confessed to still loving her, but she couldn't expect him to ignore the situation any longer. "So if convincing yourself how little you care about me is that important to you, then just say *goodnight, sir* and walk out."

You're good at that.

"Josiah, it's barely 1100."

His breath caught. Pedantry meant she felt something toward him, even if it was disdain. He could work with that. Disdain was better than indifference.

She lifted her chin. "And you can't possibly think I'm going to stand here and have a conversation about this after you—"

"Swallowed my pride?" He swallowed every bit of resentment along with it. She had every right to treat him like she was, and he had no right to be angry about it. Afraid, yes. He would allow himself to feel fear. "Told you how I feel? Yes, that would be terrible of you to extend the tiniest bit of grace right now."

"You're a year and a half too late for that!"

"Am I?" He sprang to his feet. "You're still standing here, so I'm not so sure I am."

At that, she vented what could only be called a hiss, turned her back to him, then went to work on the latch one more. But the way she was struggling with it didn't make sense. Hope had spent as much time in space as he. She shouldn't have any trouble figuring out a simple lock.

His heart skipped a beat.

"Do you need help?" He took a step toward her. "I wouldn't want you to be late."

She leaned her forehead against the steel. "I don't need anything from you."

"Could have fooled me." Another step, and then another. He hadn't been this close to her since the day they'd kissed goodbye and he'd departed for *Vigilant*. She didn't move as he reached in front of her and undid the lock, though he didn't push the door open. This close, he could smell her soap. "There. I'll see you when I see you, then."

It was only her ragged breath that could be heard throughout the silent compartment as he held his own. The back of her neck was right there, and he wanted to brush his lips down it, just to watch her shiver. *Bayonet* was always chilled, but her body was warm, and though he knew he should back off, send her off to the bridge, never think of her like this again, the only thing he could do was take a few steps away toward the opposite bulkhead.

The lock clicked into place once more.

"What do you want?" She spoke to the door, tears in the question. "Just to kill some time? Is that what this is about? You're lonely out here in space, you know no one else would ever get this close to you now that *Bayonet*'s yours, but you think I'm desperate enough and we're familiar enough to—"

"I want you. I've wanted you from the first day we met." He reached toward her and tucked that damnable loose piece of hair behind her ear. "And I want to explain. That's all."

And it's everything.

She spun around and placed her palm against his chest. "I don't believe you."

"Yes, you do. At least, you're willing to give me a chance to make you believe me. I think we've established that." Meeting no resistance, he took her by the hand and led her toward his bunk.

"I want to." Hope sat next to him without argument, only to put her head in her hands. "More than anything. But it's too late for us. You can't fix everything. You can't fix this."

After you destroyed it, he could read in her tone. *After you threw everything away, no matter what you promised before.*

"What if I could?"

She glanced sideways at him. "Then maybe you don't need to be fixing it. Maybe your fixing everything makes it worse."

His heart thumped at the accusation. Did she know why he'd left? Of course not. That was non-sense. It was the very reason he'd refused to speak with her after she'd returned to Io. Because if he had, he would have told her his reasons, and if he told her his reasons, he would have changed his mind . . .

He ran his hands over his face.

Courage, now.

"I tried to protect you." His voice was harsh and frayed as the words spilled out. "After Jonathan died, I swore that I'd never let you experience that kind of heartache ever again. I thought that was enough. That I could control the future, shield you from whatever sorrow it might bring. But then *Vigilant* happened, and I realized I'd broken that promise, that it had been naïve to begin with. Leaving was the only way I could make sure I didn't hurt you all over again. So I decided I would become nothing more than some guy you used to know, and then I left."

Hope stared at him, horror in her expression.

"I would never be sitting here like this in the cabin of *some guy I used to know*," she whispered. "I could never think of you like that, no matter how many years pass, no matter how much I try to pretend we're nothing but colleagues. Do you understand that?"

"I know that now." He reached for her, fully expecting her to pull away. Because he had done this. It had been all him who'd broken her heart, ruined his own life. He skimmed the bare skin on her left hand, and the absence of that slender piece of gold shattered the defenses he'd put up after *Vigilant*. "And I know we can still fix this."

She yanked away and pulled at her collar, but it didn't break the spell. They were right there on the edge, and he held his breath as he watched her think, as though doing nothing but taking one small sip of oxygen would change the course of their lives.

"I love you," she said slowly. "I always have, and I always will. I should have fought. I shouldn't have given up on you so quickly, on us. I should have stayed on Mars, planted myself in that hospital room until security made me leave, and told you to shove your papers into the Sun. But it was so much easier to give in from so far away, even though it wasn't what I wanted." She met his eyes, the guilt there undeniable. "We really screwed up, didn't we?"

"We did." His heart beat again. "But it's not too late to right this."

"What if it is?"

"How would it be?" He touched the name tag on her chest. "Unless I'm mistaken, it doesn't appear you've remarried."

"No." Her laugh was breathless. "I could never, you know that. But Josiah, everything is different now."

"Nothing has changed," he whispered. "Not according to me, not according to Him. And if I were to guess, not according to you, either."

Her eyes widened. "You're serious about this."

"You keep questioning how serious I am." It was his turn to laugh. "How long have you known me?"

"I can't lose you again." Hope glanced from him to the door, like she was looking for an escape route, then drew in a trembling breath. "And if this is some sort of false promise . . ."

"Not a false promise. The same one I made that day we married." He ran his finger down that devastatingly bare one of hers. "The same I've always meant."

"Okay." She touched his face, like she hadn't really believed he was sitting there in front of her the entire time, like he was about to disappear into the bulkhead, a figment of her imagination. Some reacted to space travel like that, even though she'd never mentioned it, so he couldn't blame her. "Okay," she repeated.

"Yeah?" He let the faintest wisp of a hopeful smile through. He'd gambled, and it seemed he'd won.

She didn't even pause. "Yeah."

"Then we can get the legalities worked out as soon as we get back to Mars."

"Hopefully soon." Hope's shoulders sank as she nodded. "Though I suppose soon is relative all the way out here." Her eyes widened again. "You need to tell Patrick about this. He ought to know. You know—for professional reasons."

"Do you realize the ridicule I'm going to receive?" Josiah sighed as she raised a brow in a silent reprimand. "Fine. Yes. I'll let him know next time I see him." He drew her hand toward his mouth and kissed it. Ahn, *Bayonet*, search and rescue, wormholes, and research stations—they were the last things he wanted to think about now. "I don't want to stop with these."

"But?" Her voice had been shaky for the last five minutes, but now it was hoarse.

"But," he said, dropping her hand and toying with the lowest button on her blouse, "the problem is, you don't seem like the type."

"What type is that?" Her touch met his, and before he knew it, three more buttons were undone.

"The type to screw your CO."

If his crudeness startled her, it was impossible to tell by the methodical way she led him upward, making quick work of the rest of her blouse. The fitted undershirt beneath didn't hide her curves nearly as well, but it was still too much clothing for him. Before she could protest, it joined her blouse, a navy heap on the deck.

"Well, you're right—I can't say it's ever crossed my mind." She pulled her hair free and let it tumble over her shoulders. "But I've always wondered what it would be like to sleep with a commander."

"Yeah?" Josiah glanced at the systems readout on the screen above his head, but it wasn't a lack of oxygen in his cabin that had left him so light-headed. He leaned in and nibbled her earlobe. "It just so happens I know where you can find one."

"Today's my lucky day, then."

Her grin split her face, and he couldn't help a laugh in return as he yanked off the sweatshirt he'd worn in a futile effort to prevent himself from doing exactly what he was about to do. The maneuver should have cooled him, but he was just as warm as he'd been five minutes before.

"I've missed that sense of humor like you wouldn't believe," he said, laying his palm against her cheek. "And I'm going to miss you once you walk out that door, and once we get to back to Mars, and once—"

"Josiah." She silenced him with a brief kiss. "One step at a time. We'll figure all that out later. Like we always did, right?"

"You always were the logical one." He kissed the corner of her lips, tasting coffee and strawberry lip balm. His mind knew how odd the combination was, but he wanted to drink it up, savor it forever. "Plus, you taste amazing."

"I taste like coffee." Her hand hit her mouth, and a flush began on her chest and settled in her cheeks, as if she'd only now realized. "I drank two cups before I came here. I always drink some if I think I'm going to be anywhere near you. It—it keeps me from getting too close."

"Well, that explains an awful lot. It didn't work this time, did it?" He rolled her to the bunk and pulled her against him, stifling her surprised laugh with his palm. What little resolve he'd been clinging to fractured at the feel of her skin on his. "Too bad for you I don't care about my wife's breath."

"I thought it was a brilliant plan. You can't accuse me of not trying to remain professional." She traced a line down his chest, and her touch sparked an emotion within him he would never let go of again. "The problem is, that means I really do need to be on the bridge in two hours. My husband's in command of this ship, and I would hate for it to get back to him that I was late."

"I suspect he might forgive you just this once." He left a trail of kisses along her jawline, relishing her contented gasps. "But I'll apologize in advance for leaving you wanting more."

CHAPTER EIGHTEEN_
NIMBUS STATION, ETRIK

CORALIE WAS STILL STARING AT THE GRAY CEILING over her bunk long after she'd promised to arrive in engineering. Henk might object, but then again, he'd been the one who'd initially claimed she'd had another job, and she wasn't above reminding him of it if he hassled her about not showing up in time for the monthly fire detector inspection. Besides, since she did most of that work on her own, wasn't she in charge of her own schedule?

She certainly wasn't in charge of anything else in her life. A brief visit to the security section the day before had ended up with her escorted out to the hallway, despite her pleas for help in finding the security footage from outside Kinnard's quarters that night. Whether they were hiding something or simply didn't want to deal with her, she didn't know.

But even if security wasn't hiding anything, *someone* was. Life support wasn't exactly her specialty, but that emergency oxygen shouldn't have been empty, even on a station where most of the occupants didn't need oxygen to survive—she'd stopped by yesterday and checked the install date. Even given a nominal amount of leakage, there should have been plenty remaining. No, someone had discharged it on purpose.

But who? As much as she despised Kinnard, he didn't have any motive to kill her—in fact, he had the exact opposite incentive to keep her alive. When his new subjects arrived, her life might become more tenuous, but until then . . .

She rolled to her side and contemplated getting up, but a sudden emotion had taken hold, gluing her to the bunk. Fear? There shouldn't be anything left to fear any longer, because she'd already looked death in the eye several times and survived.

Failure?

Maybe.

What would you say if I told you I'd found a way to get fifty-some new blood sources here at once —voluntarily?

Kinnard's words echoed in her mind, had been doing so all night. The fifty-some he'd spoken of had to be scientists, because who else would come all the way to Etrik voluntarily? And yet her gut told her that wasn't true. Participation in the Nimbus Station project had always been selective, required a lengthy application process and multiple interviews. It was selective enough that rumors had flown about biological weapons being produced here. Wouldn't anyone with half a brain become suspicious if they were *approached* for inclusion?

The coffee pod in the machine next to her bed dropped into the machine with a hiss, programed to brew once she moved enough to show she was awake. Coralie planted her feet on the cold concrete floor and yawned. There was no point in arguing with fate once it had decided it was time for coffee.

Cup in hand, she marched to the facilities compartment, daring anyone to challenge her and half holding her breath at the same time—both from the fear of decompression and the fear that Henk might turn her away once she got there. But he only rolled his eyes and made a comment about *working when one wasn't forced to*, which she took as tacit enough permission.

Finding an empty station, she eased into the chair and drummed a haphazard rhythm on the desk in front of her. Everything she did at a computer station was tracked, but checking the status of the environmental systems was within her area of responsibilities, wasn't it? Of course.

Flimsy excuse or not, not one of the v-words turned their silver eyes toward her as she brought up a schematic of the system. If nothing else, she could see if the oxygen in that corridor near Kinnard's quarters was the only one inoperative. No one would blame her for that.

She began with the corridors near her quarters. All green, all emergency oxygen generators charged and ready. That was surprising, but she worked her way back toward Kinnard's quarters, stopping every so often to change screens when someone walked by. But outside of the generator that had failed her the other night, the generator that still hadn't been refilled, every other emergency station appeared . . . *normal*?

Coralie checked them twice more, then leaned back in her chair with a sigh and rubbed her eyes. Maybe it had truly been an accident, a fluke, her being in the wrong place at the wrong time. And Helena? Well, Coralie *had* been exhausted, and she *had* just lost some blood, even if she'd rather pretend what Kinnard was doing to her wasn't actually happening. People had hallucinated worse than a maybe-friend, maybe-enemy during vacuum training. One of her colleagues had been so insistent that spiders were crawling over the rest of the trainees in the chamber that he had—

A hand hit her shoulder, and she barely suppressed a scream.

"That doesn't look like fire protection work," said Henk, yanking her to her feet.

* * *

Behind his desk in the private office he usually scorned, Henk tapped his fingers on his desk while Coralie sat across from him, her legs crossed and her jaw tight. If he told Kinnard, she could kiss all her system access goodbye, and being trapped at Nimbus Station, all but blind to the happenings going on around her, could be devastating. Fatal, even.

"I can't have you snooping," he said finally, twirling a stylus in between his thumbs. "Kinnard would—"

"I wasn't snooping, Henk." She leaned forward in earnest. "Someone tried to kill me the other night by discharging the emergency oxygen station by Kinnard's quarters and then depressurizing the corridor, and—" *And unlike you grotesque excuses for human beings, I need oxygen to survive,* she'd almost said. "And I have a vested interest in making sure it doesn't happen again. I only wanted to see if the rest of the oxygen generators were functional. It makes me feel more comfortable when I'm doing inspections or leaving Kinnard's quarters late at night when no one's around to rescue me."

There. Reminding him of who she was to Kinnard made her skin crawl, but Henk was almost as afraid of him as she was, so . . .

"That was an accident." Henk drew his stylus along the edge of his desk.

"Says who?"

"Security." He stopped fidgeting and focused on her. "They stopped by the next day and practically interrogated this entire division about who might have wanted to kill you, a distraction from our actual work that I really didn't appreciate."

Her forehead creased. Kinnard had taken the incident seriously?

"They did?"

"Yeah." Henk leaned forward. "And then they threatened me until I agreed to stop any rumors to the contrary that might start."

"Ah."

"So you see," he said, leaning back in his chair once more, "I can't allow that to happen. If you're going to snoop, you're going to get caught, and then I'll have more explaining to do. More interruptions to our work. I'll ban you from this office before I allow that to happen."

Coralie's stomach sank. Being banned from the facilities department meant less freedom, less access, and . . . and something less tangible. It meant less *meaning* in whatever pathetic dregs remained of her life.

"I understand," she replied.

"But I know you want answers. And I think I know how we can satisfy your curiosity and keep the rest of my department safe."

She raised a brow. "Oh?"

Henk gave her a sideways look, then slid his chair to the edge of his desk, where his tablet rested. He drew it toward him, then lowered his voice.

"If I pull the security footage, would that be enough for you to leave this alone? I don't want you going after anyone who might have been in the corridor that day, and I doubt you're going to do that, but the knowledge . . . at least you could use it to avoid the wrong people?"

Thank you.

Coralie nodded, scarcely believing what he had said. "They won't question why you're looking?"

He gave her a look. "I know how to hide my tracks."

Well. At least one of them did.

She sat back in her chair and watched him without blinking as he searched through the files, muttering under his breath all the while.

"Huh." Surprise laced Henk's tone.

"What?"

"I went all the way back to when you were brought out of the capsule. No one stopped at that emergency box. No one even looked twice at it. Not until you started clawing at it."

"But that would mean someone knew it was out of service and depressurized the corridors, knowing there wouldn't be emergency oxygen for me." The hair on the back of her neck prickled. Helena?

"Maybe." He didn't sound sure. "Or someone edited the footage."

"What makes you think that?"

"It skips." Henk pushed the tablet toward her. "See? Right as you come stumbling up to the box, there's a line where something was deleted."

Coralie stared at the video, clear as day until she entered the camera's field of view.

"Kinnard did this." Her mouth went dry. "He said he'd check the security tapes, and he must have done this instead. But I don't understand why." To discredit her? Make her think she was going insane?

But there was something else—that was it.

Helena wasn't in the picture, either.

"Henk, can I watch the past five minutes? Can you follow me out of Kinnard's quarters? I spent some time just staring out the window at the end of the corridor there."

"Sure." Henk gave her an odd look, made even odder by his silver eyes, then focused on the security tapes. "Here." He slid the tablet toward her after one of the longest minutes of her life. "This is where you come out of Kinnard's quarters."

"Thanks."

It felt odd to thank one of *them*, but he'd already done enough to deserve the single word, hadn't he? Coralie debated that as she watched herself stare out the window at the dust devil, then jump. She turned around, then apparently seeing nothing, began her walk down the corridor, muttering under her breath the entire time. The depressurization light flashed, the alarm sounded, she ran to the next door, but . . .

Helena was nowhere to be seen.

"Something's wrong." The temperature in Henk's office seemed to drop twenty degrees, even as her entire body grew hot. "I wasn't alone in the corridor that night. Helena, she—"

Her breath quickened, but there was plenty of air in Henk's office, and anyway, the chip near her lungs ensured she wouldn't feel this sick so soon. No, this was something else.

Absolute terror.

"Let me see that."

Henk took it from her hands and frowned as he watched the video again.

"Coralie," he began, "I don't see anything. No glitches, no edits. Not like when you tried for the emergency oxygen. Are you sure Helena was with you? Maybe it was another night, another corridor."

Half of her wanted to accuse him of lying to her, too. But Henk had never been like that, and even as the monster he'd become, she trusted him. More than Kinnard, anyway. Coralie hadn't realized such an emotion was still possible. Even Riley, friendly though she was now, wasn't someone she *trusted*.

"I know what I saw," she said stubbornly. "And if someone edited the later footage, why not the earlier parts? Why couldn't Helena have deleted it herself?"

"Well, to begin with, she's a life support technician."

"Yeah." Her shoulders sank. "I know."

"Tell you what." He shoved the tablet into a desk drawer and folded his hands on the desk. "I'll poke around. Ask questions. As long as you don't. Deal?"

Coralie nodded, though all she really wanted to do was go hide in her quarters.

"Deal."

CHAPTER NINETEEN_

FOR THE END OF MORNING WATCH, THE WARDROOM was strangely quiet, with only a few grabbing coffee and leaving. Josiah was staring at his second cup, bleary-eyed, when Hope slid into the chair across from him and smiled. If the coffee hadn't woken him up, the familiar liquid in her mug did—her usual chai, with the faintest hint of powdered soy milk.

"You're awful sprightly this morning," he said, running a hand across his face. *And beautiful.* "And making me look bad once again. I suppose I'll have to get used to that once more."

"Sprightly?" Her smile dissolved into a laugh. "What kind of word is *sprightly*?"

"One of a man who got about fifteen minutes of good sleep last night," Josiah replied. "Tossed and turned for hours. I'm surprised I was still functional enough to find the wardroom."

He pushed his cup to the side and folded his hands on the table. There hadn't been any vivid dreams like when *Bayonet* had transited the wormholes, but the shadowy nightmares his exhausted brain had fabricated of *Triumph*'s fate had almost been worse. A lengthy gash in her hull, passageways filled with icy, floating bodies, echoes of screams that hung in the dark vacuum like ghosts—he'd seen and heard it all last night.

Or was it *Vigilant* he'd dreamed of? Her ghosts were just as present, perhaps more so.

"Stressed?" Her forehead creased. "Anything in particular?"

He shook his head, even though he didn't want to answer. But she'd always been able to read him, and there wasn't any vulnerability in confessing to it now. Well . . . no, there was still that, but he didn't mind anymore. She could know everything about him, and it still wouldn't be enough to make up for lost time.

"It's a lot of responsibility," she added. "You'd be a fool if you weren't stressed about everything that's going on. I am, and my critical duties are over for now. Though I suppose I'll feel better once we find *Triumph*."

"We should have found her by now." He exhaled. It wasn't true, but he could still hope. "There's nothing but a bunch of empty space in front of us, all the way to Etrik. And that means—"

The coffee turned heavy in his gut; perhaps that second cup had been a mistake. There'd always been the chance they wouldn't find *Triumph*. It happened. Pirates took a ship, it disintegrated in deep space, whatever. More frequently, they found a ship full of bodies. The void didn't always wait for a rescue, not even closer to Mars.

Hope shook her head. "It's too early to determine what happened to her, if in fact anything did, and you know it. We don't know what kind of anomalies could interfere with the sensors out here, and once we reach the Etrik System, it'll be even more difficult to see her in between whatever pieces of rock might be in the way."

She didn't have to explain it to him, and yet he needed the reassurance that only she could provide. Ahn had said the same thing yesterday as they'd stood on the aft viewing deck and watched *Bayonet* make yet another turn to position her sensors away from the engine interference. Once upon a time, he'd thought it strange that they couldn't just blast through space scanning for targets left and right, but life was never that easy.

"You're right." He forced a smile that became easier when he remembered who he was smiling at. As soon as they got back to Mars . . . "And as Patrick is so fond of reminding me, I've seen worse."

"I'm glad you can smile about worse now."

Josiah waved his hand toward the door, the coffee maker, the floor. Hope knew how badly he'd handled the outcome of certain patrols, but she also knew he didn't show much emotion out here in space. Laughed about it sometimes, yes. But everyone knew that was self-protective, not sociopathic.

"What are the other options?" he asked. "Fall apart?"

Hope cocked her head in unspoken agreement. She'd been waiting at home when he'd done that once, had held him while he stared at the wall and told her about the vessel they'd found drifting just outside Pallas's orbit, the icy graveyard of twelve platinum miners from Ceres. The bodies had been warm when *Vigilant* had arrived, and he still had nightmares about the twenty minutes it had taken them to cut through the outdated hatch that hadn't had a quick release.

"Anyway, I was talking to—" she began. His watch beeped, and she glanced down at it. "Take it. This can wait, but I have something to tell you as soon as you can find a free moment."

He disagreed that more conversation with her could wait, but he swiped at his wrist with an unspoken prayer that it wasn't anything too urgent. Having breakfast with Hope, he'd decided a whole thirty seconds ago, was better than *almost* anything else he could be doing . . . and that anything else also involved her.

Need a moment when you have one, Captain. - 47610

The system's insistence on defaulting to personnel numbers instead of actual names was a frustration most alternatively laughed and complained about, but Josiah didn't have to cross-check the manifest this time, for when he glanced back at Hope, Blayne's figure in the passageway outside caught his attention.

"Yeah, I've got to take this one," he said, grabbing his cup as he stood. "I love you and I'll catch you later," he added under his breath.

"Goodbye, sir." The words were louder than necessary as she lifted her cup to her mouth, and he knew she was hiding a smile.

Always more professional than him—maybe he could learn something from her. But at least his cheeks weren't burning like hers as he stepped outside the wardroom and motioned Blayne forward.

"I've got to head up front." A lie, but he needed to be away from Hope if he was to focus. "Mind if we walk and talk?"

Blayne shook his head. "Fine with me, sir."

He didn't seem inclined to say much more immediately, and Josiah cast him a sideways glance as he strode forward. Perhaps that was simply Blayne's personality, but the heavy feeling he couldn't shake suggested there was more to it.

"How's Eshana?" he asked.

"Eshana." Blayne made an odd noise of disbelief as *Bayonet* twisted into yet another turn. "Well, Eshana should be the least of your worries right now, because there's some jacked up shit happening on this ship, Captain, pardon the language."

"Nothing I haven't heard before." Josiah's brows rose. "But for example?"

"You won't believe me if I told you."

"Indulge me."

Blayne sighed.

"All right. Somerset commed me a few nights ago, just after we transited Foxtrot. Eshana was screaming, some kind of nightmare, and she'd forgotten every word of English she'd ever spoken."

"Well, that doesn't surprise me." Josiah shrugged. Not having a Hindi speaker aboard *Bayonet* might have been a crisis. A nightmare? Not so much. "She spent a few days floating around with the bodies of her family. I'd be worried about her if she didn't have nightmares. You get her calmed down?"

"Eventually, but that's just it—turns out she hadn't had a nightmare."

"Oh?"

Josiah stopped and pressed his back against the bulkhead, out of the way of anyone else who might pass by, but the passageway was empty now. His curiosity was forced, because somehow he knew what Blayne was about to say, even though he couldn't verbalize it. Hadn't Hope all but confessed to the same thing? He didn't want to admit he'd bought her story of simply being tired, even if for the briefest of moments.

"They were pleasant dreams, she told me. Of India, and her family, and how amazing it was when she'd looked down on Earth from orbit for the first time. Nice memories, you know? She wanted to stay in them, keep reliving everything. But when she woke up aboard *Bayonet* . . ."

Josiah's heart skipped a beat.

"I imagine waking up aboard this hulk would devastate anyone," he replied, more evenly than he felt.

The joke fell flatter than it should have, and his mouth went dry before he remembered he was still holding his coffee. He took a sip, but it didn't chase away the apprehension that was only heightened by the deserted passageway that suddenly seemed to go on forever. *Triumph* had looked like this in his nightmares . . .

And ghost stories never frightened you before, O'-Donnell.

"Not just that. She remembered the details, too, like she'd actually been there, and that frightened her. And that's not the eeriest part of the whole thing, sir."

"It gets more eerie?" Josiah forced a smile over his coffee. "I hope that's not true, because you're doing a damn good job of creeping me out right now, Master Chief."

"I've had them, too." Blayne's cheeks flushed as he stumbled on, the very opposite of the man Josiah had watched board *Kamorta*. But then, some dealt with the realities of deep space, even when they included death, much better than the unseen. "Only a few times, and only inside the wormholes. Took me a while to figure out the pattern, but once I did, it became impossible to ignore."

"Well." Josiah took another few steps toward the bridge, then stopped when Blayne didn't follow. *Bayonet*'s turn stopped, too; the thrusters weakened. "Everyone's exhausted these days, right? Things like this are bound to happen."

Blayne squared his stance. "Eshana's not exhausted."

"Traumatized, then." His response was sharper than he'd intended. *Look, I'm sure it's nothing,* was what he wanted to say, but he wouldn't lie or break Blayne's trust by dismissing his concerns so easily. "Look—"

Boots seized his attention, and his head swiveled toward the sound. Could he not finish one single conversation without being interrupted? The boots belonged to the messenger of the watch, so likely not.

"I'm sorry to interrupt, sir, but you're needed urgently on the bridge." To her credit, the petty officer really did appear sorry. "The OOD pinged you twice, and Commander Ahn thought you might already be on your way, but he asked if I might—"

Josiah glanced at his wrist and swore to himself. *Of course he did.*

"Very well." He gave Blayne a quick glance, a promise to explain later. Explain what, he wasn't sure, because he didn't have any answers. "I'll be there momentarily. Care to give me a hint about what's so urgent?"

Her lip quirked up in the slightest of smiles. "We may have found *Triumph,* sir."

CHAPTER TWENTY_
NIMBUS STATION, ETRIK

CORALIE SWORE AT THE FIRE DETECTOR IN THE FOOD storage compartment as she slipped off the step stool once more. This particular piece of uncooperative equipment was installed in a wall just under an air conditioning pod, and getting her tester to the correct probe was proving nearly impossible. The v-words hadn't stopped to consider how this kind of sloppy craftsmanship five years ago would become her problem now.

She hopped to the floor between two stacks of crates labeled *powdered milk* and wiped a piece of sweat-soaked hair from her forehead. It was a darker and redder blonde than it had been when she'd left Mars—bordering on strawberry—and every so often she'd glimpse herself in the mirror and wonder who that woman was. She didn't look bad, especially for a person who'd been locked in a capsule and her blood drained for so long. But there was something old in her own eyes, mistrustful, like a beaten dog waiting to strike its abuser. She didn't necessarily feel that way, though. Because she was still waiting and learning, and eventually, when they least suspected it and she was the most prepared, she would strike.

With a sigh, she moved to climb back up and fight with the tester once more when the door to the compartment opened. The hair on the back of her neck rose, like it always did when one of the v-words caught her off guard, but it was only Henk who crept inside and closed the door behind him.

"You got a minute?" He held out a tablet.

All I have is time, Coralie wanted to say, but she only nodded.

"I poked around a little." He cleared his throat, and for a moment she saw him as the friend he'd used to be on Mars. "Discreetly. It seems there were numerous breaches in security's computer systems the night you almost, uh, suffocated in that hallway."

She sucked down a gasp. "Then you believe me."

"Just look."

Coralie took the tablet with a tentative hand and stared at the numbers that danced down the screen. She blinked at them, but they refused to meld into anything that made sense to her.

"What exactly am I looking at?"

"Those are backup files created every ten seconds by the camera outside Kinnard's quarters. You can see the timestamp there on the right side of the screen. The first file is you standing against the window beginning at 2218:17, but then it skips. A whole three seconds, and then it continues to be three seconds ahead until Kinnard drags you back in there."

Coralie sagged against the wall, then tucked her hair behind her ear to hide the unease she didn't want Henk to see. It was pointless, for his expression became sympathetic, even with those unnatural silver eyes that glowed even more against the gray walls.

"That's pretty blatant," she whispered.

"In some ways. Whoever edited that video covered their tracks well, even if the fact they edited it was pretty obvious. I don't have any better or more specific answers, unfortunately."

Well, that figured. Not that she needed to know. It was obvious Helena had done it—wasn't it?

"And your contact?" She forced herself upright. "They won't say anything to the wrong people?"

Henk's tresses blew in the breeze of the nearest vent. "I have dirt on the right people."

Coralie couldn't contain her laugh. All the ethics training they'd been subjected to, and Henk had always found a way to skirt the letter of the law.

"That doesn't surprise me." She took a deep breath, and some of the anxiety vanished. Strange how being able to breathe so easily immediately settled her nerves these days. "But I'm still concerned Kinnard will find out."

"I wouldn't be, if I were you. Personally, I don't think he cares enough to listen to whoever might tell him I was being nosy." He took the tablet back, then folded his arms. "But if you want my advice on things that might keep you safe . . . I think you should stay away from Riley Shaw."

But Riley likes *me now.*

"You know, Henk," she replied, picking the tester back up, "there seems to be a lot of people telling me to stay away from other people. And to be honest, I'm getting just a little tired of it."

"I'm trying to protect you the best I know how. You know Riley has always hated you. The entire department knows the two of you never got along, and you haven't stopped to think why that's changed?"

She turned her back toward him and climbed onto the step stool, even though it felt wrong. Perhaps Henk was the only one she felt comfortable enough to do that in front of.

"Maybe she's lonely," she tossed over her shoulder.

I sure am.

He scoffed. "Riley is a lot of things, but she's not lonely."

Coralie picked at a loose thread on her jumpsuit. "Well, whatever flings she has are different. This is friendship."

"Coralie." Henk's voice became closer, and she turned toward him, scarcely keeping her balance. "I know things have been difficult, but you can't be stupid about this. I don't want to see anything happen to you."

"Stupid?" The word was too high-pitched, and it echoed off the walls of the food storage compartment. "Tell me, Henk, why should I trust you?

What makes you any different from Riley, or Helena, or Kinnard?" *Especially Kinnard.* "You benefited from my blood when I was locked in that capsule, certain I would never be able to walk or even feed myself again, and you're implying I should trust you?"

He circled around another container to face her. "I'm not implying anything. Maybe . . . hoping?"

"I think you lost any right to hope for my trust the very second you agreed to this scheme, don't you?"

"Okay." He held up his hands, the tablet grasped in his left, and backed toward the door. "Look, I care about you, and I'm trying to help. I wish you would let me, but I'll let you come to that conclusion on your own terms."

The door slammed behind him, and for a moment Coralie could only stare at it, praying he wouldn't walk back in and try to change her mind once more. Because he'd been so close, and she couldn't let that happen. She couldn't let herself think of Henk or Riley or any of the rest of them as human, and she couldn't let her former warmth toward her colleagues get in the way of what she had to do. But Henk didn't re-enter, and after the rage in her cheeks faded away and the heat gave way to the usual chill of the compartment, her gaze dropped to the crate next to her.

Dark chocolate and almonds.

With a sigh, she popped open the clasps, grabbed the top bar, and shoved it in her mouth.

CHAPTER TWENTY-ONE_

CONTRARY TO THE MOOD JOSIAH HAD EXPECTED, THE bridge was almost silent when he waved his watch at the sensor and stepped through the door. If anyone other than the OOD acknowledged his appearance, he barely noticed through the adrenaline.

"Status? Where is she?"

"Gone, Captain." The sensor operator didn't turn around, but his fingers continued to dance over the screen in front of him as he spoke. "We caught a flicker of a hull signature, then it disappeared."

"Positive match?" Josiah hadn't needed to ask for the data to be sent to his console. By the time he sat and his eyes moved downward, it was streaming across his screen, though too quickly for him to answer his own question immediately.

"That's affirmative."

"At least we're not chasing ghosts." Josiah rubbed his eyes. That was something. "What's the scanner saying?"

"The forecasted pattern is consistent with a regular and sustained appearance and disappearance, but the computer's extrapolating an awful lot, sir. We only got five seconds of data before the sensors cut out on us."

"Which means it's in orbit somewhere."

Unless it waited until we got here to explode on us.

Now why had he thought that? A continuous pattern of appearance and disappearance usually only meant one thing, and that was that the target was being regularly blocked by and then clearing a moving object.

"Appears so, sir."

"There are a few large asteroids in the system. Definitely large enough to hide a starship's hull signature." Josiah gave a grateful look and nod of thanks as a fresh cup of coffee appeared at his console. There was never enough some days. "Did we get a distance estimate before the target disappeared?"

"Negative. Still too far away."

He swore under his breath, softly enough that no one heard. Hull signature was secondary to an engine signature anyway, which meant the engines weren't running—or were running at power too low for a proper capture. Or—and this would be the best-case scenario—it could simply mean *Triumph*'s stern, and therefore her engine exhaust ,was pointed away from *Bayonet* when the sweep hit her. Pessimism, he supposed, did no one any good.

"All right. Let's resume the sweep, and plot a course for . . ." Josiah glanced at the sensor analyst hovering nearby. "2315 YX37 is supposed to be a nickel-core asteroid, correct?"

"Supposed to be, sir." She pointed at the tablet in her hand, a smaller version of the screen he was staring at. "But the data from the NSRC is a bit unclear. They say it's small enough that it could be rock all the way through."

"It'll hose up the sensors if they're right about the nickel," he muttered to himself, searching the star map on the console. In any case, the asteroid was large enough to capture a starship with its gravity, no matter what the core was made of, so they needed to explore that possibility further. "Let's avoid it if we can, but let's also see if we can swing around and check the far side of the planet before heading deeper into the system. Somewhere like . . ." He marked the coordinate with a star. "Here."

"Aye aye, Captain."

She disappeared to her own station with her tablet in hand, already loaded with the point he'd selected. It felt like much too big of a decision to make on his own, but the sensor analyst would cross-check his selection, then the navigator would cross-check hers and plot an actual course. He debated calling Hope to the bridge and watching over her shoulder as she did it, but that would be micromanaging, and she'd no doubt call him out on it later unless Ahn did it first. Anyway, it didn't matter. He prided himself on never being more than a degree off, though, and he doubted he was much more than that this time.

Focused whispers filled the bridge as he downed his coffee and decided everyone would function better without him breathing down their necks. He could be back in less than five minutes if need be, and he could retrieve the same data from almost any console on the ship.

"I'll be on the aft deck," he called out.

The OOD reacted to his departure, but Josiah had mentally disappeared from the bridge by the time he'd stopped speaking. *Bayonet* tilted to the left as he stepped into the passageway outside, setting up for her flyby past 2315 YX37, and he placed a palm on the handhold outside the door to collect his thoughts. The sweep around the asteroid would set them back, but there wasn't any other option. There was no point in reaching Nimbus Station just to learn they'd passed *Triumph*'s actual location.

Ahn was still in Bay A when he ducked through the door, waving an idle hand at the screens and muttering under his breath. He was supposed to be sleeping, and they both knew it, but Ahn had always been one for the hunt. Sleeping through an alarm like the one *Triumph*'s brief appearance had set off was inconceivable to him.

"By the look of things, I suppose you already know." Josiah sidled up beside him and sighed at the data he didn't really want to focus on. "We lost her."

"Temporarily. We'll find her again." Ahn's claim wasn't bolstered by his weary tone or the way he was flipping through screens, watching *Triumph*'s hull signature appear then disappear, over and over again. "She didn't just completely disappear from existence right in front of us."

"I know." Josiah folded his arms and stared out into the darkness. It was the truth, and it wasn't as though he'd never gone hunting for a ship that had decided to hide on the wrong side of a planet before. But dammit, he'd thought this was *it*. "Just disappointed."

"That'll make the eventual victory that much sweeter, won't it?"

If anyone's still alive . . .

"Indeed." Josiah keyed in the coordinates for *Bayonet*'s flyby of the asteroid, then waved the map up onto the screen. "The sensor crew calculated that diverting around 2315 YX37 will only set us back six hours, maybe less if we push the engines. I don't want to do that so far away from anything, but we may not have much of a choice. Anyway, it's the best chance we have at making sure *Triumph* isn't obscured by the shadow of the rock."

Ahn murmured his agreement. No doubt he'd already scrutinized *Bayonet*'s new course on his own while he observed the operation from back here.

"Sounds like a plan," he replied. "Not that I would have expected a poor one from you."

"You don't need to butter me up." Josiah exhaled. "Or if you do, you could at least be a little more subtle about it."

A laugh. "Maybe you need some buttering up. Don't think I haven't noticed how tense you've been the past few days."

Josiah glanced over his shoulder toward the door for an excuse to stay silent, to balk at replying to the comment, to deny it completely, but they were still alone on the observation deck; not even a single pair of boots sounded in the passageway outside. And it wasn't just his stress he wanted to hide. Hope would have his head if he didn't confess to Ahn sooner rather than later.

"Yes," he began slowly. Lying was pointless, especially to Ahn. "Honestly, when we left Mars, I wanted to assume this was some sort of fool's errand. I'd hoped maybe the NSRC had given us inaccurate information and that we'd have found *Triumph* adrift but otherwise safe just past Bravo."

Spit it out.

"But there's something else, too." There had to be a good way to phrase his update. "It turns out I have some news. Good news, but perhaps a bit shocking. Something you should probably hear from me before anyone else finds out."

"News?" Ahn's brows rose innocently as he waved the screen dark; no doubt he thought he was giving nothing away. "What kind of news could you possibly have all the way out here in the middle of nowhere? A place where nothing changes and life is static, and it would take a seriously expensive probe to contact the outside world if we weren't under a comm blackout?"

"Hell." Josiah stared at him for a moment, then let his head fall forward as *Bayonet* rolled level onto her course. "You know, don't you?"

Ahn crossed his arms.

"Oh, yes," he replied, his amusement evident. "I know everything. You picked the wrong XO if you wanted to keep your shipboard dalliances a secret. I learned how to have eyes in the back of my head, thanks to a particularly young patrol out of Ceres a while back." His despair over *Triumph*'s second disappearance seemed to flee into the void outside. "Though I must say, I've been wondering when someone was going to fess up. Personally, I thought she'd come to me first. Lost the coin toss, did you?"

"One, I didn't pick you at all. And two—" His humiliation vanished in a barrage of relieved laughter. "I can't remember what two is, and I don't even care. She forgave me, Patrick. She actually forgave me. All those mistakes I made, everything I subjected her to—"

"Hot damn, brother." Ahn slapped him on the shoulder. "Congratulations. You cost me $500, but I'm happy to lose it. Don't screw things up with her again."

Josiah feigned a dramatic moan. "You set up a bet?"

"Technically, no. Captain Anderson did. Though she bet against you, too. Actually, if we're being honest, she was certain one of you would murder the other before we reached Wormhole Bravo, but details, you know."

Josiah raised his arms to the side, then let them fall. "Both still very much alive, thank you."

"So I see. Then I'll trust you both to handle things with the most discretion possible."

Josiah's brows rose. "Are you lecturing me?" *Because I probably need it.*

"Well"—Ahn's eyes still laughed—"forceful lectures are all I have right now."

"You'll get there." Josiah cleared his throat. "Anyway, as to the professional stress, there's something that's been bothering me for a while, but I couldn't figure out exactly what it was until now." He waved at the screen again and brought up a map of the Etrik System. "If *Triumph* is orbiting an asteroid, or even Etrik itself—"

"Why can't Nimbus Station see her themselves?" Ahn finished. "You're not the only one bothered by that."

"They must have some kind of orbital sensors, if only for early warning of whatever else might be out here." Though he truly had no idea. NSRC had said nothing of the sort, but *he'd* want such a thing if he was stuck on a planet like Etrik. No one was coming to help them if the worst happened.

"Maybe." Ahn shrugged. "Low power systems would prevent them from seeing much past orbit. Or maybe they don't have anything at all. They're scientists, and I doubt they're armed as well as we are. Maybe they figure an early warning wouldn't make much difference against aggressors better equipped than they."

"Hmm." Josiah scratched at his jaw, stiff with tension. Ahn wasn't wrong. Nimbus Station didn't have the armament that could be projected from

Bayonet's hull. No civilian ship or space station did. Well, no legal civilian ship or space station, and NSRC was no doubt following the rules. "I suppose we'll find out once we're in communications range," he went on. "Which is something I'm looking forward to. There's so much bizarre stuff going on here lately, it'll feel good to see other people."

He'd half expected Ahn to chuckle, but his forehead creased.

"Like?"

Josiah waved a hand at nothing and everything. The bulkhead and the deck and the abyss outside. "Just some weird-ass dreams during the last two wormhole transitions. Lots of them."

"Tired?"

"You know I don't need much sleep."

"I also know you're not superhuman." Ahn moved to recline against the bulkhead, then stopped, as though he'd finally become uncomfortable with their new relationship. "What kind of weird-ass dreams?"

Josiah's gut tightened. Seeing Hope so grieved while he sat there in his quarters aboard *Vigilant*, millions of nautical miles away from her . . . why did he have to relive that more than once? He didn't even want to think about it, much less talk about it.

"Vivid ones," he replied. "Like I was reliving things. Things I would kill to go through again and things I would kill to forget." Oh, hell, Ahn was going to think he'd lost his mind. "The thing is, it didn't just happen to me."

"Well, it's not happening to me."

"Really? You didn't have them passing through Echo and Foxtrot?"

"Ah, no." Ahn chuckled. "I was awake for every transit."

Oh.

The creeping heat that had stalked him for days finally embraced him, and everything clicked into place almost immediately—it wasn't space itself that was causing this, it was the wormholes.

"Decided they weren't so underwhelming after all, huh?" Josiah shook off the suffocating anxiety, but it clung to him like a cloak.

"Even I come around sometimes. It's a pretty amazing thing to watch, as it turns out." Ahn cocked his head, an explanation and apology. "But these dreams you've been having . . . you aren't saying you think the wormholes have been responsible for them?"

"I don't know." He didn't know anything anymore. "All I know is that Jakob Blayne had them going through Wormhole Echo too. So did Eshana. And Hope." When Blayne had summoned him from the wardroom, she'd probably been about to tell him that dozens more aboard *Bayonet* had as well. He would have to track her later and find out. "I don't know who else, but I suspect we're not the only ones. And since mine didn't start until we transited Echo . . . I don't know. I'd thought it was something more general, but it must be the wormholes themselves." He hesitated. "I sound insane, don't I?"

"'The eternal silence of these infinite spaces frightens me.'" Ahn lifted a shoulder. "Blaise Pascal. Seems appropriate, no? Three hundred and fifty years of space travel scarcely makes us experts on the universe. And outside the system? Forget it. We're mere babies."

"We've sent probes." Even as he spoke, it sounded like a weak argument.

Ahn waved a dismissive hand toward the window.

"Probes," he scoffed. "Probes don't have minds or hearts. They certainly don't dream."

"It sounds like you're becoming a poet. Maybe a wormhole did get to you."

"Hardly." Ahn's laugh was abrupt. "It's just that you can't deny that we don't know everything. Did the NSRC make any comments about weird dreams in their reports?"

"Not sure." Josiah sighed and stared at the unfamiliar stars outside as *Bayonet*'s thrusters fired. "I suppose I have some more reading to do."

"And sleep." Ahn pointed at him. "You'll need it once we stumble upon *Triumph* again, and I don't need to remind you how imminent that is."

"Is that an order?"

Ahn grinned. "Sure is, sir."

CHAPTER TWENTY-TWO_
NIMBUS STATION, ETRIK

THE KNOCK ON HER DOOR WOKE CORALIE FROM THE deepest sleep she'd had in a long time. With a moan, she clicked on a light and grabbed a fresh jumpsuit. There was another knock, harder this time, and when she opened the door, belatedly wondering why she would do so for anyone on Nimbus Station, Kinnard stood in the corridor, arms folded across his chest.

"We're going on a trip," he said. "Get dressed."

"A trip?" She raised a brow as she zipped the suit the rest of the way up. "We're allowed vacations on Nimbus Station now?"

He gave her a look as he waved a few sterile kits in a clear bag at her, though the gesture didn't appear altogether hostile. "To *Triumph*. I have some business there, and it may take some time. I'd like you to accompany me in case it does."

Coralie pressed her palm against her forehead. Too much light, not enough sleep or coffee. And was—was Kinnard afraid for her safety here?

"You're being rather polite about this," she replied, surprised by her own boldness. "What's the occasion?"

"I could be rude, if you'd prefer. But I would think you'd be grateful to not be left alone here without my protection."

She gave him a resigned nod. Kinnard pointed outside, and she followed along after a wistful glance at the coffeemaker. Silently, too, for the last vestiges of sleep were fading away, and Kinnard's silver eyes were becoming clearer in the hallway's illumination. Besides, though she didn't want to be around him at all, if he was going to be polite to her over some misplaced fear of her death, well, she wouldn't argue with him.

He led her to a chamber on an upper deck that she'd only visited once during her initial fire detector inspection. Nothing had been at the dock there that day, but today there sat a small orbital shuttle, its engine whirring in the gold of an Etrik sunrise.

Coralie took a step back from its open door. Wherever the shuttle had come from, it was unlikely it had been well-enough maintained to safely make the voyage to *Triumph* and back. The v-words didn't care about trite things like pressurizing and oxygen.

"Is this safe?" she asked.

"It's *Triumph*'s. Just get on board." Kinnard fixed her with a glare. "I don't intend to kill you yet."

I don't intend to kill you yet.

She shuffled inside and chose the first seat by the hatch, her pacemaker firing when her actual heart skipped a beat. Did that mean he intended to kill her later?

Of course not. It was simply a phrase. Kinnard, she was certain, didn't think that much about the effect his words had on her.

Still, her blood ran cold as five security individuals tromped aboard behind her. The armored shirts they wore—protection which had seemed perfectly normal on Mars—was bad enough, but they were each carrying pistols, like they expected to meet an alien invasion up in space. The last one inside locked the hatch, and though Coralie could still take a deep breath of air, it felt like everything had been sucked out into the punishing Etrik atmosphere.

"What exactly are we going to be doing up there?" She tried to calm her racing heart as he sat beside her and latched himself in. Usually it was easy to settle the pacemaker, but right now it wasn't cooperating.

"You're going to sit in a cabin and wait until I need you." Kinnard didn't even glance her way as the engine's whir turned into a screech and the shuttle lifted off.

Coralie sat silently and gazed out the window, watching the planet disappear below. She'd been unconscious when they'd taken her from *Triumph* and placed her in the capsule down below, and despite her sudden apprehension, she couldn't take her eyes from the drifting dunes and enormous mountains, the size of which surprised even someone who'd spent time on Mars.

The dusty horizon gave way to the black of space, something which had never captured her attention, and she forced her concentration back inside as the gravity cut off, forcing her against her harness. Three of the security officers were dozing on the bench seat across from her, but Kinnard had floated from his seat next to her and was deep in quiet conversation with the other two. Enhanced hearing or not, she couldn't hear their words over the engine noise, and that was likely by design. She leaned forward, but even those extra few centimeters didn't do her any good.

Not that she needed them, for it was clear what was going on. Kinnard's new blood sources—this had to have something to do with them. But *Triumph*? How did *Triumph* fit into the picture? She'd been floating in orbit since she'd arrived, empty and dark.

The shuttle decelerated as Coralie leaned back in her seat, and she folded her hands in her lap, pretending to be nothing but Kinnard's complacent, cooperative blood source. They had to know she was anything but, yet they didn't seem to see her as an *immediate* threat. That was good, she decided as they drifted slowly into a large cargo bay centered on *Triumph*'s side.

Kinnard reappeared and tossed her a suit and a pair of gravity boots as the shuttle floated to the deck. "Put these on."

Coralie's jaw tightened as she worked the suit up over her hips in silence. So, they weren't going to let her have free rein of *Triumph* like she'd had on the surface. Not surprising, but definitely frustrating. Kinnard, to his credit, zipped up the back for her, though she had to force herself to remain calm as she slid on her helmet. This wasn't a trap. They didn't *need* to set a trap to suffocate her, not after they'd just spent a few hours in space.

Still, her heart pounded and her palms perspired as they opened the hatch, revealing the dark, yawning cave of the cargo bay. Surprise flitted through her, but it made sense. With no engines operating, *Triumph* had no power, no lights, no artificial gravity. No pressurization either, but a bit of hope settled into her soul. Maybe they planned to pressurize the ship once they had power.

Kinnard jerked his head toward the door on the far side of the cargo bay as she stood there, blinking in the diffuse light from the shuttle, and two security guards appeared at each arm. Her muscles tensed, wanting to take them, but they allowed her to walk between them to a small cabin further up in the ship. She needed to rest after walking this far in grav-boots, needed to figure out what they were up to before she tried anything. Besides, they couldn't stop her from taking snapshots of the ship with her retinal implant. They hadn't even noticed her doing so.

"Give me the helmet." One of them pointed at her head. "You can keep the boots for now."

"Am I going to be able to breathe?"

He jabbed upward, at the vent in the corner of the room. "In another few minutes, you'll have all the air you want, and you'll be able to take the boots off, too. Just not in the passageway."

So, there would be no exploring after all. Discouraged, Coralie slid off the helmet and handed it over. A few minutes of low oxygen, she could handle. He didn't offer to help her unzip her suit, just tossed the bag of sterile kits into the air for Kinnard to use and stalked out the door with her helmet under his arm, his colleague on his heels.

"Thanks for the help," Coralie said to the door as soon as it closed.

She yanked off the boots and let herself float upward, but working against the zero-g proved almost fruitless. It was a workout she hadn't intended on, and if he'd been correct, she'd fall to the floor soon, anyway. Instead of fighting against it, she sank to the bunk that ran across the back bulkhead, hooked her boots back on the floor, and let her vision fully acclimate. It took ten minutes to wriggle out of the suit and put her boots back on, and she only prayed that she hadn't torn anything. They might have taken her helmet, but the suit itself could prove useful.

The room wasn't terrible either, as far as shipboard quarters went. She'd spent time in far worse between Earth and Mars. There appeared to be a washroom on the opposite side, and even better, a coffee machine on the small desk next to her. When the kits fell to the deck and her hair settled on her shoulders, Coralie jumped to her feet and searched through the drawer underneath for a pod. The washroom provided the necessary water, and she placed both in the machine, then stood back.

Power. I need power.

She cursed under her breath. *Triumph* was making some power now, as evidenced by the fact that she could breathe and walk on the floor, but apparently not enough yet for electricity. But the light above her head switched on thirty seconds later, so she pressed the switch and sat back on the bunk to inhale the heavenly scent.

There had to be a way out, she decided as the coffee finished brewing and she searched through the desk drawer for a clean cup. Yes, they'd taken her helmet, but she could survive in the corridor outside for a while, couldn't she? And there would be some other cabin she could duck inside and take a breath, some other closet where emergency pressurization suits were stored. *Triumph* wasn't some poorly equipped pleasure vessel, after all.

But then . . . that hadn't worked so well on Nimbus Station, had it?

She left the coffee on the desk and lay back on the bunk to flip through the ocular photos she'd taken on the way here. They were dark since her vision augmentation only amplified her biological sight, not the retinal camera as well, but when she squinted, she could make out the location numbers.

Deck 7, Section 17, Room 209.

That was where she was now, and that was something—if only she had a clue where that was in relation to the rest of the ship. The cargo bay was on Deck 6, Section 14, straight out the lift, but the rest of it? She didn't know. She'd been restrained to a bed and locked in a special compartment on the way here. There had been no opportunity to map any of the ship before now.

The lock on her door clicked, and air hissed toward the corridor as Kinnard slipped inside. He pushed it shut almost immediately, and the hissing stopped. She would never become used to them slipping around like this in what might as well be deep space.

"I need a drink," he said, the words infused with hunger.

Coralie clutched at her coffee. So soon? No wonder he'd brought her along—though the irreverent side of her wanted to quip that he could have just as easily had a drink on Etrik before leaving Nimbus Station. But she only nodded instead and set the coffee on the desk. Desperate or not, she couldn't enjoy it while the bastard was drinking her blood.

"How long are we going to be here?" she asked as he attached the tube. Anything to pretend it was a normal conversation. Anything to pretend she wasn't completely frozen and at his mercy.

"I don't know." He glanced around for what she assumed was a cup. Finding none, he grabbed her coffee and dumped it in the sink. "A while."

Coralie gritted her teeth, just barely refraining from telling him he owed her another coffee pod. She couldn't, anyway. That same paralysis that had started to overcome her whenever she saw a tube had forced its way throughout her body once more.

"How long is a while?" she forced out.

And will I get more coffee?

"I said I don't know."

His tone had grown sharp, so she closed her eyes as the tube clicked into her port and pretended he wasn't drinking her blood out of her coffee mug. There was no pain, just like there was never any pain, but right now she wished for it. Pain would give her something to focus on besides the way her blood was filling the tube, just like it had in that capsule, if on a much smaller scale. But it was different this time for other reasons as well, wasn't it? Today she could move her feet, could see across the cabin, would be allowed to get up and walk—

The mug hit the desk with a thunk, and Coralie looked up, mentally preparing for the conversation that was sure to follow.

Instead, he stood.

"I may be back for another drink later," he said, gliding toward the door. It was an odd movement for someone wearing work boots, but she'd long grown used to weirdness where Kinnard was concerned. "Regardless, someone will bring you food in a few hours. I don't think I need to explain that going outside this door will be detrimental to your health?"

Did he take her for a fool?

"I kind of figured that," she replied.

"Good." He cracked the door open, and despite the hiss of air escaping into the vacuum outside, she had to ask.

"Kinnard, wait."

He stopped in the doorway and stared at her, his silver eyes gleaming.

"Could I maybe get some more coffee and a clean mug?"

Without answering, he slid the door closed.

* * *

There were, thankfully, another two coffee pods in the desk drawer, and Coralie brewed them both after washing out the mug with a bar of shampoo that someone—now a near-immortal monster— had left when they'd disembarked *Triumph*. She couldn't taste her own blood in the dark deliciousness of the coffee, but she'd be lying if she didn't admit to herself that the whole thing was creepy.

The gravity remained in place as she tried to forget about the blood, though it wavered a few times, and she dragged the boots over toward the bunk, just in case. Beyond that, it was the sheer boredom of waiting that bothered her now—waiting for food, waiting for Kinnard, waiting for a ride back to the surface.

Her imagination didn't stretch any further. Whatever Kinnard was up to aboard *Triumph* was obviously too complex or just too *out there* for her to visualize. And why wouldn't it be? She wasn't the one who'd come up with the plan to hold a bunch of humans hostage on a distant planet for their blood.

With a yawn, she lay down on the bunk, contemplating sleep.

Until the emergency light above her door began to flash.

CHAPTER TWENTY-THREE_
USOGC BAYONET, ETRIK SYSTEM

Josiah jerked upright, knocking his head against the display over his bunk. The dream hadn't been as vivid as the ones in the wormhole, but he still swore he'd heard—

He fell on his back and blinked up at the computer. No, it hadn't been a dream. It hadn't even been just an alarm. It was multiple alarms, plus a host of blinking lights that coalesced into a haze of color before he blinked and realized what he was looking at.

Triumph.

He jumped to his feet, almost tripping as he pulled on his pants. On the table beside his bunk, his watch flashed a similar group of alarms. How had he slept through all this? And for how long?

No one had started pounding on his door, so it couldn't have been that long. He slipped into the passageway and hurried to the bridge at a half jog, stopping only to catch his breath on a single ladder. Unlike the last time *Triumph* had briefly appeared—only to disappear once more—the bridge was a buzz of activity like he hadn't seen since they'd first left Mars.

"Status?" He settled into his chair and inhaled the coffee already sitting in front of him.

"Scan picked up a manual distress signal twenty-five minutes ago, sir." Operations Technician Third Class Maeryn Centelles sounded sheepish. "But after last time, we wanted to verify—"

"Don't worry about that." A twenty-five-minute delay after so long was hardly worth the breath it would take to issue a reprimand. "How far away?"

"Four hours at our current speed, assuming a protocol deceleration." Centelles's backup spoke, and his confidence was a little more reassuring. "We could shave maybe thirty minutes off that, but I wouldn't recommend more."

"Then we'll stick with four." Josiah traced the flight path that appeared on his console. *Triumph*'s location was substantiated now, thanks to the distress signal alerting everything within earshot that *something was wrong, help us, please.* And she *was* in orbit around a planet, like they'd guessed. But . . .

His heart skipped a beat.

Around Etrik?

Something cold touched his soul, but he shrugged it off and took a too-casual sip of coffee. Nimbus Station didn't have sensors that could see into the sky, had no idea their missing starship was so close . . . and so what? They were on the planet to research terraforming, not to watch the stars, which was something you needed to do from space, anyway.

"Engines are running at min power, sir," Centelles added. "But . . ." She trailed off, obviously wary of overexplaining.

"But they could have been running like that for weeks." Josiah rubbed his eyes. And they didn't know if that power was enough to sustain life support, especially since the emergency transmitter had its own battery power. Months' worth.

"Possibly, yes." She tapped a bit more on her console. "We'll be close enough to pick up any heat signatures in another two hours, and with the engines running this marginally, it's quite possible we'll be able to see individual bodies. I'll send the data over to you once I have it."

Finally, some good news—though whether or not it would continue to be good news was the real question.

Four hundred seventeen aboard . . .

"All right." He drummed decisively on the console and leaned back in his chair. The familiar movement eased most of his nerves, turned him once more into the person he'd been before *Vigilant*. The man who'd been able to make decisions, long before he'd made the only one possible—but also the one which had killed seventeen. "In two hours, I want Raider 2 ready at Rescue Bay A to search *Triumph*."

"Aye aye, Captain."

The response was immediate, but Josiah could see the hesitation in Valdéz's expression. Well, the entire bridge could all think he was paranoid. If they were in his situation, they'd be the same. Not that he blamed anyone for their hesitancy right now. NSRC would be pissed about what they were about to do, but if they were offended by a forceful boarding, they could take it up with someone who didn't have to make the decision light-years away from home.

For the briefest instant, the coffee cup in his hand shook, enough that he set it down again and wound his hand around the warm aluminum. Had he let the anxiety get the best of him?

No.

Because one, even though there was likely a plausible explanation that Nimbus Station hadn't seen their missing ship orbiting on the same planet they inhabited, he couldn't shake the feeling that something was wrong.

Off.

Two, the distress signal seemed to have been manually triggered. Perhaps someone aboard *Triumph* had seen *Bayonet* enter the system, but if that was the case, why not answer any of their communications? But there was a plausible explanation for that, too. It was always possible *Triumph* could set off the alarm with some sort of proximity sensor. This was the NSRC, after all. They probably had all sorts of technology the Orbital Guard didn't possess.

And three . . . he would never admit to anyone, not even Ahn, that he was making strategic decisions based on hinky dreams, but intuition came from the strangest of places. And this decision, he was certain, was just that.

"With your permission, sir?" To her credit, Graham, hovering by the bridge entrance, didn't sound nearly as doubtful about Josiah's decision. No, there was eagerness behind the question.

Have fun, he wanted to say, but he only nodded. "Go ahead."

The door opened and then closed, and Josiah focused on his console once more. Deceleration to dock with *Triumph* would begin in just twenty minutes—he could wait and observe from up here. He wouldn't be able to focus on anything else right now, and he wanted to see everything from up here. Not that he didn't trust his crew, but . . .

His console beeped, an urgent comm through a private channel.

Feel better now? —P

Urgent, indeed.

Josiah tried to suppress a snort. Unsuccessfully, because Valdéz turned toward him, a question on his face. He waved him away and forced a blank expression. Or at least, what he hoped was a disinterested one. What next, was Hope going to comm him with a remark that would bring heat to his cheeks? He found his left hand tapping out a message to her on his private channel anyway. It was either that or pace around the bridge for twenty minutes.

You hear?

It was nothing more than a conversation-starter, and she would know it—of course she had heard. One would have had to be locked in a closet with earplugs to be oblivious to the alarms sounding throughout the ship.

Finishing up some calculations, came the eventual response. *SENSOP wanted confirmation of Triumph's location once we arrive in orbit.*

You kept me waiting, then. He looked out the starboard window at the unfamiliar stars and forced a frown to cover his giddiness at her simple reply. *That took you what . . . thirty seconds?*

I'm flattered, but it was three and a half minutes.

"Thirty seconds to deceleration."

Valdéz's call cut through the hush before he could reply, and an alarm followed it: a high-pitched, grating sound that filled Josiah's dreams some nights. Anyone in their bunk—the ones who'd slept through the alarm that had woken him, that was—had better be strapped in.

"Watch those engines," Josiah murmured to himself, but it proved an unnecessary warning.

"Helm, coolant to 100%."

Valdéz was already on it, but then again, no one wanted the engines to fry themselves halfway across the galaxy as they spooled down, and it happened more frequently than Josiah liked to accept.

"Coolant to 100%, aye."

It was inaudible on the bridge, but coolant was hissing somewhere aft of the bridge as it flooded the tubes surrounding the plasma. Hope might accuse him of being above such things, but he'd spent a few weeks in engineering over fifteen years ago now, watching the engines, life support, electrical systems, and whatever else kept them all alive in deep space. It had been, mostly, a waste of time. Even on older cutters, most everything was automated now, and he'd spent much of his time wandering in circles around various panels, trying to figure out how he would have survived if his fate had been that of an engineering officer. Did they ever see outside that compartment?

Still, he would always remember the sound—even if he'd been clinging to a handhold—that his boots ground into the deck, surprised by the force of his first tactical deceleration.

"Sir?" Valdéz asked.

Josiah glanced at his console just as the engine status flashed in the corner. It was a modern miracle, how a simple command from the opposite end of the ship could have such an immediate effect. In the early days of system travel, after the swiftness of rockets became less important than the control and duration of the plasma engines they used now, it would have taken upwards of five minutes to cool the engines for deceleration.

He dragged a finger across his throat. "Cut 'em."

"Helm, engines to zero."

"Engines to zero, aye."

Stability system or not, *Bayonet* flinched. The constant engine hum that embraced the cutter while she was burning at maximum thrust fell to a whisper. Gravity was driving now—well, more than usual.

"Check course." He risked a sip of coffee. It had gone cold, but for the first time in a long time, he didn't care. Perhaps Ahn was on to something.

Valdéz took a breath. "Helm, come left half a degree."

"Half a degree, aye."

Josiah leaned back as the sound of *Bayonet*'s thrusters filled the silence. Deceleration did that about half the time, and just one degree difference off Etrik—the star, not the planet—could land them a million miles away from where they wanted to be. Not for the first time, he didn't envy Hope's responsibilities.

"Captain, we're receiving more information on *Triumph*." Centelles sounded breathless.

"Go ahead."

"The engines, they're definitely powered up, but whether they're producing enough energy for life support is anyone's guess. Give me another ten minutes for a positive call." She tapped a few more times on her console, then froze. "And—"

When she didn't continue, he leaned forward, his mouth dry despite the coffee. "And what?"

Centelles turned toward him, pale.

"And I'm seeing seven smaller heat signatures consistent with survivors, sir."

CHAPTER TWENTY-FOUR_
NSRC T/V TRIUMPH, ETRIK ORBIT

Coralie stood in front of the door, watching the light above it flash on and off. Though she hadn't exactly made it all the way to Etrik as a guest aboard *Triumph,* she'd been through the same training as every other passenger. The flashing yellow amber signified a distress signal had been activated, and the obviousness of it was meant to reassure frightened passengers that help was coming soon.

But there was no one coming this time. Not out here.

Still, whatever the reason for the alarm, it was an opportunity. There had to be emergency suits somewhere nearby, and there was no way Kinnard would have thought to hide them from her.

Not after she'd almost died down on the surface in that hallway. In fact, she was beginning to believe it had been a setup just to dissuade her from leaving the quarters he'd stuck her in right now. They might have taken her helmet, and it would have been faster to float through *Triumph*'s corridors in zero-g, but she still had her suit and the metallic chip near her lung, and that was something.

The suit went on easier in gravity, though she decided actually zipping it up would have been a simpler task had she been able to rotate weightlessly in the center of the compartment. Still, she managed it after a bit of a skirmish with the zipper, and the familiar pressure from her ankles to the base of her neck was a comforting embrace.

Closing her eyes, she leaned her forehead against the door. It wasn't as cool as she would have expected, and as she searched through the photos stored in her ocular implant, she couldn't help but think how dangerous fire could be in space. Yes, one could evacuate the air in a specific compartment, suffocating the fire almost immediately, but what about the people inside?

Fool.

There wasn't any fire outside the door. The photos, however, showed a life support storeroom just four doors down, and if she didn't find a helmet there, at least she could make a quick retreat to her quarters and breathable air. And maybe, just maybe, there would be something else there of use to her. Even if that something useful was a coffee mug that hadn't once held her blood.

She reached for the handle, then drew her hand back and rested it against her thigh. Walking out the door wasn't like what had happened to her at Nimbus Station at all, or even outside in the scarce Etrik atmosphere. Outside this door was almost pure vacuum, space itself, and though she'd used her implants enough in training to know that they *worked* . . . trusting them in a controlled environment, with NSRC technicians hovering around inside the chamber watching her, was so much different from trusting them half a galaxy away in a black void that cared nothing for her life. She might have fifteen minutes down on the surface, but up here? Five, tops.

But five minutes would get her to the storeroom, and, hopefully, a helmet.

Before she could think better of it, she opened the door and peered down the hallway, ignoring the sound of escaping air. She left it cracked open, just in case, and took a few tentative steps aft, not bothering to take a breath. Her steps echoed in the empty corridor, and once again, she cursed gravity. Floating would have made her escape absolutely silent.

Her chest ached after less than ten meters, so she began a long exhale at the same moment her vision blurred. The corridor was already dark, illuminated by only a few yellow emergency lights, and as the doorways on either side of her turned gray, her own disappeared in a cloudy haze as she turned, searching.

Enough.

Coralie turned on her heel, gasping for breath as she stumbled back toward her quarters. The door was heavier now than it had been when she'd opened it, and her muscles screamed as she yanked on it. She fell to her knees and shoved it closed, then collapsed against it as the room refilled with oxygen.

She'd failed. She hadn't even made it halfway, and there was no way she could have walked any farther. Getting to the life support storeroom and back to her quarters if there wasn't a helmet or spare oxygen inside? Impossible.

Head in her hands, she wiped away the single tear of frustration that wet her cheek. She couldn't just sit here and wait for Kinnard to come back. He'd given her a gift of some sort by leaving her here alone, though she didn't exactly know how she could use this new freedom.

"Get it together."

Her own voice made her jump in the silence, but it anchored her, enough to make her realize she really had no plan. Steal a suit and then . . . do what? Hide until Kinnard and the security people got tired of looking for her? She'd run out of air long before that happened, because he would never let go. Not after he'd pulled her out of that capsule while condemning all the rest.

Call for help? Well, yes, that had probably been her subconscious plan when they'd landed aboard *Triumph*. But Kinnard was already doing that, for a reason she couldn't even guess at.

She jumped to her feet and paced between the bunk and the door. There was something wrong with this entire situation, but between the lack of coffee and the leftover fog from her foray into the airless corridor—

What would you say if I told you I've found a way to get fifty-some new blood sources here at once—voluntarily?

She froze in the middle of the room, fixed there by an unseen fear as surely as though her grav-boots had been activated without her knowledge. Hadn't she known the NSRC would have a hard time finding enough people with the faulty gene, especially without someone becoming suspicious and raising questions? And if someone raised questions, investigations would begin, and Kinnard would never risk that.

But if it wasn't an NSRC ship . . . no one would be the wiser.

If it was a ship that had every reason to transit six wormholes, one with a mission that no one would question? A small ship that Kinnard could easily lure toward *Triumph* with a fake distress signal?

It had to be a United States Orbital Guard ship.

Had to be.

And she was the only one who could warn them.

CHAPTER TWENTY-FIVE_
USOGC BAYONET, ETRIK ORBIT

The pressurization system hummed in Josiah's ears as he sat on his bunk, head in his hands. He didn't have the luxury for mourning, but he did have five minutes to contemplate strategy. At least, if he didn't touch the rosary in his pocket, Ahn would believe that was what he was doing. If he knew he was praying, well . . . maybe what anyone thought now didn't matter. Because four hundred and ten souls were gone, just like that.

"Seven," he said, opening his eyes. Ahn still sat in silence in his usual chair, his arms folded. "In my wildest nightmares, I never dreamed it would be only seven."

And only one survivor aboard Kamorta . . .

"You aren't the only one." Ahn blew out a breath. "I thought it was a wild goose chase."

"Maybe the rest of them found their way to the surface. Maybe this is still nothing." Even as he spoke, he knew it was a fool's hope. "You can stop me when I say something idiotic like that, you know."

"Someone needs to hope for the both of us, I suppose."

Josiah stared at his hands. There was really no appropriate response to that, for they both knew hope was futile.

And hope does not put us to shame . . .

"Perhaps." He straightened at the unheard reprimand. If he couldn't feel optimistic, at least he could pretend. He'd done it before, hadn't he? "We'll be able to raise Nimbus Station in a few hours. Let's work that in parallel to searching *Triumph*. At least they can verify the missing passengers aren't on the surface."

Ahn nodded. "There'll be a substantial comm delay for a while yet, but we'll start attempts within the hour. Maybe by the time the team is back . . ."

"Yes." Josiah stood. What else was left to discuss? "Maybe."

Ahn stood as well. "You're still planning on a forcible search?"

"Here's my concern." There wasn't any disagreement in the question, but Josiah could tell when he was being reined in. "Not even the Navy has been this far out. No one has except the NSRC. What if whatever happened to *Triumph* happened to Nimbus Station? What if we're not alone out here, and it was another entity responsible for *Triumph*'s disappearance? We'd have never heard a thing about it on Mars."

"Entity?" Ahn raised a brow. "You really think there are aliens out here?"

"Stranger things have happened, right?" Josiah rubbed his palm over his face. The stubble was getting bad; he would need to shave before he stepped outside. "The fact is, we just don't know much, and what we know is troubling."

"To say the least." Ahn made his way toward the door, then stopped. "I don't suppose you've stopped to consider that there's no way we can outgun an advanced alien civilization with a few machine guns nailed to the hull."

A pained laugh escaped. *Bayonet* couldn't outgun any of Earth's spacefaring navies, much less alien technology, but she could outrun all but the fastest cruisers, and that was all that mattered most of the time. Strange how the life he thought he'd had a handle on had changed in the few minutes it took to transit a wormhole.

"We'll deal with that when and if it happens." Josiah rubbed his hands over his cheeks once more, then pointed toward the door, forcing a smile. "Now get out of here. I need to look presentable for first contact if the aliens actually show up."

* * *

Fifteen minutes later, Josiah arrived in Rescue Bay A with a smooth face and a fresh cup of coffee in hand. Lt. Graham snared him as he stepped inside, a broad grin on her face, inconsistent with the black tactical suit she wore. It was an expression he couldn't bring himself to match, but then again, she'd been waiting for this very moment since they'd left Mars thirty-seven days ago, so he wasn't going to complain.

"Status?"

"Still no response to our hails," Graham replied. "But we'll keep trying until Raider 2 is done prepping. The good news is that *Triumph*'s got a cargo bay large enough for the MarkXVII."

"She's got her own shuttle stored in that main bay," he warned, edging his way to the screens next to the airlock as *Bayonet*'s thrusters fired, lining up for her approach. A schematic of *Triumph* was projected on the display, and his forehead creased as he examined it. "Could still be there."

"There's room." Graham sounded like she'd read his mind. "Plus a whole two yards to spare."

"Good." He curved his upper lip just enough to prove to her he could still smile when something went right—a feat that was difficult to achieve on this patrol. "And the heat signatures?"

She moved to his other side and flipped through a few screens, then pointed again. "Six are concentrated in a forward compartment. A canteen of some sort, from what I can tell. The seventh is pretty far aft, looks to be in a stateroom."

Josiah gnawed on the inside of his cheek as he stared at the schematic overlaid with the yellow heat signature images. Not for the first time, he wondered how much easier his job would be if NSRC personnel—if all Americans, for that matter —were chipped and monitored like Chinese subjects had been for centuries. There would be no heat signatures to interpret in that case, since the PLAN could identify even bodies from this distance with the right equipment. He hadn't really believed what he'd told Patrick about aliens, but those chips would even determine . . . species. But that surveillance ship had sailed two hundred years ago for the United States, and they were better off without it in most regards.

"Well, a stateroom is better than sick bay," he replied, though most of him wondered if whoever that seventh signature belonged to had been placed there alone for a reason. A contagious reason. "I suppose we'll find out for sure soon."

"That we will, sir. Excuse me."

Josiah stepped to the side as she turned away from him and keyed in a code to the arms locker. The hinged door floated upward, revealing a rack with several dozen S27's, the Orbital Guard's preferred weapon for starship boarding. He grabbed the furthest on the left and handed it over to the first one who'd lined up behind Graham—Security Specialist Second Class Michael Betschen, whose defined muscles put a weightlifter's to shame.

"The lieutenant roped you into helping, did she, sir?" Betschen asked.

"It seems I was in her way, and I think she was ready to move on with the mission." Josiah grinned despite the situation, and it felt like his first in ages. "Figured I'd better help out instead of standing around."

"It was let him help with this or let him follow us aboard *Triumph*." Graham grabbed the next rifle in line and handed it to Security Specialist Second Class Daniel Salazar, next in line. "See, I know that look on his face, but it would be rather difficult to explain to Mars that we got our captain killed. Hopefully this will quell his desire to go floating through space and onto a potentially hostile vessel."

Josiah gave a friendly scoff, but she wasn't wrong, not exactly. Well, not at all, if he was honest with himself. He would have loved to follow them aboard *Triumph* in the boat, but that broke the rules, and those rules were in place for an excellent reason.

"I hear he shoots well enough, though." Betschen hefted his rifle over his shoulder and gave Graham a grin.

Graham's attention slid to Josiah, and he shrugged. "You got me. But qualifying was a long time ago, and I had a shotgun on my shoulder from the first time I could lift it as a child."

She blinked at him, like she'd seen through his false modesty, as Betschen disappeared toward the boat, then waited for him to hand off the next rifle.

"SENSOP said *Triumph*'s distress signal didn't begin until long after we entered the system." With a frown, she finished distributing the weapons and swung her own across her back. "That someone had to have manually triggered it."

Josiah nodded, his lips pressed tight. "That's correct."

"Possibly someone who suspected we were incoming." She grabbed her helmet from the deck and shoved it under her arm as she spoke. He didn't know how she balanced all her gear while wearing a suit that weighed as much as she did.

"We're on the same paranoid page, then." He glanced at the airlock and exhaled. "Be careful, all right?"

Graham gave him a lopsided smile and turned toward the boat.

"Always, sir." She tossed the agreement over her shoulder, and then she was gone.

CHAPTER TWENTY-SIX_

CORALIE REACHED FOR THE LOCK ON THE DOOR ONCE more, then stopped. She'd been mistaken before, shouldn't have tried to make it all the way to the life support storeroom. But if her quarters were pressurized, the rest of the rooms in this corridor must be as well. It would be a straightforward process to make her way there, stopping to catch her breath behind each unlocked door. Time-consuming, but straightforward. And maybe, if she was very lucky, one of those rooms would contain communication equipment.

Her stomach churned. Broadcasting in the blind to whatever ship might be tracking *Triumph*'s distress signal—well, Kinnard would be sure to hear, and when he caught her, which he would eventually, he would show her no mercy. But if she saved lives, did it matter what he did to her? Did it matter that she would end up back in that capsule?

Yes.

It might have been selfish, but it mattered. Because she wanted to *live*.

Her heart—the real one—alternately skipped and raced as she unlocked the door for the second time in two hours, and she was almost certain it was fear. Fear had no place in this thing she was about to do, but no matter how much she tried, she couldn't control it. The pacemaker kicked in every time her heart skipped, and the uncomfortable sensation of being kicked in the chest continued as she slid the door open and stepped into the corridor.

One glance left and then another to the right assured her she was alone, and she scrambled to the next door, exhaling all the while. It was more comfortable than trying to inhale nothingness, and if she was wrong about this plan, at least she could dart back to her own quarters.

But the next door opened immediately, and she slid inside, collapsing against the bulkhead as the stale scent of recycled air filled her lungs. Behind this door was a room just like the one she'd vacated, and a quick search turned up no weapon and nothing she couldn't find in her own quarters except a pod of coffee. Coralie shoved it in her pocket and stepped into the airless corridor once more.

This time, her heart didn't want to cooperate. Her vision grayed almost immediately, and she clung to the bulkhead as she slipped toward the next doorway. Collapsing inside, she slid the door closed, then closed her eyes as the room refilled with air. She hadn't had to look around for more than a second to see it was yet another stateroom like her own.

Perhaps this had been a bad idea after all. She'd worn herself out just trying to get to the life support storeroom, and now she was going to have to wait a day to recover—if Kinnard didn't come back before then, which he likely would.

But she had to warn whatever ship was incoming. Leaving them to Kinnard's machinations was unconscionable. Exhausted or not, she couldn't do it.

She tore through the cabinets, doubling her search for a weapon. A knife would slow them down, at least. But when she opened the cabinet under the coffee machine, there wasn't only a clean mug inside.

Someone had left a pistol.

Coralie brushed the smooth metal, and the heft of the weapon in her palm soothed her raw nerves. She wasn't a *fantastic* shot, but it also wasn't as though she'd never shot a gun before. She had, though it had been years.

She stuck the gun in her pocket and brewed the coffee, a plan forming. She might not be able to kill Kinnard and the others, but she might surprise them enough to get a communication out. Maybe she'd even injure them, but she really had no idea . . . would bullets affect them at all?

The lights flickered as she sat on the bunk, consoling herself with the weight of the gun and the familiar scent of institutional coffee. It was a break she could ill afford, but as she sipped, she became more certain her plan would work. *Triumph* was huge, and if there were only five security personnel on board, she'd be able to lose them. Kinnard would be angry, but maybe he'd been enjoying her fresh blood enough to not lock her back up again.

It was a pep talk that wasn't entirely successful, but she sprang to her feet and headed for the door anyway. The life support storeroom couldn't be too far away now, and with a helmet and weapon, she would become more invincible than she'd been in a long time.

The air hissed, a sound she was growing rather tired of, and she peered outside, planning her route. The pressurization system couldn't keep up with a leak like this, but that didn't matter. Her modifications could. So she stood there, counting the paces to the next door. It was narrower than the one which blocked the rest of her view—could it be the storeroom?

She placed one foot in the corridor, then stopped dead in her tracks.

A shadow?

Silently, she pressed herself back into the cabin and looked outside, toward the t-corridor in the distance. The air still hissed through the small gap, loud enough that someone might hear, so she kicked the door open a bit more. It left her with no cover and precious little oxygen, but at least the corridor had gone silent once more.

Her heart threatened to stop, and might have, had it not been for the pacemaker.

For what had been a shadow, a potential figure of her imagination just five seconds ago, was in actuality seven figures prowling down the dim corridor.

But they weren't Kinnard and his security people, for they were wearing pressure suits, something superfluous for the v-words, even here.

And they weren't rescuers either.

They wore black, and each had a rifle raised.

Coralie gulped in a breath of what was left of the air in the cabin, then sagged against the door and forced her breathing to slow. If she moved, even to close the door, they would see her, and she couldn't let them see her. She didn't know who they were, but strangers aboard *Triumph* were up to no good.

Her hand slid to the pistol as they came closer. It might not penetrate the suits they wore, but even if it didn't, it stood a chance of running them off, and running them off was the best chance she had. With a shaking hand, she lifted it, her vision blurring once more. The gun grew heavier the higher she raised it, and she fumbled for the trigger.

"Drop it!"

More words followed, but they were lost in a gray haze. Coralie squeezed the trigger once, then fell to her knees, gasping for air that didn't exist as the bullet clanked uselessly against a bulkhead somewhere. Around her, grav-boots clinked on the deck, closer and closer. She pushed herself backward into the cabin, but even the air that still hissed through the vent in the ceiling wasn't enough to fill her lungs, implant or not.

"Oxygen," came a voice from somewhere above. "Now."

Blindly, Coralie slung a fist toward the sound. If they were human, she could do plenty of damage with one punch, as long as she hit their suit in the right place. If they weren't . . .

A plastic mask slammed against her face as her fist came into contact with nothing, and she sucked in a lungful of oxygen. It wasn't enough to focus her vision, and when the mask disappeared, she nearly cried from frustration. Would have, had she been able to breathe.

"Stop fighting and you'll get more." The unfamiliar voice, feminine this time, sounded irate. "I don't particularly like being shot at."

Well, at least she knew the modifications that filled her body weren't nearly as effective when she hadn't been able to breathe normally in something like five minutes. Silence overcame the cabin, and it took Coralie longer than it should have to realize her assailants were speaking on intra-suit comms. The door remained cracked open, leaking oxygen into the corridor, and she gasped for air once more—suffocating her was likely their intent. They couldn't know what she was capable of since the augment program was secret even within the NSRC, but they *seemed* to know she wasn't capable of anything now.

Three of them yanked her to her feet as she lay there gaping like a helpless fish, then pushed her out the door into the corridor. The mask landed against her mouth once more, and Coralie swore inside of it instead of breathing. They were going to drag her away—*to where?*—like this?

"Breathing would be more helpful than swearing at us."

The voice who spoke was garbled by a microphone. They shoved the mask harder against her face, and Coralie took two deep breaths before he yanked it away.

"He wants her brought over," came the woman's voice.

For a moment she was confused why she could hear the comment, and then it made sense. They'd wanted her to hear. Whether it was intended to frighten her into compliance or not, she didn't know, but it worked.

They pushed her another twenty-five meters down the corridor as she focused on staying upright the best she could. It wasn't easy. She could imagine what her eyes looked like after so long without proper air, though it occurred to her that regular doses of oxygen or not, she'd have been dead already if the corridor was completely depressurized. That sudden awareness tamped the panic that was building in her chest. Perhaps she wouldn't die in the next thirty seconds after all.

They entered a lift at the end of the corridor, the same one Kinnard and his goons had brought her up in. Pressure filled her ears as the door slid closed, and she scarcely had to move her diaphragm for air to saturate her lungs.

"Who—" She hadn't caught her breath enough to speak more than a single word. A few more gasps and the words came, slowly and painfully. "Who the hell are you? What do you want?"

There were a few more brief looks and silent-to-her words exchanged between the other three.

Yes, that earlier comment about bringing her to another ship had *definitely* been intentional.

"Don't play dumb," the woman replied. "Where are the others?"

"Others?" Kinnard's men? Or did they mean the others in the capsules? How did they know about them?

"There were four hundred seventeen passengers and crew aboard this ship. Strange thing is, there aren't any bodies floating around and only a handful of heat signatures. Did you shove them all out an airlock?"

The lift sank downward, stopping just one deck below, and taking Coralie's stomach with it. All this time, after everything she'd been through, they were accusing *her* of being responsible for what had happened here?

Yes, she almost replied. *I shoved over four hundred people out an airlock with nothing but a pistol and three quarters of a pressure suit.*

But the sarcasm died on her lips as they adjusted their grip and pushed her nose-first against the door. The cargo bay was just outside, and now that she'd had a taste of oxygen, she wouldn't go back into the near-vacuum easily, no matter what kind of murderer they thought she was.

"I didn't hurt them. But I know what happened." Her vision blurred, and it wasn't from the hypoxia. "I can't breathe out there. I can't breathe right now. Look, let's just—"

"You weren't suffering too badly in that corridor upstairs." The woman didn't sound like she was capable of pity. "I think you can make it another six feet."

Heat bloomed in her gut despite the chill of the lift. Did they think *she* wasn't human? But that was silly—they couldn't possibly know about Kinnard, could they? Unless these were more of Kinnard's people, in which case she was as good as dead. Well, she would be back in that capsule, which was basically the same thing. But that didn't make sense either, because Nimbus Station security wouldn't be asking about *Triumph*'s passengers and crew. Besides, these strangers were obviously human behind their helmets, and Kinnard only had one use for humans.

Which meant—

Dammit.

The door cracked open and the air hissed out, a sound that was becoming irritatingly familiar. Coralie squinted through the gap into the dimly lit shuttle bay. The NSRC orbital shuttle she'd arrived on sat there to the left, its lights dark and engine silent, but to the right sat an red and white boat, *US Orbital Guard* written on the side in letters as tall as she.

She swore again.

"You bastards." She tried to twist backward but found her boots sliding forward on the smooth steel of the bay before she could finish. "I thought you were station security! You never identified yourselves!"

"Yeah, whatever." One of them slammed the mask against her face again, let her take a few breaths, then took it away. "Don't hold your breath unless you want your lungs to explode."

Like I'm that foolish.

She exhaled the entire way to the boat, certain every capillary in her eyes had just exploded. None of her modifications had been installed for anything remotely resembling vanity. But in less than fifteen seconds, she was gasping for air against the floor of the boat and the door was sliding closed.

"Put a helmet on her," the woman ordered from outside. "Then take her back. I'm going to—" The words abruptly cut off, as though she'd realized her audience could still hear her.

Coralie pushed herself up on her hands and knees, then crawled into a seat in front of her and collapsed. At least they weren't going to take her out into open space without a helmet—that was something. Her arms were too weak to lift the helmet they handed her, so one of them latched it on and gave her a questioning thumbs-up.

"I need more air," she gasped at him as he latched her into a harness.

It began to flow, cool and dry, and she could have cried at the feel of it against her lips. Another miracle—they were letting her talk, *and* actually listening to her. The hatch opened again and four of them disappeared back into *Triumph*'s shuttle bay, leaving her with the other three. The boat lifted off the floor of the bay, as if it was programmed to do so, then floated out the door. Stars surrounded them, but that was all Coralie could see through the small window across from her. If there was another ship, and there had to be this far into the middle of nowhere, it was hidden somewhere behind the boat's hull.

"How about now?" the suited man to her left asked. "Enough?"

She nodded all too politely, the weightlessness of her body making the gesture even stranger. Even strapped in, she floated upward in the harness, but shoving herself back down to the seat took effort she didn't possess any longer. Worse than the fatigue was the fear. She'd shot at them, and they obviously hadn't taken kindly to that. As though that even mattered out here. What could they do to her that Kinnard hadn't already done? Arrest her?

Before she could come up with a more terrifying future, thrusters fired, and the boat slowed. She couldn't see much out the front window, but there were lights in the distance, an illuminated rectangle that had to mean another shuttle bay.

The thrusters became more insistent in their dance, and she closed her eyes as the boat rolled, then pitched down, maneuvering for docking. *Triumph*'s cargo bay was large enough that such maneuvers hadn't been necessary to land inside, and the constant changing motion—not to mention the apprehension of what was to come—sent her stomach into a freefall.

"Don't throw up inside that helmet," a voice on her right warned.

Coralie shook her head and opened her mouth. But before she could ask what would happen after they landed, the boat hit the deck with a *thunk*.

CHAPTER TWENTY-SEVEN_

JOSIAH COULDN'T GET TO THE BRIG FAST ENOUGH, had already tripped climbing up one ladder. There had been no time to wait for a lift, and his unease was getting the best of him. Graham was still aboard *Triumph*, clearing the rest of the ship, but Betschen and Salazar had brought one passenger—who'd drawn attention to herself by firing on Raider 2, of all things.

Still, it was a start, though he suspected anyone with enough animosity to shoot at law enforcement wouldn't be as talkative as he needed her to be. He tapped an urgent message to Ahn to meet him here as soon as possible—for moral support, though he'd never admit that to anyone, even Ahn—then nodded at Betschen, standing guard outside the door.

The chill of the compartment hit his face at once, but it only took one look at the detainee in the first cell to figure out why they'd adjusted the temperature like they had. Her light red hair was thick and soaked with sweat, which wasn't surprising considering what she'd been through. For some strange reason, he'd expected her to be middle-aged, but she was only twenty-five perhaps, with the pale skin anyone would have expected of someone who'd been on a transport ship for as long as he supposed she had.

But pale skin or not, she looked otherwise healthy, and that was what bothered him the most. Betschen had said she'd shot from behind an open doorway into a nearly airless corridor, but that should have been impossible. How had she been conscious long enough to do so without a full suit? The corpsman had found no injuries besides a few burst blood vessels, frostbite, and some kind of port in her chest, and that didn't make sense either. Her lungs should have exploded.

"Are you responsible for this?" she demanded before he could introduce himself.

No, her lungs definitely hadn't exploded.

Josiah drew himself up. "Responsible for what, exactly?"

"Oh, I don't know." She jabbed a finger at Betschen. "For them roughing me up, then dragging me through a depressurized corridor of a starship in orbit. For locking me away in here. For giving me no answers. Should I go on?"

"The corpsman saw you. What else do you want?"

She gaped at him.

"You shot at them," he went on when she didn't reply. One of the few things he had little tolerance for. "How did you expect them to react?"

Or me, for that matter?

Her jaw tightened. "I didn't hit any of them."

He almost laughed. Who knew an inability to stay somber was a side effect of this new job?

"So?" he asked.

"I didn't harm them." Her eyes flashed. "Not like I thought they intended to harm me. A group of people dressed in black, skulking through a dark starship—they could have been anyone. What was I supposed to think?"

"I should have thought that would have been obvious when they identified themselves as Orbital Guard."

"They never told me who they were!"

"Is that so?" He glanced behind him at Betschen, who gave an offended shake of his head.

"Well—" she cut herself off. For the first time since he'd stepped inside the brig, she sounded uncertain. "Maybe they did. I was pretty dizzy."

Betschen cleared his throat, and Josiah made a *knock it off* gesture behind his back.

"You could have killed someone," he said, "shooting into the black like that."

She sank to the bunk. "But I didn't kill them. And I didn't kill the others, either." The latter protest was a whisper, spoken to her hands.

The others?

"Everyone else aboard *Triumph*, you mean?"

"She said I must have shoved them all out an airlock." Her tone was distant. "But even I couldn't have done that by myself. Everyone's down on the surface at Nimbus Station. And no one believes me that I had nothing to do with any of this."

"Everyone?" Josiah glanced behind him, looking for answers that didn't exist. Was she drugged? Altered respiration might account for her survival in near-vacuum, though he'd never heard of such a thing before. "Then why a distress signal?"

She shook her head.

"Is the rest of my team in danger?" That was all he really wanted to know. Graham and the remainder of Raider 2 hadn't returned; she'd told Blayne there was still more of the ship to sweep. He hadn't immediately worried. *Triumph* was large. "The ones still aboard *Triumph*?"

"Yes," she replied simply. "They are."

"How?"

Her mouth opened, and were those tears? Holy hell, but his patience here was wearing thin.

"Look," he said, "right now I have enough to turn you over to the authorities on Mars. They can figure everything out."

"I . . ." Any color that had clung to her cheeks immediately faded.

"Just tell me what happened." It was a tone the crew of *Bayonet* probably recognized, but she seemed immune to it. "You'll feel better once you do, and maybe we can work something out."

She sucked in a breath and spoke to her hands once more. "I left Mars last February aboard *Tri*-

umph. I was supposed to fill an assignment as a facilities engineer. But it turns out they needed my blood more than my engineering skills."

"Your blood?" Josiah raised a brow as Ahn appeared by his side.

"They needed it after we passed through the wormholes." Her inhalations grew so sharp and rapid he was afraid she was about to hyperventilate. "Otherwise, they would die."

Die?

His throat seemed to narrow in panic.

Kamorta.

The dead passengers, the sole survivor.

His chest became tight, and he forced his breathing to slow. Now he was afraid *he* was going to be the one to hyperventilate.

"We ran across another ship," Ahn said, saving Josiah from gasping for air as he spoke, "just past Wormhole E. Almost the entire crew was dead of liver failure. Is that how it happened with *Triumph*?"

"Yes." She blinked at them both. "I have a gene they don't, so the wormholes don't affect me."

"And if they get your blood, then what? It prevents liver failure somehow?"

She crumpled forward, clutching her arms around her chest.

Panic attack?

"Open it up," Josiah said to Betschen. The force field dropped immediately, and he sank to the bunk an appropriate distance from her. "Look, forget what I said about taking you back to Mars. I'm just a little apprehensive about everything that's gone on here lately. What happens if they get your blood? Why do they want it so badly? That's what the port in your chest is for, right?"

"It is now," she whispered. "But not before."

"How did they do it before?" Somehow, he'd wandered into a nightmare. Blood and wormholes and liver failure—none of it made any sense, but he couldn't deny that her story corroborated too strongly with what had happened aboard *Kamorta* to dismiss immediately. And by this point it was obvious there was more going on than an overdue starship, and *Bayonet* was caught up in it.

"I had a private cabin. There was a lottery, and I thought I'd been lucky. But after we transited Echo, security arrived. They said some predeparture medical tests had come back concerning, that I needed to be quarantined in an improvised sick bay away from everyone else."

A tear slid down her cheek. Josiah couldn't help but wonder about the change in her—from the woman who'd shot at his team to the person sitting here now, about to break down in tears. But then again, maybe it wasn't so odd. Some survivors crumpled like this once they knew they were safe. It was the adrenaline crash to end all adrenaline crashes.

"They handcuffed me to the bed and began to take my blood, lots of it. Said it was necessary to treat me, and I knew they were lying, but I was so sedated that I couldn't fight them or break free." Her fingers wove in between each other. "Anyway, once I arrived on the surface, they locked me in a capsule. Like those imaging machines they use in older medical clinics, but worse, because I wasn't allowed out. I couldn't move, I wasn't permitted to eat, no one heard me scream."

Her body shook, and though he couldn't see her face, he could tell she was sobbing. "And while I laid there and stared at the ceiling for months on end, they drained my blood and used it to keep themselves alive."

"Months on end?" His lengthy hospitalization after *Vigilant* had been bad enough, but even he hadn't been confined to his bed—much as he might have wished otherwise during rehab. A chill ran down his spine, and he somehow doubted it was because of the unnecessary cold in the brig. "That seems excessive. How long until they're cured? And why keep you locked up like that?"

"They knew I wouldn't agree to do it for them otherwise. I was a prisoner. Worse than a prisoner. Just a thing for them to use for what they needed. No longer a human being, not anything they bothered wasting space and emotion on." She looked up at him, but it didn't appear as though she actually *saw* him. "You don't understand, do you?"

"I suppose I don't."

"They are desperate for my blood. If they keep drinking it, it doesn't only ward off the liver failure. I don't know exactly how it works, but . . ." Her stare seeped into his soul. "They can stay alive forever."

Mother of God.

"You're saying—" Josiah glanced up at Ahn, hoping for a laugh that would ease his mind, but his face was devoid of humor. "That if the passengers aboard *Triumph* drink your blood, they don't die? Ever?"

"I know what you're thinking," she replied, a light defensiveness trickling into her voice. "But it's not like those old stories from Earth."

The eternal silence of these infinite spaces frightens me . . .

"You're going to have to dumb it down for me then, because it certainly sounds like vampires to me."

"They're human. They never stopped being human, even though most of the time I feel like they have. They just need a protein in our blood to survive what the wormholes did to them, and it has a bit of a side effect."

"A bit of a side effect is an understatement, don't you think?"

She shrugged.

Ahn lifted a brow. "Our blood?"

"Yours too, you know." Finally, she sounded like she'd found a bit of confidence. "That faulty gene I have? The one that kept me from dying when we went through the wormholes? You have it, too. Both of you. All of you on board this ship, if you're still alive, you have it. Otherwise . . ."

The word, the implication, the threat—it all floated there in front of him as though the gravity generators had collapsed.

"Okay. I believe you." Josiah sighed as he stood. He didn't, of course. There was no question she was traumatized by something, but there was also no doubt her story had holes and embellishments and whatever else. Hell, it sounded like a complete hallucination, and he'd learned a long time ago not to argue with unstable people. "Patrick?"

With Ahn on his heels, he fairly fled into the passageway, away from the brig, away from the icy air, away from the woman who claimed there were—what, *vampires*?—aboard *Triumph* and down on Nimbus Station.

"Whatever she's been smoking," Ahn began as Josiah paced in a circle outside the door, "I'm sure it's illegal."

There it was again—that pained laugh he was becoming so familiar with. "Well, that's not our problem anymore, thankfully. We'll turn her over once we get back to Mars and be done with it." She might object to thirty-plus days in the brig on the way there, but that wasn't his problem either.

"Indeed." Ahn stepped in front of him, cutting short his third aimless circuit. "And *Triumph*?"

Josiah wanted to bang his head against the bulkhead but settled for leaning against it and folding his arms, the very picture of someone who knew exactly what to do.

"We'll let them clear the rest of the ship, find those other heat signatures. Not that I expect anything but more of the same. I wonder if they stumbled upon *Triumph* and decided it would be a good place for a rave. *Kamorta* was past the wormholes, so it's not outside the realm of possibility that someone else is, I suppose. While they do that, we'll run her name through the system and see if we can figure out where she came from."

"But it doesn't explain what happened to everyone else."

"You really do like to deliver bad news." Josiah sighed. "I suppose it doesn't. Which means all we do is take her at her word—and visit Nimbus Station."

CHAPTER TWENTY-EIGHT_
USOGC BAYONET, ETRIK ORBIT

They hadn't believed her.

Coralie stared unblinkingly at the opposite wall, as though if she did so long enough, they'd come back and tell her this had been a mistake, that they believed her, that they'd already taken care of Kinnard and were ready to find the others. She'd had a nightmare once, back in her quarters on Nimbus Station, that the military had shown up on Etrik, guns blazing, then laughed and left when she'd told them what had happened. This wasn't quite the same thing, but close enough that she might as well be reliving it.

But what else could she do? She'd been honest from the start, but they obviously hadn't forgiven her for shooting at their people. Could she blame them for that? Not really. If she could take that back—but she couldn't. Fixing it? They'd never accept her apology and move on. That O'Donnell man had stared at her like he'd just as soon murder her than forgive her. Since he probably had six inches and sixty-five pounds on her, he probably could have, too.

Still, if they were here after *Triumph*, their lives were in danger, and she needed to make them see what was really happening here—partly because her life was in danger as well, for Kinnard would find her if she went back to Nimbus Station alone. But maybe that didn't matter, because there were still people from *Bayonet* aboard *Triumph*, and Kinnard would find them first.

You can't save the world.

But she had to save her colleagues, and she'd been unsuccessful so far on her own. Well, she hadn't actually planned anything, much less implemented it, but maybe that was for the best. Because now she had help, actual help with guns and everything, if they would just listen.

Coralie hopped to her feet and stuck her nose as close to the force field as possible. Even her modifications wouldn't help her now. No, being thrown against the opposite bulkhead by an electrical charge wouldn't kill her, but it didn't sound appealing either.

She took a step back, even though there wasn't anyone in the vestibule outside to reprimand her for standing so close, just a single empty chair and bare white bulkhead with a locked door on the other end.

Locked. How ridiculous. Like anyone in the galaxy could escape from a ship filled with armed individuals in orbit. Probably not even Kinnard.

"Hello?" she called. Surely they hadn't left her alone, even if it was just some sort of camera tracking her every move and sound. "Is anyone there?"

A long silence greeted her, broken only by the constant flow of air and a beeping somewhere in the distance that could have meant anything. Her fist hit the bulkhead before she could stop herself, and she shook out the pain, cursing under her breath. Every minute she spent here, every hour, Kinnard could be—

The door clicked, then slid open. Coralie stuck her knuckles in her mouth, but that didn't appear to have hidden her impulsiveness from the man who entered. Not O'Donnell, but younger and shorter and just a bit heavier—though something told her the extra weight wasn't from idleness.

"You don't need to break bones to get someone's attention." His name tape said Hackett, and in one hand he had a mug of something steaming, in the other, a plate. "I was getting some breakfast for you. It's eggs today. Powdered, naturally, since we've been out here a while. Hope you don't mind."

"I don't mind." It wasn't as though Nimbus Station had chickens running around. The NSRC training center on Mars hadn't either. She didn't think she'd had real eggs since Mexico. "I didn't realize it was morning."

"On board it is." Hackett reached through the field—obviously keyed to his DNA—and handed her the plate and mug. "As of two hours ago."

Coralie's stomach growled, so she sat back on the bunk and glanced between the eggs and coffee. The eggs won out, and she dipped a tentative fork into the pile and examined it. There seemed to be something off about accepting food from the people who'd locked her up here.

And starving yourself won't help.

"I don't know how the day worked aboard *Triumph*," she admitted, shoving a forkful of eggs into her mouth as delicately as she could. They were definitely powdered, bright yellow and unnaturally fluffy, but they were the best powdered eggs she'd ever tasted. "I—"

Why was she bothering to explain her background? That O'Donnell man who'd stopped by first hadn't cared, and this man wouldn't either.

"I'd assume watchkeeping aboard *Bayonet* is the same as any starship." If he was taken aback by her abrupt silence, he didn't show it.

"*Bayonet*." She tasted the word, then swallowed another bite of eggs. "Out of?"

"Mars." He cocked his head. "Bonneville Orbital Docks. That's—"

"Somewhere high above the Bonneville crater, I would assume." Her chest wanted to cave in at the familiarity.

"Yeah." He dragged a chair in front of her cell and sat, and despite her dread, she couldn't take her eyes from how his muscles flexed as he did. "You're familiar?"

"I trained on Mars." *At least, the person I used to be did.* "And before, I was at Valles Marineris University."

"For?"

"Mechanical engineering."

Hackett whistled. "You don't look old enough."

The coffee cooled, so she tested a sip. It was as bad as she'd expected, but somehow the best she'd ever had. "And you don't look old enough to be sitting here guarding me."

"Well, you got me there. What was it like, being on the surface for so long?"

He smiled as he asked, and something inside of her cracked. It was genuine emotion, true kindness, and she hadn't been the recipient of that in so long. Even Henk, close as they'd once been on Mars, had distanced himself from her on Etrik. She understood, even if she hadn't liked it. And now Hackett was sitting there looking at her like perhaps they had made a mistake and she wasn't a criminal after all . . .

"Three years isn't so long." She looked at the deck. "Though I suppose I was on Earth for most of my life before that. You grew up in space?" She didn't really care where he'd grown up, but perhaps making nice was her best bet of earning another smile, one that told her she was still human.

"I was born on Ceres, and then . . . yes, I suppose. Mostly. My parents ran mail from Earth to Saturn, and it was sort of a family affair. I learned to hate the surface. Too confining."

Coralie set the eggs down and took a deep breath. Maybe there was someone who would listen to her after all. "Then you've seen weird things out here."

"I suppose that's true as well." Hackett's expression grew guarded, but he wore the look with unease. "Just last year, we intercepted a stolen merchant vessel just off Phobos. Me and the others hop in the MarkXVII, ready to fly on out, and wouldn't you know it, we heard knocking on the outside as soon as we pushed back from the cutter."

"Knocking?"

"Like someone outside hitting the hull with a hammer. We came back, did a full mechanical and visual inspection, found nothing. Launched again, same thing. That time we pushed through it and got on board, but I had nightmares for a week." He leaned forward, toned forearms on his knees, then pointed at her. "Someone was outside that boat."

Oh, please.

She tore her gaze away from his muscles and her brain away from whatever ghost story he'd just told. "Then you have to understand what's happening down on Nimbus Station. You have to believe me. And the rest of your people on *Triumph*, they're in danger, too. Imminent. If you don't care about what's happening on the surface, at least listen to me about that!"

He almost, but not quite, rolled his eyes. "Look—"

"I need to talk to your captain."

"You already talked to the captain."

Coralie's forehead creased. O'Donnell had been the captain? He hadn't even introduced himself.

"What about the guy who was with him? Tall, black hair?"

"That was the XO."

Crap. Probably not an ally, then.

"So can I talk to the captain again?" She pushed the eggs toward the force field for him to take— her appetite was gone. "Please?"

Hackett sighed as he stood. "I'll see what I can do."

* * *

Coralie was staring at the ceiling when she heard the cough. It had been hours since Hackett had disappeared, and even though she hadn't truly expected him to talk the captain into speaking with her once more—wasn't there some sort of chain of command that prevented that?—she couldn't control her weariness with the entire situation. She'd been so close to figuring out how to rescue the others, and now she was further away than ever, a disaster of her own making. If only she hadn't fired upon them. If only she'd gone running toward them instead.

Whoever it was coughed once more when she didn't react, so she sat up. It was O'Donnell who stood there outside the force field just like he had before—except now his complexion was pale and his eyes, which had been a piercing blue before, were dark. And there was something else about him, something undefinable. He was almost *too* put together, like he was pretending to be calm for her sake.

"Tell me exactly what happened," he said quietly. "From the time you began training on Mars."

"All of it?"

"All of it."

Coralie rocked forward, hands around her knees. Keeping secrets didn't seem to matter anymore.

"I volunteered," she began, "for an experimental NSRC program meant to investigate how certain bodily modifications could advance human space-flight. It was . . . confidential. Not even most in NSRC knew about it. My first few weeks there, they implanted what we call augmentations." She pointed at her eye. "I have an implant here that can snap photos that are then stored in a chip near my optic nerve. I can access them the same way. I have small capsules of a special coagulant floating around in my blood stream to keep me from bleeding out if I'm injured."

He was better at hiding his disgust than most, but she saw it. She always saw it. Even the doctors who'd performed her surgeries had felt the same about their own work. *Better her than us*, was the usual sentiment. They never seemed to accept any accountability for their Dr. Frankenstein work, though whether that was out of guilt or something else, she'd never been able to figure out.

"I have an implant near my lung," she went on, "that allows me to breathe in low oxygen environments. For a while, at least. Hard vacuum for more than a few minutes will kill me just as surely as it'll do you in, but down on Etrik, it's possible for me to function for short periods of time. And some other things. Muscle enhancements that increase my strength, a pacemaker in case my heart stops."

"And this is why your lungs didn't explode aboard *Triumph*."

Coralie nodded.

"And *Triumph*—" She ran through the voyage, the wormholes, the way the medic and the rest of the crew had developed silver eyes once they'd passed through Wormhole Echo. "Then, once we reached Etrik, Thomas Kinnard, the director of Nimbus Station—he locked me in that capsule."

"Where they took your blood. And drank it."

"Well, no." His brows rose, and she hurried on before he decided everything she'd said was a lie. "Only Kinnard drinks it. The rest take pills made from blood. I've never seen where they're made, and I don't care to. But yes."

"And this gene?"

"I'm not a biologist. I don't understand it all. What I know is there's a necessary protein we're able to manufacture and they can't. It's rare, too, maybe only five percent of the population has it. And without it—"

"Liver failure."

"Yeah," she whispered. "I know this all sounds crazy, and you have every right to question every bit of my story, but I've seen them walking around on the surface of Etrik like you or I would do on Earth. I've seen them die when the blood pills are withheld." Those unwelcome tears fell, even though she'd sworn they never would again. "I still have nightmares about what it was like to be locked in that capsule for months."

He opened his mouth.

"And the worst part is," she said, before he could say anything, "there are three more just like me trapped on the surface. I have to free them. I have to. I made a promise to myself, and I can't leave them there. But Kinnard told me he had a plan to get even more blood sources here of their own accord, so no one would suspect any of this was going on."

And you're them.

O'Donnell paled even further, enough that she could see a thin scar on the edge of his jaw.

"Do you believe me now?" she asked.

He nodded, silent.

"Why? What changed your mind?"

Even as she asked, she knew.

"Because the rest of my team aboard *Triumph*," he replied, rubbing the back of his neck, "has gone missing."

CHAPTER TWENTY-NINE_

To her credit, the girl kept up with him as Josiah led her through what she must see as an impenetrable rabbit's warren. The brig was about as far from Rescue Bay A as one could get, but she didn't complain or fall behind his pace as she followed him in a seemingly random pattern aft and upward inside *Bayonet*'s guts. She didn't say anything either, and for someone who'd seemed desperate to help just ten brief minutes before, that was odd.

He hoped she wasn't taking pictures of everything with that unnerving implant of hers.

Physically biting his lower lip to keep from asking, Josiah pulled open the last door and gestured her inside the hangar bay. *Triumph* was visible in the distance through the larger window, and she glanced at it once, then looked away—though her gaze didn't land on anything in particular. It just refused to focus on *Triumph.*

"How much of the ship did you actually see?" He waved a hand at the screens on the bulkhead. They sprang to life, *Triumph*'s schematic immediately appearing. "Before or this time?"

She twisted her hands together, any confidence he might have imagined earlier gone. "Some. On the way here, I spent the entire trip flat on my back in a compartment they called sick bay but was almost deserted, and when they brought me up last time, they took me straight to a stateroom." Her eyes went blank for a moment. "Deck 7, Section 17, Room 209."

"Okay." Josiah shook off the eerie sensation he'd gotten watching her undoubtedly check the chip near her . . . what had she said? Optic nerve? "Any idea where the others might be?"

"The bridge?" It sounded like a guess.

"Okay," he repeated like a fool, glancing around for Blayne. "That makes as much sense as anything else, I suppose. Want to go along?"

"Yes." Her eyes, her real eyes, grew wide. "But why? What are you going to do?"

"We're going to—excuse me." Leaving her there by the bulkhead, he hurried over to Blayne, who'd slipped inside the bay almost silently and was digging through the arms locker. "Master Chief. Got a companion for you."

Blayne yanked out a rifle.

"Her?" He motioned at Coralie with his chin. "I hear she's got a bunch of body modifications."

"Don't be such a puritan." Josiah feigned a laugh. "I dislike it as much as you do, but she might be helpful. Apparently, she can take pictures with that implanted lens of hers. Could be useful."

Blayne gave him a look and tossed another rifle over his shoulder. "That violates a whole bunch of laws, Captain. Not to put too fine a point on it or anything."

"I know. And even more importantly, NSRC knows, which means there's likely nothing we can do about it." Josiah shrugged. He wasn't above using the technology in her body while he could. "But we're well past worrying about it, aren't we?"

"Yeah, yeah." Blayne sighed. "She's not getting a gun."

"You'll get no argument from me there. Keep her in the middle, but listen to her. I don't know if she knows more than she's letting on, but there's no point in not using whatever knowledge she has. And maybe she'll remember something useful as you clear the ship. Hell, maybe she's involved, and it's possible she'll slip and confess if she's there."

"Maybe." Blayne's jaw tightened. "I've never seen personnel beacons up and disappear unless something went really wrong. Even if they were lost or injured—"

"I know." Crushed under a grav-boot or intentionally wrapped in foil, well, that would destroy the signal. "Let's just see what we find and go from there."

"Aye aye, Captain." The rest of Blayne's body stiffened. "You know, I met Roselyn Graham three years ago on Deimos. One of the sharpest officers I've ever met. Made me wish I was that competent at her age. She didn't screw up. And she certainly didn't lose her beacon."

The weight of the entire ship seemed to settle on his chest as Josiah motioned him into an empty corner of the bay.

"Look, before everyone gets carried away with this," he began. There was no point in hiding anything, not when rumors flew as fast as they did. "There's reason to believe that the others aboard *Triumph* and most of those down on Nimbus Station, they might not be, uh . . ." Blayne was going to think he was insane, and he wouldn't blame him. "They might not be entirely human."

Blayne cocked his head. "Not entirely human?"

I'm sure Coralie Frazer would be thrilled to tell you the details . . . probably in a dark passageway.

"It seems the wormholes may have changed something in their DNA. It's why the crew of *Kamorta* died of liver failure, and I believe it has something to do with the dreams we've all been having. Ms. Frazer—they've been using her to blood to stave off the liver issue, and therefore death, indefinitely."

There.

That hadn't sounded too insane. Not mutiny-inducing-insane, at least.

Blayne shrugged in response, a surprisingly composed gesture for someone who'd just been told there might as well have been vampires on a spacecraft he was about to board.

"If that explains those dreams, Captain, I won't argue with you. Better than aliens, right? Do bullets work on them?" He patted the rifle, belated though the concern was.

"I don't know yet." *And I don't really want to find out.* "I'd say I wouldn't count on it, but the truth is, I have no idea what to believe anymore. Just get in, find them, get out. No screwing around, no matter what she tells you. We'll deal with the rest later."

"Aye aye, sir." Blayne turned around and whistled for the rest of Raider 1.

"Hold on, Master Chief." Indecisiveness was the word of the day, it appeared. "Look, the fact is, we don't know what we're going to find over there, and no one would blame you if—"

"They wouldn't leave me over there." There was kindness, not judgment, on Blayne's face. "Wouldn't leave anyone else, either. Besides, if you're not exaggerating about what's going on over there, I rather think we're all a little screwed at this point, right?"

"I had to give you the option." Josiah's heart beat a little slower. "Good luck."

He didn't watch them board the boat on the other side of the transparent bulkhead, even though he knew he should. As soon as alarms blared and the boat floated into the blackness outside, he turned back to the console by the airlock and stared at the schematic of *Triumph,* the flashing beacons of Raider 2 conspicuously absent.

But McArthur had arrived, and she was already muttering data to Blayne. She gave him a brief nod, and though he wanted to ask for an immediate status, he bit his tongue. There was nothing new for her to tell him until the boat reached *Triumph,* and his very presence was probably a distraction for her.

He flashed five fingers in front of her—*back in five minutes*—then headed toward the door for a brief walk. Anything to clear his mind and allow him to focus on the mission at hand. Not wormholes which forced him to relive some of the best and worst times of his life, not blood-drinking former humans, not the now-orphan the corpsmen were entertaining in sick bay, and not . . .

. . . not Hope.

"Hey." She gave him a grim smile as she appeared through the door.

"Hey." He glanced back at the screens on the other side of the bay, willing the beacons to flash again. "You shouldn't be here right now. Go get some sleep."

"You've been stalking my schedule? Well, sleep is always attractive, I'll say that much." A thermos of coffee appeared in front of his face. "But I suppose that means I should take this with me when I leave."

His gaze slid slowly back toward her, and for the briefest instant, he forgot about *Triumph*. "You're manipulating me," he said, waving her out into the passageway.

"Hardly. And if I am, it's because it's so easy to do." Her laugh was familiar and comforting as she shook the coffee in front of him. "You want it or not?"

He seized it from her hands and took a sip. "Thanks. I feel ragged as hell."

"You look it." She folded her arms and moved against the bulkhead, letting a group of technicians into the bay. "How are you holding up?"

Another sip. He didn't want to answer.

"Yeah, that's what I thought." Her expression turned morose, but that made sense. He'd seen her eating with Graham more than a few times in the wardroom. "Nothing yet?"

"Boat just launched," he replied quietly. "Probably another five minutes until they dock. I needed a quick break."

"You don't have to explain anything to me or anyone else." She turned away, then stopped. "Good luck. I won't be getting any sleep, so if you have a moment later and need someone to talk with—"

"I'll be in the wardroom in an hour." The smile he attempted felt more like a grimace. "It'll be time for more coffee."

"It's a date." The barest flash of a grin crossed her face, and then she was gone.

CHAPTER THIRTY_
NSRC T/V TRIUMPH, ETRIK ORBIT

THIS TIME, THEY'D CONNECTED THE communications inside her helmet, and listening to the casual chatter of the Orbital Guard team eased Coralie's nerves. They knew what they were doing, and even better, they seemed to have some sort of plan. Not that she understood the jargon and phraseology. They also had rifles across their laps, and though she was certain it would require more than a few bullets to take down Kinnard and his goons, it was a start.

They hadn't given her one, of course. Didn't seem to trust her at all, really, though Jakob Blayne, seated on her left, patted her leg and gave her a thumbs-up sign as they'd glided into the sleek darkness. Coralie returned it, but she would never admit she appreciated the concern.

She did, however, snap a photo of each of them with her implant, something she should have thought to do back on *Triumph*. It seemed idle, but at least she'd have names. There was Blayne to her left, one of the few who'd actually introduced himself. Hackett, straight across from her, a crooked smile focused in her direction. Stephens, to her right, cradled a tablet with orbital diagrams on it. Peyer, by the airlock, studied his gloves. Sprenger, next to Hackett, whistled something in silence inside his helmet. McArthur, on Hackett's other side, sat absorbed in the view out the window. Coralie wished she knew their given names. It would have humanized them.

"Once we land," Blayne said, oblivious to her work, "I want you to wait here until we clear the cargo bay. There's liable to be some surprises up there, and I don't want you in the middle of it. Shouldn't be more than a few minutes. If you hear anything that sounds remotely off before I tell you it's safe to disembark, just smash that emergency button on your shoulder."

"What happens then?" There hadn't been another boat in *Bayonet*'s rescue bay. Perhaps there were more? She strained her neck to see the window, but the angle was all wrong.

"Someone will come get you."

"Before or after Kinnard does?" She hadn't meant to sound frightened, but her voice cracked on his name.

There was a long pause, broken only by the sound of air filling her helmet.

"You're afraid of him." The tone of Blayne's voice changed, like he'd switched to a private channel.

"Yeah." She glanced around, but no one else appeared to be paying attention to the conversation. "I am. He won't give up what he has here, and if I don't play along, he won't risk me ruining things. He won't risk you ruining them, either. And I don't think your captain believes what I've been through—what Kinnard is capable of."

"Hmm. He gives off that feeling, doesn't he?"

"You might say that."

Blayne laughed. "You've had how long to come to terms with what's going on down on Nimbus Station? Months? A year? We've had something like a day. It's not that he doesn't trust you—though that might be part of it, and I'll remind you he has every reason not to after you shot at us. But it's more that you've called into question everything we once thought we knew, and no one wants to hear that their grip on reality wasn't as strong as they once believed."

"I think I can understand that." She could, if she tried. "But you have to believe me . . . I'm only trying to help. And yes, I need your help as well. Those three down there—I can't leave them. I won't. If I do, there's no way I'll ever be able to free them, and I won't let them suffer like that for the rest of their lives. Not when I was expecting a hundred years or more."

His jaw tightened. "Your lifespan is enhanced as well?"

"A little." She gritted her teeth. Non-augmented humans never felt comfortable with any of this. "It's nothing over-the-top. It's mostly because wounds that would otherwise be life-threatening don't faze me much, and diseases—same thing. I have capsules of antibiotics and anti-virals in my bloodstream to supplement my immune system. It's nothing like what Kinnard is doing."

"That sounds useful, if I'm being honest." Blayne smiled. "And awfully illegal, I might add."

"Useful is the purpose of the program. Legalities, well, yes. I can't argue with that. And I under-stand that bothers people, but there's good being done in the program. Perhaps one day—"

"Perhaps one day they might be mandated of us again." His voice chilled. "I'm not thrilled with the idea of compulsory implants."

"I understand." She folded her hands in her lap as the boat rolled once more. There was no point in aggravating him further, not when he clearly had different views on the sweeping cultural changes that had nearly torn the country apart. "What happens after you clear the bay?"

His voice became scratchy again, and she knew the rest of the team had been looped back into their conversation. "We'll sweep the ship and make sure no one's left. O'Donnell wants you with us while we do that, in case you have information stored in that chip of yours that might help. It could get rough, though."

"I told him I only have a few photos between the cargo bay and those quarters." She flipped through them once more, pretending to focus on her gloves while she did. The blank stare would only creep Blayne out more. "And those don't show much."

But if you think I won't be taking more once we land, you don't know me at all.

"Well, it's something." Peyer gave Coralie a lop-sided grin. "If you can't keep up, let us know."

She gave the briefest smile in return. Peyer was certainly not augmented. Keeping up wouldn't be an issue now that she had mostly recovered from her time in the capsule.

"I think I can handle that much," she replied. She stretched her neck the best she could inside her helmet as the boat rotated level. *Triumph* loomed large in the starboard window as the thrusters hissed, lining them up to intercept the cargo bay. It yawned in the distance, a gaping black hole against *Triumph*'s gray hull, and for a moment it looked like a monster waiting to swallow them. The tips of her fingers grew cold, even though the air in her suit hadn't changed temperature since they'd departed *Bayonet*.

Why wasn't the cargo bay the same dull gray as the rest of the spacecraft?

She leaned forward, and when the yawning blackness was pierced by a small white flash, she was sure.

"Blayne." Her palms began to sweat. How could she have been this wrong? She'd been certain Kinnard wouldn't go anywhere without her. "Coming out of the cargo bay—that's the shuttle I came up on."

Blayne unlatched himself and stepped across the boat to peer through a window, then swore. "*Bayonet*, we've got a problem."

He tapped on the controls beside the window, and the thrusters fired so aggressively that the boat seemed to come to a halt right there in space. Coralie slammed against her harness, catching his movement too late to brace herself against the seat. Not that there was much of a chance of that, even in a spacecraft this small.

"You sure that's it?" he asked.

She nodded, then remembered the helmet made such a gesture pointless—and that Blayne no doubt already knew the shuttle was the only atmospheric-capable ship aboard *Triumph*.

"Positive." Her stomach clenched. Surely the boat was armed. If not, *Bayonet* was probably equipped enough to vaporize the shuttle with one effortless shot. "Unless another one landed after I was left."

Blayne's jaw clenched, obvious even through his helmet. "*Bayonet*, any record of another shuttle docking with *Triumph*?"

"Negative." The reply crackled in Coralie's earpiece. "Zero contacts logged since we picked her up."

Blayne swore again. "Sprenger, put one across their path."

"Aye aye, Master Chief."

After the briefest moment, the sound of gunfire tore through the boat. Coralie had the immediate sensation of being flung the wrong way before the thrusters fired again, even more violently than before, stopping their backward plunge into nothingness. Her stomach rose, but Blayne hadn't even flinched at the aggressive movement.

"What was that?" Her eyes were wide. "You could have hit them!"

Hackett chuckled from across the boat, as blasé as Blayne had been. "Hardly. The computer won't let itself hit what we don't want it to hit."

"And if you wanted to?" How could it be this hard to breathe inside a helmet that was pushing air into her lungs?

"Smithereens." He shrugged as much as was possible in his suit. "*Bayonet* could turn it into smaller ones, of course."

Of course.

The ill feeling returned. The boat was the smallest spacecraft she had ever been in, but even it had more firepower than she'd seen in her life. Kinnard's shuttle seemed to be unconcerned by the shot. For an instant it pulled away, but the boat accelerated, letting off another shot as it closed in once more.

"They're not slowing down." Stephens swore as she examined a screen. "*Bayonet*, Raider 1, permission to follow?"

Coralie's heart thumped. The boat became quiet, except for the sound of thrusters keeping it stable after its last shot. Tumbling toward the planet in pursuit of another ship was the last thing she wanted to do, but it wasn't as though they were going to drop her back off on *Bayonet* first.

"Negative, Raider 1," came the immediate answer. "Proceed to *Triumph* as instructed and remain clear of the target."

Coralie glanced at Blayne, wide-eyed.

"They can't fire at it!" Six heads swiveled toward her as she forced down bile. "He's got them. He wouldn't have left otherwise. He wouldn't have left *me*. I am telling you, your people are not aboard *Triumph* anymore. They are on that shuttle."

Blayne swore under his breath. "And I assume you're sure about that, too."

"Yes. And I want them back as much as you do."

He exhaled, fogging up his helmet for the fraction of a second. "*Bayonet*, hold your fire. It's likely there are hostages on that shuttle."

"Acknowledged." The line went silent for a moment. "Stand by, but do not approach the shuttle."

Coralie unlatched herself and pressed her nose against the window as much as she could wearing a helmet. The shuttle seemed to fall toward the planet, accelerating as it broke free of *Triumph*'s interference. But there was something wrong, something she couldn't identify at first.

"Blayne." Now it made sense. "I don't think they're heading toward Nimbus Station. Close, but look at the angle."

"No?" He appeared beside her and squinted at the red dust below. "I do believe you're correct. Get a track on that shuttle," he called over his shoulder.

"They just cleared us down to flight level 500," Stephens added.

"They're not headed for Nimbus Station," Coralie murmured as she stared out the window, wishing she could scratch her ear. Did Kinnard have another base somewhere? Of course not. She'd have known about that, wouldn't she? Even rumors would have spread. "Very close, but too far east. Could that warning shot have damaged their guidance and navigation systems?"

"Unlikely. Anything's possible though, I suppose."

Blayne sounded certain, but the shuttle kept its descent, spiraling closer to the planet. And to where? Could the Orbital Guard find them once they'd landed? They didn't perform search and rescue on the surface, though perhaps they could if pressed. Still . . . they were halfway across the galaxy with limited crew and absolutely no support.

The boat descended, though Coralie was able to stay upright as it did, her hand gripping the support next to her. Etrik grew large below, and the chatter that had filled the boat when they'd first launched grew almost silent.

Guilt settled onto her shoulders. Blayne thought he knew what fate awaited them, and she was sure that was bad enough for him, but . . . she *knew*, and that wasn't something she could just shrug off. Tears welled up as she tried to blink them away, and in that moment, she hated the helmet more than she appreciated its ability to keep her alive.

"It's gone," she said under her breath to herself as the shuttle vanished into the swath of mountains and red dust below. It had descended farther than she'd imagined possible in just a few minutes, but picking out the metallic craft among the ground clutter seemed impossible—for her, at least. *Bayonet* had eyes, didn't she? Probably the boat did too, for Stephens still looked absorbed in one screen or another.

"Who was left aboard *Triumph*?" Hackett asked.

Blayne didn't hesitate. "Lauren Graham, Jairus Halley, Martin Caldwell, and David Landolt."

Coralie jumped as her earpiece crackled.

"Raider 1, *Bayonet*. We're seeing an explosion at 32.42, -110.73. Confirm if feasible, but do not descend lower than current altitude."

Explosion.

She turned toward the bulkhead before anyone else could see how puffy her eyes had become.

Her throat closed up, even as she turned the dial to increase her oxygen.

"*Bayonet*, Raider 1 . . . say again, please?" Stephens asked.

"Correction, Raider 1. Ground blast consistent with the destruction of an atmospheric shuttle confirmed at 32.42, -110.73. Do not descend past current authorized altitude of 500. Return to *Triumph* and execute prior instructions, no delay."

Coralie sank into her seat, numb despite the adrenaline. She and every other person on the boat looked toward Blayne, like he could change what they'd heard. He only jerked his chin at Stephens.

"Did you copy that, Raider 1?" came the crackling inquiry. "Respond."

Stephens blew out a deep breath, then clicked her comm switch. "Copy that, *Bayonet*."

Heavy silence filled the boat, then Blayne spoke as the thrusters fired.

"You heard them. It's time to head back up to *Triumph*."

* * *

No emergency lights flashed outside as the boat settled onto the deck in *Triumph*'s cargo bay. The trip back into space had been almost silent, broken only by hushed sentences of planning between the team that Coralie hadn't been privy to. Blayne seemed to have forgotten his earlier order for her to stay on board the boat until his team had cleared the cargo bay, for he motioned her off and into zero gravity as soon as the door opened.

The light on the side of her helmet cast a narrow beam of yellow as she floated behind Hackett, but it wasn't enough to pierce the darkness that clung to either side of her—and her soul. Kinnard hadn't been suicidal, and the shuttle had been in decent enough shape when they'd departed Nimbus Station. Of course, things happened to even the most well-maintained spacecraft, and if the boat's firing calculations had been off . . .

But she hadn't *seen* a direct hit on the shuttle, she realized as she trudged down the corridor, and they'd been close enough that it would have been obvious. Perhaps a mechanical issue was the most likely cause after all, but—

"Ms. Frazer."

Her head jerked up as Blayne called her name. The team had stopped in front of the stateroom

Kinnard had initially left her in, and she glanced from it to the door, silent.

"Any idea why Thomas Kinnard chose this state-room to stash you away in?"

Her forehead creased. "I have no idea. Closest to the lift?"

"Except it's not," Peyer replied, clicking his boots onto the deck. "Not even close."

She tried to shrug, but the pressure suit they'd given her aboard *Bayonet* had almost no give. "I honestly couldn't tell you. Maybe he realized he had to stash me somewhere, and this was the most convenient spot."

"Sprenger, Hackett, check it out."

"Aye aye, Master Chief."

Sprenger tromped inside, and Coralie followed Hackett after attaching her boots to the deck. A sterile package of tubing Kinnard had left behind floated by her head as soon as she stepped inside, and for one idle instant she wondered why she'd bothered with the boots, since the sight had cemented her to the deck just as surely. It drifted behind her and out of sight, and she squeezed her eyes closed as she turned back to the door. She didn't need to be in here.

"What's that?"

She flinched at Hackett's voice.

"Medical tubing." Sprenger sounded dismissive and very, very far away. "Just more trash they left behind."

The stateroom seemed to spin about her, even though *Triumph* wasn't capable of such a maneuver without tearing herself apart in the vacuum. Coralie glanced at her boots, but they were still latched to the deck, along with the two larger sets in the very corner of her vision. Adrenaline pulsed through her.

More tubing.

She steadied herself. This time, Kinnard wouldn't get what he wanted. This time, she would fight him.

A hand landed on her shoulder, substantial even through her suit. Her heart thumped, and she spun around toward the offender, her fists raised. For the briefest of moments her vision blurred, then she blinked.

"Hey, now." Hackett stood his ground, even as she braced herself to strike. "What's going on?"

She couldn't speak. He shoved her hands to her sides before she could get off a punch, then grabbed her by the shoulders and pulled her toward him. She took one stumbling step forward, her left foot still attached to the deck. He let go, and she took a deep breath.

"I'm fine. I'm sorry. I just—"

He narrowed his eyes at her, but Sprenger motioned him away with his chin before he could say anything. They cut her from the comms, so Coralie wandered over to the coffee machine and pretended to examine it. She couldn't tell if they knew what had happened to her or were truly interested in something they'd found, and she didn't care. She picked up the coffee mug and hooked it to the machine. Not a trace of her blood remained, and she found herself wishing it did. They'd have no choice but to believe her if it did.

"What are you looking for?" she called over her shoulder as her heart rate returned to normal.

Sprenger ducked his head inside the washroom, then shrugged. "Stuff."

It was obvious he didn't want to answer, so Coralie plodded back into the corridor and unlatched her boots from the deck. Weightlessness was better that having to focus on every heavy step she took.

"Bridge," Blayne said as Hackett followed her out. "Ms. Frazer, stay in the middle. Be ready to duck."

Are you serious? Coralie wanted to ask him. *Be ready to duck?* But there was probably no precedent for dragging a civilian around with them. From the time every human had entered Wormhole Echo, everything had been without precedent for all of them. What could she do but try to help the best she could?

She fell in behind Hackett once more, McArthur behind her, and tried to keep from flinching each time they turned around the corner and the helmet lights illuminated one more shadow that turned out to be equipment or an open door. Sprenger raised his rifle once, but otherwise they appeared more composed than she—perhaps *Bayonet* had determined no one was aboard any longer, or at the very least not in their path as they headed to the bridge. They floated forward through *Triumph*'s guts, and Coralie took a few photos of location placards, though it was mostly out of habit. Clearly the team had a map stored in their comm watches, because they turned left and right with scarcely any hesitation at all.

"Master Chief." Stephens grabbed a handhold on the bulkhead and pulled herself to a stop. "That compartment twenty minutes ahead isn't on the schematic. And it appears to be shielded."

"NSRC is holding out on us, are they? Why am I not surprised anymore?" Blayne glanced at Coralie. "Any ideas?"

"No." Her heart pounded; it knew exactly what was inside, even if she didn't want to admit it. "I told your captain I didn't exactly have the run of the ship on the way here."

Blayne tilted his head to the side. "Oh?"

Coralie nodded. It was obvious he didn't believe her, but her heart was already beating faster than it should have been, thanks to the pacemaker that hadn't approved of that one skipped beat.

"Then we'll check it out." He gave Peyer a decisive nod. "See what there is to see."

"You think someone's in there?" she asked.

Blayne's stance widened. "If anyone's still on board, yes, I think they might be in there."

"Okay," she said under her breath.

What else was there to say? Nothing, except *please don't let anyone be in there.* She drifted to the top of the corridor and grabbed a handhold as Blayne and his team advanced on the door. Sprenger floated up like she had, but unlike her, he pressed his back to the ceiling and aimed his rifle at the opening. She lost track of the others; though she knew they hadn't gone far, they seemed to vanish into the shadows of *Triumph's* bulkheads.

The door clanged, echoing down the corridor, but she couldn't see who was responsible. It was the loudest thing she'd heard in days, and she flattened herself against the bulkhead, wishing she could disappear into the darkness as well.

"Open it," came Blayne's voice in her earpiece.

Metal clanged again, then the distinctive sound of a lock releasing filled her helmet. Sprenger floated forward, followed by the clomp of grav-boots. Their helmet lights flashed on, dancing across the bulkheads and shouts of *Orbital Guard* filled the corridor—the warning she obviously hadn't heard when they'd found her.

Her breath became short. She clung to the handhold and tried to freeze the best she could, make herself invisible to anyone who might come out of that compartment, but her body wanted to roll backward. Finally tucking her foot behind her opposite knee, she peered into the darkness ahead and forced her implants to adjust.

Indistinguishable figures were visible in the compartment now, but even her modifications didn't allow her to see much more. Some equipment, perhaps. A cot and some tubing and—

Her stomach churned, and she closed her eyes. Memories washed over her, even though she tried to focus on the air flowing into her helmet and the sound of the people inside the compartment.

The dreams. Of Mexican sunsets and Martian sunrises. Of the silver eyes that had suddenly appeared in the faces of *Triumph*'s crew. Memories of fighting them once she'd realized something was terribly wrong, of being restrained and drugged and shoved into that capsule.

Someone called her name in the distance, and she squeezed her eyes even tighter. She hadn't been able to fight them off back then. Why would she think otherwise now?

"Ms. Frazer." Blayne stood below, his boots locked on the deck and his hand out. "Ms. Frazer, I think you should see this."

Coralie blinked away the visions of silver. Her mouth was so dry she could scarcely swallow, but she nodded, sank to the deck, and latched her boots to it. The retinal implants were at full strength now, and she could see the others milling about just outside the door, all but two locked to the deck. She didn't have a chance to flip through her photos and figure out which two were floating in the corridor, for as soon as Blayne guided her inside, there was no doubt.

This was where she'd been.

This was where she'd spent much of the trip from Mars, hooked up to a machine that had taken her blood before she'd even understood why.

The compartment spun around her, and unable to move against the bulkhead quickly enough to restore her balance, she collapsed forward, her soles still stuck to the deck. Hackett crouched behind her and clicked the emergency release on her heels as her shins shrieked to be set free, and she rolled forward in midair, her arms wrapped around her chest.

"I've got you. You're okay."

His words were muddled as he spun her upright with a light hand on her arm, but the underlying concern wasn't. Coralie tried to shake him off, but he shook his head and his grip tightened. She twisted backward, then froze as he floated in front of her.

"You're going to pull a hose loose if you keep that up. Don't make me cuff you."

It wasn't the warning that stopped her. No, it was his eyes—a deep, warm brown like dried oak leaves, inquisitive and compassionate, so far from the cold, penetrating silver of everyone on Nimbus Station that she couldn't help but stare.

"You—" she began, then shivered. "You're not them."

"No." Hackett swore as the curiosity in his eyes turned to understanding. He held up his gloved hands and gave her a forced smile. "No walking around without a suit for me. Or any of us."

Coralie gulped for air and focused on his pressure suit. Deep black like the void, nothing a civilian would wear. Hard, reinforced fabric that didn't drape over his muscles but created an entirely new silhouette. His name in small white letters, just visible enough if you knew what you were looking for.

"They wore gray," she stammered. "Gray jump-suits, because *Triumph* was pressurized then. Ones that matched their eyes once we transited Echo."

Hackett glanced sideways, then back to her. "No one with silver eyes in this compartment right now, yeah?"

She closed her eyes and shook her head—in refusal, not agreement.

"Come on," he replied. "Look around and tell me what you see."

His flashlight illuminated the starboard bulkhead when she opened her eyes. *Dark.* It hadn't been dark in here on the way to Etrik. There hadn't been any need for flashlights. There had been gravity too, but now she could only feel the sensation of falling.

And the figures. She searched each visor in turn, taking in the eye color. Hackett was right. Brown, mostly, like hers. Blayne's, she noticed for the first time, were blue.

But no silver.

"I'm sorry." She took a few slow breaths. "I really thought I was back here before."

And now I feel like such a fool.

Hackett patted her on the shoulder. "Nothing to be sorry for."

"There was blood on some of the equipment," Blayne broke in like nothing at all had happened. "We've got some samples, and we'll try to run them once we get back to *Bayonet*, confirm they're yours—though I have no doubt."

"Yes." Coralie struggled upright, and Hackett let her drift toward the overhead. "They're mine."

"We took pictures," Peyer said from somewhere behind her. She was too dizzy to turn around and face him. "Do you want to take your own?"

"No!" Having those stored on her chip was the last thing she needed, but he couldn't possibly understand that, even now. "No. I don't. As long as it's good enough for O'Donnell to trust me, to believe what I'm saying—"

"It was always enough." Blayne motioned her toward the door. "It just takes him a while to come around sometimes."

CHAPTER THIRTY-ONE_
USOGC BAYONET, ETRIK ORBIT

His quarters weren't meant for this many people, but Josiah couldn't very well order Ahn off his bunk since Coralie Frazer had claimed his usual chair. Blayne stood against the door, his arms folded, wearing the same grim expression Josiah was becoming all too familiar with.

"I owe you an apology." They were words so many people found difficult, but what was the harm in apologizing to her? He'd been awful to her, hadn't believed her, had accused her of—well, he couldn't even remember anymore. Lots of stuff it didn't seem she was guilty of. And the things she *was* guilty of? They mattered little right now. "Both for not believing you and wasting your time. It was unproductive and unfair, and I'm sorry."

She cocked her head at him and nodded. Her cheeks were flushed, which wasn't unusual for someone who'd been inside a helmet as long as she'd been, but he suspected that wasn't the only reason she looked so bad. He also suspected she'd been pretending to be more courageous than she actually was as he'd flicked through the photos Blayne had taken.

But then, perhaps she *was* that brave.

"All right." He waved on the bulkhead display. "*Triumph*'s shuttle crashed in a remote canyon three nautical miles from Nimbus Station." His chest tightened. His people had been aboard that ship. "Though I suppose everywhere on Etrik is remote from everywhere else."

"Only *crashed* seems to be the wrong word." Ahn pointed. "The flight path looks to be stable. Exactly what you wouldn't see from an out-of-control spacecraft."

"Nominal angle and velocity, right." Josiah chewed on his lip. It was too much to hope for, but the data didn't lie. "The explosion could have been unrelated to a crash. Could have been intentional, too."

It had happened before—pirates, among others, preferred to destroy small spacecraft rather than leave evidence for the Orbital Guard or whoever else to use against them. But faking a crash was more difficult than the perpetrators always assumed it would be.

"You're saying it didn't crash?" Frazer wound her hands together.

God willing.

He glanced at Ahn. "Now that we've been able to run the scans and analyze more of the data . . . yes, I suppose it's a possibility that the shuttle made a safe landing, emergency or otherwise."

Frazer's expression didn't turn relieved like he'd expected.

"In that case, Kinnard might have them by now," she replied.

Josiah nodded. "And I need to know from you what kind of danger they're in."

"He's not going to kill them. I don't know much, but I know that." The answer came too quickly. "I swear to you, that's not what he wants with any of us."

Though they might be better off if they were dead, he swore he heard in her voice.

"You think they'll head for Nimbus Station?"

"I don't know." Her gaze blanked, and he looked at Ahn to give her privacy while she checked through whatever she had stored in her brain. "I don't have any information on that area of the planet. You didn't see another vehicle on the surface?"

"Not immediately, but the analysts are going through the scans again. Likely they won't find anything from this altitude." He ran a hand over his face. They'd be doing so throughout the next watch—something that would be much easier if they were in orbit over, say, Mars or Jupiter. Anywhere but this exotic planet whose only photos had come from the NSRC. An organization he no longer trusted.

"What can I do?" she asked. "There must be something."

"For now . . . rest. Recover." Josiah sighed. There wasn't anything else he could ask of her. She was a survivor, not a member of his crew, no matter how much information she might have, or how much she might want to exact revenge or whatever else on the people who'd done this to her. "Master Chief?"

"We'll take care of her." Blayne straightened. "Ms. Frazer? Let's find somewhere more comfortable than the brig for you to relax, shall we?"

Josiah cracked a smile, but it immediately fell once the two stepped into the passageway and closed the door.

"What do you think the odds are that they're still alive down there?" he asked.

Ahn shrugged. "You're the pessimist. You tell me."

"I want to say ten percent." His jaw tensed. "Only I feel like they're a whole hell of a lot higher than that, and I'm not sure I want them to be. Halfway across the galaxy, no backup, and no way to call for help. What are we supposed to do?"

"Leave them."

Josiah scoffed.

"Or don't leave them. I believe those are our only two options."

"I'm open to your counsel, then."

Ahn pushed himself to his feet and paced in the largest circle the compartment would allow. "There will be fireworks on Mars either way, you know."

"Maybe I don't care," Josiah replied.

And he didn't. They would praise him for his decision aboard *Vigilant* and in the next breath judge him for making the best of a no-win situation here? Well, of course they would, because that was how the Orbital Guard worked, but he didn't have to concern himself with their capricious reactions when lives were on the line.

"Didn't figure you did. Which makes the decision somewhat easier, of course, because it's only your own conscience you have to satisfy. And *Vigilant* aside, satisfying your conscience has never been much of an issue for you, has it?"

Josiah narrowed his eyes. "Why am I starting to feel like I'm at confession?"

"That's your own guilt talking, I believe."

"Not that you would know anything about that, sounds like."

"Eh." Ahn collapsed into his usual chair. "Thankfully, I don't have to make those kinds of decisions right now. I won't even attempt to goad you into the correct one—mostly because I can tell you're mulling it over already."

Ahn wasn't wrong. There was truly only one option here, and he'd known it since he asked for advice. Even if leaving his own crew was for the best, even if no one would criticize him for retreating to Mars and coming back later with more firepower, Coralie Frazer had said there were other captives down on Nimbus Station, and he had every obligation to rescue *them*.

Whether he could do it without sacrificing more of his own people was the question, because he would never ask them to accept more risk than he would accept himself. And that, of course, was a straightforward thing to do as long as he sat up here aboard *Bayonet*, relatively safe.

"I only have nine left out of my two boarding teams," he replied. "Even if I had the rest of them, that's hardly enough to . . ."

Enough to what? Storm a station on the surface of a planet only a thousand people had ever set foot on? He couldn't ask them to do that. Blayne would volunteer, of course, and the others would likely follow, but . . .

"Does Ms. Frazer know what the security situation is there?" Ahn asked. "It might not take much to slip in and slip out."

"I'm assuming it's light, since it's not as though they have outsiders coming and going, but we'll see what she knows." Josiah gnawed on the inside of his cheek. "But I'm not sure a light security presence makes much difference when you're dealing with a thousand . . . uh, near-immortal scientists."

"Near-immortal scientists." Ahn stared at his hands, then blinked. "You realize how this report is going to sound, don't you?"

Josiah exhaled.

Oh, yes. He knew.

And he knew what would come afterward, too.

They would take *Bayonet* away from him once he told them what had happened on Etrik, that much was for sure. They would question his mental status, his fitness for command—not just that, but for duty, period. But wasn't that what he'd wanted for the past year? Zero responsibility? No power of life or death over anyone under him? The enforced inability to foul things up as badly as he had aboard *Vigilant*?

They would question his mental status . . .

His muscles tensed, and suddenly his quarters, which had been his sanctuary on this patrol, seemed smaller than usual. Why hadn't he put two and two together before now? Of course they would believe him—but they'd also never admit it.

"Somehow," he began slowly, "I think they might find it more credible than either you or I would like to believe."

"I'm sorry?" Confusion splashed across Ahn's face. "You've lost me now."

Josiah stood, if only to keep his foot from tapping the deck. "Do me a favor—can you call Hope in here?"

Ahn's forehead creased. "I'm more than willing, but why can't you?"

A weak laugh escaped as he leaned against the bulkhead. "Just humor me."

"For the love of all that's holy and decent." Ahn burst into laughter as he tapped at his wrist. "You need to make certain she knows it's not a date, don't you?"

Despite the revelation whirling in his mind, Josiah smiled. "Has anyone told you it's improper to read minds?"

"Part of the job description, I might remind you." It was Ahn's turn to scoff. "But if you keep questioning my soft skills, you'll find out how useless I am without them." He cleared his throat. "She's on her way. Care to give me the advance explanation of what's going on here?"

"I already told you." Certainty weighed down his shoulders. "Before we even left Mars. Remember? I mentioned how odd it was that the three of us had finally ended up on the same ship. And you—"

"Called you paranoid, even though every single person aboard *Bayonet* is still healthy and happy and not dead of liver failure. Well, perhaps not happy, but we can pretend that much." Ahn let out a long thread of vulgarity. "This was a setup. But how?"

"Damned if I know." Josiah ran his hands over his face again as a knock echoed on the door. He needed to shave again, but shaving seemed like an insignificant waste of time now. "Let her in."

Hope stepped inside and looked between them, her curiosity turning to something else in an instant.

"Did I miss something?" she asked.

"Oh, yes, I would say you missed something," he replied without any warmup. She raised her brows at his acerbic tone, so he hurried on.

"Though to be fair, so did everyone else. You, me, Patrick, all aboard *Bayonet* together. Strange, isn't it?"

"Of course." Her brows drew together. "I suppose. But I stopped questioning things like this a long time ago. There's really no point in focusing on bizarre coincidences or orders that seem illogical, especially where the Orbital Guard is involved. I'd lose my mind if I allowed myself to have reservations about circumstances that don't make sense."

Ahn chuckled. "I always told you she was smarter than us."

"That's why she's saner than us, too." Josiah frowned at her. "Except it's not a coincidence, Hope."

"I see." Her green eyes, bewildered and exhausted, flickered between the two of them. "Look, I've been up for eighteen hours now, so if this is that important, could you just—"

"Liver failure," Ahn broke in. "None of us are dead of it, even though something in the second to last wormhole seems to precipitate it in those of us who don't have a certain mutated gene."

"A gene that, according to our survivor, only five percent of humans possess," Josiah added.

"Which means the odds are astronomical that everyone aboard *Bayonet* has it," Hope murmured, her calculating eyes focusing on the deck. "I'd go so far as to say impossible, even. Which means someone had to make sure the crew was hand-selected, not for any kind of skill that might be needed for a mission like this, but for their genetic makeup."

"Bingo." Josiah pointed at her. "Who that might have been is irrelevant right now, I suppose, but it means I have zero ethical, moral, or professional obligation to follow through with their plans for us."

"Plans that involved us ending up in those blood-sucking capsules down on the surface, I assume," Ahn added.

"No doubt."

Rage built inside of him. He had known from the beginning, over twenty years ago, that he was risking his life doing this mission in deep space. Everyone on board *Bayonet* had known the same, and yet . . . and yet none of them had signed up for *this*. Someone had just used their willingness to volunteer to condemn Graham and half of

Raider 2 to a fate that had shaken Coralie Frazer so badly she had cried while detailing it for him, and he couldn't leave any of that unpunished. But right now there were, unfortunately, more immediate problems than dealing with a conspirator—or, God forbid, *conspirators*—in the Orbital Guard back on Mars.

Hope exhaled. "We can't leave them down there."

"No," Josiah replied. That much was clear now. He hadn't needed Ahn's counsel after all. At least, his subconscious hadn't. "We can't, and we won't."

"Then what's your plan?" She exchanged a look with Ahn—one that was indecipherable, even for him.

A frantic heat washed over him. Even in his wildest nightmares, rescuing hostages from a research station hadn't so much as flitted into his mind when *Bayonet* had departed Mars, and he hated himself for that shortsightedness—a liability no cutter captain should be allowed to possess. Perhaps the swiftness of *Vigilant*'s emergency had been a gift from on high, for he doubted he'd have made the same decision if he'd had a few days to think about it.

His chest tightened, a sensation he was growing rather tired of. Did that mean everyone else had been right? Hope, the doctors, that insufferable chaplain, everyone else who'd praised his actions that day. That he hadn't personally sentenced seventeen of *Vigilant*'s crew to death but had saved untold more by undocking her when he had?

You deserve it. You need to believe that. Unless you can, things will never get better for you.

Hope's admonition lingered in his mind as he stared at her.

"I don't know yet," he said. "But I'll figure out something."

CHAPTER THIRTY-TWO_
USOGC BAYONET, ETRIK ORBIT

Coralie took a step inside the compartment McArthur had motioned her into, then stopped. Another starship, another bare room, the bulkheads sterile and white and unforgiving. This one was larger than her quarters on Nimbus Station—also larger than the compartment aboard *Triumph* where Kinnard had left her—and *definitely* larger than the brig aboard *Bayonet*. Even so, it made her feel shuttled about, like a problem they had and didn't know what to do with.

Well, that wasn't quite true, because it was obvious they knew exactly what to do with her. Rows of empty bunks set back into the bulkhead stretched farther than her muddled brain could count right now, crisp blue blankets folded atop each. She'd wondered if and where *Bayonet* had space for more than a small starship's worth of people they might run across, and here was the answer, complete with groupings of empty tables in the narrow space between each side of beds that might have seemed prisonlike in any other circumstance.

But on second thought . . .

She dropped her clean jumpsuit to the bunk nearest the door. "I suppose I shouldn't be surprised you have space for me."

"And a hundred of your closest friends." Hackett stepped inside behind her.

"A hundred?"

"Give or take." He leaned against the bulkhead and shrugged. "Not that it's meant for long-term accommodations. It would give anyone claustrophobia."

Coralie stared down the aisle, trying to focus on the bulkhead at the opposite end. The emergency berthing seemed to take up the entire length of the ship, and though it was narrow, claustrophobic wasn't what she would call such a large space.

"It's . . ." How could she phrase it without sounding ungrateful? "You probably won't believe me when I say this, but it's almost too large after being on the surface. I feel as though I might float away all the way to the bow."

"Nimbus Station isn't known for its luxurious quarters, huh?" McArthur asked.

The blood drained from Coralie's cheeks until she was certain she blended into the bulkhead, and McArthur swore under her breath.

"Dammit. I didn't mean—"

"Still hard to believe, isn't it?" Coralie sank to the bunk. "Sometimes I wonder if it was a nightmare, but—"

"But it wasn't." Hackett sighed. "Sorry. Didn't mean to interrupt. Just didn't want you to feel the need to justify yourself again."

Coralie didn't doubt he'd seen worse. At the very least, there hadn't been bodies floating throughout *Triumph*'s corridors. But there was also, she knew, something ordinary about a human being who had died in a most typical manner in space—and that there was nothing mundane about what Hackett and his team had seen in that compartment there.

"I appreciate that." She couldn't help a yawn. "It's nice to have someone finally believe me."

"It's not that no one believed you." McArthur unlocked a cabinet across from her and stared inside, then yanked out a fabric bag. "Toiletries. Shower is down the passage and to the right. There are instructions printed on the bulkhead, but if you have trouble, just hit the comm." She glanced at her wrist comm, then handed the bag to Coralie. "Blayne's looking for me. If you need anything . . ."

"I'll let someone know." Coralie rubbed her eyes, and when she looked up, McArthur had vanished. "I didn't mean to make her uncomfortable," she said to Hackett.

He waved a hand. "She'll get over it. Everyone steps on toes sometimes, and I promise you she'll have forgotten about it by the time you see her again."

"Good." A yawn threatened to split her face, even as she tried to suppress it.

"You tired?"

"I should be, shouldn't I? But I don't think I could sleep right now if I tried."

"Adrenaline."

A laugh escaped. "Yeah. Enough of it for the rest of my life, I'd say."

"Hungry?"

"Hungry is the one thing I'm not." She narrowed her eyes at him—he hadn't moved from the position against the bulkhead. "Really, I'm fine. You don't need to coddle me."

"It's not coddling. Okay, maybe a little," he replied with a grin. "But you can't blame me."

"Because I had a flashback?"

"Because if I wasn't down here fussing over you, I'd be up above doing . . . well, something much less desirable."

Coralie gave him a friendly scoff. "Like what?"

"Er . . . swabbing the deck?"

"It's a starship, Hackett." She rolled her eyes. "Water tends to break things."

He raised a brow. "Ethan."

"Excuse me?"

"It's Ethan."

She blinked at him. It was nothing more than a name, but no one on Nimbus Station had invited her into their life in such a fashion. Even Riley, as superficially approachable as she'd become, had kept her distance somehow. Down there, they all knew what Coralie was, that her purpose on the station was utilitarian only, and they would never forget it.

Take a breath.

"It's a starship, Ethan." She burst into laughter at the idea of him washing a metal deck, then sobered. "How did you know what happened to me aboard *Triumph*? That I was having a flashback?"

Hackett pushed himself off the bulkhead and settled onto the bunk beside her. "A while back—well, it doesn't matter what happened. Not really. But I learned enough about trauma reactions and how to handle them." He swallowed. "What did it for you?"

"Plastic tubing," she whispered to the deck. "Floating around in that cabin, and running through *Triumph*'s bulkheads, and attached to this cursed port." She yanked her jumpsuit down, and heat filled her eyes as she drew her thumb across the plastic. "Every time I see it, I think I'm back in that capsule."

"That's got to be hard."

The words sounded flippant on the surface, would be to anyone as cynical as she'd become, but his tone was anything but as he took her hand in his and tugged it away from her collarbone. Coralie expected him to let go, but his grip tightened, and before she knew what she was doing, she was clinging to him. His touch wasn't sexual or even romantic—though she would never deny how attractive he was—but more of a declaration.

You're human. And I see you.

"Yeah," she replied, dissolving into tears against his shoulder. "It is."

For a long time, Hackett was silent, holding her as she shook. She supposed she should have felt like a fool, but the embrace was mutual, and as his heart beat against her, real and undefiled and organic, she didn't care that she'd broken apart in front of another person. Because someone had finally seen her as just that: a person.

"How about we see if the corpsman can remove that tomorrow?" he asked as her sobs faded. "I have no idea what's possible and what's not, so no promises, but there's no reason we can't at least try, right?"

Coralie drew her first steady breath in what seemed like forever and nodded. "That would be perfect."

* * *

Etrik almost filled the floor-to-ceiling window in *Bayonet*'s aft observation deck, so much like Mars it made Coralie's soul ache. All this way, and yet some things were so familiar she couldn't help wondering if they'd transported into another reality instead of another part of the galaxy. But when she focused on the surface, the canyons were all wrong, and the red of Etrik was just different enough from Mars that it brought her current situation into sharp relief. This was not Mars, and she would not be returning to her flat on the surface anytime soon.

"It's rather lonely, isn't it?" Blayne leaned against the bulkhead beside her and handed over a cup of tea.

"I thought it would be an adventure." Coralie inhaled the tea but didn't take a sip. They'd been over-hospitable with the food and drink for the past six hours, and she wasn't sure her body could handle another ounce. "Not a nightmare."

"They got the port out all right, though?"

"They did." She shuddered. In the end, it hadn't been so bad physically, just a few injections of painkillers and some ice packs afterward. But her mind had wandered over and over to that day Kinnard had removed the tubes from her thighs, and it had only been Hackett's presence that had calmed her enough to go through with the procedure. "But it shouldn't have been inside me in the first place, and that part of it was all my fault."

"We all make mistakes."

"Like this one?" Her lip curled upward. "I doubt that you've done anything as reckless as I did in coming to Etrik."

In believing all the lies.

"You'd be surprised," he replied. "Though I suppose some of our choices have worse outcomes than others."

"Oh? You sound like you know what you're talking about."

Blayne chuckled. "I was young once and pretty irresponsible. You, at least, had the excuse of wanting to make a better future for humanity."

She turned and gave him an unforced smile. "Do tell."

"You'll think less of me."

"I doubt anything you could tell me would make me think less of you."

"Well, then." He cracked his knuckles. "When I was seventeen, and living on Deimos, I hung out with the wrong crowd."

Coralie shrugged. "That happens."

"Sure does. But this crowd liked guns."

Her jaw dropped. "You killed someone?"

"No." His eyes crinkled in amusement. "But one day we found an airlock with a busted alarm—exactly the thing you don't want a bunch of nosy kids to find. We stole some pressure suits, which was child's play on an airless moon where they're a dime a dozen, then climbed on out and secured ourselves to the roof of the habitat."

Coralie glanced out the door, but they were still alone. "Should you be talking about this here?"

"Please." Friendly mockery laced the word. "As though I'm the only one on board to have done something like this. Anyway, Deimos Organization was in the process of decommissioning a commercial port that hadn't been used in a few years—problem was, not all the owners had heeded the order to get their ships out of there, and a half dozen were still moored there up above, empty."

"You didn't," she breathed.

"Hell, yeah." Blayne glanced toward the door. "Shot every single one full of laser and bullet holes. They never figured out who did it, but we were the talk of the station for a long time."

"I bet you were."

"And you better believe the owners got their ships out of there in a hurry afterward. We were practically heroes. But I was already committed to the Orbital Guard, even though it was tough to leave Deimos afterward."

Coralie laughed. "They probably limit what you can shoot at, don't they?"

"Fortunately. But I love space. It grounded me, in an odd way. You can screw up on the surface, even on a bare moon like Deimos, but space forces you to sit up, watch what's really going on, and think about your actions prior to doing them. Mistakes will get you killed. It was what I needed, and I suppose I got used to it."

"Definitely dumber than signing up to work on Nimbus Station. And possibly even less legal than what I agreed to." She looked out the window. Now that people knew what she was, people with law enforcement authority, she would have to answer for it. Someone had to, and it would never be the doctors or the NSRC.

"I doubt you'll end up in much trouble for that," he replied. "And if you do, you have a bunch of people ready to speak for you."

Coralie shrugged. It was pretend to not care or tear up. "Even after I shot at you?"

Boots resonated throughout the observation deck before Blayne could reply, and she blinked before greeting the owner—O'Donnell, of course. He had, she was learning, a talent for showing up at the most inopportune times.

"You win," he said to Blayne, after a curt nod in her direction. "I'm authorizing a team to the surface to verify the status of *Triumph*'s shuttle and survey the area. We need to find out if the individuals on board headed for Nimbus Station or somewhere else."

"They're headed to the surface?" Coralie interrupted before Blayne could reply. Her pulse began to race. "Then I want to go along."

"I can't allow that."

"You have to let me, because I'm going."

O'Donnell made a derisive sound. "It's my operation, so I can certainly say no, and I am."

"You sent me onto *Triumph* with them, and I don't see the difference between that and this. What if they need me?"

He hesitated, and she realized that had a been a mistake to him. One he wouldn't make again.

"They won't need you, like they didn't end up needing you aboard *Triumph,* and my duty is to keep you safe, not to send you down to a planet where every single inhabitant wants to lock you in a cage for the rest of your life."

"Might I remind you they want to do the same thing to you and your crew, Captain." She swallowed. "And yet you and they are taking that risk."

Blayne cleared his throat.

O'Donnell shot him a look. "That's their job."

"Great. Which means they volunteered, just like me."

His shoulders sank. "That's different, Ms. Frazer."

"You know it's not."

The observation deck went silent, and though she hadn't known him long, Coralie was certain he was debating with himself—and that she would win. She had to win. This was her fight, not theirs. Well, partly theirs, but only out of obligation.

His gaze didn't leave hers. "You'll follow all of Master Chief Blayne's instructions to the letter."

"Yes."

"And you realize the risk inherent with letting you tag along?"

"Yes." Coralie raised her brows. She knew more than anyone. "Of course."

O'Donnell shook his head and muttered something under his breath. "Take her along, then. Just try not to lose her, okay?"

"Aye aye, Captain."

Coralie clenched her hands by her sides to keep from clapping as Blayne led her through another maze of corridors. "He didn't really want to let me go, did he?"

Blayne pointed, and they turned another corner. "He feels responsible for your safety. Is responsible for your safety, I suppose."

A chill ran down her back as they entered Bay A. "He doesn't think we'll come back, does he?"

He glanced sideways at her. "What makes you think that?"

"If we don't, no one will ever know what happened to me, and his conscience—and record—will be clean."

"His record, perhaps, but not his conscience." Blayne stopped her inside the door and lowered his voice. "This isn't the first crisis he's dealt with nor the first people he's lost. Though unlike before, he may still salvage this mission, given enough luck and time and grace from the God he worships."

"What happened before?"

"Just prior to taking command of *Bayonet*, he was the XO on a cutter out of Mars. At the start of the last patrol before he was to return home, a terrorist group rammed them in port with a skiff full of explosives. O'Donnell was on the bridge, called for them to undock. Killed seventeen when the ship fell from the clamps, but saved even more. He spent a long time in the hospital . . . this is his first assignment back. He won't risk his people unnecessarily. Nor his conscience, which is battered enough as it is."

"Wow." It explained a lot about him—or at least, she suspected it did. At the very least, she felt compassion for him slipping in.

"All that to say"—Blayne pointed her toward a cabinet on the port bulkhead and yanked out a pressure suit—"don't get lost. I'd hate to be the one to tell him."

"I won't." Coralie took the suit. It was heavier than the one Nimbus Station had provided, and that was reassuring. "We're leaving now?"

"Before he changes his mind, yes. It's a little trick I've learned over the years." He grabbed a suit for himself and pointed toward the group hovering on the other side of the bay, handing out weapons and laughing. "Put it on and meet us over at the boat when you're done."

Coralie did what he asked, her heart and pacemaker thumping and skipping and overcompensating the entire time. Memories of walking on the surface with Riley Shaw came to mind again and again, and by the time she'd zipped up her suit and grabbed a helmet, she was sweating. Had she put a hole in this one, too?

Not useful.

She ignored the building anxiety and headed toward the boat. It wasn't as frightening this time, though she wondered if anyone else had qualms about walking in the low oxygen dust of Etrik. McArthur's usually placid expression was tight, and Sprenger's grip on his rifle was tense, but their apprehension could have been from anything.

"You talked the old man into it, Master Chief." Hackett slapped her on the shoulder and looked her up and down, from her boots to the helmet under her arm. "Who'd have thought?"

"Must have caught him in a weak moment." Blayne tossed a few metal crates into the boat's cargo area and nodded at them. "He made me promise not to lose her, so don't lose her, okay?"

"We'll try," Hackett replied. Blayne gave him a look, and he cleared his throat. "Don't lose the engineer, aye, Master Chief."

"Good. Now get inside. You, too," he added to Coralie. "I wasn't joking about him changing his mind, and we need to be off before he does."

He probably wasn't wrong about O'Donnell, but she hesitated. "Will Nimbus Station see us coming?"

"Unlikely." Blayne shook his head and headed onto the boat. "It doesn't appear they have the sensors to do so," he called over his shoulder. "And weapons are even more unlikely."

"But Kinnard knew to head up to orbit and manually trigger the distress signal to lure you and your ship closer into the system." Her breath grew short.

"Maybe." When she didn't move, he took a few steps back toward her. "Look, let's cross that bridge when and if we come to it, all right? Him knowing we're around might work out for the best, anyway."

"Yeah." Coralie's shoulders relaxed, though she didn't know why. "You're right."

She followed him onto the boat on legs that felt like they might collapse. But as she harnessed herself in between Blayne and Hackett and yanked on her helmet, reality seeped through her, from her head to her icy toes.

Kinnard would pay for what he'd done.

Somehow, she would make him pay.

CHAPTER THIRTY-THREE_
ETRIK

R‍ED DUST FLEW INTO THE AIR AS THE BOAT SETTLED on the ground, momentarily obscuring Coralie's view outside. The engines became powered down, and as the landscape cleared, she took what seemed like her first breath in hours. Through the forward window, sharp cliffs edged the canyon where *Triumph*'s shuttle had supposedly crashed, and through the window across from where she sat, a mountain rose in the distance, all but blocking out the weak sun.

"The goal here is to confirm the survival of the shuttle." Blayne adjusted something on his rifle. "And determine if any man-made structures exist that might provide shelter to whoever was on board. We're not going to go far—Peyer, you, McArthur, and Sprenger go north. Hackett and

Stephens, you're with me. You too, Ms. Frazer. I want everyone back in fifteen minutes."

"Report back?" Sprenger asked.

"Back. As in, boots standing inside this ship."

There was a chorus of agreement, and the four others trudged off. Coralie took a careful step onto the red dirt, all too conscious of the last time she'd stood on Etrik's surface. Blayne wouldn't lead them that far from the boat and its lifesaving oxygen, but then, she hadn't been that far from Nimbus Station when her suit had failed before.

And about Helena? Don't trust her.

Riley's words echoed in her mind as she followed behind Hackett, swiveling her head from side to side. This part of the planet was desolate and rough compared to the wide, flat plain on which the research station sat. Here, boulders slowed their pace, and jagged, sedimentary bluffs hid the expansive view in the distance.

"Wreckage should be a hundred yards in front of us," Blayne said. They were the first words he'd said since stepping off the boat. "Unless it's buried in dust."

As if challenging him, a dust devil whirled up, covering Coralie's helmet.

"It's that easy?" she asked under her breath before realizing it was the radio transmission he'd wanted to cut short.

"No." He turned briefly, flashing her a self-effacing smile. "Well, yes, if there's absolutely no man-made ground clutter, the atmospheric conditions are just right, and we don't care about using sensors that are banned by a dozen countries. We wouldn't have gotten such an accurate fix on Mars, for example."

"You intentionally degrade your capabilities?"

"Have to," Stephens broke in. "China won't allow ground surveillance by the Allies inside Jupiter, and even in the outer system, there are still enough legal restrictions and spacecraft to make it difficult."

"That's all academic, since we haven't actually found the shuttle yet. Coordinates are meaningless unless we find the wreckage." Blayne checked his wrist computer. "That's five minutes."

Coralie's left foot caught a rock, and she stumbled forward. Hackett caught her at the last minute.

"You'll rip that suit doing that," he warned.

"I know." She shrugged off his help and scanned her gloves for cuts. "But it's happened before, and I survived."

"Yeah?"

"That's enough chatter," Blayne's voice cut in. "Just over that rise, keep an eye out. We're running short on time."

The gloves looked to be intact, so Coralie scrambled up the boulders behind Hackett, not daring to hope. *Bayonet* had been high above the planet and though there was no metal or anything else synthetic lying about, there were plenty of boulders and cliffs and—

Her throat closed up as she crested the rise.

—and an orbital shuttle, sitting in the shadow of a large overhang.

"Peyer." Blayne's call was curt as he typed a rapid stream of numbers into his wrist computer. "I'm sending you coordinates. Get over here and be ready to drop a beacon."

"On the way."

Blayne looked toward her. "That's it?"

"That's it." She rocked back on her heels. "Is there anyone inside?"

Stephens squinted at her own computer. "Unlikely, but with as much shielding as it has, we can't tell from here. Master Chief?"

"We'll have to assume it's occupied." Blayne licked his lips, suddenly reminding Coralie how dry the air inside her helmet was. Rocks scattered behind them, and he turned toward the other four approaching. "Spread out. You—" This to her. "Find a boulder."

Coralie gave him a thumbs-up sign and plodded behind the nearest large rock, one that looked like it would protect her from gunfire or worse. Sitting was out the question in the suit that prevented her from doing anything as physical as squatting, but as long as she kept her legs stretched out, she could lounge under a smaller rock behind it. It wasn't the most flattering position, but her muscles were screaming for any kind of rest.

The team went silent as soon as she disappeared behind the boulder, and she craned her neck, trying to hear anything they might be saying or doing. But radio silence apparently meant strict radio silence, and even their boots had faded away into the howl of the wind and the constant hissing of air inside her helmet.

Well, they would confirm what they'd found inside the shuttle soon enough—and yet somehow, she already knew they'd find it empty. Why would Kinnard fake a crash only to be sitting inside once the Orbital Guard reached it? No, he and *Bayonet*'s missing crewmembers were long gone. To where was the question.

A loud bang echoed through the canyon, and after she stopped flinching, Coralie risked a look between the boulders toward the shuttle. She couldn't even identify them as individuals from this distance, but their raised rifles and the way they slunk inside meant business, there was no doubt about that.

It was too hard to keep from asking what was happening inside, and even though she was nearly certain they'd cut her from the communications, she turned away from the shuttle, desperate for something else to focus on. It wasn't difficult, because even though she'd already spent months on Etrik, this kind of freedom was unheard of, even during her little expedition with Riley.

Dust whipped up again, obscuring the shuttle, and she drew calculus equations into the sand with her glove, pretending she was here as a visitor. Someone who would be shown around to all the interesting compartments on Nimbus Station, fed decent food, and then whisked back up to space and back to Mars when the time was right.

Her fingers hit a sharp rock, and her throat closed as she yanked her glove in front of her helmet to check the seams. Nothing appeared broken, but she took a shallow breath as she checked her wrist computer for the suit's status.

Nominal.

Well, at least something had gone right. She moved to brush the offending rock away with a larger one, just in case. The dust had settled, and when she squinted down at the ground—

Metal?

It had to be something that had fallen off the shuttle. Carefully, Coralie edged off the rock where she'd been sitting and settled to the ground beside it. The latest dust storm must have been violent before they'd arrived, for the shiny material was covered in almost ten centimeters of red dirt.

Forgetting the helmet for just long enough, she blew on the metal, then glanced around to make sure no one had seen her foolishness. But the sound of dead space on the comm line still overwhelmed her, so she swiped the dirt to the side.

Heat bubbled up from her core.

It wasn't metal, or at least not metal from the shuttle. Three hinges lay flush with the ground, and a lock flashed red on the opposite side.

A warning rose in her throat, but she bit her lip to keep silent. Blayne was supposed to have muted her, but she couldn't risk distracting them if Kinnard or anyone else was still inside that shuttle.

Silly.

Because no one was inside that shuttle anymore. They'd all gone underground now.

"Blayne," she called quietly. "Sorry to interrupt, but I'm guessing that shuttle's empty."

Static crackled in her ear before he replied.

"How did you—" He appeared over her shoulder before she could answer, Hackett on his heels. "Well, damn."

Coralie stood, though not nearly as gracefully as she might have wished. "We're several kilometers from Nimbus Station, though. I can't imagine they walked the entire way there underground."

Like moles.

"It could be another station altogether." Hackett hoisted his rifle on his shoulder, and she wondered how he could be so blasé about that kind of weight resting on his pressure suit. "Or something that predates the NSRC expedition."

Blayne nudged the hatch with his boot. "I'm not sure that's the reassurance you mean it to be, actually."

"It's not aliens. It's NSRC." Coralie suppressed a sigh of relief as she pointed. "The lights there, they're typical of Nimbus Station security systems. And NSRC facilities on Mars, for that matter."

"Which we've probably tripped by now." Stephens appeared on her other side.

"I don't—I don't think so. Not yet, at least." Coralie stared at it. "If we tried to open it, perhaps it might send a signal back to Nimbus Station. But a proximity alarm would be unlikely . . . it's just not something I've ever seen before."

"And you're that familiar with Nimbus Station's security?" Stephens sounded doubtful. "I thought you spent most of your time locked up."

"Yes." Coralie forced away the memories. "Once Kinnard let me out, I settled into the position I would have had if things hadn't gone the way they did—fire protection. I had free run of the station, almost. Believe me, I'm very familiar with how they're providing security."

"Well, everyone's curiosity will have to wait," Blayne said. "We're not going to open it now."

"Why not?"

"Yeah, Master Chief," Hackett parroted. "Why not?"

"Let me count the reasons: cameras, security, no plan, and oh, yeah—a bunch of scientists with little to lose." Blayne ticked each one off. "We'll come back when we're better prepared."

"Doesn't get much more prepared than this," Stephens replied. "And look at this." He held out a scanner. "Four heartbeats down there. We can take them."

Dust flew into the air as a crackly silence settled between the group.

"Peyer, where are you?" Blayne glanced at his wrist computer.

"At the boat," came the reply. "You find the shuttle?"

"And something even more interesting. I'm sending you the coordinates now—meet us here as soon as possible."

"We're going inside?" Coralie's heart skipped a beat, followed by the punch of the pacemaker.

"Unless I want a revolt on my hands, it appears we are." Blayne shook his head in feigned disapproval, but she could see the hidden enthusiasm there. "Sprenger, grab the camera. We'll look before we open that hatch."

"Already got it." Sprenger sidled in between her and Blayne, Peyer and McArthur next to him. "What's this?"

"Hatch." Hackett knelt and held out his hand. "She says it looks like NSRC equipment. Master Chief thinks it's Nimbus Station property, but I think it might be aliens. You know, I once saw a vid-program about—"

"Mmm." Sprenger crouched beside him and brushed the never-ending dust away. "I like that idea better."

"Shut up, Sprenger." Blayne coughed. "Just get that camera through and see what's inside."

Sprenger set the end of the flexible cable in Hackett's hand, then pulled a small drill from his pocket.

"You're going to put a hole in it?" Coralie asked.

"We'll plug it when we're done, and they won't be any the wiser." McArthur shrugged. "Can't just barge in a small hatch like this without knowing what's on the other side."

The drill spun against the metal, albeit silently, and Coralie's cheeks flushed, despite the cool air in her helmet. McArthur sounded confident enough, but this was Etrik, not Mars. It wasn't even Uranus or its moons, and that, she suspected, was the most hostile environment they'd dealt with before now. And they knew what might be on the other side of that hatch, didn't they?

"That was thin enough. I'm through." Sprenger set the drill in the red dirt. Drifting dust immediately covered it.

"It isn't as though they need protection from the elements." Coralie took a step back, as though Kinnard might smell her through the pinhole. "I suppose they just don't want dust filling up whatever's down there."

"We'll be fast enough that it won't." Hackett's jaw tightened as he threaded the camera through the hole. "Okay, flip it on," he added, nodding at Sprenger.

The screen in Sprenger's gloved hand lit up, revealing a gray corridor that could have been ripped straight from Nimbus Station itself. Below the hatch, a set of narrow, low stairs led to a steel floor that headed south, toward where *Triumph*'s shuttle was parked. No one was visible, and the floor was devoid of red dust, which likely meant no one had been down here lately.

"That corner at the end," Blayne said under his breath. "Will the camera reach?"

"Let me try." Hackett fed it along the ceiling, toward a hallway that was illuminated as though from an inside source. "Too short, I think."

"Wait." Sprenger pointed at this screen. "There's a door at the end. Closed, appears to be locked, judging by the lights."

"A door," Coralie murmured. "I don't suppose you can drill your way through that one?" she asked Hackett.

"No," he replied, finessing the camera a few centimeters farther. "But I can take some pictures, at least."

"We'll head down and check it out."

Her head swiveled toward Blayne.

"What? Four individuals aren't impossible to subdue, and that door inside just gave us an extra measure of surprise."

She wanted to argue, but Hackett was already drawing the camera back up through the hole. Stephens handed him a silicone cap, and he pressed it against the metal, sealing the hatch once more.

"There," he said. "Might not hold forever, but I don't particularly care."

No, she couldn't imagine that they cared. Especially since they were about to—what? Pry it open? Unlock it? Shoot holes in it until it was damaged enough to walk through?

Peyer waved behind him. "Okay, everyone, time to back up."

The order was so abrupt that Coralie took a step backward without checking behind her. Her ankle twisted on a rock, and by the time she caught her balance and tested her weight again, the hatch was lying on its side.

"How did you do that?"

"Secrets." Hackett wriggled his fingers at her. "Pay more attention to where you're stepping next time, and you might find out."

Coralie narrowed her eyes at him.

"Enough jokes." Blayne's rifle was pointed toward the dark hole that gaped where the hatch had once been. "Let's get a move on."

"Wait." She stepped toward him, suddenly noticing how the sun had dropped closer to the mountains in the distance. "You can't leave me here."

"Oh, I don't plan to." With a fluid movement, he unholstered his sidearm and held it out in front of him. "You know how to use this, I assume?"

"I think I can figure it out." Coralie's fingers closed around the grip. Had he both forgotten and forgiven her for shooting at the other team? "But we still don't know if this will stop them."

He lifted a shoulder. "I guess we have to figure that out at some point, don't we?" He nodded at her and disappeared down the stairs, leaving her standing on the surface with Hackett and Stephens.

"Ready?" Stephens asked.

Coralie nodded at her, took a step toward the hole, then froze. If Kinnard was down there—if anyone was down there—would she react like she had aboard *Triumph*? Then she would become a liability, and she couldn't be a liability. She was supposed to be *saving* people, not getting in the way.

"We can wait," Hackett added.

"No." Coralie shook her head. "I don't need to wait."

She gathered all her courage and stepped onto the stairs, propelling a cloud of dust into the passageway below. Blayne and Peyer and the others were already turning the corner, but she leaned against the wall and closed her eyes as Stephens and Hackett passed by her to meet up with the others.

The sound of a door creaking seeped through her helmet, followed by shouts. Coralie stepped around the corner and blinked. Whatever was past the door was only barely lit, but the lights on their helmets danced across the far wall, enough to illuminate—

She retched inside her helmet.

Illuminating a row of capsules.

CHAPTER THIRTY-FOUR_
USOGC BAYONET, ETRIK ORBIT

ETRIK'S STAR PEEKED OVER THE PLANET'S HORIZON once more through the bridge's forward window. Josiah had almost forgotten what such brilliance could look like. On Mars, the Sun was smaller than Luna was from Earth, and he'd pretty much forgotten that now, too.

What he hadn't forgotten was how his crew was dwindling. Four on the surface somewhere—or worse, dead. Coralie Frazer had assured him death wasn't in Nimbus Station's plans, but the fact was, they'd all been lured here for their blood. Yes, she'd said that was Thomas Kinnard's plan all along, and he mostly believed it now, but who knew what could have gone wrong down there?

Blayne and his team hadn't reported in, but that wasn't unusual—or so he told himself. The dust storms that seemed to kick up on Etrik's surface had a tendency to degrade handheld communications beyond use, and the team hadn't been gone long enough to worry. Worry was all he had now, though. Well, to be technical, he had a whole lot of worry and an entire suite of high-powered comm equipment that wouldn't have any trouble reaching Nimbus Station itself. And it was time.

"Comm, see if you can raise Nimbus Station." He wet his lips. "Put it on my console when they answer."

If they answer.

"Aye aye, Captain."

He was beginning to doubt they would, but if that was the case, he had every right to send a team down there. Just to check on things. Just to make sure something catastrophic hadn't happened. *Bayonet* was well outside the Orbital Guard's physical jurisdiction, but Nimbus Station was still an American facility, and not a soul would criticize him for making sure everything was safe down there.

"Nimbus Station, this is the US Orbital Guard cutter *Bayonet*, how do you hear?" The comm operator cleared his throat. "If you can read this, reply on 2085.68." He repeated it three times; nothing but silence answered.

"No answer, Captain."

"Keep at it." His jaw tightened. "Their comm station might ordinarily be unmanned." It was probably wishful thinking, but he didn't really care anymore if they answered or not. If nothing else, they'd eventually tire of the calls and answer—or their continued silence would give him even more of a reason to search the station.

"Unmanned, huh?" Ahn edged beside him.

"It would make sense." Josiah rubbed the back of his neck. "Who would they be expecting?"

"They did send a probe," Ahn said.

"Sure. Which wasn't actually sent with the most honorable of intentions, I might remind you."

Ahn tapped the edge of Josiah's console. "What do you plan to say if they answer?"

What, indeed?

"Well, I'd planned to start by asking how they weren't aware that *Triumph* was orbiting right above them. Then I figured I'd ask if their emergency equipment is up to date. And then . . . I suppose I thought I would end things by demanding to know where my missing crew is."

"So there is a plan."

"No." Josiah glanced at him and shrugged. "But I'm glad I did a good job at pretending."

"I'm sorry, Captain, but we're receiving a reply."

He shot Ahn a grin. "Send it over."

"*Bayonet*, Nimbus Station security here," the voice from the surface was saying. "I think there's been some sort of miscommunication . . ."

The rest of the transmission was garbled and broken, but the audio delay was short, so he took a breath and said the first words that came to mind.

"Nimbus Station, you sent a probe reporting one of your transports overdue and requesting assistance. We have an obligation to investigate the call. Now, if there was some sort of mistake, we can discuss it."

Ahn cleared his throat in a *good luck* sound Josiah knew all too well.

"*Bayonet* . . ." Another long crackle. "The probe was sent mistakenly, and *Triumph*'s passengers and crew are here on-station as planned. We're sorry for the misunderstanding, but again, there is no emergency. *Triumph* came into comm range shortly after the probe was deployed, and we were unable to recall it. Everyone is safe on the surface."

Josiah leaned back in his chair and shrugged at Ahn. "Interesting claim. I can't imagine how they believe we'd buy it."

"Desperation, maybe," Ahn replied. "Or a lackey who doesn't know we've already been aboard their ship. Or that Ms. Frazer has told us everything that's going on down there."

"Suspicious and completely illegal is what I'd call it." He keyed the mic again. "Nimbus Station, we'll be sending a team down to confirm."

"Negative." A woman's voice came on the line, harried and rushed. "This facility is limited to National Space Research Council personnel, and we will take appropriate measures to ensure its security if forced."

Josiah snorted out loud, drawing looks. "Unacceptable, Nimbus Station. Per 72 USC 522(a) you are subject to inspection. You have twelve hours to be ready for our arrival."

"We will file a complaint with your superiors."

"Your objection is noted." *And subsequently ignored.* "I'll see you in twelve hours." He muted the audio once more and turned to Ahn. "I don't get it. If they want us for their little science experiment, why the pushback? You'd think they'd be dying to get more people down there."

"Sounds like they're in over their heads, and their best-laid plans are going awry. Or maybe this scheme is on a need-to-know basis and the comm people don't know."

"Possibly." Josiah yawned. "Let's get some air."

Ahn followed him dutifully off the bridge, but Josiah leaned against the bulkhead just outside the door instead of continuing to a compartment that might give him more breathing room.

"Blayne's still on the surface as of an hour ago," he murmured, "so Nimbus Station has bought themselves a little more time, though I hope they don't realize that yet."

"Nothing from them?" Ahn's brows drew into a frown.

Josiah shook his head. "But I'm not worried yet."

"You are."

"What gave me away?"

Ahn pointed toward his cheek. "You're grinding your teeth right here in front of me."

Josiah wiggled his jaw from side to side like a snake, but it did little to ease the tension. Ahn wasn't wrong, but there wasn't any point in confessing to it. Why would he verbalize his concern, especially when there was nothing he could do about it?

On his right, the door to the bridge slid open, and a young petty officer made to step outside before drawing up short. Josiah didn't have to ask why—the flashing lights above front viewscreen inside meant the boat was about to dock.

"I'll meet them back there," he said before she could say anything. He'd already taken three purposeful steps before she spoke.

"They're still fifteen minutes out, sir. They asked for a corpsman to meet them as well. They wanted you to know about the request before they arrived."

Josiah swore under his breath. "Did they say why?"

"No, sir."

"Very well. Send one up and let them know the corpsman is on their way—and find out why."

He stalked aft toward Bay A with Ahn beside him, his heart pounding. *Be careful*, he'd told Graham. What insipid, pointless words those had been—though he hadn't known just how pointless. Would he have sent Raider 2 had he known exactly what was waiting for them aboard *Triumph*? Of course not. Then again, Graham would have probably insisted anyway, out of adventure if not duty.

And now—

Well, how could it be worse than four of his crew locked in capsules and being drained for their blood? Death, he assumed, was supposed to be worse, but was that actually true? Frazer might disagree.

"No one's dead yet," Ahn said. "They wouldn't have asked for medical if that was the case. Don't borrow trouble."

Josiah's head jerked around. "Not yet. But I'm not sure that matters at this point."

"Of course it does." Ahn stepped aside to let him through another door. "Everyone needs some good news, including you."

Snarling at him was out of the question and probably undeserved, so Josiah ignored the platitude.

The corpsman joined them as they turned the corner into the passageway that led to Bay A.

"One casualty," Luis Flores said, anticipating Josiah's question. "Not serious, from what I understand, but they were rushed in their comms. I'll be able to tell you more once they dock."

Ahn gave him a look of muted smugness, but the air had been sucked out of Josiah's lungs. Good news, indeed.

"Did they say what happened?"

"Said they found a . . ." Flores glanced between him and Ahn. "I don't want to repeat bad information, Captain."

"If it sounded odd—" Josiah sighed, not caring how resigned he sounded. "It probably wasn't bad information. Out with it."

"They called it a cache, sir. Of sorts."

"A cache," he repeated numbly, already knowing.

"That's all I know besides the casualty." Flores's pace quickened. "I'm sorry."

Josiah let him go, though he stayed on his heels until they reached Bay A. The boat was floating to the deck as he entered, and the instant oxygen flooded the landing pad, he darted toward it behind Flores. The hatch swung open, and before he could worry once more what the latest set of bad news might be, figures dragging a gurney rushed through it.

That made him stop, and he ground his boots into the deck to keep himself from getting closer. No sense getting in the way.

"I'm fine! Stop acting like I'm that badly injured!" The voice from the gurney was stronger than he'd expected—and *definitely* irritated.

And it was Roselyn Graham's.

Josiah hurried toward the group. Graham's hair was tangled, dark circles ringed her eyes, and he was afraid to ask what other injuries were concealed by the pressure suit they'd somehow gotten her into, but she was *alive*.

But of course she was alive. Frazer had said she would be.

"They won't let me walk," she went on, glaring up at the corpsman. "It's ridiculous."

"That's because you can't walk, ma'am." Blayne hopped to the deck behind them, helmetless, wiping sweat from the back of his neck.

"You wouldn't even let me try." She pushed herself up on her elbows, then collapsed under the weight of the suit.

"Yeah," Blayne replied as the corpsman began scanning her. "At least I made one good decision down there."

"What the hell happened?" Josiah asked.

"We found an auxiliary site, not too far from where *Triumph*'s shuttle landed. You were right, it didn't crash."

All sorts of good news.

He turned to Graham. "Please tell me you remember what happened."

She shook her head. "They injected me with something, knocked me out. I woke up in that capsule."

"She should be okay." The corpsman gestured with his head toward the door. "But I want to run some tests, and judging by the wounds in her thighs, she will *not* be walking anywhere anytime soon."

"That'll be my decision," Graham replied through gritted teeth.

Good luck with that no walking thing, Doc.

"And the others?" he asked Blayne as they dragged Graham from the bay, still arguing.

"She was in the first capsule we checked." Blayne looked at his feet. "We got her, uh, disconnected, then went to work on Caldwell. But I don't think he recognized us, because he freaked out, started fighting us. Slugged Hackett pretty good. I was afraid he was going to pull out all that tubing and bleed to death, so we shoved him back inside."

A wordless plea flashed through his mind, the barest sensation of an appeal to a God who hadn't listened to his prayers before. Why would He start now?

"You did what you had to do." The claim didn't help Josiah's building nausea. "Then what?"

"Figured we'd let him calm down and that we could try again after we released Halley, but there was an alarm before we could open the third capsule. We grabbed the lieutenant and ran like hell." Blayne hadn't looked at him once while he'd recounted the story, but now his focus was intense. "And now we're going back for the others."

Josiah steadied himself. "I'm sorry, but you're not."

"Excuse me, sir?" Blayne glanced behind him, as if the actual captain of *Bayonet* would appear out of the ether and issue the orders he wanted to hear.

You heard me.

"Look." Josiah softened his tone. "If there was an alarm, odds are they've already heard it and they've either moved the hostages or they're lying in wait, and I won't permit you to walk into a trap like that. I can't."

"We can be in and out before they know we're there."

"Not anymore. They know we know what's down there now, and they're not going to lose more of their—whatever they want to call them."

"Then, with all due respect . . . what do you plan on doing?"

Josiah swallowed. "We're going to pay Nimbus Station a visit."

"We?"

"Don't worry, Master Chief." He gulped down the rest of his misgivings. "Because you're going with me."

AHN CLOSED THE DOOR TO JOSIAH'S CABIN BEHIND them and folded his arms.

"Tell me you're not serious," he said without preamble. "Because this isn't you."

"I'm not exactly sure what you're talking about." Josiah took an automatic step backward.

"You damn well know what I'm talking about." Ahn raised his voice. "Are you trying to get yourself killed?"

"I think we've established that no one's getting killed down on Etrik."

I hope.

"Court-martialed, then. Which, as much as I hate to agree with you on the outcome of this idiotic decision, even tacitly, is more likely at this point. Hell, it's guaranteed, if we want to get technical."

"Then they can go ahead and do it." Josiah yanked off his shirt and tossed it to the bunk. He was going to do this with or without Ahn's blessing.

The challenge should have made his gut drop, but there was something undeniable about it—something relieving and terrifying all at once. And *that* was even more terrifying. Because Ahn was right. If Mars got wind of this, his career would be over. Probably his freedom as well. So why was he so certain about what he planned to do?

"I don't know why you'd do this. Even if nothing happens down there . . ." Ahn swore under his breath. "You got a second chance, and I won't let you throw it away, even if you're bent on destroying your own life."

"Look—" Josiah exhaled. "Do you trust me? Even the slightest bit?"

"No." The answer was immediate.

"That's not the correct answer."

"It's the truth. If you just wanted someone to give you the answer you want to hear, well, that's not me. And you ought to know that by now."

Josiah rubbed his forehead. "Just let me do this one thing, and whatever happens on Mars happens."

"I won't bail you out."

"I don't expect you to."

Ahn shrugged, and Josiah recognized the capitulation. He dug the fitted orange bodysuit from a drawer under his bunk and stepped into it as Ahn eyed him with trepidation. His heart should have been racing at the idea of heading to the surface, but for the first time in days, he wasn't questioning his next steps—though whether that was because Nimbus Station had backed him into a corner was debatable.

"When's the last time you wore that?" Ahn asked.

"This?" Josiah drew the silky fabric over his shoulders and shook the sleeves down to his wrists. "Would you believe there's still a tag on the collar?" He scratched at the back of his neck. "Itches like hell, I'm telling you."

"*Now* you decide to develop a sense of humor." Ahn crossed his arms. "There's no need to walk straight into even more trouble than you're already in."

"Who says I'm walking straight into trouble?"

"Well, to start with, if you weren't expecting problems, you'd be wearing utilities and not an armored pressured suit."

"We're about to conduct a safety inspection, and I'm arriving from orbit on a ten-person boat, so I'd be a fool to not be safe about things. It would set a terrible example, Patrick," he added with a deadpan expression. "Whatever would the NSRC think of us?"

Ahn threw his hands in the air. "A safety inspection which both you and Nimbus Station know is a pretense."

"Good." Josiah shoved his rosary in the zippered chest pocket, then yanked on his regular shirt over the orange fabric. There was no reason to alarm everyone aboard by traipsing down the passageway like he was about to do a spacewalk. "Because I'm no longer in any mood to indulge them."

A sigh. "Somehow I doubt you ever were."

"Oh, I gave them the benefit of the doubt right up until they snatched my boarding team off *Triumph* to be used for their blood." His pants didn't fit over the suit quite as easily as his blouse had, and he collapsed to the bunk and swore at them. "So, yes. If Nimbus Station knows our visit is a pretense, I'll find a way to make that work in my favor."

"Even if they meet you at the airlock with rifles?" Ahn raised a brow.

"If I didn't know better"—Josiah jumped to his feet and forced the pants over his waist—"I'd think you were still trying to talk me out of this."

"Is there anything I could say to you that would?"

Out of habit, he strapped on his watch, even knowing he wouldn't need it inside the suit Ahn was so concerned about. "I won't lie, the idea of being met with rifles isn't all that appealing. But Jakob Blayne has arrived at the shoot-first-and-ask-questions-later stage, so I'm not too worried. Besides, I suspect Nimbus will make a show of compliance at first, possibly to chase us back up to orbit."

"May I remind you that chasing anyone who was cursed with this gene back up to orbit is not their ultimate goal?"

"You may."

At last, his hair stood on end. But he would not walk into a trap, even though there was no way of convincing Ahn otherwise. He controlled the situation now, even if Thomas Kinnard thought he did. He would make certain of that.

"And?" Ahn moved away from the door, like he'd completely given up.

"And I won't end up in one of those capsules." Josiah stepped outside. "Neither will anyone else, if I have anything to do with it."

Ahn kept pace with him as he headed aft. "And the three hostages Frazer says are still down there?"

His heart thumped. "Maybe our inspection will be more detailed than the NSRC would prefer."

"Great. Say you find them. Then what? As I understand it, they're not ambulatory, and there's no way Nimbus Station will let you take them without a fight."

"For the love of—" His voice was too loud, so he stopped and pressed himself against the bulkhead. "Look, I understand what you're trying to do, and I appreciate it. No one's going to hold you accountable for what's ultimately my decision and my decision alone."

Especially if none of us make it back to answer for any of this.

Ahn blinked at him. "I'm not questioning your competence."

"I know you're not." He resumed the mazelike path to Bay A. "And I won't say I'm not just as apprehensive about the entire thing. But to come so far, and be so close—"

"Josiah."

Josiah froze.

"This is about *Vigilant,* isn't it?" Ahn had stopped three paces back, just before the passageway turned, the last sequestered spot before the commotion of the bay. "You think if you save those people down there, it'll make up for what happened before? It won't, you know. You'll go on feeling just as guilty as ever until you realize that what happened was not your fault. You didn't load those explosives, you didn't pilot that skiff, and you certainly didn't smash it into a cutter with a hundred and seven souls aboard. You didn't kill the ones who died either, not intentionally or otherwise. I've told you this, and I know Hope's told you this."

"It's not about *Vigilant.*"

"You're lying."

Hope's very same words.

Josiah took two deep breaths. "What if I am? You weren't there. You never went through what I did, so your conscience is clear and your motivations are pure. So tell me, would you make a different decision right now?"

"No." Ahn hesitated for a moment. "I'm only saying that unless you're doing this for the right reasons, whatever plan you have is going to fail. Blayne might have his doubts, but he's also trusting enough to go along with it. But me? I've known you too long. I won't let you do that to yourself or anyone else."

The right reasons.

Did they exist anymore?

"There are three people down there being held in conditions that would probably give me nightmares for the rest of my life." He swallowed at the thought. "If nothing else, we owe them enough to check things out and see if there's anything we can do without walking straight into the same circumstances ourselves. This is about them, nothing and no one else."

"Then that's good enough for me." Ahn cleared his throat. "Good luck."

"I'll see you soon." Josiah patted him on the shoulder. "Take care of my ship."

* * *

Nimbus Station security did not, as it turned out, meet them at the airlock on the east side of the station with rifles. Just two unarmed men with security badges on their black fatigues stood on the other side of the glass, seemingly unconcerned by their visitors who looked, Josiah had to admit, like they were prepared for a small war. Not that he much cared. As much as the use of intimidation bothered him occasionally—albeit very, *very* sporadically—it came in useful more often than not.

"This really isn't necessary," the one on the left said as Blayne, McArthur, and Sprenger pushed by him without a word and headed down the corridor. "I believe you were informed as such."

For a moment, Josiah wondered why the man had addressed him, then remembered his light gray pressure suit—his personal evac gear—was far less threatening to anyone than the black the boarding teams wore. He glanced beside him at Frazer, attired in the same, less the sidearm he carried. They would recognize her eventually, especially if she took her helmet off, but right now the pair appeared too distracted to notice.

"Where's your director?" he asked.

The other man sighed. "Right this way."

With Frazer, Peyer, and Hackett behind him, Josiah tromped after station security in boots too substantial for this pressurized corridor, desperate to remove his gloves and regain full use of his body. His pistol was designed for someone wearing full vacuum gear, but there was something so incredibly vulnerable about being here . . .

"Captain," Blayne broke over a private channel, "they've been pretty cooperative so far. Just as irritated as anyone else would be, but cooperative. I'd say they're up to something, but I honestly think most of them here just want us gone as soon as possible. Almost like . . ." The signal crackled as he paused. "Almost like they don't know that we were summoned here on false pretenses."

"Copy that," Josiah muttered under his breath. It wouldn't surprise him if most of the station didn't know. Frazer had only mentioned Thomas Kinnard's involvement, and surely most of the scientists must know the blood would run out eventually, though whether they knew *Bayonet* had been lured here was a different story altogether.

"Just around the corner here," the security guard said, gesturing toward a metal door halfway down a bland, sterile corridor.

"Look familiar?" he asked Frazer. "Or is this some sort of trap?"

"Mmm." She glanced up at him with uncertainty, then back at Hackett. "I never visited him in his office, but this is the administration area."

"Good enough for now." If anyone planned on jumping them, they'd likely choose a more logical place for it. A research compartment, maybe. Not somewhere with secretaries wandering around. Did Nimbus Station even have secretaries?

But Kinnard did, Josiah discovered as the guard pulled the door open, revealing an outer office with a silver-eyed woman behind a desk. To her right was a large window with a spectacular view of Etrik's surface, and to her left was another door, this one open. The man who he assumed was Thomas Kinnard emerged from that open door with a frown.

He held up a hand, stopping Kinnard before he could speak. "Let's dispense with the excuses and games right now, shall we, Mr. Kinnard? The rest of my team is searching your station as we speak, and we all know what they're going to find."

Kinnard's brow furrowed. "And what's that?"

"Captain—" Frazer interrupted on the private comm.

He gave her a quick shake of his head, unable to risk moving his lips silently in front of Kinnard. "You're denying that you've kept Americans here against their will?"

"It's a long way back to Earth or Mars." Kinnard glanced at Frazer, but Josiah couldn't decide if he recognized her. "I'm sure there are some on Nimbus Station who wish to return to a more established planet, but their employment contracts forbid it."

"You can't keep people on a planet where they don't wish to stay, signature or no signature." He wasn't an expert on contract law, but there was no way an employment agreement with illegal terms was enforceable.

"Perhaps not. I had no hand in writing the contracts." Kinnard shrugged. "Even so, the logistics of such a voyage preclude it. We simply don't have ships or flight crews to spare. Don't have any, actually. Every person here knew the trip was one-way."

"*Triumph* is still in orbit," Peyer broke in.

"In due time, she'll be dismantled for parts like the others. We have to make do with what we have out here—fuel issues preclude a return as well. Some of our budgets are smaller than the Orbital Guard's."

In Josiah's left ear, Hackett made an unflattering, derisive sound.

"Odd you say that, since you sent a probe reporting her overdue. Oh, I know," he said before Kinnard could reply. "That was a mistake, and she showed up afterward . . . isn't that what your security group said?"

"Yes." Kinnard leaned against his secretary's desk, his hands in the pockets of his gray jumpsuit, utterly composed. "There was a miscommunication regarding her ETA, and I apologize for any confusion. I will take full responsibility for any discipline that results from that falsified report."

"He wants you to go away, I think." Frazer turned her back to the door, facing away from Kinnard, and her voice was a rush. "He wasn't expecting you to show up like this, and now he's decided confining all of you isn't worth the risk. Bird in the hand and all that."

Josiah swiveled toward her. "Well, he's not going to keep the birds he has, either." A strange sensation twisted through his gut. He reached for the oxygen dial on his hip, but it wasn't a lack of air that had left him suddenly nauseated.

You rescue those hostages, and you condemn every other person on the station to death.

Heat washed over him, even though the inside of his suit was cool. Somehow, it hadn't occurred to him until now that by rescuing the others and his own team, everyone on the surface would suffer a protracted and unpleasant death. But he wasn't supposed to care about that, was he? By all measures, what the NSRC had done here on Etrik was unethical at the very least and beyond evil at most.

The problem was, he did care. He'd saved pirates and smugglers and worse from situations where the void could have easily taken them. He could have simply waited and let them die, and yet no one would have expected that of him. Would have reprimanded him for it, no less—probably worse.

But he couldn't leave anyone here to be trapped inside a capsule and drained of their blood for the next fifty years, either . . .

He turned back to Kinnard, dizzy. His ethics training had never included leaving over a thousand to perish. "We'll discuss *Triumph* after we finish the inspection. I assume we'll receive full cooperation from your staff?"

"I'll send out a request." Kinnard folded his arms, a smug expression plastered across his face—a face Josiah suspected usually looked that way. It was a wonder Frazer hadn't ever slugged him. "I can't guarantee it'll be followed, though. You know how it goes."

Josiah couldn't help his even smile. Criminals were all the same. Whether they were in deep space or orbiting above Mars, whether they were hiding drugs, weapons, or people . . . they thought they were smarter than everyone else.

And that was always their downfall.

"If I get the faintest hint that you're hiding anything from me," he said, "I'll make sure you realize you crossed the wrong person."

Breathless, Josiah stalked out into the corridor without waiting for Kinnard's reaction to the threat. Frazer darted to his side, questioning and giving what he suspected was probably rather valuable advice, but her words were lost in the hazy fog of his mind.

"Hey, Master Chief?" he called through the team's private comm. He didn't wait for an answer. "Send me a location ping, because we're going to head your way. Kinnard denied the entire thing, pretended he didn't even know Ms. Frazer. Screw caution and restraint. We're going to tear this station apart until we find them."

Nothing but silence greeted him on the comm, and his heart thumped.

"Blayne? Give me status."

"Not sure why he bothered lying to you," Blayne finally replied. "Because thanks to Ms. Frazer's information, we just walked in on his stash of blood donors."

CHAPTER THIRTY-SIX_
NIMBUS STATION, ETRIK

O'Donnell swore under his breath, then turned to her. "You know where they are?"

Coralie nodded, pointed, and darted down the corridor. "One level up, three sections aft. There's a locked door that requires a handprint and code. How they did they get inside?"

Peyer laughed in her earpiece. "You going to tell her, Captain?"

"I'm glad you find this amusing," O'Donnell replied, "but Ms. Frazer doesn't need to know everything about operational matters."

Little late for that, she wanted to reply, but she only stopped at the lift and slammed her gloved hand against the button. The four of them barely fit into the small compartment, and not for the first time, she wished she could take her helmet off.

"Don't even think about it." O'Donnell nudged her with his elbow. "Kinnard could depressurize this entire wing before we knew what was happening. In fact, I'm pretty sure that's what he was counting on. Turn up your air if you need to."

"How—" The door slid closed and her breath came even shorter, even after she adjusted her airflow. "How did you know what I was thinking?"

He chuckled. "Because I'm thinking the same thing."

"But you practically live in space." Coralie glanced at the ceiling as the lift rose, the acceleration scarcely perceptible.

"Thankfully not in a pressure suit." O'Donnell made a motion that looked like he was trying to roll his shoulders as the lift came to a stop. "Peyer, Hackett, be ready."

He hadn't even needed to tell them, and Coralie backed into the corner as they lifted their rifles. She doubted Sanchez and his people would stand a chance against *Bayonet*'s crew, but betting the integrity of her suit on that seemed unwise.

The three exited the lift in front of her, then waved her out. She breathed easier at the emptiness of the corridor, though her legs shook as she scurried aft toward that steel door, flipping through the photos stored in her data chip the entire time.

The schematic of the fire protection system she'd copied in the facilities department office caught her attention, and she enlarged the picture to squint at it, even though that didn't make sense— the images appeared in her mind, not in front of her eyes. She hadn't noticed before, but the fiber line that connected the entire system, the cable that allowed the entire station to be monitored by Henk's people . . . it led west, toward an unlabeled connection.

Kinnard's second cache?

Voices interrupted her scrutiny of the diagram, and when she looked up from her boots, the door compartment she dreaded was open, the flickering amber light from inside spilling into the corridor.

But the door was never open.

And the light never spilled outside.

She blinked the tears away before they could become obvious through her helmet.

You can do this. You're so close to what you set out to do.

She took a deep breath and stepped inside. Her implants didn't even need to adjust, because the lights from *Bayonet*'s team provided enough illumination that the compartment appeared to exist in a different reality than she remembered. But the look on Sprenger's face as he turned toward her from inspecting the second capsule on the right—that was familiar. She wished she could promise him he'd forget soon.

"There should be three." She stepped past O'Donnell, who'd pressed himself against the door and was watching the corridor with the attentiveness of a hawk. "At least, there were. No more ships since *Triumph*, correct?"

"No more ships." Blayne straightened from where he'd been examining another capsule. "We can get them out of the capsules, but getting them into pressure suits in this condition is another matter. And if they fight like Caldwell did—"

"The corridor is pressurized," she replied. "And the gurney floats, so it scarcely needs any attention at all. You won't need pressure suits for them, and I doubt station security can stop you, armed like you are."

"Pressurized for now." Blayne blew out a deep breath. "That can change in an instant, and as for trying to stop us, they probably will. They're going to be desperate, and desperate adversaries can be unpredictable."

"Yes, but—"

A bullet flew by her head, piercing the steel wall above the capsules with a ping she heard through her helmet. Coralie froze, more terrified of it puncturing her suit than her body, then broke into a fit of giggles at the ridiculousness of that fear. She scarcely had time to glance down at her wrist computer and check the integrity of her suit before Hackett pushed her against the wall.

"Stay there and don't move." He took up a ready stance against the far bulkhead, opposite the door from O'Donnell. "Captain, that's an S27."

"They took those rifles from your people on *Triumph*." The horrifying realization slammed into her. They weren't just dealing with a few security guards with handguns anymore.

"Yes." O'Donnell's hand hit the keypad, and the door slammed shut. Another volley of pings sounded on the other side as the lock engaged. "And now they've got us trapped here unless we can get rid of them."

Coralie sank to the floor. The pressure suit made the motion difficult, and it wasn't a comfortable position, but her legs wouldn't keep her upright any longer.

"Can *Bayonet* help?" she asked.

O'Donnell's mouth opened, and for a moment she thought he was going to make a smart remark, but then he shook his head.

"We couldn't contact them if we wanted to," he replied. "From the boat, yes, depending on atmospheric interference, but in here? Not going to happen."

Another bullet hit the door. Coralie flinched, but so far the door was holding, which wasn't a surprise. The v-words would have made sure nothing could get through.

"There's no other way out of this compartment?" Blayne asked.

She pointed to the hatch that led to the drop ceiling. "That hole there gives access to the machinery above. There's a bulkhead just above us, but I'm not sure how thick it is. It might even have access to the corridor."

Peyer's eyes flicked upward. "If we can get out that way, that means they can get in."

Oh.

Her mouth went dry. She hadn't thought of that.

"Hackett—" O'Donnell pushed himself off the wall. "Check it out. Get rid of them if you can."

"Aye aye, Captain." He bounded toward the ladder without hesitation.

Coralie found her feet. "I'm going with you."

Hackett turned toward her and shrugged. "Sir?"

"Yeah, no." O'Donnell shook his head. "Not going to happen, Ms. Frazer. You'll stay right here."

She edged away from him. Modifications or not, he'd probably have no trouble throwing her to the ground, and while he didn't carry any handcuffs that she could see, Blayne's team did. There was a limit to her strength, especially when she was half-sick with fear.

"Look, I've been up there before," she replied, "and I have pictures of all these areas. If he gets up in the ceiling and can't find his way back, I can help." Not that it would come to that, and she could see in Hackett's eyes that he knew she was making things up, but it made a nice story for O'-Donnell. "And I can see in the dark. And shoot a gun."

Hackett choked down laughter. "Captain, I—"

"Reminding me of your lack of skill with a handgun is probably not the way to convince me." O'Donnell waved a gloved hand. "Whatever. Go. Don't do anything I wouldn't do."

She didn't ask why he'd caved so easily, just scrambled up the ladder behind Hackett into the mechanical area above. One quick blink and she could see as easily as downstairs, though judging by the cautious way Hackett settled onto the beam, he was struggling.

"You can flip a light on," she said under her breath, even though it didn't matter inside their helmets. But another round of bullets hit the door below them, and she wondered how true that was. "This area is shielded well enough that they won't see you."

"You're useful." A moment later, a red light illuminated the batches of tubes and wiring. "Glad I talked him into letting you come along."

"Pretty sure I did that. Though he agrees more easily to things than you seem to believe." She glanced down at the open hatch, half expecting to see Riley waiting down there for her like she had been before. Nothing but Blayne's concerned and helmeted face greeted her, and she took a deep breath. "Okay, turn to your right. The bulkhead is three meters forward. See it?"

"Yep." He grunted as he maneuvered toward it, crouching awkwardly to protect his suit. His rifle banged against the ceiling once, and he shifted lower. "Think I can hold my breath all the way back to the boat if I tear this suit moving around up there?"

"Be more careful about what you're doing, then." She laughed. As if *careful* mattered now. As if a ripped suit was the most they had to worry about. "You know, that gun banging about on everything is going to alert them."

"Your talking is going to alert them," Blayne interrupted from downstairs.

"Aw, you know they can't hear us talking." Hackett came to a stop near the bulkhead and leaned up against it, then flicked a button on his arm. "Busybody," he added on a private channel to her.

"Think they might decide to just wait us out?" Coralie slid by him and ran her gloved hands across the bulkhead. All of this would have been easier without the plastic and fabric that encased her, but the gunfire downstairs had only slowed, not stopped, and the suit would at least help protect her. "The blood itself is harvested from another compartment. Theoretically, they could just let us starve."

"Then they wouldn't get our blood."

"Maybe they're angry enough to not care. They've already got three blood donors downstairs, three more in that auxiliary cache, and there's ample historical precedent."

And you know Kinnard's got to be furious with me . . .

"Like where?"

"The nineteenth-century American Midwest, for one." She blinked, but the bulkhead remained a dark gray outline. "Potawatomi warriors trapped a group of Illiniwek atop a sandstone cliff and laid siege there until they died of hunger. They called it Starved Rock for centuries."

"That never happened," O'Donnell broke in.

"Excuse me?"

"I'm from Illinois, I know the history, and I'm telling you it's a myth. If you're going to make poor comparisons, the siege of Leningrad would be more apt. At least there's historical evidence for that one. But you were told to stop the small talk."

"Fine. Whatever. They could mostly starve us, then." Coralie blinked again, but in the red light, the implants didn't compensate as well as usual, a bug she'd never understood. "There's an access panel along the top of the ceiling."

Hackett shifted to face the bulkhead. "Not something we can fit through, it seems."

"It's just thin aluminum. I think I can peel it down."

"You're sure there's another access shaft on the other side?"

"The tubing for the blood runs aft, into a compartment about ten meters away. None of the electrical goes the same way, so there's got to be some sort of space. Whether or not we can fit . . ."

She tugged downward on the metal, just enough to peer through the crack she'd created. On the other side of the bulkhead lay Hackett's desired access shaft, and even though she hadn't dared to hope for more luck, it was even wider than the area in which they currently crouched.

"Would you look at that?" He yanked the nearest corner of the bulkhead down toward the beam as another bullet slammed into the door beneath them. "And not a moment too soon."

"They've got to give up eventually." Working cautiously, she bent the metal until they had a human-sized hole in the bulkhead. "Or maybe not."

Coralie balanced on the edge of the beam as Hackett lowered himself to his belly and hauled himself through the makeshift door. She'd been certain they would hear him from below, but another bullet pinged against steel, and it became clear just how silently he could move. He disappeared into the shadows, and she followed him, crouching to keep her suit intact. There was no talking on her end anymore—she could scarcely draw a breath in case they heard. Hackett apparently had no such fear, more trusting of the sound dampening technology in his helmet than she.

"You want to work that magic on the ceiling?" he asked.

Her eyes met his as she dragged her gloves along the metal. There was no access panel in the ceiling to pry open like there'd been in the bulkhead, but—

But there was a smoke detector.

"I'm going to pry this out, but I need to disconnect it from its power supply first. You got a knife?"

He handed it to her, hilt-first, and her heart thumped as she envisioned dropping it, imagined the sound it would make. The ceiling wasn't reinforced like the door down below, and if they shot upward . . .

Coralie squeezed her eyes shut and found a better grip on the knife. She didn't know how anyone could manipulate something so slender in these gloves, but it slid through the wiring like it was made of thread. She handed it back to Hackett before her nightmare of dropping it came true.

"I'm ready to remove the sensor," she whispered at him. "But once I do, they'll be able to see the hole if they look up. You ready?"

He swung toward her, his rifle pointed at the floor. "I was born ready."

Coralie suppressed a snort. The grip on her gloves slid off the plastic coating twice, so she slipped the right one off and laid it next to her after checking her wrist computer. For some reason, the section was still pressurized. Free of that impediment, she grasped the outer case and turned it. It loosened immediately, and she drew it upward and set it next to her glove.

"There you go." She backed away and shoved her glove back on her hand. It sealed with a satisfying click—because once Hackett fired, there was no doubt station security would try to vent the air up here.

"Sir?" Hackett sounded unsure for the first time; his voice was low. "We've moved forward into the access shaft just above the shooters. Two of them, three yards from your compartment."

Another bullet pinged off the doorway below.

"Get rid of them." O'Donnell hadn't even hesitated.

"Aye aye, Captain." Hackett drew a breath; his comm clicked over to a speaker. "You've got two seconds to put that gun down on the floor."

Asking so politely wasn't *quite* what Coralie suspected O'Donnell had in mind, but she didn't have time to question it further. The figure glanced down the corridor, then toward the ceiling, bringing the pistol upward.

Hackett's rifle flash, a bolt of lightning in the darkness, nearly blinded her.

CHAPTER THIRTY-SEVEN_
NIMBUS STATION, ETRIK

Shards of concrete exploded on the floor of the corridor beneath her, drowning the profanity from the men below. One of them was Sanchez—Coralie recognized his stocky build and the gray streak in his hair. He went down heavily in a cloud of white dust, then lay there as it settled, unmoving. The other glanced around, panic-stricken, and then up, meeting her eyes.

His gun rose.

Her pulse thrashed in her ears.

"Hack—"

Lightning flashed again.

This time, the mist was red. The glint of a rifle lying on the floor caught her eye, and her stomach churned. Even closing her eyes didn't erase the sight of the two figures down there. They had been alive just five seconds before, and she had played a part in ending their lives. A small one, yes, and it wasn't as though they would have done any better to her, but did that matter?

"Stop torturing yourself." Hackett slid backward and slung the rifle to his shoulder. "Plug that hole back up and let's get out of here."

Coralie didn't bother to remove the glove. The sensor slipped straight back into the hole, and she stayed right on Hackett's tail as he slithered back into the compartment above the capsules.

"Captain, we're coming back down," he said. "Probably only bought us fifteen minutes though, so we've got to be fast if we're going to get the first one out of here."

Silence fell over the room as Coralie made her way to the ladder. She skipped the last three rungs and landed heavily on the floor. All this, and they'd only gained fifteen minutes.

"We have to try," O'Donnell replied, sounding like he'd made the final decision. "Without knocking them out, please. I don't want to do any-thing that might affect their respiration in case we end up dragging them out through hard vacuum."

Hackett shifted from boot to boot.

"Let me." Coralie spun toward the capsule holding the man she'd spoken with so long ago. He couldn't have heard them even if they hadn't been in suits, but his heart rate was steady and those deep blue eyes weren't wild like they'd been before. Today they were . . . resigned. "Crack them open one at a time and let me talk to them. Maybe I can calm them."

"Worth a try, Captain." McArthur sounded like she was more than willing, even if the rest of them weren't so sure.

O'Donnell nodded. "Open it."

Coralie stood back while McArthur cracked the capsule open—in a stroke of luck, the doors to the capsules themselves lacked locks. His heart sped up, so she unlatched her helmet and removed her right glove and set them on the floor. O'Donnell might object, but this part of it, she would do her way.

"Hey." She reached through the small opening and touched him on his shoulder. He shuddered but didn't otherwise move. *Couldn't move,* she reminded herself. "I promised I would get you out, and I'm back to make good on that promise. Do you remember me?"

"He screams and you slam that door shut," O'-Donnell said from over her shoulder.

Coralie gave him a look, then turned back around. "But I need you to do me a favor, okay? They're going to pull you out, and—and I know they look frightening, and I suppose I do too, for that matter, but they're here to help you, I swear. But for them to do that, you have to do your part. Can you do that for me?"

His eyes flickered toward her, even though he couldn't move his head, and he gave a guttural moan as they locked on hers.

"Good. Can they pull you out the rest of the way? Get you disconnected? I'll stay right here with you, I promise."

The man blinked but didn't make another sound, and she took that for a yes. Backing up a pace, Coralie nodded at Blayne, and he pulled the gurney out. She grabbed the man's clammy hand and squeezed as hard as she dared, but he still shook with quiet tears as McArthur removed her gloves and maneuvered the tubing over the edge of the silken cocoon.

Coralie's stomach lurched at the sight. Everything in the compartment seemed to disappear except for the plastic that connected him to whatever unholy machine spun and cleaned his blood.

No time for this . . .

Hackett swore out loud, forcing her back to reality. "Should have brought a corpsman."

"Shove it, Hackett." Still, McArthur's hands wavered over the man's left leg. "Dammit, this could get messy. I need someone to apply pressure once I pull these out."

Coralie's head swung in her direction. "You got Lieutenant Graham out just fine."

"She hadn't been in there as long. Less blood. Less tissue damage. Less a lot of things." It was McArthur's turn to swear under her breath. "Here we go."

Coralie turned away and squeezed her eyes closed. She could feel the pain of the plastic sliding out of the wounds in her legs and wondered if she had cried out as loudly as he did. She suspected Kinnard had mocked her, but who really knew anymore?

"Okay." McArthur stiffened. "That should hold." She looked up at Blayne, questioning.

"We're going to have to take them to the boat one at a time," he replied. "You and Sprenger take him. One of you stay, the other get back here as soon as possible. If they try to stop you, do whatever you need to do to get through."

"Gotcha, Master Chief." Sprenger sounded thrilled at the prospect of a fight as he followed McArthur into the corridor beside the floating gurney.

"Get that door closed. We'll have to hole up here until they get back." O'Donnell sighed. "We'll work on getting the next one out of the capsule while they do."

Coralie darted for the door, waterfalls of blood dancing in front of her vision. When Kinnard removed her from the capsule, it had been a slow, intentional procedure, not the rushed affair they'd been forced into now. Would the man they'd just rescued bleed out before he reached *Bayonet*? Zero-g could be devastating on wounds like this, and that was if they got him to the boat in the first place.

She slammed her palm against the button to close the door as footsteps echoed outside. Not Sprenger and McArthur's heavy boots that had disappeared down the corridor just thirty seconds before, but light steps, feminine and quick.

Please hurry, you cursed slow door.

Pale fingers slithered inside before it could slam close and lock, stopping the steel's movement like it was paper. The sound of rifles being readied echoed in her brain, and she held her breath, frozen.

"Coralie!" The voice from outside was familiar. "I know you're in there, and so help me, I'll pry this door open if you don't let me in!"

Coralie took a step to the side. "Helena?"

"Yes. And listen, we need to talk. Let me in."

Coralie glanced backward, into the gloom of the compartment. Her helmet and missing glove were so far away, lying on the floor behind the second capsule where Peyer and Blayne now worked. What had O'Donnell said? He'd warned them. Taking away their air was the only way Nimbus Station could stop them.

O'Donnell slid beside her as she contemplated darting for the rest of her gear, then shoved her out of the way and leaned against the door.

"Back away from this door." He raised his pistol, just out of striking range. "Now."

"You won't do that." Helena's face wasn't visible, but her smile was audible.

"You want to find out?"

The hiss of the pressurization filled Coralie's ears.

"No." Helena's answer was curt. "But I need to speak with her—and you. Your people? I know where they are. I can help you find them."

"She's lying, Captain." Blayne still wore his helmet, and his warning was confined to Coralie's earpiece.

"No kidding." O'Donnell steadied himself. "You've got three seconds to back off and let us close this door."

Helena didn't move. "Coralie, I am telling you, I'm here to help you."

"Why?" Hackett appeared beside her, her glove and helmet in hand, and she slid both on. "Why would you do that?" Her voice sounded odd now, projected from the speaker on the side of her helmet.

"Because you were right." Helena glanced down the corridor, then took a deep breath. "Everything we've done to you, it was horrible. Maybe most of them can live with that, but I can't. Not anymore."

"You help us rescue them and you die." O'Donnell hadn't lowered his pistol. "You'll excuse me if I don't believe a word you say."

"We have stores of criexain pills, enough to last awhile. And the scientists have been working on a better solution ever since humans first arrived here. They're going to have a breakthrough eventually, and none of this will be necessary anymore. Kinnard might hate giving up his fresh blood, but he doesn't need it."

"McArthur's on her way back for the second survivor," Blayne said into Coralie's ear. "You need to get rid of whatever she is fast."

O'Donnell turned toward her so Helena couldn't see his lips. "How do you feel about luring her away from here?" he asked through the intercom. "If she's lying, we need to get her out of here, and if she's telling the truth, so much the better."

Coralie gave Hackett one last look. "Let's do it."

CHAPTER THIRTY-EIGHT_
NIMBUS STATION, ETRIK

O'Donnell's boots echoed in the empty service corridor that ran from just outside the capsule compartment along the very edge of the station, and Coralie couldn't help but wonder if hers were as loud. Helena led them forward as he followed behind both of them, swiveling his head behind him every so often. She and Helena had to slow down every so often to let him catch up, and she suddenly felt sorry for the unaltered human in a heavy pressure suit.

"You're not used to being on the surface," she said to him through the private channel inside her helmet. "Are you?"

"Hardly." He hesitated, and for a moment she didn't think he'd say anything else. "Earth, yes, when I was a child. But I haven't spent more than a few months on Mars in years, and even a sprawl of interconnected habitats is hardly the surface."

"We used to go for long hikes in the craters for training." She could feel the sore muscles, could still remember the decompression sickness that had descended on her once during a failed prebreathe. "You weren't missing much except a lot of rocks and red dust. Space is full of possibilities."

"'The heavens are telling the glory of God; and the firmament proclaims his handiwork.'" He gave her a reluctant glance, almost as though he was ashamed by whatever words they were. "But the only thing I see in the heavens anymore is death."

"Jakob told me what happened above Mars." She couldn't imagine the guilt O'Donnell must feel— or maybe she could, in a way, for hadn't she felt guilt over being free and relatively happy while three others languished in those capsules? They weren't dead, no, but she would have welcomed death had she spent much longer in the same circumstances. Perhaps she already had. "I'm so sorry."

"It happens." His voice was steel. "Space is unforgiving. Always has been."

He didn't really believe that. She could tell by his tone and the manner in which his gait had turned stiff, something not explained by the suit he'd already been wearing for hours like a professional.

"It wasn't space that caused that disaster. And you'll forgive me for speaking of something I know little about, but I doubt it was you, either."

O'Donnell held up his hand, and she flinched. She'd gone too far with a virtual stranger, but perhaps it was *because* he was a virtual stranger that she could see the pain he was hiding. Would anyone else dare call him on it?

"They got the second one to the shuttle," he said instead of launching into an admonishment. "One more to go. At least luring her away from that compartment accomplished something."

"They may have sent her after the trying to shoot us failed, but I don't actually think she was lying." Coralie's pace faltered the slightest bit as she flipped through the fire detector schematics once more. "I've been searching through some old photos I took of the fire protection system diagram in my department's office, and I think—" The crackle of empty air on the comm line filled her ear as she thought, familiar and soothing. "I think that cache we found is actually part of the station, however remote."

"Master Chief, how many miles did you say that was?" O'Donnell asked. They crossed through another door as he spoke, and Coralie wasn't surprised when no one answered, given the number of walls now separating them. Even so, the silence was disconcerting. "Raider 1, you still reading me?"

"Three, I think," Coralie replied to break the silence. "Well, maybe a bit farther."

"Seems ten times as long," he huffed.

She laughed inside her helmet. Even with her modifications, not to mention the oxygen being forced into her suit, she was winded when she spoke. Etrik's gravity was too high for anyone who'd spent so much time on Mars—not that the scientists minded. Pacing around a laboratory or sitting in front of a computer didn't require that much exertion.

"Why haven't I heard anything about this new replacement blood?" she asked Helena.

Helena turned briefly, then continued her trek down the corridor. "No one's supposed to know.

Kinnard's afraid if word gets out, there will be a revolt. If it happens, it happens. If it doesn't, he doesn't want people panicking."

"Then how did you find out?" O'Donnell asked. "Are you working on the project?"

"I know one of the research biologists." She didn't seem inclined to say anymore, and Coralie knew that was answer enough. "Here," she added. "There are only two more doors, but the last stretch of corridor doesn't have power or air. It's how Kinnard keeps people from snooping."

"Don't tell me you're afraid of the dark." O'Donnell chuckled.

Coralie laughed out loud, and she didn't care if Helena saw.

"What?" he asked her. "Not sure why something as trivial as no oxygen would stop them."

"You just saw Hackett stop two of them," she said into his earpiece. "They're *mostly* undying but still human, and it takes a lot to undo millennia of self-preservation. I would be nervous coming down here in their situation."

"Would be?" He glanced her way. "Does that mean you're not?"

"Well." She stopped beside him as Helena keyed a long code into the keypad beside the door. "I'm a little nervous, but admitting that doesn't do us much good, does it?"

"Coralie." Helena motioned her over toward the keypad. "We have a problem . . . I can't get it to unlock. I think they changed the codes."

Coralie's stomach sank.

"Try again?" She planted her boots on the concrete to keep herself from running in the opposite direction and clicked on the private channel once more. "I suppose that wouldn't surprise me," she said to O'Donnell. "If they've realized there's not much they can do to prevent the loss of the other three, and that your people are more than willing to fight their way out, they're going to lock down this compartment even harder."

"That's partly good news," O'Donnell said quietly in her ear. "It means their attention is focused here and not on what's going on in the main station. Likely they've given up on stopping Blayne and his team. Yes, definitely good news," he repeated.

Good news?

Her breath caught.

He was willing to lose his people as long as the civilians made it to orbit. And maybe himself?

"We can save both," she replied under her breath, even though Helena couldn't hear anything through their suits' comm system. "We will save both." Sensing he was about to argue, she turned toward Helena so any response would be visible to her. That would stop his argument before it began.

"There." The flashing light above the door turned green, and Helena breathed a sigh of relief. "Backup code worked."

O'Donnell lumbered through the door first, then stopped and sniffed inside his helmet as if he was testing the air in this new, hostile part of the station. Trapped inside her pressure suit, there wasn't any noticeable difference to Coralie. The same gray concrete floor and steel walls stretched almost as far as she could see; the same bare light bulbs hung a regular distance from each other, though they weren't illuminated here. She flicked on her helmet lights in deference to O'Donnell, even though her implants had already adjusted.

"Pretty eerie watching her walk down this corridor without a suit." He glanced at his wrist computer. "Because it's most definitely not pressurized."

Coralie licked her lips. They were already cracking. "I walked on the surface beside one of them, and let's just say . . . at least here we can pretend. Out there, I had to wonder if I'd stepped into some kind of nightmare."

He held up his hand again, and she was starting to understand that he meant it more as *hold on* rather than *shut up.*

"Do you hear that?"

Coralie shook her head. Helena didn't seem to hear anything either, had continued padding along the corridor without slowing.

"Footsteps," he went on.

Her skin grew clammy in the dry air of her suit. "Helena suggested no one else had access to this area."

"No one?"

"Well, Kinnard would, but I rather suspect he's busy trying to figure out what happened to his security department. I suppose some of the facilities people would have access, but—"

She skidded to a stop. O'Donnell had disappeared from her side, and when she turned around in search of him, he'd taken a few paces back the way they'd come, his pistol raised. She craned her neck, but she couldn't see anything in the darkness. Couldn't even hear the footsteps he claimed he'd heard. Space did that to people, though. Imaginations ran wild. The lack of up and down gave rise to hallucinations.

But on Etrik?

Her chest constricted in confusion just seconds before she went crashing against the wall. Not even steel all the way down here, but solid concrete, enough to send shock waves through her suit. Metal would have been soft by comparison, she thought as her helmet slammed against her head once more.

Behind her, a thud. She twisted her head around toward the sound, straining a muscle she hadn't realized she possessed. O'Donnell was face-first on the ground, and Helena—

Helena's hands were on the seal of his helmet, working to unlock it.

Coralie sprang at her, knocking her to the concrete floor. No air hissed from the maybe-broken seal around O'Donnell's neck, but as she grabbed Helena by the wrist and tried to hurl her a safe distance away, he didn't move.

Her breath fogged the inside of her helmet, but Helena pounced at her before she could figure out how to clear it in the unfamiliar suit. The boots that had seemed so heavy just five minutes ago couldn't hold her down any longer as Helena smashed her into the concrete over and over. It didn't make sense. She had bodily modifications. Illegal ones. Numerous ones. She'd taken Kinnard. Not for long, no, but she should have a *chance* against Helena.

The suit's integral computer was screeching something at her, but her head swam as Helena pounded her against the wall once more. It was, Coralie realized somewhere in the pain and her altering vision, protecting her from the near-vacuum but also limiting what her modifications could help her with. If only she could—

She brought her hands together in front of her and let Helena throw her to the ground.

There. One glove clanged to the floor, followed by the second. Coralie reached up, grabbed Helena's forearm and flung her as hard as she could, ignoring the unmistakable sensation of air escaping from around every part of her.

Well, not ignoring. She couldn't ignore the pressure in her eardrums, or her eyes, or in her chest.

But even down here, just like up on Etrik's surface, there was still a bit of oxygen. She could still take a breath, and freed from the unrelenting protection of the suit, she could use her enhanced strength against their attacker. Helena was stronger, of course, but it might not take much. All O'Donnell had to do was get up. Or at least find the strength to fire his pistol.

"You couldn't leave well enough alone." Helena flung a glove at her as she paced back to O'Donnell's limp body. "You're going to kill us all!"

Coralie held her hands in front of her. "What about the replacement blood?"

"They can't make it work," Helena snarled at her. "Can you believe that? All this time, all these people, and they can't make it work yet. And you don't care what you're condemning us to."

"I do care." Coralie blinked, but the implants were already at full strength. Still, she could tell there were unfamiliar shadows behind Helena, something that shouldn't exist unless there was someone else in the tunnel. She slowed her heart rate with a few deep breaths. Helena was going to trip over O'Donnell if she kept backing up like she was, and then she would spring. "But I am telling you, I will not live like this for the rest of my life. I won't be threatened and imprisoned and tormented by you and your games anymore."

"You would trade our lives for yours?" Helena's face turned crimson, and her lack of denial regarding the holey suit and missing emergency oxygen was confession enough for Coralie.

"I'm not trading anyone's life," Coralie replied, suddenly dizzy.

Helena crouched over O'Donnell and went to work on the helmet seal once more, oblivious to the interlopers approaching behind her. "Take our blood away and that's just what you're doing. You know it, and you don't care!"

"That's a problem you created for yourselves." Coralie took another step toward them. "And you're creating another one right now—you take his helmet off here, and he'll die. I don't think that solves anything, especially since you know what Kinnard will do if he finds out you did this."

"Kinnard." Helena's lip twisted up in an imitation of a smile. "Not everyone is as afraid of Kinnard as you are. Besides, a brief period of anoxia won't kill him, and who needs a functioning brain inside a capsule, anyway? It was a terrible idea for Kinnard to keep the blood sources conscious in the first place, and this one will probably be better off not knowing what's going on around him. I'm saving him from the horror, really. He would thank me if he could."

The shadows in the distance flickered, then formed a new darkness, one that could only be caused by the solidity of figures. The darkness strengthened until finally it coalesced into a familiar gait that sent a rush of relief through Coralie.

Riley.

And—

The relief faded.

And Kinnard beside her?

Her lungs expanded, searching for every available molecule of oxygen, though how she was still breathing was a mystery. Maybe fifteen minutes had been conservative. She didn't know. The only thing she knew was that she needed to get her hands on O'Donnell's pistol.

"Get away from him, Helena."

Helena spun around at Kinnard's order.

"Kinnard." Her crimson cheeks turned pallid. "I found her trying to escape with him. Trying to get to the other three. They're going—"

"I don't care." Kinnard's jaw was tight. "Shaw told me about the hole in Frazer's suit the day they went outside the station. Along with the breaches in the security tapes the night she almost suffocated in that corridor. You know how vulnerable our existence is here, and you tried to murder one of the people keeping us alive?"

"You're the only one who gets her blood!" Helena screeched. "It wouldn't kill you to take pills like the rest of us. Don't pretend her death would be a substantial loss. We've all survived without her just fine for months."

"You don't get to make that decision." Kinnard's response was calm.

Coralie stared at O'Donnell's pistol, lying just beside him, too close to Helena, then glanced up at Riley.

I need your help.

As if she'd recognized the plea, Riley nodded, almost imperceptibly.

"I just did, since you won't make the correct one." Helena sat back on her heels. "And it all ends now."

It all ends now?

Before Coralie could figure out what she had meant, Helena swiped O'Donnell's gun and raised it into the air. Kinnard launched himself at her, and she screamed a string of curses, swinging the pistol from Coralie to him.

The shot exploded in the concrete and steel corridor, not as much of a sound as a blast that wrecked what little hearing Coralie had left after destroying the integrity of her suit. She blinked twice, fighting against her ocular implants' inexplicable desire to recede against the diffuse flash, just as Kinnard sagged to the floor.

Helena stumbled to her feet, raised the pistol again, and aimed it at Kinnard's chest.

Coralie found her footing. Her suit was armored, was designed to protect her from a bullet, though at this close range?

No time to think about that.

She flew at Helena, but Riley got to her first. She shoved Helena to the side, and they both stumbled against the wall, caught in a reciprocated hold. Before Coralie could move toward them—or pull O'Donnell away—another blast of the pistol shook the corridor.

Helena fell to her knees just beside O'Donnell, blood pouring through her jumpsuit, the pistol that Riley had turned toward her chest still in her hand. She dropped to the concrete and reached out a hand toward his neck. Riley sagged against the wall, shaking but otherwise uninjured.

"You don't want to do this, Helena." Coralie's pacemaker fired, but her legs were too heavy to move. Blast it, her whole body felt like the concrete that surrounded them. She dragged her feet forward. It wasn't enough to close the gap between her and O'Donnell quickly enough, she could already tell. "Just let him go, and then you can have me."

"No." Helena looked up at her one last time with glassy, unfocused eyes. "I can't."

And then she twisted the latch around O'Donnell's neck.

CHAPTER THIRTY-NINE_
NIMBUS STATION, ETRIK

JOSIAH'S EYES FLICKERED OPEN AS AIR HISSED FROM his helmet.

Just let him go, and then you can have me.

He could have sworn he'd hallucinated the words, but Frazer stood a few feet away, screaming something he couldn't quite understand at someone he couldn't see. He tried to roll to his side, then to his knees, then to his feet, but something heavy stopped him before he could budge.

Vigilant.

The memory swirled around him in the dark. He'd lain like this on the bridge, pinned down by that display until help had arrived thirty minutes later. He'd wanted to move, just like he wanted to move now, only it wasn't just the weight that prevented him from getting up. His chest was tight as well, in that familiar yet unwelcome feeling of a suit leak.

He reached out a hand, dragging his useless glove across the concrete. His pistol was somewhere, and he needed—

The lock around his neck clicked. His lungs moved again, sucking in precious oxygen that he'd thought was gone for good. Frazer appeared beside him, her lips moving soundlessly, and he risked the use of his throat.

"What happened?"

She leaned down and lifted him against her shoulder, then sat him up.

"Helena tried to kill you. She got your helmet almost all the way off before Kinnard and—and a friend showed up." Frazer glanced behind her at a tall woman with dark skin and silver eyes. "Helena's dead. So's Kinnard."

"How?" His head spun, but a few deep breaths steadied it. "And this friend?"

He blinked as she placed his pistol in his glove without answering, and his fingers curled around it. The light on his helmet wasn't working anymore, but hers was, and along the wall lay two bodies, just as Frazer had said: Thomas Kinnard and Helena.

"Riley. She's going to help us with your people. But we've got to hurry."

Every bone in his body seemed to creak as he stumbled to his feet. "No offense, but I've stopped trusting your friends."

"You can trust this one."

She seemed certain and refused to say anything else, so he staggered behind the two of them toward the door at the end of the corridor. It opened into a large concrete vault, twice as high as his head and probably ten feet wide. Capsules lined the far side. Not as many as in the main side of Nimbus Station, but the flickering amber light from within three told him they were occupied.

"We can't get them out." His heart broke in two as he sagged against the wall. All this way, and they were still trapped. "There's no way station security will let us through now, and I can't risk impeding Blayne's evacuation."

"You're right. But *Triumph*'s shuttle isn't far." Frazer marched to the nearest capsule and peered inside. "And it's functional."

"Through a low oxygen environment." A headache was building. "They don't have suits, and that's if they could even walk. Taking them outside is going to kill them after what they've been through."

"I have one." She yanked off her helmet and shook out her damp hair. "Look, this compartment is pressurized, so we're good for now, and I can breathe outside. But only for around fifteen minutes, so I need you to work on getting the first one out of that capsule while I doff this thing. We can put him in it, carry him to the shuttle, let me recover a bit, run back, let me catch my breath again, and then do it two more times."

He focused on the concrete, running through her plan in his mind. She was making a few assumptions, namely that *Triumph*'s shuttle hadn't been disabled, but—

Better than nothing.

"And her?" He nodded at the other woman. He hated speaking about her like she wasn't there, but he couldn't afford more emotional involvement. He had to think of her as someone not quite human, or else . . . "What's her motive for helping? What's she getting out of it?"

"I can't live like this," the woman replied before Frazer could answer. "I thought I could suppress my conscience, but in the end, who can? Sociopaths? And you can believe what you want, but it's impossible to gather a thousand of those in one place."

It sounded like a practiced answer, but somehow he trusted Frazer enough by now to nod. She set her helmet on the floor and removed the rest of her suit while he cracked open the nearest occupied capsule. Caldwell had fought their rescuers the first time, Blayne had said, but when Josiah pulled out the cocoon-like gurney, he did nothing but stare up at him and blink.

He clicked on the speaker on his helmet. "Hey there, Caldwell. You ready to go home?"

Caldwell licked his lips. "As long as I can sleep in a cargo bay instead of my bunk on the way back to Mars, sir. I've kind of developed a bit of claustrophobia."

Josiah couldn't help his laughter. "I think we can arrange that."

Frazer and Riley appeared on the other side of the gurney, both in the usual gray Nimbus Station jumpsuits—Josiah knew he'd never become used to them walking around and breathing where he could not. Frazer dropped a stack of pressure bandages on Caldwell's chest, paler than he'd ever seen her. Hackett had told Blayne about the flashbacks she'd had aboard *Triumph*, and Blayne had informed him in turn. He suspected she was having one now, but what could he do?

Well, there was one thing . . .

Riley busied herself with the tube inserted into Caldwell's left leg. "Just make sure you've got a good grip on it and pull it *straight* out toward his ankle," she told Josiah, demonstrating with the other tube. "It's not been that long, so there shouldn't be major issues with removal."

Like everyone else aboard *Bayonet*, he'd had basic field trauma training, but this was far beyond anything he'd done in the past. But the right tube slid out as easily as the other, and it only took a minute for the blood to stop seeping through the pressure bandage. It was good enough. They could fix it more permanently aboard *Bayonet* and then for good on Mars.

Riley maneuvered the pressure suit to the end of the gurney, and Josiah glanced at Caldwell's face. His eyes were squeezed closed, and by the way he shook, it was obvious the tube removal hadn't been painless.

"This might be uncomfortable," he said. "But we've got to get you in this suit to get you out to *Triumph*'s shuttle. Lots of pain meds aboard *Bayonet*, don't forget. Just give it another hour, and don't move while we do this."

Caldwell's mouth opened, then shut. "Yes, Captain."

"We've got to finesse this," he told Frazer as she threaded Caldwell's feet into the suit and worked it up toward the wounds. There was so much more he wanted to say, but there wasn't any point in frightening a kid who was in enough pain as it was. "Here, let me work that side up before you go any further."

Riley leaned against the rear access door while they worked, her ear against the steel. She looked preoccupied with her guard duties, so he risked the question to Frazer.

"Seriously, though—why help us? She's only harming herself."

Caldwell moaned as Frazer sat him up and worked the suit over his shoulders. "It's like she said." She didn't meet his eyes. "She decided immortality wasn't for her."

"And she believes she's godlike enough to make that decision for every other person on the station?"

His stomach seemed to fall all the way to his boots. There was no way she did, and with that realization, he knew. It had been tingling in his brain for a while now, ever since he'd insisted to Ahn that he didn't care about a court martial, but until now, his mind hadn't settled enough for him to consider it.

He couldn't return to *Bayonet* with the others. He couldn't leave Frazer here, as traumatized as she was. He couldn't doom over a thousand people to their deaths, even if they'd done terrible things—things he could never have imagined before a few weeks ago.

He couldn't lose more people.

"Let's lay him back down and get the helmet on," he said to Frazer, his voice shaking. No matter. She would assume it was only the physical exertion that made him sound like this, because in truth it *was* difficult doing this dressed as he was.

Frazer looked at him oddly but helped him get Caldwell flat on his back once more. The helmet went on easier after that, the gurney floated toward the exterior hatch with even less effort, and before he knew it, they were standing there at the top of the stairs ready to open it.

"You got enough air?" he asked her. "We'll be quick about it, get the shuttle spooled up and give you a break inside, then run back here."

"I'm ready." Her words were clipped.

Josiah lifted the hatch above his head in response, and the dim light of a distant star flooded his eyes.

He would die here, he realized as he and Frazer floated the gurney out into the red dust that looked so much like Mars but wasn't. Not today, and maybe not in a year, but eventually his body would wear out from being constantly drained of blood, and that would be it. He could live with that, as long as he'd made up for the lives he hadn't saved aboard *Vigilant*, and Hope would understand . . . eventually.

Triumph's shuttle sat where she had landed, and his heart beat easier as they floated the gurney inside and he started the engines from the remote keypad in the small cargo deck. Frazer collapsed in a jump seat and took a dozen deep breaths as air flooded the shuttle.

"Wow." Her color became healthier right there in front of him. "You have no idea how fantastic that feels."

Josiah forced a smile he didn't feel as he removed Caldwell's helmet and eased him out of the suit into a reclining position on the deck.

"I think I can imagine. Here," he added, handing the suit over to her. "At least you won't have to walk back all exposed."

She took it gratefully and slid it on once she caught her breath. Red dust swirled about them as they returned to the bunker in silence. They removed Halley and Landolt with Riley's help—also in silence—and finally collapsed back aboard *Triumph*'s shuttle in what passed for a waning sunset on Etrik. Neither had fought like Caldwell allegedly had the first time Blayne had tried to remove him, and all three were in good spirits, all things considered. It happened that way much of the time, and after *Kamorta*, Josiah hadn't realized how much an unsuccessful rescue took from him. He would live off this accomplishment for a while.

"Riley wanted to give me something." Frazer stood as he contemplated how he would tell them he wouldn't be returning to *Bayonet*. "I'll be back in five minutes. I assume you can program a route to *Bayonet*?"

"You're not suited up for that. I'll go back and get it and tell her goodbye for you." Josiah pushed himself to his feet and hurried between her and the door that led to the aft airlock. "You look like you could use some more rest anyway. You definitely don't need to fight that suit to get it on again."

Her shoulders sank.

"Maybe you're right," she said with what sounded like the greatest of reluctance. "But let's get that route programmed in first. I don't want any surprises when you get back."

Josiah nodded in agreement as he passed by her, feeling foolish about his suspicion. Of course she wasn't planning to stay behind on Etrik, because that would be idiotic. So was removing his helmet when he'd be headed back to Nimbus Station shortly, but he needed a break from the claustrophobia, so he detached it and set it on the bench outside the flight deck before collapsing in the pilot's seat.

"Here we go." He waved his hand at the console and blew out a deep breath as the navigation system sprang to life in front of him, all foreign stars and calculated flight paths and the white ellipses of standard orbits. "*Bayonet* will be on the lookout for any traffic leaving the surface, especially this shuttle, so it's not as though we can get lost. All we need to do is—"

That same heavy silence he'd felt in the kitchen the day Jonathan had died overcame him. He spun around, expecting to see Frazer watching him silently from the doorway, but the door must have slid closed while he'd been studying the chart projected in front of him. She hadn't even come inside?

Heat coursed through him as he jumped to his feet and darted out the door, only half surprised his helmet wasn't sitting outside where he'd left it. He swore out loud as he rounded the corner into the cargo bay, already knowing what he would find.

Well, that wasn't quite true.

Because even in his worst nightmares, Coralie Frazer pointing a pistol at his head from the aft end of the shuttle wasn't *exactly* what he'd expected.

"Look." He raised his hands. "Whatever's going on here, whatever you think you need to do, it doesn't have to happen. You don't need to destroy the shuttle or whatever else you're planning. We can talk through this, make it right."

"Destroy the shuttle?" The amusement in her voice made him cringe. "Such an odd accusation from someone who knows exactly what I'm planning to do, because he's planning to do the same thing."

His heart threatened to stop.

She knew.

"Captain?" Halley shifted to a sitting position on the metal deck, like he was a half second away from lunging at her. "What's she talking about?"

"You haven't figured it out yet?" Her tone was light. "He has some sort of problematic conscience, and he's realized if he doesn't stay on Etrik, he's condemning over a thousand people to death. And he would be correct, except that he seems to have forgotten about me. That I also have the protein they need and absolutely no motivation to return to Mars. Your captain, on the other hand, is trying to sacrifice himself out of misplaced guilt over something he had no control over."

"Ms. Frazer. Coralie." Josiah knew his face was pale. "You can't do this. You know you can't."

"Why not?"

"Because you called us here."

"I didn't. Not personally. I think we've established that distress signal was fake."

"That's not the point." He took a step toward her as the shuttle jerked into the sky and hovered a bare foot off the dusty ground. "You're actually going to stand here and tell me you don't want to leave? That you're just fine with staying on Etrik, knowing what you know now? You don't owe them anything, especially this."

"It's not about owing. It's about not being responsible for more death, something you would never understand. No," she added before he could argue, a little more loudly, "you don't, because you've never been responsible for any deaths in the first place. And that means you still have a life to live now. A full one—I think Lieutenant Commander O'Donnell would agree with me there. But me? When I left, I knew I would die on Etrik. It was the plan, and it's the plan now. And no offense, but heading back to Mars instead with a bunch of cops and illegal modifications in my body isn't high on my list of fun things to do."

"You can't do this." He would murder whoever had told her about Hope and given her the idea that she needed to sacrifice herself for *him*. "You know what they'll do to you!"

"Hardly." She backed toward the rear airlock without taking her focus from him. "Kinnard is dead, and in case you've forgotten, Nimbus Station is full of scientists working on a synthetic protein to save their own lives. Yes, they've failed so far, but they won't. Helena just let her fear get the best of her. And until they come up with something, I'll make sure they live long enough to do it."

"Ms. Frazer, listen to—"

She didn't listen.

She flung the pistol at him instead, and Josiah ducked just in time to allow it to bounce off the far bulkhead. Caldwell flung himself at her ankles as she disappeared into the airlock, but at that moment, she was the most agile person aboard the shuttle.

"Captain?" From his position on the deck, Landolt sounded exhausted. Josiah didn't know how any of them were still conscious. "There's an open hatch alarm for the aft airlock—I think she's planning to jump. And that's the good news."

He couldn't take his gaze from the airlock. "Then what the hell's the bad news?"

"She programmed the shuttle for polar orbit, then locked us out. Said she was programming a rendezvous with *Bayonet* for once you returned, but she did it right in front of us, while you were up front. I've tried to override it, and no luck. We're just along for the ride now."

Josiah was certain he hadn't said so many profanities in one sentence in ten years, but he couldn't stop himself as he ground his boots into the deck and pressed himself against the window of the steadily climbing shuttle. For a long second, Frazer was motionless on the ground as he held his breath. They were too high for anyone else to survive jumping now, perhaps thirty feet, and that faraway star had almost disappeared below the horizon, casting a golden light across her gray suit as she climbed to her feet.

Two figures appeared in the distance while he stared down at the surface—Riley and a hulking man with blond hair to his shoulders. Frazer nodded at them as they flanked her and helped her limp toward the bunker, only to stop and look skyward before they reached it. She gave Josiah the briefest wave, standing there in that red dust that looked so much like Mars but wasn't, then the shuttle banked to the right.

And she was gone.

CHAPTER FORTY_
USOGC BAYONET, ETRIK ORBIT

Josiah tried to yank his arm free once more, but Somerset forced it down against the edge of the sick bay gurney and lined up a needle with his vein until finally, he gave up. It wasn't worth arguing with corpsmen. He'd lost before, every time.

"This isn't going to hurt much," she said. "Unless you keep fighting, in which case I make no guarantees."

"How much blood do you plan on taking?" he asked warily. "Because I've got to tell you, I'm a lot less willing to share than I used to be."

But that wasn't true, was it? He *had* been willing to share, but Frazer had been right—it had been for the wrong reasons. Somerset didn't need to know that, though. No one needed to know that. Not yet, anyway, and since he hadn't mentioned a word of his plan to anyone . . . maybe no one ever needed to know.

"I suspect everyone aboard feels about the same, including me." She laughed under her breath. "Just a few vials, though. I want to make sure you're not having any complications from lying in that tunnel without a helmet."

"It never came off completely, and I can breathe again. Have been able to for a while now." He waved the sensor on his finger at her after a quick glance at it. "And even with no medical training, I suspect this reading is adequate enough to make you happy."

"You're probably right." She drew out the needle, slapped a bandage on his arm, and set the pulse-ox meter and two vials of dark blood aside. "I'll get this run as soon as I can. How do you feel?"

"Bit of a headache," he admitted. It was an understatement, but anything more truthful would lead to—well, he didn't want to imagine how long Somerset would keep him in here if he confessed to how badly it was pounding.

"I don't doubt that." A frown. "If you think you need more oxygen, let me know—but with everything else going on, I somehow suspect it'll only take the edge off."

Right.

Josiah swung his feet to the deck and stared at the opaque screen cordoning off a small section of sick bay. Behind it lay Caldwell, Halley, and Landolt, awake and alert, but in rougher shape than they had first appeared. Frazer's three companions were even worse. And it wasn't hard to guess what Somerset wasn't saying—the rumors aboard *Bayonet* right now must be something else.

"That bad?" he asked.

"Commander Ahn's been outside for a while, sir." She didn't meet his gaze. "I'm not sure he's willing to wait much longer."

"And?" It was obvious there was more.

Somerset cleared her throat. "And Commander O'Donnell as well."

Fantastic. Not only were they going to scold him together, but Somerset's tone implied she knew exactly who Hope was to him. Well, of course, she'd *known*, since the Orbital Guard wasn't large and gossip was gossip, especially when it came to a marriage that had met a public and flaming end, but . . .

Oh, hell.

"Very well. I'll handle them." He sighed and hopped to his feet, wincing at how the motion jolted his sore brain. "Let me know right away if there are any changes here."

"Captain, you really ought—"

Josiah waved off her objection and opened the door into the main passageway like a man headed to his death. Well, perhaps not quite that reluctantly, for the smell of antiseptic was making him nauseated, and Somerset had bigger worries than him. At least he was walking.

"You made it back," Ahn greeted him.

"Told you I would." Josiah barely glanced his way, even to scrutinize the flat tone, for Hope was leaning against the opposite bulkhead beside Ahn, her eyes wide and dark. Suddenly, his vow to keep secret what he'd almost done vanished into the shadows outside. She deserved more than a lie, and so did everyone else. "Let's talk in private. Both of you."

He led them to his quarters in silence, then locked the door behind him. Hope sank to his bunk and watched him with a hawklike stare, and Ahn leaned against the door and did the same, but neither of them said a word while he paced in a circle for what seemed like an hour. He didn't want to imagine what they were thinking. Probably the same thing he was.

You screwed up again.

Finally, he swallowed his regret and faced them.

"I almost stayed," he said. It was one of the most difficult confessions he'd ever made. Maybe the most. Or was it the easiest? "If Frazer hadn't reprogrammed that shuttle for orbit then jumped, I would have."

Hope's breath caught.

"You lied to me." Ahn's flat expression hadn't changed. "You told me it wasn't about *Vigilant*."

"Yes." Josiah rubbed his eyes. "I lied to you. And it was a mistake."

"Why?" Hope asked.

He spun toward her, but the pain in her expression was too much to bear, so he closed his eyes and pretended he knew what to say.

"I couldn't let them die," he replied. The only thing left was the truth. "You know that. I couldn't let anyone else die."

Her boots squeaked as she stood. "You couldn't stop it, either."

"I know." The lie slipped through his lips, transforming into the truth as it drifted into the space between them. "I know that now."

"Not Jonathan or *Vigilant* or whatever's happening down there on the surface," she went on. "All of it—out of your control. You have to stop blaming yourself. You did everything you could and more. More than anyone has ever asked of you."

Your captain, on the other hand, is trying to sacrifice himself out of misplaced guilt over something he had no control over.

Her words echoed Frazer's so perfectly that for a moment he wondered if they'd spoken to each other. But likely not. His missteps were simply that obvious to everyone but him.

"Yes." He reached for her hand, then dropped it. Ahn was still here, after all. They could talk later. About their past, their future, their mistakes, their promises. "And I swear to you, I will try to remember—as long as you're around to help me."

"You won't get rid of me that easily again." Hope touched a light finger to his cheek, then reached for *Great Expectations*. "May I?"

He nodded like he was in a dream. The book fell open straightaway when she slid it from the desk, its spine cracked and loose after years of use. Her curious gaze swung from the underlined paragraph inside to his face, but he stayed silent.

"'And then I looked at the stars,'" she read, "'and considered how awful it would be for a man to turn his face up to them as he froze to death, and see no help or pity in all the glittering multitude.'" She set the book back on his desk and slipped beside Ahn once more. "Josiah, by that measure, you've succeeded more than you seem to understand."

"I know that, too." And somehow, in the midst of that glittering, hostile multitude, he did.

"So we're good?" Ahn asked.

A sharp breath. "We're good."

"And Nimbus Station? Coralie Frazer?"

Josiah focused on the deck, the strategy coming together in his mind. Most of him wanted to head back to the surface, grab her, and take her back to

Mars. No one would blame him for attempting it, but if he did . . .

She would never forgive him, and rightly so.

"With her voluntary participation and Thomas Kinnard's death, Nimbus Station is better positioned in the search for a treatment than they were six months ago," he said slowly. "And more motivated. I have no doubt they can make something work, given enough time." Frazer had gifted them just that. "But we need to get Eshana back to populated space, and *Bayonet* has six people who need medical care more advanced than we can provide onboard. Right now, that's our priority."

He smiled. "Patrick—let's go home."

ACKNOWLEDGMENTS_

It's an incredible cliché that no book is created in a vacuum, but I am here to tell you that some take a *lot* more assistance than others. *Vortex* is one of those stories, and I am forever grateful to the people who helped get me to publishing day.

Thank you to Lauren, Brittany, and Sophia, my early readers. You all gave me the encouragement to keep going on a story I was unsure about for so very long.

Jasmine and Ed, thanks for finding all those missing words and extra commas. Any further errors are my own!

Meghan, I don't know why you're still willing to read all my first drafts, five years on, but your critique and cheerleading is invaluable.

Hope, thank you for letting me borrow your name. You get more action in the second book, I promise.

Mindy, thank you for helping me out when one of my main characters decided he was Roman Catholic.

Cathy, your pep talks and lectures are probably the biggest reason I worked up the courage to go through with this—and I still can't believe your determination in finding a resource for your poor Navy brat and Air Force spouse friend who found herself writing about a futuristic . . . Coast Guard.

Tim, thank you for agreeing to be that resource and for your willingness to read a complete stranger's unpublished book.

Dad, you wanted to be listed in these acknowledgements as "an old dirt sailor whose seagoing knowledge ended when he got a commission," but you minimized that knowledge. Thanks for sharing it.

And finally, Andy. You've listened to me talk about this book for entirely too long, and I hope it doesn't disappoint. I love you.

ALSO BY ANNE WHEELER_

'Last Mission'

Crownkeeper

The Brightest Void

Resonance (2024)

Crownkeeper Novellas

Treason's Crown

War's Crown

Queen's Crown

Shadows of War

Asrian Skies

Unbroken Fire

Shattered Honor

Faded Embers

The Star Realm Saga

The Stars Wait Not

A House of Nebulas

ABOUT THE AUTHOR_

Anne Wheeler grew up with her nose in a book but earned two degrees in aviation before it occurred to her she was allowed to write her own. When not working, moving, or writing her next novel, she can be found planning her next escape to the desert—camera gear included. A commercial pilot, jet engine geek, and occasional flight instructor, she currently lives in Georgia with her husband, son, and herd of cats.

For more information:
www.anne-wheeler.com

facebook.com/annewheelerbooks
instagram.com/annnewheelerbooks